You wouldn't want to send me back to Polk without exploring this thing between us, would you?"

He grinned, the slow, sweet grin she was sure he'd inherited from his charmer of a father. "For all you know, this could be fate."

"Or a disaster."

His grin broadened. "At worst, we'll have some fun."

No, at worst, she could get her heart broken. Falling in love with a soldier who was raising a two-year-old daughter on his own . . .

Practicing a relationship with Keegan was one thing. All she'd planned to do with him was get herself accustomed to being single and available and looking again. A date, sure. Dinner, some kisses, naturally. Sex? Judging by how much she'd wanted him to kiss her the night before, almost a guarantee.

But a real relationship, risking her heart, risking the already fragile situation in her home . . .

"Things happen when they happen," Keegan said. "You accept it and take advantage of it, or you don't. And if you don't . . ."

She would wonder. Always wonder. And regret.

ACCLAIM FOR
A HERO TO COME HOME TO

"Pappano shines in this poignant tale of love, loss, and learning to love again...[She] creates achingly real characters whose struggles will bring readers to tears."
—*Publishers Weekly* (starred review)

"Pappano's latest is a touching story about loss, love, and acceptance. Tender to the core, her story is filled with heartwarming characters who you can't help but fall in love with, and she tells their stories candidly and poignantly. The ending will simply melt your heart."
—*RT Book Reviews*

"A wonderful romance with real-life, real-time issues... [Pappano] writes with substance and does an excellent job of bringing the characters to life."
—**Harlequin[]Junkie.com**

"Poignant and engaging....Authentic details of army life and battle experience will glue readers to the page."
—*Library Journal*

A Man to
Hold on To

Also by Marilyn Pappano

A Hero to Come Home To

A Man to Hold on To

MARILYN PAPPANO

FOREVER

NEW YORK BOSTON

Forever
Hachette Book Group
237 Park Avenue
New York, NY 10017

www.HachetteBookGroup.com

Printed in the United States of America

First Edition: February 2014

10 9 8 7 6 5 4 3 2 1

OPM

Forever is an imprint of Grand Central Publishing.
The Forever name and logo are trademarks of Hachette Book Group, Inc.

The Hachette Speakers Bureau provides a wide range of authors for speaking events. To find out more, go to www.hachettespeakersbureau.com or call (866) 376-6591.

The publisher is not responsible for websites (or their content) that are not owned by the publisher.

For every man and woman who has served in the United States Army, Navy, Marine Corps, Coast Guard, National Guard, and Air Force.

For every parent who has said good-bye to their children, sending them off to a life far from home to protect and defend their nation.

For every spouse who has left family, friends, and jobs to move from one duty station to the next in support of their service member.

For every child who has lived the nomadic military lifestyle through no choice of their own but adapted anyway because that's what military kids do.

And especially for those who served with the following commands, keeping my husband, Robert, safe while he did the same for you:

1st Marine Division, Camp Pendleton, CA

1st Marine Division (REIN)

2nd Battalion, 1st Marines, Vietnam

Naval Air Station, Beeville, TX

USS Sierra (AD 18), Charleston, SC

*Fleet Aviation Specialized Operational
Training Group, Pacific*

*SERE School, Naval Air Station North Island
and Warner Springs, CA*

*Dwight D. Eisenhower Army Medical Center,
Fort Gordon, GA*

2nd Battalion, 8th Marines (SOC), Camp Lejeune, NC

5th Battalion, 10th Marines, Camp Lejeune, NC

*Headquarters, 6th Marine Regiment (SOC),
Camp Lejeune, NC*

And, as always, for Robert, who took a timid small-town Oklahoma girl off to see the country. The experience taught me strength and independence (and a whole new language) and gave me an enormous sense of pride in our troops, their families, and the sacrifices they all make.

People talk about the one-percenters who share most of the nation's wealth. To me, our troops are the one-percenters who *are* our nation's wealth.

Thank you.

The strength of our soldiers comes from the strength of their families.

—U.S. Army

You never know how strong you are until being strong is the only choice you have. My choice was simple. I was not going to give up.

—Jessica Villarreal,
wife of wounded warrior
Corporal Anthony Villarreal, USMC (Retired)

Chapter 1

The first thing Therese Matheson did when she arrived at Tulsa International Airport was head to the bathroom and blot her face with a damp paper towel. She should have taken an extra antianxiety pill this morning or skipped the pancakes and blueberries for breakfast. Maybe she should have stopped off somewhere for a fortifying drink, even though it wasn't yet noon, or guilted one of her friends into coming along.

"It's not that scary," she whispered to the pale reflection staring wide-eyed at her. "You're just picking up the kids after their spring break trip, Paul's kids."

Usually, reminding herself that Abby and Jacob were Paul's kids helped calm her. Paul had been the love of her life, and when his ex-wife had sent the kids to live with them nearly four years ago, Therese had embraced the opportunity for a ready-made family. When he'd deployed to Afghanistan not long after, she'd promised to keep them safe for his return. When he didn't return, well, she'd been shocked that their mother didn't want them back, but she'd done her best. They were his kids, after all.

Now, she'd used the time they were gone to seek advice about giving up custody of them.

Shame crept into the reflection's eyes. She'd promised Paul. She'd wanted to love them. She'd tried, God help her, but in the end, it had come down to two choices: keep them or find some much-needed peace. Break her promise to their father or break her own spirit.

She was surviving Paul's death, but she wasn't surviving life with his angry, hostile, bitter children.

Child, she corrected. Before they'd left for the visit with their mother, Jacob had shown her some sympathy, even some respect.

It was Abby who was breaking her.

With a deep breath, she forced the shame from her gaze, then left the bathroom and took the escalator to the baggage area above. There weren't many people waiting for the incoming flights. She missed the happy reunions that once were common in airports. Getting off the plane and finding someone waiting for her had been part of the fun.

Someone who was happy to see her, she amended when passengers started appearing in the skywalk from the main terminal. She wasn't happy to see Abby, already texting on her cell, strolling lazily, mindless of the people who dodged her snail's pace, and the swell of pleasure brought by the sight of Jacob wasn't really happiness. It was a start, though.

Tall and broad-shouldered, Jacob had a pack slung over one shoulder—his only luggage for the six-day trip—and buds in his ears. A person could be forgiven for thinking him six or eight years older than his eleven, not only because of his size, but also the look in his eyes, the air of having lived about him. He looked so much like his father that most days seeing him made Therese's heart hurt.

Next to him Abby looked even more petite than ever—and less angelic. For once the bright streaks that sliced through her blond hair were gone, and the blond was platinum instead. It had been cut, too, in a sleek but edgy style, sharp angles, short in back, longer in front, no bangs but a tendency for the entire left side to fall over her face—her *made-up face.*

Her clothes were different, too. Therese had seen swimsuit bottoms that covered more than Abby's shorts, and the top looked more like a beach cover-up than a blouse except that it was too short to cover anything adequately. The bright print was semi-transparent and kept sliding off one shoulder or the other, revealing the straps of her new black bra.

Therese's efforts to breathe resulted in a strangled gasp. Another pill, two more pills, and definitely a drink, or maybe she could borrow a sedative. Surely someone in the Tuesday Night Margarita Club still had a stash of sedatives somewhere.

She couldn't pull her gaze from her stepdaughter even when she had to move left or right to maintain line of sight. Abby's skin was darkly tanned, a startling contrast to her white shorts and platinum hair and her shoes—

Another strangled sound escaped. White leather, heels adding at least four inches to her height, skinny straps crisscrossing her feet and wrapping around her ankles to end in bows in back.

Oh, my God.

Beside Therese, the conveyor belt rumbled to life and

people began nudging her aside to get prime spaces for reclaiming their bags. She took a step toward the kids as they neared, digging deep to find a neutral expression and to stifle the shriek inside her. *What was your mother thinking?*

Abby barely slowed when she reached Therese. Recently manicured nails didn't pause in typing as she said, "My bags are pink. I'll be waiting at the door."

Therese turned to watch her go, then whispered, "Oh, my God."

Jacob stopped beside her and pulled the buds from his ears. "Scary, isn't it?"

Forgetting Abby for the moment, she studied her stepson. He looked exactly the way he had the day he'd left. He might even be wearing the same clothes. Whatever effects the visit with Catherine had had on him, they weren't as painfully obvious as with Abby.

She wished she could hug him or even just lay her hand on his arm to welcome him back home, but he kept enough distance between them to make it difficult. "Did you have a good time?"

He shrugged. "It was okay. We didn't do much."

Of course not. By the time Catherine had bought new clothes and shoes for Abby, taken her to a tanning salon and gotten her hair cut and colored, there probably hadn't been much time left over for Jacob.

"If you want to go on and get the car, I'll get her bags."

"Okay." Therese took a few steps, then turned back. "Why are her bags pink? She left with black luggage."

He grimaced. "Mom bought her new ones. She said only—"

After a moment, Therese said, "It's okay to say it."

"Only boring people use black luggage."

She forced a smile. "Well, I never aspired to be exciting. She did bring them back, didn't she?" Black though they were, the suitcases were sturdy and still had a lot of miles left on them.

At the hopefulness in her voice, he grinned. "I did."

"Thanks." This time she did touch his arm, just for an instant. "I'll meet you guys out front. Make her carry her own, will you?"

He grunted as he stuck the earbuds back in.

A warm breeze hit Therese as she walked out of the terminal, then crossed the broad street to the short-term parking lot. Her flip-flops keeping familiar tempo, she pulled out her cell and dialed her best friend back in Tallgrass.

The call went straight to voice mail. No surprise since Carly had gotten engaged just a few days ago and was still celebrating. After the beep, Therese said in a rush, "I know you're probably busy with Dane, so don't call me back. I won't be able to talk for a while anyway. I'm at the airport, and oh, Carly, I sent a wholesome sweet-looking thirteen-year-old to visit her mother and got back a tarted-up twenty-three-year-old streetwalker-wannabe! Makeup, high heels, platinum hair! I'd be afraid she's got tattoos or piercings or something even more inappropriate except that there's not enough of her clothing to cover anything like that!"

She drew a deep breath. "Okay, I'm breathing, I'm in control. I'm not going to explode. Yet. I'll call you later."

Once she reached the mom van, she buckled herself in and practiced a few more breaths. As she flipped down the visor to get the parking ticket stub, her gaze landed on the photograph of Paul she always kept there. He'd been in Afghanistan, smiling, full of life, in a khaki T-shirt and camo pants, with dark glasses pushed up on top of his head. He'd e-mailed the photo to her, then followed it up with a print copy, where he'd scrawled on the back, *Major Paul Matheson, Helmand Province, counting the days till he sees his beautiful wife Therese again.*

"Oh, Paul, I wish you were here. You were the only person in the world who loved both Abby and me. Maybe you could negotiate a truce, because, sweetheart, we are facing a major battle. Send me some strength, will you?"

She sat there a moment, wishing she would actually feel *something*, just some small sign—a bit of warmth, encouragement, hope.

The only thing she felt was sorrow.

It took a few minutes to exit the lot and circle back around to the loading lane in front of the terminal. She was breathing normally, and a glance in the rearview mirror showed her shock was under control. It also showed the grimness in her eyes, dread for the upcoming skirmish.

The kids were waiting, Jacob with the suitcases, Abby still texting. She did pause long enough to open the rear passenger door, slide inside, and fasten her seat belt, then she ducked her head and went right back to it.

Therese helped Jacob load the luggage. The black one was easy to lift, since it contained nothing but the other empty black one. His muscles bulged as he hefted the matching pink ones inside. "Thank you, Jacob."

He started to go around to the other passenger side, then stopped. "Can I ride in front?"

Her first response was a blink. For years, she'd chauffeured the kids nearly everywhere, with emphasis on the hired-driver concept. On the rare occasions it was just her and Jacob, he sat in the front seat, never talking to her but listening to music and playing video games, but if she had both kids, they always sat in back and pretty much pretended she wasn't there.

"Sure. That's fine." It wasn't much, but as she'd thought earlier, it was a start.

* * *

Jessy Lawrence rolled onto her side with a groan and opened one eye. All she saw was pale aqua with a strip of brown on one edge. Closing her eye again, she digested that bit of information. She was lying on the couch, and it was daytime. Late morning, judging by the light coming through the south-facing windows of her apartment. It was Saturday, so there was nowhere she needed to go, nothing she needed to do.

She did a little shimmy, just enough to realize she was wearing clothes and not the tank top and boxers she normally slept in, and a flex of her feet revealed she still wore the heels she favored to disguise the fact that she was vertically challenged.

That little movement was enough to make her aware of the queasiness in her gut and the throb in her head. She hadn't felt so bad since she'd gotten the flu last winter. She'd stunk of sweat then, too, and had been certain that the slightest movement would make her puke.

Slowly she nudged the pumps off, and they fell to the floor with a thud muffled by the rug. Her arches almost spasmed in relief. Next she rolled onto her back and opened her eyes, then oh so slowly she sat up. Her stomach heaved, the sour taste making its way into her throat, making her clamp her hand over her mouth, and *that* movement sent daggers through her head. She could only hope the brain tissue they destroyed was nonessential, but she wouldn't count on it. After all, this wasn't the first time she'd done this to herself.

The absence of sound in the apartment both soothed and pricked at her. It was always so empty, and it made her feel even emptier. She lived there alone. Slept there alone. Got sick there alone. Grieved there alone.

Home was the second floor of an office building in downtown Tallgrass. Originally, an abstract company and a dentist had shared the space, then a dance school, but after it had stood empty for twenty years, the owners had converted it into residential space. It was the first place she and Aaron had looked at when the Army had transferred him to Fort Murphy, and the last. She'd loved it on sight, with its high ceilings, tall windows, and ancient wood floors. She'd loved the old architectural details of the moldings and the couldn't-be-more-modern kitchen and bathroom and the convenience of being within walking distance of restaurants, shopping, and clubs.

Aaron hadn't loved it so much. He had wanted an extra bedroom or two for kids and a yard to mow and play in, but he'd loved her so he had agreed to the apartment. It wasn't like it was permanent, he'd said. They could always move as soon as she got pregnant.

She hadn't gotten pregnant.

He had died eleven and a half months into a twelve-month tour in Afghanistan.

And she was so sorry that she was drowning in it.

It was too early to start feeling bad—worse—so she carefully pushed to her feet, swayed a moment, then started toward the bedroom. She was halfway there when the doorbell rang, the peal slicing through her. Cursing the day she'd given her friends keys to the downstairs entry, she reversed direction and went to the door, opening it without looking through the peephole.

Ilena Gomez stood there, blond hair loosely pulled back, face pink from the exertion of climbing the stairs. Her hands were in the small of her back, and she was stretching, making her pregnant belly look huge compared to normal. She greeted Jessy with a smile, all white teeth and pleasure, and said while patting her belly, "Hector and I are starving. Are you ready?"

Jessy tried to erase the dull look she was certain glazed her eyes while searching her mind for a clue. Starving meant food, obviously she had agreed to go to lunch with Ilena today. She must have been insane at the time—or as fuzzy as she was right now—because Saturdays were never her best days.

But she couldn't renege. Sure, Ilena would understand, but that was rule number one in Jessy's life these days: never fail to be there for any member of the Tuesday Night Margarita Club, also known around town as the Fort Murphy Widows' Club. Without them, she wouldn't have survived the past year, and by God, she would return the favor.

"Give me ten minutes. Come on in and sit it down." As quickly as her stomach and head would bear, Jessy went into the bedroom, then the bathroom with an agenda. First: take aspirin. Second: brush horrible taste out of mouth. Third: shuck clothes and give sigh of relief that everything was fastened properly and she still wore her underwear. Fourth: shower, dress, and apply makeup. Fifth: avoid looking in mirror until absolutely necessary.

Missing her target by only four minutes, she returned to the living room. She wore one of her girl-next-door outfits: cargo shorts, T-shirt, sandals with a thin sole. Her red hair was short enough that all it needed was a finger fluff, and her makeup was minimal to go along with the innocent look.

She would feel more innocent if she could remember what she'd done last night.

Ilena was sitting on the couch, holding the digital picture frame from the end table and gazing at some of the photographs Jessy had taken over the years. "You take beautiful pictures. Majestic. Haunting."

"Sometimes I feel like a queen," Jessy said flippantly.

"And sometimes like a ghost?" Ilena's look made it clear she found that odd. That was okay. A lot about Jessy was odd, but they hadn't stopped loving her because of it yet.

She found her purse on the dining table instead of hanging from its usual hook near the door and slung the strap over her shoulder, then went to help Ilena up from the too-comfy couch. "What does Junior want for lunch?"

"My boy may be here by way of Guadalajara, but we need some pasta and cheese today. How about Luca's?"

"Sounds good." Comfort food, and she definitely needed comfort.

*   *   *

"You should take her with you."

Keegan Logan secured the duffel that held his clothes, then rummaged through an olive-drab backpack to check its contents: laptop computer, power cords, paperwork, a handful of CDs. After zipping it, he finally met his mother's gaze. "It's a nine-hour drive."

"You can stop every few hours to give her a break."

"That would make it an eleven- or twelve-hour drive."

When that didn't faze Ercella, he made another excuse. "She's not comfortable alone with me."

Ercella gave him a dry look. "You mean you're not comfortable alone with her. You could fix that if you just tried. Get down on the floor with her. Play with her. Talk to her. Bounce her on your knee. Lord, Keegan, you know how to act with babies. I've seen you with your sisters' kids."

"Yeah, you saw me ignore their existence until they were old enough to be fun. Besides, they're boys." Both his sisters lived in Shreveport, so he didn't see their kids that often. And he was good at doing boy things. And his nephews didn't look at him like they'd summed him up and found him lacking. They didn't narrow their eyes into little squints and let out shrieks that could shear metal.

They didn't look lost and alone, the way Mariah sometimes did.

"Besides," he went on before Ercella could speak, "I want to check this guy out. I want to see..."

His mother's eyes narrowed into little squints, and she held the baby a little tighter. "Are you sure...Have you really thought about this?"

Hell, he'd done nothing but think about it for the last month. He woke up wondering what to do about Mariah, and he fell asleep considering the same thing. He'd been going into work late and taking off early, talking to social workers and a lawyer and the chaplain in his unit at Fort Polk. He hadn't done a damn thing besides think about Mariah.

And regret the day he'd ever met her mother, Sabrina. He'd loved her, he'd hated her, and since she'd abandoned Mariah with him, he'd been furious with her. Not that she knew or cared, since he hadn't heard from her for more than a year before she'd decided to take a vacation from being a mother. He hadn't even seen the nearly three-year-old Mariah until the day the social worker had led her by the hand to him and performed the introductions.

If he could get his hands on Sabrina...

He risked a look at the little girl, settled into his mother's arms as if she belonged there, blond hair curling delicately around her chubby-cherub face. Her brown eyes watched him with a seriousness no two-year-old should ever know, and he wondered for the hundredth time what was going through that little brain of hers. Faultfinding? Her mother had certainly excelled at that. Disillusionment? Sabrina had that in spades, too. Wariness that, like her mother, one day he and Ercella would disappear from her life without notice?

Guilt prickled his neck because that was exactly what he planned. If everything checked out in Oklahoma, she would be going to another family. Another man would get on the floor and play with her, talk to her, and bounce her on his knee. Another man would fall in love with her and do his best to protect her and keep her safe.

Keegan wasn't meant for that role. He wasn't father material. Especially for another man's daughter.

Deliberately he shifted his attention from Mariah and that line of thought. "When are you guys going home?" Home for Ercella was Natchitoches, fifty miles from Leesville, half that again from Shreveport. She had more or less moved in with him when Mariah had come, but with him out of town, she was happy to be returning to her own place.

"Soon as I get her stuff packed. I'm going to show her all the places my other grandkids—I mean, my grand-kids—love and all the places you knew growing up." Regret pinched the corners of her mouth. He'd warned her before she'd come here that Mariah's presence in their lives was short-term, and she'd insisted that she understood. Still, it hadn't taken her more than about five minutes to get totally charmed by the kid. Left to her, he would be Mariah's father, despite proof to the contrary, and Sabrina's daughter would be a Logan forever.

But it wasn't just for himself that he was heading off to track down her father. She deserved to be with real family. She deserved to know who her people were, and they *weren't* Logans.

"Okay. Well. Guess I'll take off." He circled the dining table and hugged his mother, inhaling the scents of bacon lingering from breakfast, perfume, and clean laundry and recently bathed baby.

Ercella squeezed him tightly, then forced a big smile for Mariah. "Sweetie, want to give Keegan a hug good-bye?"

As usual, the girl studied him, fingers stuffed in her mouth, as if he were an alien creature. She wasn't going to give him a hug, say good-bye, or do anything but look at him and judge him, and his mom both knew it.

This time, she surprised them both. Just as he started to step back, she pitched forward, tumbling out of his mother's arms and landing in his, her arms wrapping around his neck.

Keegan froze, not quite sure what to do. Her solid little body felt foreign—too soft, sweet, innocent. He'd never held her, not once, because she hadn't allowed it, because he hadn't wanted it. She'd never spoken to him, never touched him, never done anything but watch him warily, and now she was holding on as if she might never let go.

It felt . . . nice.

Aw, hell, he really needed to get on the road.

He was about to tug loose and return her to Ercella when she reversed her earlier move, leaping into his mother's more familiar embrace. His throat tight, he forced a smile.

"Gotta go."

"You call me as soon as you get to Tallgrass. And be careful."

He nodded, picked up his bags, and left the apartment. His destination was programmed into the Garmin: 718 Cheyenne, Tallgrass, Oklahoma. He felt bad about leaving Mariah, though she was happier with his mom than she was with him. It was necessary, though. Since Sabrina had named him as father on Mariah's birth certificate, no one else was much interested in finding her real father. Besides, like he'd told his mother, he wanted to check the guy out. He wanted to make sure he was a good fit for Mariah. Wanted to be sure she would be welcomed into his family.

And if he decided she didn't belong there? she had asked. *Then what?*

"I'm not her father."

Too bad that didn't solve the problem.

And way too bad that saying the words didn't ease the guilt still prickling at the back of his neck.

* * *

On the hour's drive northwest to Tallgrass, Therese asked the kids if they wanted to stop for lunch. Jacob declined, and Abby ignored her. She asked if they'd taken lots of pictures. Jacob said no, and Abby ignored her. She asked how their mother was. Jacob grunted, and Abby ignored her.

Once they got home and she told Abby that she wouldn't be wearing those clothes or that makeup for at least another few years, Abby would no longer pretend Therese didn't exist. Therese half-wished she could do the ignoring and just close her eyes to what the girl did, but there was no way any child in her care was going to leave the house looking like that.

Tallgrass was a small and lovely old town, dating back to Oklahoma's pre-statehood days. Its early purpose had been to provide for the area ranches and the settlers brought there by the land run. Later it had supported the oil-field workers, as well, and for the last sixty years, it had been home to Fort Murphy, which tripled its population.

Paul had been transferred there four years ago, and she'd fallen in love with the place. They'd bought a house big enough for his kids and the babies they'd intended to have together, with a manicured front lawn and a big backyard for play and family cookouts. But there hadn't been any babies, his kids weren't interested in outdoor play, except for Jacob's football and baseball teams, and Abby never missed a chance to remind her that they weren't a family.

Someday the kids would be gone. Either their mother would take them back, or her parents, or maybe Paul's parents. Or maybe Abby would miraculously start behaving like a human being, or Therese would find peace with the idea of putting her in foster care. Failing all that, if she could hold herself together for five more years of misery, then she could be free.

Freedom had never sounded so good...or seemed so impossible.

As she shut off the engine in the driveway, she said, "Abby, put the phone away, take your stuff inside, and unpack."

Abby either didn't think Therese saw the face she made or simply didn't care, but she tucked the phone into her tiny purse before sliding to the ground and stalking to the back of the van. The high school boys sitting on the porch across the street came to sudden attention, eyes popping, mouths gaping.

Oh, Lord, please not that. Therese had enough worries without adding males to the list.

Abby dragged her pink bags into the house, leaving the door standing open, and the boys slowly sank back into lethargy. Therese wanted to yell at them, *She's thirteen!* She wanted to go upstairs to her room and march back down with the .40 caliber handgun locked in Paul's gun safe and warn them what would happen if they even thought about his baby in that way.

She settled for scowling at them, then jerking the black bag out, slamming the hatch, and following Jacob inside. He went to the laundry room off the kitchen, unzipped his backpack, and dumped the contents into the hamper there. After grabbing a bottle of water from the refrigerator, he headed past her with a grunt on his way upstairs. Within minutes he would be on the computer, headset on, jumping with both feet into the game he'd last played six days ago. He wouldn't make another appearance until hunger drove him to it.

Therese put her purse and keys in the kitchen, blew out

a breath, and much more slowly climbed the stairs. Abby's door was open, and she was reclining on the bed, one sandaled foot on the white spread, the other stretched high so she could admire the shoe. As usual, she was talking on the phone to Nicole, her BFF and, until very recently, the coolest kid in town. No doubt, Abby now felt that title belonged to her.

"—so much fun," she was saying when Therese stopped in the doorway. "I can't wait till you see my hair and all the clothes she bought me. And the shoes! They make me taller than you. We spent a whole day at the spa, and I've got the best tan ever, and the cutest outfits! It was the best week of my life."

Therese waited, hands hanging limply at her sides. She really wanted to fold her arms across her chest and scowl as hard as she had at the boys outside, but there was no reason to start off openly aggressive. They would get there quickly enough.

Tiring of admiring her right foot, Abby lowered it to the mattress and raised the left one, twisting her ankle this way and that. It was a pretty ankle, a pretty leg, all bronzed and lean and leading to a compact lean body. She was more assured at thirteen than Therese had been at thirty, more aware of the attention she received from others. The teenage girl Therese had once been envied her; the woman charged with overseeing her welfare was cringing in the corner with her hands over her eyes.

Trying to feel more like the woman, she moved into the room and picked up the larger of the suitcases, set it on the foot of the bed, and unzipped it.

Frowning at her, Abby said, "Gotta go, Nicole. See you tomorrow." She set the phone on the nightstand, then sat up, arms folded over her middle. "Those are my bags. They're private."

"You live in this house. Nothing is private beyond your journal, if you keep one, your purse, and, to some extent, your room, so long as you don't give me a reason to reconsider that." She flipped open the suitcase and saw nothing but unfamiliar clothes inside. She shook out the top garment. "Is this a dress or a shirt?"

Abby rolled her eyes. "A dress. Duh."

With a nod, Therese laid it to one side. Next came a pair of jeans so skinny that only through the miracle of stretch fibers could they possibly fit her stepdaughter. They were the start of a second pile. The tiny shorts that measured the width of Therese's hand from waistband to crotch joined the dress, along with a couple of tops too fitted and too revealing for any child.

"What are you doing?" Abby finally demanded.

"Sorting out what you can wear and what's going into storage."

Abby surged from the bed and nearly lost her footing. She wasn't quite as accustomed to those four-inch heels as she'd thought. "You can't do that! They're mine! My mother bought them for me."

Therese reached the bottom of the suitcase and picked up a handful of undergarments. No, not undergarments. Lingerie. Matched sets. Bikinis. Thongs. Push-up bras. Black, royal blue, red, purple. They were prettier, sexier, and more revealing than anything she owned, including the lingerie she'd bought for her honeymoon.

Struggling to keep her hand steady, she began repacking them in the suitcase. Out of the twelve garments and the lingerie, she left only two or three pieces on the bed.

"You can't do that!" Abby repeated, grabbing for the bra in Therese's hand.

Therese shot her a look so hard that Abby should have fallen backward from the impact. Sullenly, she let her hand drop, then took a few steps away, her bottom lip poked out.

After a moment's stare, Therese looked at the bra. Catherine hadn't bothered with Victoria's Secret, judging from the padded cups, red lace edging black satin, and breakaway front clasp. She'd gone straight to Frederick's of Hollywood. For her thirteen-year-old daughter! She dropped it into the suitcase, closed the flap, and zipped it before reaching for the smaller bag.

Quivering with anger, Abby went to the closet. "You have to let me wear them." She threw open both bi-fold doors, then clenched her fists. "I have nothing else. I left all my other clothes there because I knew you would do this. I told Mom so."

She wasn't exaggerating by much. Except for her school uniforms and the dresses she wore to church, her closet was practically empty. A few pairs of jeans, a couple of old T-shirts that had sentimental value but no fashion sense, two hoodies. There were gym shorts and underwear in her dresser, but she'd taken practically everything else with her.

"You'd better call your mom and ask her to ship them back, then, or you're going to get awfully tired of wearing the same things all the time." Therese sorted through the second bag, confiscating three more pairs of ridiculous heels, two more bags of cosmetics, and—she gulped silently—two of the skimpiest swimsuits she'd ever seen. She was surprised thunder didn't roll across the plains from Paul's roar of disapproval.

"I can't do that, because we threw them away."

Therese hoped she was lying, but it sounded like exactly what she and Catherine would do. Catherine might be Abby's mother, but she didn't want to be. Occasional friendship without real responsibility better suited her nature, and conspiring with Abby to thwart Therese would be an easy way to cement that friendship.

"If that's the case, you'll have to buy new clothes from your allowance."

She expected another roar, but the girl just stared at her. In that moment, there was nothing of Paul's baby in her, just quiet fury. Malevolence. Sheer hatred. Her eyes were like chocolate ice, her rage unflinching, but when she spoke, her voice was far calmer than the shriek Therese was used to.

"You know, I don't pray very much because I don't think God really listens, but I do pray for one thing every night. I pray for you to die."

Chapter 2

All his life, Dalton Smith had found comfort in the Double D Ranch. He lived alone, worked too hard, and didn't make much more than a living wage, but it didn't matter. This was where he was born. Where he was raised. Where he was meant to be.

His parents had left it. Once they'd been sure the ranch was in capable hands, they'd invested in an RV and had been seeing the country ever since, winters down south, summers up north, stopping off at any place that caught their fancy and had hookups.

His little brother, Noah, would probably leave, too. A sophomore at Oklahoma State, Noah had decided he wanted to be a vet. While he said of course it would be around Tallgrass, Dalton knew his brother liked a lot of things, and small-town living wasn't one of them. Besides, Tallgrass already had enough vets.

His other brother, Dillon, was gone, too, but what was the saying? Good riddance to bad rubbish.

And what was that other saying? A bad penny always comes back.

Nah, Dillon would never return, and if he did, Dalton would meet him at the property line with a shotgun. More likely, he would just beat the tar out of him and throw his worthless carcass into the bar ditch on the other side of the road. It would be easier than explaining to his mother why he'd shot his twin brother.

With a brother like that, he didn't need enemies.

He rocked back, the creaking noise an accompaniment to the breeze blowing from the northwest and the soft snoring of the dog on the floor beside him. The Australian shepherd had wandered down the road yesterday morning, burrs in all four paws, flea-bit and tick-bit and twenty pounds underweight. Dalton didn't want a dog; he had enough four-legged creatures depending on him already, plus one two-legged, since he was paying for Noah's schooling. But the dog didn't understand he wasn't wanted, or just didn't care.

So it appeared Dalton had a dog.

The floorboards inside the house creaked, too, a moment before the screen door was shoved open and Noah stepped out. He was home from college for the weekend and had done more than his share of the work today. Unlike Dalton, who'd sunk down in the rocker afterward with a bottle of cold water and hardly moved, Noah had showered and changed into clean, pressed indigo jeans and a pearl-snapped shirt. He wore a rodeo championship buckle on his belt and his good boots and carried his good hat.

Dalton knew from the clothes that Noah was partying in Tallgrass tonight. Local girls seemed to appreciate the genuine cowboy look more than they did in the cities an hour away in each direction.

The scent of cologne reminded Dalton that he stank, his skin was taut from the gallons of salt he'd sweated, and his clothes could probably stand on their own. His mother would have thought twice about letting him inside even the back door.

Noah sat on the rail. "Me and some guys are going out to dinner, then hitting some of the clubs. Wanna come?"

Dalton gazed to the west. He was twelve years older than Noah and his buddies. He'd likely changed diapers on every one of them when he was a kid. They would eat like refugees, party it up, and at least some of them would find girls who appreciated genuine cowboys to spend the night with.

Would one of them be a pretty redhead with exotic green eyes? Willing, wearing clothes that fit her hard little body as if made just for her, tossing back more than a few drinks with them before singling out one and suggesting the nearest motel? And would she forget their names before the booze was out of her system, the way she'd forgotten him?

"No, thanks."

"Aw, come on. You haven't gone out drinking in longer than I can remember."

"Maybe that's because you go out drinking too much."

Noah didn't even have the grace to make his grin abashed. "College," he said, as if that explained everything. "You can at least have dinner with us. Anywhere we go's got to be better than what you fix."

"Nah. I'm tired."

Noah pushed away from the rail, tall and lanky, strong

but leaner than Dalton. "You know the Smith family motto. Work hard, play hard, live hard, love—" Abruptly his face turned red, and he clamped the hat on his head. "If you change your mind, you've got my number."

Love hard. Dalton had done that twice. He'd loved Dillon like a best friend and his wife like his life. Dillon could be dead for all anyone in the family knew, and Sandra *was* dead, buried in a sunny plot at Fort Murphy National Cemetery. She'd died in Afghanistan.

Because she hadn't loved him enough to live.

Grimly, as Noah drove down the gravel lane, Dalton shoved to his feet and stomped to the door. He stopped long enough to toe off his boots, then shucked his dirt-crusted jeans and left both in a heap next to the door. In grimy socks, ripped T-shirt, and boxers, he stepped inside, then scowled at the dog. "You coming?"

As if he'd been extended the most gracious of invitations, the mutt got up, trotted across the threshold and down the hall to the kitchen.

Yep, Dalton definitely had a dog.

* * *

It was five thirty, and Therese was curled in her favorite easy chair in the living room when her cell phone rang. She didn't have to look to see it was Carly. "Happy Together" was the song she'd programmed in for her best friend just yesterday. She considered leaving the phone there on the table, on top of the Bible she'd been trying to find comfort in, but it was a general rule that she didn't ignore her margarita sisters.

"Sorry I missed your call earlier." Carly sounded the

same as always, just somehow lighter. Happier. A few months ago she'd been in the same situation Therese was in, minus the Princess of I-Hate-You, then Dane had come into her life and suddenly she wasn't alone anymore. She wasn't just a widow. She was a woman in love with a man who loved her every bit as much. It made Therese happy and sad and so very hopeful.

Not for herself. She wasn't looking for love. She just needed courage and sanity and peace. But Fia, Ilena, Marti, Lucy, Jessy—all the other members of the margarita club—deserved it. They were all too young, even the oldest ones, to live the rest of their lives alone.

"Don't worry," Therese said drily. "I'm sure you had way more fun this afternoon than I did."

"I know a place just outside town that's isolated. Do I need to bring over a shovel and a flashlight?"

Therese's smile was faint. "She's much too alive to bury. Though if you made the same offer to her, she'd probably take you up on it since she's been praying for me to die."

There was a moment's silence, then, "Aw, Therese."

The sympathy in Carly's voice was almost Therese's undoing. Her eyes grew damp, her nose got stuffy, and she was sure she would cry if she gave herself half a chance. And what good would it do? How many gallons of tears had she cried over Abby, Jacob, and Paul, and how much difference had it made?

"So tell me about the platinum hair and the streetwalker clothes. And just what size are those high heels? I know I could never squeeze into even two of her outfits, but my feet just might fit the shoes, and Dane has this thing for trampy shoes."

Therese chuckled. "Don't ever tell anyone I said this,

but she really looks amazing. The teenage boys across the street were too stunned to move when they saw her. But she's thirteen. It would break her daddy's heart to see her dressed like—like her mother." Of course Catherine had approved the clothes. It was her own style. Fine for a thirty-some-year-old woman in most universes. Not for a barely adolescent child.

"Did you take the clothes away?"

"I did. They're in the attic, in the dustiest corner in a box marked Old Drapes." Therese heaved a sigh, massaging her temples with her free hand. "So what have you and Dane been up to?" The last time she'd seen Carly was Tuesday, when Dane had gone down on his bionic knee and proposed to her in front of everyone on the Three Amigos restaurant patio. Carly wasn't the only one who'd gotten teary-eyed at such a public profession of love and commitment. "He took you home?"

"He did." Small words to contain so much pleasure.

"I noticed your car was still in the parking lot Wednesday night. Or was it Thursday?"

"I picked it up Wednesday night. Very late Wednesday night."

"I guess sex isn't on the list of things you miss anymore."

A loud rumble came from across the room, and Therese looked up to see Jacob coming down the last few steps. His scowl was tinged with red. "There are kids in the house, you know."

A comment from Jacob when normally he would have walked past without noticing her. Better, a comment lacking the sullen tone both kids affected so well. "Sorry, Jacob."

"He asked me to marry him, Therese," Carly said with a sniffle.

"I know, sweetie. I was there."

"He wants to set a date. He wants to buy a ring. He wants to meet Jeff's family and mine. He *really* wants to marry me." She sounded so full of wonder and awe. Therese understood. She'd felt that way when Paul had proposed to her. It seemed an eternity ago, so special and amazing that she wondered if she could possibly ever feel that way again.

At that instant, a door slammed upstairs and footsteps that would do a dinosaur proud headed down the steps. She couldn't be in a worse possible place for even thinking about falling in love. She had nothing of herself left to offer. It took all her strength to get through everyday life, and even that required medication. Her only list right now consisted of things to survive. Romance, sadly, didn't make the cut.

Abby stomped down the stairs and turned down the hall toward the kitchen. She didn't spare even a glance toward the living room, but Therese felt the hatred radiating from her. A direct look from her enraged brown eyes probably would have pulverized Therese where she sat. *Nothing left but a layer of dust,* the cops would say, shaking their heads in amazement while sweet, angelic Angry Girl looked on from the sidelines.

Forcing her stepdaughter from her mind, Therese concentrated on Carly. "Have you set the date yet?"

"We're thinking the first weekend of June. I know that seems fast since we only met in March, but..."

She didn't need to say it. Life was short, time was fleeting, and so on. No one had ever expected Jeff and Paul and all the others to die as young as they did. That was why so few of them had started a family. They had plenty of time. One deployment here, another there, the war would surely end, the troops would draw down, their husbands would come home. There was always next month, next year, the next duty station.

Except when there wasn't.

"Will it be here in Tallgrass?"

"Yes. My friends and church are here. His friends are all over the world. His mom can come up from Texas, and it'll do my family good to come out of their labs into the real world for a few days." Carly hesitated. "I told Mia and Pop. We cried. But some of it was happy tears."

Carly had remained very close to her former in-laws. Therese envied her that. About the only contact she had with Paul's parents involved their grandchildren, whom they didn't want to raise, but they didn't believe Therese was doing a competent job, either.

Her latest decision regarding the kids would probably sever contact between them forever. At the moment, she couldn't decide whether that would be a good thing or a bad one.

"You know Jeff's parents will always love you, and it sounds like Dane's willing to include them in your lives." *I want to have little Jeff Juniors and Dane Juniors and Carly Juniors to chase after with you,* he'd said when he'd proposed. He knew she'd loved Jeff dearly, and he didn't feel threatened by it because he also knew she loved him dearly.

Could Therese ever have that again? Maybe when the kids were gone. Maybe when she'd regained control of her life. But perfect loves weren't out there floating around for the taking. She'd already had one. Unlike what happened with Carly, one might be all she was entitled to.

"They're going to come down before the wedding so they can meet," Carly was saying when Therese tuned in again. "It's going to be fine, isn't it? We're all adults, and we can work things out."

"It'll be better than fine. Mia and Pop already love him just for making you happy, and they'll love him even more for himself. They'll probably adopt him for their own, the way they did you."

"From your mouth to God's ears," Carly murmured. "Is there anything I can do to help with Abby?"

"Just pray."

"I always do. Is there anything I can do to help you?"

With a sigh from deep in her heart, Therese repeated the answer. "Just pray." For strength, for courage, for wisdom.

* * *

Saturday night in Tallgrass, Oklahoma, was like being nowhere at all.

But almost immediately Keegan contradicted that. Tallgrass was much bigger than Leesville, where he lived, and offered a lot more than miles of businesses butted up to one busy road. He arrived around sunset and drove through the town. There were the usual fast-food restaurants, bars, and churches that any town had, but also a sense of a real town, not just a place that existed to support the Army base. It had a thriving downtown, and there was action other than prostitutes and drugs—restaurants open, a few shops getting ready to close for the day, regular people strolling the sidewalks.

Murals of oil rigs, cowboys herding cattle, wild horses, buffalo, and Indian encampments covered entire brick walls, along with old-timey ads for soda fountains and cigars. The downtown area looked solid, as if it had endured the Dust Bowl, drought, and tornados just fine and wasn't planning on surrendering to any other disaster. It had a sense of permanency that appealed to him.

He'd driven down Main Street from one end to the other, past the national cemetery and the two main entrances to Fort Murphy, then took First Street all the way from the south edge of town to the north. He would find food, then a room, just as soon as he checked out something else.

The address was already in his Garmin, and the cheeky Australian voice he called Matilda led him through a few blocks of commercial property, then into residential neighborhoods. The houses in this part of town were mostly old, mostly well maintained, with mature trees that towered overhead and neatly mowed yards. The farther north and east he went, the bigger they got, the pricier, until finally he found himself at the curb across the street from 718 Cheyenne.

It was two stories, white wood, dark shutters, redbrick steps and foundation. The porch ran the length of the house, but it wasn't very wide, not like the porch on his mom's house that functioned as an outdoor living room. There was a swing and a wicker chair at one end, two wooden rockers at the other, with big pots of red flowers evenly spaced along the porch.

In the dim light, a piece of metal gleamed dully on the supporting post at the left of the steps, an anchor for hanging a flag. Flower beds lined the porch and the sidewalk that led to the driveway, where a silver minivan was parked in front of the garage. There were no toys visible—no three-wheelers or bikes, no basketball hoop, no abandoned skateboards. Inside, lights shone through sheer curtains in various rooms downstairs and were muted by blinds in one upstairs room.

So this was where Mariah's father lived. Keegan didn't know much about him beyond his name, and what he did know wasn't encouraging. The guy had been married when he'd gone to Fort Polk for training and hooked up with Sabrina. Then he'd come back home to Fort Murphy, and she'd never heard from him again. He hadn't even had the decency to respond when she told him she was pregnant. One e-mail going astray, maybe, but four? All going to his army.mil account? Not likely.

The house was nice, one Keegan couldn't afford on his salary. Of course, majors made significantly more than sergeants, and the major's wife probably had a job of her own. And kids of their own, judging by the size of the place. He'd guess four, maybe five bedrooms.

His chest tightened, and he shifted the air-conditioning to high, turning the vents so they blew straight at his face. There had to be room in a house like that for Mariah. Her father might have ignored her existence until now, and his wife might not know a thing about her, but things were about to change. Things *had* changed, the day Sabrina dropped her off and kept going.

Guilt settled in his gut, and he would have cursed his mother for putting it there if he hadn't been afraid God would smack him down for it. He wasn't Mariah's father. He'd dated her mother for two years, lived with her for one before she confessed to her affair with the major. That didn't make him responsible for her child. It wasn't his job to find her real family. It was just something he needed to do.

He was going to talk to her father, scope out the situation with his family, to make sure they would provide a good home for her. He wasn't abandoning her, because she wasn't his to abandon.

Now, if he could just get those damned big, solemn brown eyes out of his mind...

He'd sat there long enough to see everything and learn nothing. Shifting into drive again, he eased from the curb and headed back to Main Street. After a stop at a drive-in for a cheeseburger and onion rings, he drove a few more blocks to a motel on the west end of town. It was a genuine old-fashioned motor court, or at least made to look like one, with tiny individual structures for each room. A metal lawn chair in familiar faded green occupied each stoop, and neon buzzed and perfumed the air.

The metal key to Room 9 was bent. Getting it into the lock required a little jiggling, but soon enough the tumblers fell and he opened the door. Nothing luxurious—he'd known that from seeing the outside. But the room wasn't shabby. The vinyl floor was clean, the area rug showed marks from being recently vacuumed, and the bed was neatly made. Instead of stale-motel, it smelled like something baking—his mother's sticky buns, maybe.

The window air conditioner cooled with a hum instead of the deafening racket he'd expected, and the sofa was comfortable. With a tiny kitchenette—dorm fridge, two-burner cooktop, sink—he'd do fine for however long he had to be here. Best hope: a day. Realistic hope: a week or more.

That was okay. He had forty-five days' leave on the

books. If it took every one of them to get Mariah settled elsewhere, so be it.

After eating dinner, he brought in his bag, then pulled out the phone to call his mother. She'd already let him know, not long after he'd hit the interstate, that she and Mariah were back home in Natchitoches. *Call me when you get to Tallgrass,* she'd instructed him again. He grinned at the thought of all the times she'd told him that. *Call me when you get to basic training. Call me when you get back from leave. Call me when you get to Iraq. Call me when you get to Afghanistan.*

He had four brothers and sisters to prove there'd been a father in his life, but not one that had mattered much. Ercella was twice the man Max Logan was, mother and father to her own kids, now to Mariah. *Isn't it possible she's yours?* she'd asked more than once. *I think I see your eyes in hers.*

It wasn't possible. Not unless Sabrina had had the longest pregnancy on record, or the shortest with a healthy, full-term baby.

"I'm in Tallgrass," he said when his mother answered the phone.

The television sounded in the background, along with kids' voices. It didn't matter where Ercella went, she always attracted kids. With her own grown and her grandkids living an hour or more away, she entertained the neighborhood kids on Saturday nights and most any other time they wandered over. "Is it nice?" she asked over the noise.

"Well, it's no Natchitoches," he said drily.

"Naturally. Have you decided how you're going to…"

He silently finished the question for her: give away the grandbaby who wasn't her grandbaby in any place except her heart. "I thought I'd go by and meet the guy tomorrow afternoon."

"What? And just say, 'Hey, remember when you had an affair with my girlfriend? Well, here's a cigar, it's a girl'?"

His scowl fixed on the silent television. "I haven't exactly figured that out."

"Be up front. 'You got a two-year-old daughter and her mama doesn't want her and I don't want her and—' "

Keegan heard a sob before Ercella clamped off the words. It both pained and frustrated him. "Mom, I'm sorry—"

"I know." Sniffly noises, as if she was wiping her nose. "You don't wanna raise a kid who's not yours. I understand that. It's expensive. Lots of responsibility for a lot of years. It's not your job. I get it, Keegan."

But in her heart, Keegan knew, she really didn't. She might have in the very beginning, when he'd first told her the situation with Mariah, when he'd asked for her help. But now that she'd gotten to know the little girl, of course she'd fallen in love with her. How could she not? She was a mother deep in her bones, to any kids who needed mothering.

God help her, Mariah needed mothering. She'd had so little of it in her life.

"I'll call you as soon as I talk to the major, okay?"

"Make sure you do." Ercella breathed deeply and made an effort to sound normal. "I've got to shoo these kids home and get Mariah bathed and ready for bed. You want to say good night to her?"

Before Keegan could say no—he was ashamed of it, but there it was—his mom's voice distantly said, "She's listening. Say something."

"Hey, Mariah." He cleared his throat. "Sounds like you're having a good time. Good night and…sleep tight and…" Before he could remember the rest of his mother's nightly routine with her kids, the phone hit the floor with a thud.

A moment later, Ercella came on again. "She was listening. She recognized your voice. I could see it in her little eyes."

Of course she recognized his voice. She'd heard it talking around and about her every day for the past month. "I'll talk to you tomorrow, Mom. Love you."

After her *love you, too,* he laid the phone aside and stretched back on the bed. Best hope: a day. Realistic: a week. Worst: having to turn to the authorities to get Mariah's father to accept responsibility for her. Even though it would break his mom's heart, he didn't have a choice.

Because he wasn't Mariah's father.

* * *

Sunday morning services were one of the highlights of Therese's week. The church she attended occupied an entire block on the fringe between the business district and the houses that edged downtown. Broad concrete steps led to an old sandstone building with classrooms and a gym on the lower level and a sanctuary with arched stained glass windows filling the upper level. Her regular seat was a pew about a third from the back on the left, which she shared most Sundays with Carly, while Abby and Jacob sat elsewhere with their friends.

She wasn't surprised this morning that Carly was absent. Still floating somewhere in the stratosphere with Dane, she supposed as she settled on the bench alone.

The solitude didn't last long. She'd just set her purse aside when the cushions gave slightly and a familiar voice greeted her. "Hello, Therese. How are you?"

Loretta Baxter was a major and one of the few people in Therese's life who created incredibly bittersweet feelings just by existing. LoLo had been the CNO—casualty notification officer—who had notified Therese of Paul's death, so she was associated with the worst moment of Therese's life. Afterward, though, she'd provided counseling, support, and friendship that had helped Therese keep her sanity on more than one occasion.

She was also one of the rare people outside of the margarita club to whom Therese didn't have to lie. "Things could be better. I'm not sure they could be worse."

"I noticed Abby's new hairstyle. And color. And the tan." LoLo glanced at her hands, folded in her lap. "And her manicure looks better than mine."

"Did you also notice the rage in her eyes?"

"I thought she looked a little testy when we passed in the aisle. So the visit with her mother wasn't a success."

"The visit was fine. The coming home sucked pond water." Therese gazed at an arch of Jesus with the children. *Suffer the little children…to come unto me*, He'd said. *Suffer* seemed such an appropriate word at the moment.

"Have you made any decisions?"

Therese's fingers tightened on her Bible. While the kids were in California, she'd had an appointment with the Judge Advocate General's office—the legal office—on post, and she'd talked with LoLo. It seemed everyone knew of her desire to reclaim her life by giving up custody of Paul's kids. Except the kids.

"Not yet. I actually feel like I'm making a bit of

progress with Jacob. It—it would be okay having him." She stared harder at the image, the colors so vibrant, the love so obvious even in glass. Such serenity.

When was the last time she'd felt serene? Long before Paul's death. Being a military wife wasn't ever easy. The moves, the training, the deployments, the forced independence, the loneliness, the ever-present fear of loss. Her last moments of serenity had likely been when they'd moved to Tallgrass: a new post, a new town they both loved immediately, new opportunities, and plans to get pregnant as soon as they settled in.

Then had come custody of the kids.

Then the deployment.

Then his death.

"But you can't stop thinking about how that would make Abby feel," LoLo said quietly.

Abandoned by everyone. Rejected while Jacob was accepted. Even more unwanted and unloved than she already felt.

Therese sighed heavily as the choir filed onto the stage and the pastor moved into place behind the pulpit. "It's a hard decision."

LoLo squeezed her hand. "You'll make the right one. I have faith in you."

Though she dutifully bowed her head as the pastor requested, inside she was silently scoffing. Faith? In her? She didn't even have that herself anymore. Once she'd thought she could rule the world, but truth was, she hadn't faced any real complications in that world. Life as she'd known it was easy.

Lord, I'm not asking for easy again. Just bearable. I can live with bearable. Please.

After prayers and songs, the congregation split up for Sunday school, kids and young adults streaming out the side doors, mothers taking their little ones to the nursery, singles and seniors heading for their own classes. Therese remained where she was, her gaze following Abby as she shuffled along behind Nicole, head down, full lower lip stuck out. She looked miserable, so at odds with her delicate beauty. An angel whose burdens had become unbearable.

The Sunday school class was interesting, the sermon inspiring, the singing the best part of the service. Old hymns spoke to her soul, and this morning they were all old. They gave her peace, at least, until the closing prayer was echoed with *Amens* around the room.

LoLo hugged her when they stood. "If you ever need anything…"

"I've got your number." Therese returned the hug.

"And I've got your back."

LoLo wandered away to visit with other members. The congregation was a nice mix of civilian and military, families who'd lived there a hundred years and families who would move on in three years. Therese and Paul would have moved on by now if things had been different. She would have been teaching in a new school, the kids adjusting to their own new schools and the knowledge that, in a few more years, they would move on again. Nomads, gypsies. She thought Jacob was well suited for the life.

Abby, not so much.

After speaking with the minister and his wife, along with the youth minister, Therese located the kids outside and motioned them toward the car. About halfway there, they fell into step, a silent group. Therese knew how the next few minutes would go: she would ask, *What do you want for dinner?* Jacob would grunt, and Abby would ignore her. She would throw out some suggestions; Jacob would grunt, and Abby would ignore her. She would finally make a choice, and Jacob would say nothing, and Abby would sniff scornfully.

Since Carly was usually with them, the routine hadn't bothered Therese so much, but Carly wasn't there today. She might stop going to church completely, or she might go elsewhere with Dane. She might prefer to develop her own family's Sunday routine over being a part of the dysfunctional Mathesons'.

The possibility hurt somewhere deep inside Therese. Carly was her best friend, and nothing could end that. But Carly being in love and happy with Dane could change it.

When they reached the minivan, she beeped the doors, and Abby climbed into the backseat, per usual. Jacob hesitated, then, once again, slid into the front passenger seat. "Can we have Mexican for lunch?"

Therese stilled in the act of putting on her seat belt. A flicker at the rearview mirror showed Abby was surprised, too, and peripherally Therese saw the hint of a flush darkening Jacob's cheeks. She forced herself to go on as if nothing unusual had happened, clicking the belt, starting the engine. "Sure. You want Three Amigos, Bueno, or something else?"

"Three Amigos." Jacob shrugged. "You go there every week, so we hardly ever do."

It was true. They ate at home practically every night, even if it was just frozen pizza and a quick-tossed salad. Considering how uncomfortable their family meals were, she preferred to hold them in private. "You have any problem with that, Abby?"

Her only answer was silence. Therese backed out of the parking space, joined the line of cars waiting to exit the parking lot, then smiled at Jacob. "Three Amigos it is."

The restaurant, a bright dose of primary colors in the middle of a strip parking center, was popular, and Sunday post-church was no exception. Therese gave her name to the hostess, then joined the kids near the blue-tiled fountain in the middle of the lobby. Abby was already texting, and Jacob was staring into the water, his hands shoved into his pockets.

He glanced at Therese when she stopped near him. "Why do people throw money in fountains?"

"It's tradition. Throw in a coin, make a wish." Since it didn't seem a reasonable response to him, she went on. "Some ancient cultures believed water was sacred. If you sacrificed something you held dear to the deity that lived there, you'd get something in return. What do people hold more dear than money?"

"Throwing a penny into water is a stupid way to make wishes come true." His shoulders hunched forward, in a subconsciously defensive gesture that she'd seen in him since they'd met. A little boy who didn't understand why Daddy moved away, why he was living with another woman; a frightened child who'd been taken from the only home he'd ever known and sent halfway across the country; a boy who'd stood stoic but heartbroken at his father's graveside.

Therese didn't know what to say. She laid her hand on his shoulder, half afraid he'd shrug it off, and squeezed. "I know. But sometimes it's fun to do things that are stupid or silly." A pause, and she withdrew her hand. "You threw pennies in there the first time your dad and I brought you here. You wished for a new bike and a new game."

He tilted his head so he could see her without quite looking at her. "Did I get them?"

"Not then, but for Christmas. Though, by that time, you wanted a different game."

After considering it a minute, he shrugged. "But those are things. Things aren't real wishes."

No. Things could be bought, borrowed, traded, and sold. Real wishes were rarer, more precious, lasting longer...or not nearly long enough.

"Matheson, party of three," the hostess called, saving Therese from having to respond to Jacob's last words. She smiled at him, and together they circled the fountain to reach the young woman, Abby trailing silently behind.

Chapter 3

It had been a long time since Keegan had had an entire morning to himself with nothing to do. He slept in late—a clock down the street was chiming eleven when he woke—then ran a few miles, bought a protein bar and a Red Bull from the convenience store on the corner, and made it lunch out on the stoop. The old metal chair was rusted, the paint sun-faded, and it creaked when he shifted just like the ones in his mom's yard.

The house where he'd grown up was nothing special: maybe fifteen hundred square feet, three bedrooms, a living room, dining room, and kitchen that had seen a lot of hard use. The front porch was broad with mismatched chairs, screens to keep out the bugs, and a paddle fan to help cool the heat. Around back was a large yard where grass never grew, thanks to all the playing that went on there, another assortment of odd chairs and tables, a clothesline Ercella still used, and toys: a swing set as rusted as this chair, old bikes, a sandbox, a wading pool.

She'd worked hard to raise him, his brothers, and his sisters. Keegan didn't remember a lot about their father even though he was the oldest of the five. A wandering man, she'd called Max Logan. A no-good waste of air, their Granny Dupree said. Ercella must have agreed with her mother eventually, because after baby number five, she'd given up hope of him ever coming home to stay. She'd never divorced him, though, and she still thought of him fondly, at least from time to time.

And she'd never, ever made Keegan or any of the others feel unwanted. Hell, she couldn't even imagine not wanting a kid.

So what was he going to say to the major? And what if the major didn't want Mariah? Didn't remember Sabrina? Didn't want his wife finding out he'd been unfaithful?

What if he refused to take her? Even the courts wouldn't force a child on an unwilling parent. The Army would make him provide for her, and she'd get all the benefits any other dependent got. But benefits wouldn't make up for not having a family.

Wearily, he gathered his trash, went inside, and stripped for a shower. If he didn't come up with a way to break the news to Mariah's father before he left the motel, he'd do it on the drive over. He always worked best under pressure.

He shaved, dressed in jeans and an old gray-and-black PT shirt, put on running shoes. After staring at himself in the mirror a minute or two, he set his jaw and turned away. It was time to go. No point in putting off the inevitable. Time to fulfill his sole duty to Mariah.

It was harder than he'd expected to walk out the door, lock up, and get in his car. The farther he drove, the slower he drove. It *was* inevitable, right? He didn't want to be a father. He *wasn't* a father. And this could turn out to be the best thing in Mariah's life. Her father and his wife might welcome her into their family. They might be the parents she deserved. They might love her and pamper her and treat her like a princess.

And then Keegan could go on with his life. Best outcome for everyone.

The minivan was in the driveway again. He pulled to the curb, this time in front of the house, and shut off the engine. Took a deep breath. Swiped his hands on his jeans. Took his keys. Got out.

The yard was green, and flowers were blooming in the beds. Some of them smelled sweet as he walked past. Others didn't smell at all. The flag was flying this afternoon—or, more appropriately, hanging. Not even a breath of wind stirred the air. The flowers on the porch glistened with water that pooled around the bottoms of the pots from a recent watering. Music sounded faintly from inside.

He stood in front of the door, raised his finger to the doorbell and, wishing he was back home in Louisiana, pushed it. The chimes echoed distantly. He'd gone past second thoughts and was on to fourth and fifth ones when the door was jerked open.

"*What?*" Standing across the threshold was a girl, somewhere between twelve and twenty, blond and petite and pretty. She had the same coloring, the same pouty lip, as Mariah. Her hip was cocked out, one hand resting on it, and she wore an expression of boredom and annoyance and seething. His sisters had seethed a lot when they were her age.

"Is Major Matheson here?"

Her brown eyes narrowed to slits, and she squinted at

him like Mariah did, as if she'd summed him up and found him lacking. God, was Mariah's ear-piercing shriek going to come from this girl's mouth next?

It did, but not directed at him. She tilted her head toward the rear of the house and screeched, "Tuh-*reese!*" Without waiting for a response, she spun and stomped up the stairs.

So Mariah had a half-sister who was either having a really bad day or really needed her butt swatted. Great. Every little girl needed a big sister, right? A moody, bratty big sister, in this case, but still a sister.

The door opened into a long hallway that led to the kitchen. A double-wide door on the left opened into the living room, and another doorway showed a bit of the dining room. The floors were hardwood with area rugs, the furniture was good, and the family portraits were plentiful. The major, his wife, one girl, one boy. Both kids looked like their dad.

So did Mariah.

His gaze swept the living room again, jerking to a stop on the mantel. Another photograph, the major in his dress uniform, looking stern, and beside it a display case with a flag and a bunch of medals and ribbons. A photo of him in ACUs, sunglasses shoved up on his head, grinning. Next to that—

"Can I help you?"

His jaw clenched, he forced his gaze to the woman who was approaching down the hall. She was tall, slender, with brown hair swept back from her face. She wore faded jeans that fitted snugly and a T-shirt identical to his own. Her husband's, he thought, judging by the size, then he looked at the mantel again. "I . . . I, uh . . ."

As she waited for an answer, her brows arched over

hazel eyes. She was pretty, not like her pouty daughter but in a rounder, more womanly way. And she was starting to look wary.

"I was hoping to see Major Matheson," he said. The next natural thing was to ask if he was home, but he couldn't force the words out. Not when he already knew the answer.

Emotion flashed through her eyes, and she swallowed visibly before forcing a sad smile. "You don't know." She said it as fact; then, with the faintest tremble in her voice, she went on. "Paul was killed in Afghanistan."

* * *

Killed. Aw, jeez. Of course, Keegan had known it the instant he'd seen the Gold Star flag on the mantel. Blue Star flags were for the families of service members—his mom had one hanging in the front window—and Gold Star flags were for the families whose loved ones didn't come back.

He'd never considered the possibility that Major Matheson was dead, that that was why he'd never contacted Sabrina, why he'd never acknowledged Mariah. He'd just assumed the major was like any other bastard who'd run around on his wife: ignoring the consequences of his infidelity.

Dead. That was a hell of an excuse for ignoring his daughter.

The major's wife—widow—was waiting for a response from him. It took him a moment to find the proper words. "I'm sorry." Even as he said them, even as she nodded as if she'd heard them a thousand times, he felt guilty for them. He was sorry. He was even sorry the major had been killed.

Too damn many people had died in the war, and every single one of them was a loss to the country.

But mostly he was sorry for himself. Sorry that his plans had just been shot to hell. Sorry that he couldn't say, "Here's your daughter; her name's Mariah; take care of her." It might have gone over all right with the major. He seriously doubted it would fly with his widow.

"Thank you," she said politely. She hesitated a moment, then took a step back, gesturing toward the living room. "Would you like to come in?"

"Sure, thanks," he answered mindlessly when what he really needed was someplace quiet to think and figure out what to do now. He'd been counting on this trip working out successfully. He'd thought Matheson might balk, but he'd been convinced that in the end, Mariah would have a new home.

So much for hopes. There was no father for Mariah. No easy way out. Maybe he should spend the rest of his leave trying to find Sabrina, but she'd abandoned her daughter once before. How could he know she wouldn't do it again?

Besides, Sabrina had spent half her life running and hiding. The four years she'd lived in Leesville were the longest she'd spent in one place since she was fifteen. She had no family to speak of, and she'd had a million dream places to live: Los Angeles, San Diego, New York, Chicago, Miami, Las Vegas, Honolulu, Acapulco.

"I'm Therese Matheson," the major's widow said as she led the way into the living room. She put a slight emphasis on her first name, *Tuh-race,* correcting the seething teenager's mispronunciation. She offered her hand.

"Sergeant Keegan Logan." He kept his handshake brief, the way he'd hoped to keep all his contact with the Matheson family brief. Even in those few seconds, though, he noticed that her hand wasn't as soft as he'd expected. The skin was warm, a little callused, her nails pale pink tipped with white. She wore a ring on her right hand, gold with a fiery orange stone, and a bracelet with the same stones linked end to end.

And a wedding ring on her left hand? He checked as he stepped back and saw, yes, a gold band, along with a second band bearing a chunky square cut diamond. It was impressive, but it didn't suit her. A delicate hand like that needed a more delicate stone.

And he needed to focus on the problem at hand. No distractions caused by any pretty woman but especially the widow.

Releasing her hand, he felt the need to swipe his palm on his jeans. Huh. He couldn't remember the last time a handshake had made him sweat.

She sat in a chair near the fireplace, the comfortable sort that his mother cuddled all the kids in, and crossed her legs. He chose the opposite chair, not nearly as comfortable, and sat stiffly. "Can I ask when...?"

Sadness crept into her hazel eyes. "Three years ago. An IED."

"Sorry," he said again.

"You knew him through the Army?"

He didn't like to lie, but what was the point of the truth? *Actually, no, I know of him because he slept with my girlfriend. He betrayed your marriage vows, he betrayed you, and he has a baby girl who needs a home.* The truth would serve no purpose but to hurt her, and she'd already lost her husband. Hadn't she been hurt enough? "I was in Iraq and Afghanistan. It must have been tough for you and your children." He gestured toward a family photo, the girl happier than she'd been today but not by much, the boy looking grim, too.

Therese looked at the picture for a moment or two before smiling faintly. "It was very difficult for Paul's children. They miss him very much."

Paul's children. Not *our* or *my*. She was raising her husband's kids from another relationship. Not lucky enough to have any of her own, assuming she wanted them, but surrounded by her husband's kids.

"Are you stationed here at Fort Murphy?"

"No. I had some leave and thought I would look him up. I'm at Fort Polk now."

She smiled faintly. "He went down there several times for training. He didn't like the place, but I always thought being that close to New Orleans would make up for anything lacking in the town and the post."

Keegan swallowed back irritation. He might not love Leesville, either, but he was entitled. It was his state. Let Matheson find fault with his own home state before he started on someone else's.

"What do you do there?"

"My MOS is Sixty-Eight Whiskey." Military Occupational Specialty was the Department of Defense's way of saying job specialty. Why speak in full words when acronyms and numbers would do?

When she raised a brow, he added, "A combat medic."

A flash of sympathy crossed her face, and he knew what she was thinking. A medic, combat tours, the things he'd seen, the lives he'd saved and the ones he couldn't do anything for but send on down the line or be with them while they died. Other than the danger, that was the thing that worried his mom most: how he dealt with the inability to save everyone.

"Tough job."

"They all are."

She studied him a moment, tilting her head to one side, before asking, "Is that why you wanted to see Paul? About something that happened while you were deployed?"

So Matheson wasn't the sort to be friendly with a non-commissioned officer. That didn't surprise Keegan. A lot of officers mistook subordinate for inferior. They gave orders to the enlisted people under their commands; they risked those people's lives; but they didn't become friends with them.

"Yeah." It wasn't a lie. He had been deployed when Matheson had done his last training at Fort Polk, and something had damn well happened. But if she believed he'd wanted to discuss some combat incident, let her. He was fine with misdirection.

Pushing forward, he stood, and she automatically rose, too, a fluid movement that reminded him not of a dancer's grace but a dancer's strength. Therese Matheson was a strong woman. Some wives found their strength when their husbands deployed, some when they died, but his guess was that she'd nailed hers long before she'd even met her husband. "I'm sorry to have bothered you." His mom's manners forced him to go on. "I'm sorry about your loss."

"So am I." She walked to the door with him, arms folded over her stomach as he stepped out onto the porch. "Have a safe trip back to Fort Polk."

"Thanks."

But it wasn't the trip back that concerned him.

It was what to do about Mariah.

* * *

Therese closed the door behind the visitor, then stepped to the side to watch him through the sheer curtains over the narrow window there. More than three years, and telling someone Paul was dead never got easier, whether it was an old friend of hers, an old friend of his, or a total stranger.

Keegan Logan. Nice name. It suited him. If he wasn't thirty, he was close. His sandy brown hair was a high-and-tight in need of a trim, his skin deeply tanned, his eyes surprisingly blue. Even in casual clothes, he had that Army Strong look—erect posture, chiseled muscles, square jaw, a compact body to do a uniform proud. He wasn't overly tall, maybe five ten, and under normal circumstances he probably exuded confidence, assurance, and charm.

Under normal circumstances, he probably fluttered the pulses of every woman in a hundred-foot radius. Therese's pulse had been unflutterable for a long time. Though when—if—it did flutter again in response to a man, it could be a man like him. She did have a weakness for blue eyes and chiseled muscles.

She watched him climb into his car, shiny and black, then pull away from the curb before leaning against the door, considering the future. However distant it might be, someday she might find herself in Carly's position, interested in, sexually attracted to, in love with another man. A part of her wanted it intensely. A part of her wasn't sure she could handle loving another man, because as she'd learned too well with Paul, love came with the risk of loss. She wasn't sure she'd ever be up to that.

When a noise from upstairs drew her gaze that way, unease curled through her stomach, leaving sourness in its wake. There had been a time in her life when uneasiness was a rare thing—nerves over a school test, regret for an argument with a friend, fear that her college boyfriend was seeing someone else. Now it was a constant. Nerves strung tight. Queasiness. Uncertainty. Dread.

"Who was that man?" Abby stood on the landing, glaring down at her like an enraged demigoddess. How difficult had it been for her, opening the door to someone asking for her father? Logically, Therese knew it must have been tough—it had been tough for *her*—but she saw no outward sign of hurt on Abby's face. Just anger.

"He was a friend of your dad's."

"How could he be a friend and not know that Daddy's dead?"

Daddy's dead. The kids usually didn't use that phrase. They usually didn't talk about Paul's death at all, but when they did, it was with euphemisms. *Dead* sounded too harsh. Too final.

"People lose touch. They met in Iraq. Your dad came back here. Sergeant Logan went wherever he was assigned. Their paths didn't cross again."

"So they weren't friends."

"Just because you lose contact with someone doesn't mean you stop caring about them. I haven't seen my best friend from high school in ten years and haven't talked to her in five, but if we got together again, it would be like nothing had changed."

"Things *have* changed or you would have seen her and talked to her." Abby snorted. "What did he want?"

Sometime in the past moments, Therese's head had begun to ache. It was Abby's tone of voice, just the right pitch and level of snottiness to zero in on her eardrums with laser precision. She pressed her fingertips to her temple, but it did nothing to ease the throb. "To touch base." She guessed. People who'd been in combat together always had memories to discuss, maybe questions to answer or sorrows to share.

With a dramatic *hmph!* and a toss of her hair, Abby spun around and disappeared down the hall. Predictably, a moment later her bedroom door slammed, the exclamation point at the end of the longest conversation they'd had since her return.

Therese needed aspirin, caffeine, and sugar. After lunch, she'd stopped at CaraCakes, her favorite bakery in town, and picked up fresh-baked bread and cookies. Cookies never failed to improve her disposition. In the kitchen, she poured a glass of mint tea brewed with simple syrup and took her first cookie from the pink and black CaraCakes box. By the time she began the second cookie, the oatmeal, raisins, and brown sugar had worked their magic, rendering the aspirin tablets unnecessary.

She was a creature of routine, and except for church this morning, today had broken routine. The things that usually occupied her time—laundry, paying bills, getting ready for work—had been done during spring break. Except for the dirty clothes Jacob had brought home with him, there was nothing requiring her attention. She could read a book. Go for a walk. Talk on the phone with that old friend she'd mentioned to Abby.

Instead she stepped outside. The house had a great front porch but only a square slab of concrete out back. It was one of the projects she and Paul had planned: jack-hammering the cement, putting in brick in a herringbone pattern, building a low wall around the perimeter to hold flower beds she would fill with something lovely and creeping, like phlox or ivy. They'd intended to reseed the yard, too, and add crape myrtles along the fence. She liked the vibrant colors and the papery peeling bark, and he'd liked the alien-looking seed pods left behind after the blooms.

All they'd managed was to invest in a nice set of outdoor furniture. Here it was April, and she hadn't bothered bringing out the yellow floral cushions for them yet. Hadn't considered hiring someone to replace the patio. Hadn't even looked at flowers or crape myrtles.

What did the state of the backyard matter when she hadn't yet reached a decision about the kids?

Even though her tea was in a tall insulated glass, sweat formed on it in the time it took to pull a teak chair into the sun and drag over another to prop her feet on. She sat, eyes closed, face tilted back, absorbing the sun's warmth and concentrating on settling the disquiet inside her.

It was impossible, though. The first step in giving up custody of Abby and Jacob would be talking to their mother to see if she would take them back. Therese did her best to avoid talking to Catherine. The woman was the role model for selfishness and irresponsibility. Needing *me time* when she had two small children to raise. Refusing to be there for them when their father died because *she* was grieving too much herself. Oblivious to Abby's unhappiness and uncaring that neither child wanted to live with Therese. And those clothes she'd bought Abby...

Selfish and irresponsible. And yet Therese would return custody to her in a heartbeat. Did that make *her* the role model for evil stepmothers everywhere?

Catherine was their mother, the small voice inside her

insisted. But another small voice disagreed. Catherine gave birth to them. She hadn't mothered them in the past four years. They were, for all practical purposes, orphaned. She had left them willingly, Paul unwillingly, but the results were the same.

Paul had left them with Therese. He'd entrusted two of the three people he'd loved most in the world to the third. He'd believed in her so much that she'd believed in herself. It hurt that she'd lost faith.

"Are you taking a nap or getting an early start on a tan?"

"Me, tan? Don't you know that's unhealthy for you? I'm getting my daily dose of vitamin D." Slowly Therese opened her eyes to find Carly standing in the doorway. "Grab yourself a glass of tea and bring those cookies on the island out here."

When her friend settled in the chair that had minutes before supported Therese's feet, Therese gave her a long look. Carly wasn't an impressive beauty, the kind who made men and women both take a second or third look, but Therese had always thought her delicately pretty. This afternoon she was downright radiant, and it had nothing to do with the sun.

"Being in love agrees with you." Therese hoped her friend didn't hear the envy in her voice.

"Being in love with someone who loves me back agrees with me."

"How is Dane?"

"Recuperating," Carly replied with a grin.

The man had spent months dealing with the loss of his leg, and the long months before that, he'd been in Afghanistan. He probably hadn't had sex in longer than most men thought possible, until a few nights ago, and

Carly had been celibate even longer. But no more. Therese sighed, not caring if her envy sounded loud and clear. Carly and Dane were going to live happily ever after. She would probably be pregnant before the wedding next month. They would find bliss and joy in every moment they could because they both knew how fragile life was.

Yep, Therese was jealous. All the margarita sisters were. Very happy for Carly, but jealous just the same.

"I missed church this morning. And dinner."

"We missed you, too."

"I don't plan to stop going. To church or to dinner with you guys."

Therese wanted to say the thought had never occurred to her, that she'd known things would change with Dane in Carly's life but she'd also known it would never change their friendship, but she couldn't without lying. The main group of the margarita club had discussed that very thing a while back—ironically, on the very day Carly met Dane. At the time of the conversation, none of them had guessed that she'd just met Mr. Right—more appropriately, Staff Sergeant Right—least of all her.

Even so, there'd been a little fear. All of the group, but especially Carly, Jessy, Ilena, Fia, Marti, Lucy, and Therese, had helped each other through their husbands' deaths. They'd become best friends, sisters, family. They had assured each other that a new man in their lives wouldn't affect them, but they worried anyway.

Because she couldn't say anything without giving away the relief that filled her at Carly's words, she settled for leaning forward and squeezing her hand.

After selecting a cookie from the box, Carly glanced toward the house, then said in a low voice, "Abby answered the door. Gorgeous haircut. She looks so grown up and beautiful. The boys at school tomorrow are going to be tripping over their tongues."

"Oh, gee, thanks for reminding me of that. You just brought back my headache."

Carly didn't look the least bit apologetic. "I want boys. Little girls are so sweet and adorable, but then they grow into teenage girls and you have to deal with teenage boys. I want boys."

"Paul never thought about her growing up. In his mind she was always Daddy's girl. If it ever occurred to him that someday she'd be dating, having sex, falling in love, he shoved it out of his mind. If he saw her today, he wouldn't be able to live in denial anymore." She paused to sip her tea before drily adding, "If he'd seen her yesterday, she'd be locked in her room for the next ten years. Oh, Carly, am I really considering sending her back to live with the mother who dressed her like a hooker?"

Carly's gaze remained steady on her. "I don't know. Are you?"

Some decisions were so easy to make. When she'd been offered a job in Georgia after college, she'd taken about sixty seconds to consider accepting, even though it meant moving far from Montana and her family, and she'd never regretted it. When she'd met Paul after he and some buddies helped her with a broken-down car, she hadn't thought twice about his invitation to dinner—or to bed. She'd never regretted that, either.

Not even when she'd stood beside his grave, clutching the flag presented to her by a solemn-faced general.

"Every thought I have about the kids makes my stomach hurt, whether it's keeping them or sending them away. I

think of five more years like the last two, until Abby goes
to college, and I can't stand it. I think of not seeing them,
not knowing what's going on with them, whether they've
been abandoned again, and I can't stand that, either." Her
eyes grew damp as she spoke, and the tightness in her chest
made a deep breath impossible. "I think about what Paul
would say—" She finished with an inhale so sharp her
throat burned with it.

"Oh, honey, Paul would say that you've done the best
you could. You've provided them with a home and security.
You've taken them to counseling. You've tried, Therese.
That's all anyone can do." Carly's expression darkened.
"That's more than their mother or grandparents have
done."

The words reassured her—a little. But there was so
damn much doubt as she stared across the yard at the bare
wooden fence that separated it from the neighbor's. The
unfinished yard, the forgotten plans, the disappointing life.
Everything was on hold, it seemed, waiting for her to find a
solution she could live with. Nothing was going to change
unless she changed it, and she didn't know the right way to
do that. "I just feel so conflicted."

"You know I'll support whatever you do," Carly said.
"But, sweetie, if you're this torn, maybe you're not ready
to make a decision yet. Maybe you should pray more, think
more, do the counseling bit more. I don't know, maybe you
should even set the kids down and tell them their options—
straighten up and act human, be a responsible member of
this family, or go away."

That was most of her friends' opinion—at least, the
straighten-up-and-act-human part. How many times had
she heard it? *I'd smack any child who spoke to me like*

*that. My mama never would have put up with such a smart
mouth. They have to learn that behavior has consequences.*

She could have been tougher on them. Of course she
knew that. But, as the chaplain, the psychologists, and the
therapists had repeatedly reminded her, they were grieving children. She was the adult. They'd advised cutting the
kids some slack, and she had done it. She'd let them get
away with things Paul hadn't tolerated. They'd pushed the
limits of her control, and she had never raised her voice,
much less a hand, to them in anger.

Abby couldn't make the same claim. Therese imagined
she could still feel the tenderness in her cheek from the
slap Abby had once delivered in a fit of anger. The breaking point in their so-called relationship.

Which begged the question: if the relationship was broken, why hadn't she called Catherine yet?

*   *   *

After leaving the Matheson house, Keegan turned onto
Main Street, found a parking spot at the back of the Sonic
drive-in, and ordered before dialing his mother's number.
Ercella answered on the second ring, not bothering with a
greeting. "Did you talk to him?"

He removed his sunglasses and pinched the bridge of his
nose. "No. He's dead."

"He's— Oh, Lord, bless his heart. And his family's."
She murmured more, a prayer for Matheson's soul, no
doubt. A month ago she'd been angry that he refused to acknowledge his daughter. Every few days since, she'd asked
how in the world any man worthy of the name *father* could
not want to be with a precious little girl—sometimes as

much a dig at Keegan, he thought, as Matheson. Now she was praying for the man.

Honesty forced Keegan to admit that she'd probably been praying for Matheson from the first time she'd heard of him. She believed God answered prayers.

"Did you meet his wife?"

"Yes."

"Poor thing. Finding a stranger on her doorstep asking for her dead husband."

Poor thing. Not the first thought Therese Matheson brought to his mind. Pretty. Contained. Grieving, but going on with life. Staying strong. Raising his children from a previous relationship. Had she wanted children of her own? Matheson's children?

With a bratty teenager and a son who looked a few years younger, did she miss the cute cuddly days of toddlers?

Don't even think it. If Therese didn't know about her husband's infidelity or his illegitimate daughter's existence, damned if he would be the one to tell her. He wasn't about to tarnish her hero's memory for her.

His mother echoed his thoughts. "Does she know about Mariah?"

"Hard to say."

"And you can't just come out and ask. If she doesn't, it would probably break her heart. So what now? You gonna spend the night before you come home?"

The car hop, a young redhead so pregnant she looked as if she might pop right there, tapped on his window, and he rolled it down. "Hold on, Mom."

"Cheeseburger, tots, large cherry limeade," the girl said cheerfully, trading him the bag for a ten-dollar bill. She was probably an Army wife working to make ends meet.

Defending your country didn't pay as well as it could, especially for families.

"Keep the change," he said before picking up his phone again.

"Well?" Ercella prompted.

Going home. There was no reason not to. No reason to even bother spending the night. He wasn't tired. He could be in Leesville in time to sleep in his own bed.

He didn't have to be back at work for a couple more weeks.

He hadn't taken time off in a while.

He could probably find some old friends at Fort Murphy, or at Fort Riley a few hours north, Fort Sill a few hours southwest, or definitely at Fort Carson a long day's drive west. He could even hang around Tallgrass and see what this part of Oklahoma had to offer.

"Well?"

"I don't know, Mom. I think I'll wait...Maybe Matheson's got parents somewhere or a brother or sister."

There wasn't any kind of physical connection between them, so how could she make the phone vibrate with her disapproval? "This child shouldn't be raised by grandparents."

"You're raising her."

"I'm helping out. She needs parents young enough to do things with her, to have fun with her, who won't be on Social Security before she even gets out of grade school. She needs a regular family."

"And we're not it." Immediately he regretted the words, the tone. She loved Mariah and considered her family even if he didn't.

Before he could apologize, Ercella stiffly said, "According to the State of Louisiana, we are. *You're* listed as father on her birth certificate. *You've* got custody of her. She's your legal responsibility even if she isn't your daughter."

"And I'm trying to do what's best for her—find her real family. Mom, I warned you..." The day he'd asked for her help, he'd stressed it would be temporary. Not to get too attached. That he intended to find Mariah's father and turn her over to him.

But telling Ercella Logan not to get attached to a kid who needed her was like telling the fish in Saline Lake not to rely too much on the water they lived in. She'd known it. He'd known it.

"I know." She sounded weary, and fairly so. They'd had this conversation too many times before. "I just wish..."

That Mariah *was* his daughter. Her granddaughter.

There had been a moment, back when Sabrina broke the news that she was pregnant, that he'd wanted it, too. He hadn't been looking to become a father, not yet, though he'd always figured he would. They'd had a solid relationship. They'd had fun together. Good times, good sex, a good commitment.

In that moment, he had thought they'd get married—his mother would've had his hide if they hadn't—and by the time the baby was born, he would have been ready for fatherhood.

Then, less than five minutes later, she'd blown that thought out of his mind.

I'm six weeks along, Keegan. You're not the father.

Again he removed his sunglasses and pinched his nose. It had taken him some time to understand what she'd meant. The concept of infidelity was familiar, of course. His father had run around on his mom, and the first man his sister had fallen in love with had slept with her best friends—three of them. They'd both had their hearts broken, and he had learned the real meaning of commitment.

I met this man while you were gone. He's a major. He's the father.

Too bad Sabrina hadn't shared his idea of commitment.

Ercella's sigh was as heavy as the Louisiana air. "Your food's getting cold. Go ahead and eat, and call me when you decide what you're going to do. I'll give Mariah a hug and a kiss for you."

He thought of the hug Mariah had given him yesterday, the first time she'd touched him, how soft and warm and foreign it had felt. Those pudgy little arms wrapped around his neck, that sweet baby girl smell of her, the overwhelming sense of obligation to her.

"You do that, Mom," he said quietly. "I love you."

Grimly he disconnected and reached for the paper bag that held his late lunch or early dinner or whatever the hell it was. God, he just wanted life to go back to normal.

Somehow he didn't think that was going to happen.

Chapter 4

The cookies had been banished back to the kitchen, what was left of them, and their glasses were empty when Therese finally broached the subject of her visitor that afternoon. "Something kind of awkward happened earlier. A man came to the house looking for Paul. Abby answered the door and bellowed at me, then stormed upstairs and left him standing there. By the time I got to the door, he was looking mortified."

Carly's forehead wrinkled sympathetically. "He saw the Gold Star flag."

Therese nodded. "He was...Shocked wouldn't be understating it. Then he felt bad, and I felt bad, and after we talked a few minutes, he left."

Carly stared down into her glass for a moment, clinking the last bits of ice, before leaning over to set it on the cement. "The first few months after Jeff died, it seemed everywhere I went, everyone knew. People would look at me. Sometimes they'd say they were sorry. Sometimes they couldn't meet my gaze or get away from me fast enough."

Therese nodded again. She knew those looks. They'd followed her through the halls at school, in the businesses she frequented, whenever she ran into soldiers from Paul's unit or especially their spouses. They were sympathetic and awkward and sometimes fearful but also relieved, because what happened to her and Paul could happen to any of them, but hadn't yet.

"The first time we met..." Carly gestured with her left hand, and for just an instant it struck Therese how odd it looked without the wedding band she'd just recently switched to her right hand. "I went to your class to ask you to dinner, I told you my name and said, 'My husband was...' and you knew. You said, 'I know. Mine, too.'"

"It was hard not to know." The post school where Therese taught kindergarten and Carly third grade was large, but with the population entirely military dependents—and many of the teachers—a combat death couldn't go unnoticed. At the time of Paul's death, there had been more than twenty teachers at the combined elementary/middle/high school whose spouses were deployed to Iraq or Afghanistan. More than twenty people living in fear of that casualty notification call.

Carly had been lucky enough to get hers at home after school—if anything about the experience could be considered lucky. Therese's had come in the middle of the day: a knock at her classroom door, the principal asking her to accompany him to his office, where two solemn-faced officers in dress uniform waited. Her first hope when Mr. Hopkins called her from the room was that some minor accident had affected one of the kids, but in her heart, she'd known it was Paul, and seeing the officers had confirmed it.

Her heart had broken, her life ended, in the principal's office.

Not ended. Just ... redirected.

At least, that was her prayer.

"So ... this man ... did he say what he wanted with Paul? Was he in Afghanistan with him?"

"Yes. He's a medic. Stationed at Fort Polk now. His name is Keegan Logan."

Carly nudged her with one sandaled foot. "Is he as handsome as his name?"

Therese made a big show of rolling her eyes. "Need I remind you that you're engaged to be married?"

A flush of sheer pleasure washed over Carly, brightening her face, lightening her eyes. "You do not. But I know available women. Is he?"

"Available?"

"Handsome. You're avoiding the question, so I'm going to assume the answer is yes, very." Slowly Carly smiled, her expression shifting from teasing to serious. "When was your last date, Therese?"

She bent to pluck an early-blooming weed from the lawn at the edge of the patio and fixed her gaze on it. "I have no time or energy for or interest in dating. You forget, I have enough drama in my life with Jacob and the princess. Besides, even if I were interested, it wouldn't be another soldier. And Sergeant Logan isn't even stationed here. I won't ever see him again."

"Maybe not." Her friend's smile returned. "Though I wasn't looking for another soldier, either, and when I met

Dane in that cave, I thought I'd never see him again. Look at us now."

"Disgustingly in love, I know. But it's different for you." Carly had only the memories of Jeff, what they'd had and what they should have had, to deal with. The major impact of getting involved with another man was on her and no one else.

"You're a stepmother, Therese, not a nun. You agreed to take care of Paul's kids, not give up your own life for them. Besides, a father figure might do them some good."

The mere thought of introducing a man into Abby's and Jacob's lives made Therese shudder. Her relationship with Abby was a certified disaster, and things with Jacob were iffy. If they thought for an instant she was trying to replace their father with another man...

"I'm not saying this Keegan guy is the man for you. There's that little problem of living eight to ten hours apart. Though," Carly said reflectively, "we do it all the time. My point is, you noticed him as a man, in a gee-he's-handsome-and-I'm-a-living-breathing-woman sort of way, and that's a start. The next man you notice might be one right here in town, one who's available and worth the risk of getting involved."

"I can't imagine it," Therese said stubbornly. And she really couldn't, not with things the way they were. But her friend did have a point: she *had* noticed that Keegan Logan was handsome, and that she was a woman still living and breathing, no matter how hard it was at times. And there was certainly an allure to the idea that, sometime in the future, she might share her life with someone.

Before she could get all wistful thinking of not being alone anymore, Carly sighed and got to her feet. "I've got to get home. Thanks for the cookies. Next time I'll bring them with me."

Therese started to rise, but Carly waved her back.

"I know the way." Unexpectedly she bent for a hug. "Everything's going to be good again someday, sweetie. With you, with the kids, with life in general."

Therese clung to her a moment, savoring the simple embrace, the closeness, the affection. Her voice was a little husky when she asked, "Are you sure about that?"

It took Carly a bit after she straightened to reply, thoughtfully, positively. "I am. Hey, life's nothing without hope, right?"

After saying good-bye, she went into the house. A moment later, Therese imagined she heard the click of the front door, though of course she hadn't. Only Abby's vigorous slams were loud enough to hear out back.

Life's nothing without hope. Carly was right. That was why Therese felt so edgy and empty and bleak these days. She'd lost hope. Part of her was convinced that giving up the kids was the first step to finding it again—both hope and her life. Part of her thought if she could just hold out until Abby was on her own. Part of her didn't have a clue.

"Lord, if You want to send down some answers, I'm here waiting," she whispered, her gaze shifting automatically to the sky. It was a beautiful vivid blue, with clouds so fat and white they didn't look real. Far above, the contrails from two jets formed intersecting wisps, and right next door a bird sang in the branches of the neighbor's maple.

Peace. Even without an answer from God, that was what she should have been feeling on such an afternoon, but it eluded her. It had for a long time.

Wearily she stood and gathered the empty tea glasses. At the door, she hesitated, her lungs tightening, that familiar sensation fluttering in her chest. Her home wasn't a refuge, as it should be, but a place she dreaded being.

Monday morning and work couldn't come soon enough.

* * *

Monday morning always came too soon.

Jessy dragged herself out of bed after hitting the snooze button on the alarm three times for an extra thirty minutes of sleep. She was achy, stiff, and stuffy when she went into the bathroom. Her hair stood on end, the red so bright that it hurt her eyes this early in the morning, and made her face look as washed out as a jar of paste. There were shadows under her eyes and lines bracketing her mouth.

She must be coming down with something. She hadn't slept well. She wasn't getting enough exercise, and her nutrition sucked. All combined, it was taking a toll on her, and it showed. At least, that was what she told herself.

Damn it if she'd admit, even to herself, that it was a lie.

She showered, dressed, applied makeup with lots of concealer to hide the shadows, then went into the kitchen to scrounge up something for breakfast. Resolutely she ignored the empty bottle of scotch on the counter, took a candy bar from her snacks cupboard and a can of pop from the fridge, and promised herself she'd eat better for lunch.

The only good thing about Monday was that it was always followed by Tuesday, and that meant the weekly meeting of the Tuesday Night Margarita Club. It was the highlight of her week. Going out partying Friday night and

Saturday night and polishing off the scotch for dinner last night were the lowlights.

Grimly she acknowledged, as she locked up and headed down the stairs, she'd had lower moments. There were still depths she could sink to, but she'd avoided them this past week. Who knew how she'd do with the upcoming one?

Jessy hated her customer-service job at Tallgrass National Bank. She'd told her friends so often, and yet hadn't done anything about it, that they didn't take her seriously anymore. It was just all so routine. Open accounts, close accounts, make transfers, set up automatic withdrawals, answer the same questions over and over with a smile and not even a hint of the frustration that lived inside her, then repeat again and again. About the best thing she could say for the job, in fact, was that it was convenient, seeing that the bank was only a few hundred feet from her apartment. Close enough to walk in heels, in good weather and in bad, in sickness and in health...

"Get a grip, Jess," she murmured as she pushed open the door that led onto Main Street. The morning was so bright that she automatically reached for her shades, muttering a curse when she realized she'd left them upstairs and had no time to go back for them. Thanks to the extra hits on the snooze button, she was going to be late as it was, only one of the many things her supervisor held against her.

A breeze tousled her hair as she headed toward the intersection of Main and First. Oklahoma, wind, plains... it wasn't often the air was really still. She liked the wind, though. Liked the weather: the hundred-plus-degree range in temperatures, the hard pellets of winter ice, the fat flaky snows, the unforgiving summer sun, the furious storms, the delicate but too short springs and falls.

Oklahoma weather reminded her of herself: extreme, ever-changing, rarely doing anything halfway.

She said hello to everyone she passed on the way: the regulars headed to work, the early shoppers, the unfortunate folks with early appointments. As much as she disliked work, she loved the building where she did it. It stood on the southwest corner of the main intersection in town, two stories built of sandstone chipped into 8-by-12-inch blocks, with sections of smooth concrete arching above the windows and doors and wrapping around the corners. It dated back to the first year of statehood—1907—with the year chiseled above the main entrance, and every large window was topped with a leaded-glass panel that scattered light inside in prisms that danced on wood floors and marble counters.

When she'd first started working there, she'd taken hundreds of pictures, both inside and out. She had even gone to the roof and hung over the edge for upside-down shots of the cornices circling the top floor. She'd documented the building thoroughly, always when it was empty. She didn't care much for people in her photographs.

Jessy breezed through the leaded-glass double doors with their polished brass push-bars, across the vestibule and through another more elaborate set of doors into the lobby. All of her co-workers were at their places, including Mrs. Dauterive, her supervisor, who scowled at her from her office. Giving her a smile and a wave, Jessy hurried to the break room, stuck her pop in the fridge, and shoved half of the candy bar into her mouth, chewing quickly, before she went to her desk in the northwest corner of the lobby.

"You're late."

She stashed her purse in the bottom drawer of her desk

before giving Mrs. Dauterive another phony smile. "I'm so sorry. I was halfway down the stairs when my mom called on the landline to give me an update on my father. He's in the hospital, and she's been so worried about him. I couldn't just let it go to the answering machine, and Mom never remembers my cell number."

The older woman's gaze was glacial, but a tiny nerve ticked at the corner of her eye. She wanted to call Jessy a liar, anyone could see that, but two things held her back: common courtesy and an unwavering loyalty to family. She'd given up a career in New York—and a serious romance, according to gossip—and returned to Tallgrass to care for her mother, to whom she was devoted. With all of Jessy's flaws, her own "loyalty" to her family was the only trait Mrs. Dauterive appreciated.

After a long moment, Mrs. Dauterive said, "Ask the hospital staff to program your cell into her phone." She turned curtly and was several steps from the desk before she grudgingly added, "I hope your father is improving."

So many lies, Jessy thought as she logged on to her computer. She didn't have a landline or an answering machine, and though she did have parents, her father was healthy as a horse and her mother didn't call her middle daughter. Not ever.

She was going to go to hell for lying—among other things—but not today.

A short while later, a customer walked into the lobby and made her question that. It was Dalton Smith.

She considered sliding bonelessly out of her chair into the protected space underneath the desk just until he was gone. Only a few customers seated in the chairs at an angle to her desk, waiting for loan officers, would actually be able to see her, and odds were they would look at her funny but not say anything. She could huddle there, listening to the hollow clunk of his well-worn cowboy boots on the wood floor, until they clunked right on out of the bank.

She didn't do it, of course. Not so much because it was a juvenile response but because she couldn't make her body relax enough to slide anywhere. Her muscles were clenched, her spine rigid, her heart pounding hard enough to echo in her ears.

The first time she'd seen him, they'd had lunch and too much booze and spent a few sweaty hours in the seedy motel across the parking lot from Bubba's. The next time, only a week later, she'd been waiting for a pick-up order at Serena's Sweets down the block from her apartment and he'd been paying for dinner. His younger brother had been with him—no question they came from the same parents—and Dalton had looked at her, not as if he'd never seen her before but as if he'd seen way too much of her and never wanted to again.

He'd made her feel an inch tall and about as desirable as something he would scrape off his boots after working with the cattle.

He wasn't the first man who'd wanted nothing to do with her after, well, doing her. Maybe she should change her behavior so he was the last.

The phone on her desk buzzed, and she automatically answered, propping the receiver between her ear and shoulder. "This is Jessy," she said in her fraud voice.

"I see you're doing the same thing I am." It was Julia, the account rep whose desk sat catty-corner from Jessy's, near the massive stone fireplace. With her name and fragile magnolia appearance, people often mistook her for a Southern belle, but her nasally Boston accent quickly cleared up that matter. "That is one handsome cowboy, and you know, I do love me a cowboy."

"You do love you a man, period," Jessy said. "His name is Steve, and he's in Korea." Though Julia talked a lot, she never acted on it. She was too crazy in love with her husband.

"I can look, as long as I don't touch. You, on the other hand…It's about time that you looked *and* touched."

Thankful Julia couldn't see her, Jessy winced. Every woman she knew thought she'd remained faithful to Aaron's memory, even her margarita sisters. She felt crappy for lying to them, but she didn't want them to know what kind of person she really was. They wouldn't understand, and they might not want her around anymore.

Without them in her life, she would break apart into a thousand little pieces, each one sorrier than the one before, and simply cease to exist.

"It's time for me to get some work done," she said primly.

"Yeah, I saw you were late again. One of these days, Jessy…" Julia's voice lowered. "Gotta go."

Jessy hung up, then glanced over her shoulder. The vice president of investments had come out of his office, only a few feet from Julia's desk, and was leaning over to examine her computer screen. Relieved the conversation was over, Jessy turned back to her own work…and found Dalton standing in front of her own desk.

His glower was world-class, making the strong lines of his face look granite-hard. In her brief experience, hard looks and hard actions were normal for him, though she suspected they had been the norm only for the past four years, since his wife had died in Afghanistan. What had he been like before then? Had he smiled, laughed, unbent that spine, and had a little fun?

She would never know, and somewhere deep inside, she regretted that.

Steeling herself, she politely asked, "Can I help you?"

* * *

She may not have had a clue who Dalton was last Saturday night when she'd been flirting with Noah at the café, but she remembered him now. Just for an instant, when she'd looked up and seen him standing there, panic had flooded through her green eyes.

He didn't know whether the odd churning in his gut was satisfaction that he wasn't so forgettable, after all, or annoyance that the sight of him was enough to panic her. Did she think he was thrilled to run into her again?

Deliberately he looked around the lobby. Two desks were empty, and the woman at the fourth desk was busy with some suit leaning over her shoulder. He could wait until she was done—though how middle-school did that sound?—or he could take care of business and get back home to work.

He pulled back one of the two chairs that fronted Jessy's desk and sat down. Unlike the other desks, there was nothing personal on hers: a pile of folders, a phone, a nameplate with only her first name. No picture of her dead husband in uniform. No pictures at all except one of the bank itself, a black-and-white print with storm clouds looming overhead. With no people or vehicles in it, no sign of power or phone lines, it was impossible to tell if it had been taken this year or fifty years ago.

Realizing she was waiting, and none too easily, he pulled a piece of paper the teller had given him from his pocket. "I have a problem with one of my accounts."

He set the paper on the desk, and she picked it up, then turned to the computer on the L-shaped extension and began typing.

"I didn't know you worked here."

She gave only the faintest response to his remark: her jaw tightening, the tip of her ear turning pink. "I didn't know you banked here."

The sad truth was, neither of them knew anything about the other, except that her husband and his wife had died in the same faraway place, that they took flowers to the graves and liked greasy burgers and, at least on occasion, drank too much to retain any good sense.

Two people should know more than that about each other before they have sex.

That Saturday afternoon hadn't been one of his better moments.

"What's the problem with the account?" she asked, barely glancing at him before looking back at the computer.

"There was supposed to be an automatic transfer made Friday from my savings account to that checking account. It didn't happen." Noah had stayed over last night, leaving at dawn to get back to Stillwater in time for his morning classes, only to find that the power at his apartment was off: no coffee, no cooking breakfast, no lights to shave and no hot water to shower. Turned out, the payment he'd made Friday had been denied due to lack of funds.

The kid did a pretty good job of limiting his expenses so his education didn't cost Dalton any more than necessary, and he'd been apologetic about the complaint. Dalton didn't care. The money came from Sandra's life insurance. Hell, something good should come from her death.

Thinking about Sandra, even vaguely, while sitting across from Jessy gave him an itch in the middle of his spine. He shrugged, then fixed his attention on Jessy again. She was clicking through screens, occasionally pausing to type a few characters.

"There was apparently a glitch in the system, but it's fixed now." She clicked one final time before swiveling her chair back to face him. Not exactly look at him. "Is there anything else?"

He thought of the last time they'd met, when she'd paid so much attention to Noah, who was obviously way too young for her, and pretended she'd never seen Dalton before—hell, pretended she'd hardly seen him even then, standing a few feet away—and he stiffly got up from the chair. "Just one thing."

That brought her gaze to his, surprise in her eyes.

"Leave my brother alone. Don't flirt with him. Don't try to charm him. And don't even think about doing anything else with him."

His warning left her at a loss for words, momentarily, at least. Her cheeks paled, and her mouth opened as the air around her turned electric. She moved as if to rise from her chair, anger fairly humming along her skin, but he didn't give her the chance. He'd said what he wanted.

He turned his back on her and walked away.

He was at his truck half a block down the street before he realized his hands were clenched. Forcing his fingers to uncurl, he pulled out his keys and beeped the lock, rousing the dog sleeping in the passenger seat. He stood, stretched, then sat down again with a yawn. Dalton hadn't intended to bring the mutt into town with him. He'd just jumped through the driver's door before Dalton could stop him and settled in the other seat with a try-to-make-me-move look on his ugly face.

Maybe one of these days Dalton would come up with a name for the animal, if it didn't wander on down the road first. It seemed everyone else did.

After sliding behind the wheel and buckling his seat belt, he drew a deep breath and inhaled regret with it. Had the warning to Jessy been a mistake? Would she take his advice and stay away from Noah, or was she just stubborn enough to accept it as a challenge? He didn't know.

He did know Noah, though. His brother was a sucker for a pretty woman, and he didn't always think with his brain when he met one. A woman like Jessy could tie Noah in knots and hurt him bad.

Besides, Dalton had been with her first. While little details like that hadn't mattered to Dillon, Noah had a stronger sense of loyalty. Hell, this stray dog that he'd spent more hours than he'd had to spare doctoring, feeding, and bathing had more loyalty than Dillon.

Good or bad, what he'd said to Jessy was said. He couldn't recall the words. But he could keep an eye on Noah the next few times he was home, and if need be, he would tell him just how he knew her. Given the fact that Noah viewed Dalton about as much father figure as brother, that would be more than enough of a gross factor for him to keep his distance from Jessy Lawrence.

Just as Dalton intended to do.

*   *   *

Therese and Carly stopped in the doorway of the elementary school building, shifting bags, looking for keys. The hallway behind them was empty, and no sound came from the classrooms. Most of the teachers had left for the day, and the ones still working were doing so in silence—a valued commodity in a school.

"What are your plans for the rest of this beautiful day?"

Therese looked out at the rain steadily pouring, leaching the vibrant spring colors from everything it touched. In recent years, much of Oklahoma had suffered from drought, so she wouldn't wish for the rain to go away, but if it stopped long enough for her to run errands and get home, curling up in a chair and watching it fall was one of her favorite pastimes.

It showed no signs of letting up at the moment.

"I have to go to Walmart. Did I tell you that after her mother bought her all new thongs and push-up bras, Abby left her own underwear there, along with the rest of her old clothes?" She and Carly both rolled their eyes at the same time. "Yesterday morning she tried to persuade me to give her just one set for church, preferably the lavender satin or the red ones with black lace, or she'd have to go without. Unfortunately for her, there were two pairs of white cotton panties left in her drawer and one sports bra. She's going to be so unhappy when she sees what I come home with."

Carly shook her head. "I can't believe her mother— Well, actually, I can believe it. Catherine seems to think Abby's her new best girlfriend or her latest dress-up doll. The girl's no one's doll, and she's got friends. She needs—"

A mother. Therese adjusted the straps of her shoulder bag and the tote that carried her papers over her shoulder, then shoved the door open. Quickly, before the rain could do more than sprinkle against them, she popped open the giant umbrella she kept in her classroom and made room under it for Carly to join her.

"What she needs right now is underwear that covers the essentials and doesn't look like it belongs in a porn film," Therese said as they started toward the parking lot. "She called her mom yesterday—got her voice mail—and very reluctantly asked her to return her clothes if she hadn't already thrown them out. According to Catherine, they weren't even worthy of donating to a homeless shelter."

"Do you think she'll send them?"

"Find a box, shove clothing into it, tape it, address it, and take it to the post office? Nah. Way too much trouble for her only daughter. She probably thinks I'll give in and let Abby wear the stuff she bought her." Which proved just how little Catherine knew.

Water streaming from the parking lot down the sidewalk seeped into Therese's shoes and dampened the hem of her pants. If she had a pair of the heavy-duty, knee-high rain boots she'd worn on the ranch when she was a kid and a good slicker, she would take a long walk to simply enjoy the wetness and blurriness and freshness of the deluge. While she did have a slicker at home—hot pink with yellow madras lining—she lacked the boots. She'd been happy to leave them behind when she'd left Montana. No more mucking stalls and trudging through mud or slush for her.

There were a lot of things worse than muck and mud.

They hurried to their cars, parked four spaces apart, and Therese waited while Carly unlocked her door and tossed her bags inside. "Have fun shopping. And be sure to take cover when you give Abby the new undies."

Therese grinned evilly. "I'm getting cotton. White. Granny panties."

With a wince of sympathy, Carly slid into her car, and Therese splashed the short distance to her own. She closed the umbrella, gave it a good shake, then put it in the passenger floorboard and slid her purse and tote onto the other seat. Damp and feeling as if everything about her were curling, from her hair to her clothing to her toes inside her shoes, she wished she could go home. But since Abby going commando wasn't an option, neither was going to Walmart.

The store was located a few blocks south of Main on First. Though the post exchange and the commissary sold pretty much the same stuff, it was easier sometimes to stop at the supercenter. The nearest parking space she could find was miles from the entrance, of course, and by the time she reached it, her pants and feet were soaked.

So were the shopping carts. Bypassing them, she headed inside and straight to the lingerie department. They had a more varied selection than she'd expected, and she made her choices quickly, though she didn't opt for plain white, as Abby deserved. With a pink bra and a pale yellow one dangling from hangers, plus a half dozen pairs of bikinis in stripes and polka dots, she went to the checkout and was standing in line when the clearing of a throat—a male throat—caught her attention.

Keegan Logan stood next to her, his black T-shirt darker where it was wet from the rain, his hair darker, too. His khaki shorts were splattered, along with his calves—nice calves—and his shoes looked even wetter than her own.

Who would have thought looking like a drowned rat could be a good thing?

Heat went through her as she looked at him. Not much. Just enough to send up a little steam from all her wet parts. Wet *clothes*. Wet skin. Not parts. That sounded...wrong.

"Sergeant Logan."

"Mrs. Matheson."

"Therese," she corrected him.

He nodded. "Keegan."

His gaze shifted to the garments in her hands, and the heat intensified. "My stepdaughter spent spring break in California with her mother, who bought her a lot of, uh, inappropriate clothing, then encouraged her to leave everything she'd taken with her there." TMI, she could hear Abby saying rudely. *Too much information.* Besides, anyone with the vaguest sense of proportion could tell the delicate bras wouldn't fit her.

Her cheeks burning, she laid everything on the conveyor. "I didn't realize you were staying in Tallgrass awhile."

"Such beautiful weather, how could I leave?" His expression was desert-dry, then, after she'd gazed toward the gloomy scene outside the big glass doors, a slow smile curved his mouth.

And what a smile it was. Charming, sweet, a little wicked. She loved a man with a wicked smile.

As her purchases inched toward the checker, he reached past her for a small plastic divider bar. She caught a whiff of cologne and did her best not to breathe more deeply. It was a wonderful smell, musky and spicy and warm, and she hadn't been close enough to a man to really smell his cologne in a long, long time.

As he withdrew, she allowed herself another quick breath, then watched as he laid his items on the belt: a twelve-pack of bottled water, a box of protein bars, coffee, energy drinks, and an assortment of fresh fruit. No chocolate, no cookies, and no bagged popcorn—all things she bought on a regular basis.

Which explained why she was soft and rounded and he wasn't.

Civilians automatically thought of everyone in the military as strong and fit. She had enough years as an Army wife to know that wasn't the case. Not everyone in uniform had physically demanding jobs; not everyone PT'ed— short for physical training—regularly; not everyone could resist the better foods in life.

There was no doubt that Keegan fit the popular image. She didn't need to touch him to know that he was rock-solid...though her fingertips tingled at the idea of feeling it for themselves.

What was up with her? She hadn't noticed such things about any man other than Paul in years, about any man at all in nearly ten years. It must be Carly's talk yesterday about opening herself to the possibility of getting involved with a man again. Nothing more.

Convinced of that, she breathed and glanced his way as the checker started ringing up her stuff. For about the millionth time, things fluttered inside, but unlike the usual first sign of panic, this was a pleasant fluttering. It made her smile, though that fluttered, too. "Are you just waiting for the weather to clear, or have you decided to spend a few days?"

"Damned if I know." The words sounded cranky, but his easy shrug immediately dispelled that notion. "I'm on leave. I'm just taking things as they come."

"Must be nice." At his look, she offered her own shrug. "When you're a single parent, you don't get many chances to just do what you want. Kids take planning."

"Do you have family around to help out?"

The checker read out the total, and Therese swiped her debit card, then picked up her bags, shifting far enough that he could move up to the small shelf next to the screen. "No. My family's in Montana, and Paul's parents live in Illinois. The kids' mother is in the Los Angeles area, and her parents alternate between Chicago and Miami."

"Tough," he murmured. "But it's got to be tough anyway, raising kids who aren't yours."

This was the point where a good stepmother would say, *Oh, but I love them like my own.* Wishing she could say it and mean it, she smiled faintly instead. "You do what you have to do." Fingers tightening on the plastic grip of her umbrella, she summoned a smile. "I should be go—"

"You want to get a cup of coffee?"

She blinked. The best-looking man she'd seen in a long time was asking her to have coffee with him. Not a big deal. Certainly not a date or anything like that, but still...Coffee. Wow.

But because she had a ton of things to do—get home, change into dry clothing, see about dinner, face off with Abby over the underwear—and no matter what Carly said, this wasn't a good time for interest in the opposite sex, she opened her mouth to refuse.

Her words surprised her. "Sure, I'd like that. You want to go to McDonald's or someplace in town?"

His gaze traveled past her to the McDonald's just inside the entrance, and a skeptical look crossed his face. "Doesn't Tallgrass have a Starbucks or something?"

"We do, out by the main gate on the east side of town, but there's a Java Dave's just down the street."

The checker called out his total, and he swiped his own card. Even if she wasn't looking, Therese would have felt the instant his gaze left her. It was a heady thing, being the focus of a handsome man's attention. There was something electric and flattering and hopeful about it.

Something sweet. Bitterly so.

"Sounds good. I'll meet you there."

A lump formed in Therese's throat, making her sound hoarse. "Turn right out of the parking lot, two blocks, on the right." Before she could think better of her decision, she clenched both bags and umbrella tighter and walked to the exit with long strides. Just before passing through the automatic door, she glanced over her shoulder. He was talking to the clerk as he picked up his bags from the revolving rack. Charming her, too.

But he'd asked Therese to have coffee with him. Wow.

Chapter 5

There's response to his comment about raising her stepkids hadn't been encouraging, but at least Keegan had learned that Paul Matheson's parents were still alive. Mariah had grandparents in Illinois. Were they active in their grandchildren's lives? Would they be interested in taking custody of the granddaughter they didn't yet know existed?

He didn't have a clue, but talking to Therese over coffee might give him one. That was why he'd suggested it. No other reason.

By the time he left the store, there was no sign of her or her giant umbrella. He jogged across the parking lot, though there wasn't much left on him to keep dry, and deposited the bags in the backseat before escaping the rain himself.

It took maybe three minutes to navigate out of the parking lot, down the street, and into a space near the coffee shop. It occupied a storefront on the ground floor of a building dating to 1926; the year was spelled out in bricks on the second-floor level. The air inside smelled warm, rich, sweet...kind of like the woman waiting at the counter. She greeted him with a polite smile that made him faintly uneasy—not the smile itself. His reaction to it. Like a pretty woman had never smiled at him before, when that was so not true. Women liked him. Pretty women liked him a lot.

As he joined Therese, she turned that same smile on the teenage kid behind the counter who offered her some kind of fussy drink in a clear cup, with lots of froth and whipped cream. Keegan glanced at it before ordering. "The strongest roast you've got."

"I'll get a table," Therese said, scooping up napkins along with her drink.

He watched her weave between the tables to a cozy table for two next to the plate glass window and continued to watch until the kid cleared his throat. "That'll be two and a quarter."

Keegan slid his card through the reader, took his foam cup, and murmured thanks before following Therese. He slid into the chair across from her, glanced out the window at the rain, sipped the steaming coffee, and nearly burned his tongue. Though she didn't say anything, her faint smile showed she'd noticed.

"So...you're from Montana." *Really smooth, Logan. What are you—fifteen?*

"I grew up on a ranch outside Helena."

"Beautiful country."

"You've been there?"

"Not even close."

Her brows raised, then she smiled for real. It made her

look a few years younger and a lot of burdens lighter. "You're right, though. It is breathtaking."

"But you decided not to go back there when…" He shifted his gaze to his coffee. He had no tact for talking to a widow. He couldn't remember ever even meeting one, other than his fourth-grade teacher, when he'd been too young to really grasp the concept, and a few aunts whose husbands had earned gray hair and retirements before their deaths. He'd known plenty of guys who'd died—a hell of a fact, considering he was only thirty-one—but he hadn't known their wives.

"When Paul died." Her voice was steady; so was her gaze. "It's okay to say it." She sipped her coffee, then set it down again. "No, I didn't think about it. It would have been nice to be close to my parents and my brother, but I'd been living out of state for several years before I met Paul. Jacob and Abby had already been through so much, what with moving here, their father's deployment, then his death. I thought it was best at the time not to move them again.

"And it gets damn cold up there. I'm not a snow-and-ice girl. There's nothing quite like chopping holes in six-inch-thick ice so the cattle can drink. Or digging a path from the house to the barn, taking care of the animals, then digging out the path again to get back." She sighed. "Sun, sand, a gentle breeze…"

"Doesn't it get cold in Oklahoma?"

"Yeah, sub-zero from time to time. But it's not as if winter moves in to stay. We may go from ten below to ninety degrees within a couple of days. We do get snow and ice, but usually nothing major." She popped the plastic top off her cup and used the straw to scoop out piles of whipped cream. "Your accent says you're from the South. Not Georgia, I'd guess. I was teaching in Augusta when I met Paul."

"Louisiana. Natchitoches."

"How long have you been in the Army?"

"Six years."

"There's a big risk in joining the military when the country's at war."

If the comment had come from anyone other than another service member—or the widow of one—his response would have been short. *No shit.*

"I was already doing medical stuff and occasionally getting shot at." At her raised brow, he shrugged. "I was a firefighter and paramedic. We did a couple runs where the guys who set the fires weren't too happy to see us putting them out." One was hoping a little arson would save him from bankruptcy, while the other was counting on the charring of his wife's body to disguise the fact that he'd beaten her to death.

She shifted in the chair, and it made the little squeaky noise he associated with rocking chairs, ancient wood floors, and home. "Why the Army? You were already being a hero."

Keegan hoped his snort wasn't too obnoxious. "I was doing a job. I liked the medical aspect of it better than the running-into-a-burning-building part, and . . . A guy I went through the fire-training center and worked at the same station with was a reservist who got activated and sent to Kandahar Province. He didn't come back."

Therese's features softened. "I'm sorry."

"Yeah, me, too. I figured . . . when someone falls, you've got to have someone else to take his place, so . . . I enlisted. It's been an experience." Mostly good, but parts of it would haunt him for the rest of his life.

"Thank you." Simple words, spoken with complete sincerity. They raised a heat on the back of his neck that crept up and around toward his jaw.

"You're welcome."

He got thank-yous from total strangers—in airports, on Memorial Day and the Fourth of July and Veteran's Day. Elderly men, veterans themselves, didn't need a special day to shake his hand and express their gratitude. It always made him stand a little taller, feel a little prouder, but at the same time, a little self-conscious. He always remembered that there were thousands of people, like his friend Todd or Therese's husband, Paul, who didn't get to hear those thanks.

All gave some. Some gave all.

He'd given some—six years—and made some good friends and acquired some bad memories, but he was alive. He was here. *Thank God.*

"How long were you and the major married?" he asked, the need to change the subject burning hot on his throat.

"Five years."

Carefully he parroted her words back to her. "There's a big risk in marrying someone in the military when the country's at war."

"Oh, but when you're young and in love, you don't think about things like war, death, separation, ex-spouses, stepchildren. You're so starry-eyed you only see the good possibilities." Therese finished her coffee, crumpled her napkin, and stuffed it into the cup, then pushed it aside. "I love to indulge in that stuff, but once it's gone, I can't stand the smell of it."

He took the cup and tossed it into the trash can a few feet behind him, then waited to see if she would go on.

After a moment staring out at the rain, she sighed. "My friends and I were all crazy mad for our husbands when we married them. We knew there was a war going on; we understood that they'd leave us to deploy; in our heads we knew there was a chance they wouldn't come back, or they'd come back drastically changed. But we loved them, and we were proud of them, and we were willing to take that risk to be with them while we could. Even if it was far too short."

Sabrina hadn't loved Keegan like that. She'd had so little love and commitment in her life that he didn't think she was capable of it. She'd wanted to marry him, but it had more to do with the fact that he was Army—the whole man-in-uniform thing, the benefits she would receive as a dependent wife, the access to a mostly male population—than it did with honest feelings about him.

"What about your friends?" he asked, rubbing his hand over the knot in his gut. If he didn't know better, he'd think he was a little jealous that Matheson had had a wife like Therese and captured Sabrina's attention, too, but Keegan didn't do jealousy. It was more likely too much strong coffee with too little food in his stomach. "Have they gotten their husbands back?"

Her smile was faint and sad. "No. That's how we became friends. We call ourselves the Tuesday Night Margarita Club and meet every week at Three Amigos for dinner and drinks. If you stay in town long enough, you'll probably hear someone else refer to us as the Fort Murphy Widows' Club."

Widows' club. Just the sound of it made the muscles in his jaw clench, which was really a stupid response. Didn't all clubs and groups form because of common interests or

situations? And it was a sad fact that some of those interests or situations were brought about by tragedy. Parents
of murdered children. Families torn apart by drunk drivers.
Victims of violent crime.

Why shouldn't women who'd lost their husbands to war
have a social group of their own? God knew, they needed
the support, and who better to understand than someone
who'd been through it herself?

"How many?"

She shifted again, the chair creaking again. Like Granny's
rocker, the wood worn silvery gray from decades on the front
porch, its squeaks punctuating every conversation she'd ever
had, every bedtime story she'd ever told, every gospel hymn
she'd ever sung.

"There are about twenty of us here in town. Seven of us
never miss a Tuesday night or any of our adventures. The
rest come and go as their schedules allow, or as their needs
require."

Twenty dead soldiers. Twenty grieving widows, and at
least two grieving children. *War is hell,* General Sherman
had said.

Damn straight.

* * *

With a reluctant sigh, Therese checked the watch on her
left wrist. It was after five o'clock, making her an hour late
in getting home. She'd told Jacob before he caught his bus
this morning that she had an errand to run and had left a
note on the refrigerator door to remind them. Still, it was
time to go home.

The rain hadn't let up, falling steadily enough that it

had finally overwhelmed the drains along the curbs and crept up over the sidewalk in places. The street outside was a blur of headlights and early dusk, and the people leaving work wore slickers or trench coats or huddled beneath mostly drab umbrellas.

"I should go," she said. *Should.* Didn't want to. It had been so long since she'd sat in a quiet place and enjoyed coffee and conversation with a man, unless she counted her last visit home and her father. Though she loved her dad dearly, Keegan was a whole different kind of man.

A handsome, charming, appealing man who could remind her she was a woman with nothing more than a look.

She didn't make a move to rise, and neither did he. She did pull her keys from her purse and noticed that he'd parked one space down from her. They could share her umbrella on the way out. Funny that the thought caused the sweet, unfamiliar, not-a-panic-attack fluttering. Hadn't she just shared the umbrella with Carly a short while ago?

Don't play stupid. Carly's your best friend. Keegan is not. Carly is a woman. Keegan is definitely not.

"Are the kids old enough to stay alone for a few hours at night?"

Her throat tightened, and so did her fingers, until the bite of the keys forced her to relax. Was he asking just for general conversational purposes, or did he have something in mind?

Something in mind. It was hard to just say it: dinner. More time together. A date. She didn't even think of herself as a dating sort of person. Dating was for people who didn't have the obligations she did, or the past, or the uncertain future.

"A few hours," she said, wondering if her voice sounded as choked to him as it did to her. "As long as I'm in town. If I go out of town or it's going to be longer than that, they go to their best friends' house down the street. Their mom and I trade off sometimes so she and their dad can have date nights."

Apparently, she'd developed the habit of talking too much when she was nervous. Why hadn't someone pointed that out to her before?

Keegan was quiet, focused on gathering what little trash there was. When he'd done that, he looked up. "Could we have dinner? I'd be happy to get a pizza or take-out for the kids."

Therese's nerves tingled as if an electric current hovered in the air, about to disperse its energy at any instant, setting her hair on end and her heart to pounding and maybe scorching her in the process. She should say yes. All the best friends in the world couldn't disguise the fact that she missed having a man in her life. She *wasn't* a nun. She *was* alive and breathing. And she liked Keegan.

The kids didn't get take-out that often. Jacob wouldn't care, and Abby would be so busy acting out that she wouldn't notice. They would appreciate that there'd be no table to set, no blessing to sit through, no cleanup. They wouldn't miss her.

She refused to acknowledge the tiny prick of disappointment inside her.

"All right. What are you in the mood for?" Her lips trembled into a sort of smile. "Please don't say Mexican. That's what Jacob wanted for dinner yesterday and the margarita club will be having for dinner tomorrow."

"Lucky for you, I'm not hungry for Mexican." He stood,

and she pushed to her feet as well, reaching for the umbrella she'd leaned against the wall. "You have any place that serves catfish?"

She gave it a moment's thought—a couple of barbecue joints, plus at least two home-style cooking restaurants. She chose Paul's favorite, though. "Walleyed Joe's. It's on the northeast side of town. I can give you directions or I can pick you up after I take dinner to the kids and change clothes."

"Or I can pick you up. I don't need directions to your house," he pointed out.

Pick her up. Like a real date. A real man-woman thing. She needed to go by the house anyway. He might be comfortable in damp clothes and shoes, but she wanted something dry against her skin. She could grab food for the kids, deliver the undies to Abby, and have an excuse for not sticking around for the fireworks.

"All right." She started toward the door, and he fell in step with her. "Give me fifteen minutes."

He checked his watch. "How about twenty? I'll go by the motel and change."

"All right," she said again.

With the awnings over the portion of sidewalk nearest the building, she didn't bother to unfurl her umbrella. When she came even with her van, she dashed and splashed through the rain, climbed in, and started the engine. The windows immediately started fogging, probably from the heat radiating from her, from the excitement that she had a dinner date.

Not that she was looking for a relationship yet. Not that she even wanted a relationship with another soldier, as she'd told Carly. American troops might come home from Iraq and Afghanistan, but as long as one group of people held a grudge against another, as long as their solution to problems was violence, an American soldier would never be completely out of danger. As Carly sometimes said, she'd been there, done that, and had the posthumous medals to show for it.

But she could think of this as a practice date, for the time when she eventually—hopefully—met someone not in the Army.

Before backing out of the space, she called the house. Jacob answered on the third ring to the sound of doors closing and dishes rattling. He was predictable: if he wasn't doing homework or playing games on the computer, he was on a search-and-devour mission in the kitchen. For an eleven-year-old boy, he ate an enormous amount of food. Granted, he was a head taller than Therese and broad through the shoulders.

He was his father's son.

"Hey, Jacob, it's Therese. I'm not going to be home this evening, so I thought I'd pick up dinner for you and Abby. What would you like?"

A chugging sound came over the phone—milk, drunk straight from the carton—then a burp. "I don't care. Anything so long as it doesn't take forever."

"Starving again, huh?"

"Yeah. I haven't had anything to eat since I got home besides some cookies. And a frozen waffle. And some cereal. We're almost out of milk."

"Put it on the list. Want to ask your sister if she has any preferences?"

After a moment's silence, a bag rustled in the background. He'd found the potato chips, apparently. "Yeah, do

I have to? If she's hungry, she'll eat whatever you bring. If she's not, I will."

Abby wasn't quite so malleable, as they both well knew. One week she might love pizza; the next, all that cheese and fat would be disgusting.

"How about Chinese?" Jacob suggested. "I'll call it in."

He was eleven, Therese reminded herself. And he was trying. She could look ahead six months, a year, three or five, and see him in her life: acing middle school; making the football team; starting high school; getting his driver's license; playing baseball the way his dad had; graduating.

No matter how she tried, she couldn't fit Abby into the picture.

"Thanks. I'll be there soon."

* * *

Soon translated to ten minutes. Added to the time she'd sat in the van, Therese had about seven minutes to change clothes and deal with Abby.

She hustled from the driveway to the front door, juggling bags, then gave herself a shake on the rug in the front hallway. Jacob climbed over the back of the couch, where he'd been lying, and met her with a grunt that she took for hello, claimed the food, and headed for the kitchen.

"Good evening to you, too," she called after him.

Without turning, he raised one hand in a wave, a habit he'd picked up from his father.

Therese kicked off her shoes and climbed the stairs to the second floor. At Abby's door, she knocked, waited a moment, then opened it. "I'm going out for a while. I brought Chinese, and I got you these."

Her stepdaughter was lying on the bed, an old pair of running shorts exposing most of her legs, a ratty hoodie swallowing the rest of her. She'd stuffed pillows behind her back, had earbuds in, her phone in one hand, and a biology book propped open against her knees. Her disinterested gaze locked on Therese for a long moment before she pulled one bud loose. "You say something?"

Therese considered her response a smile, though it was really only the baring of her teeth. "I'm going out. I brought Chinese. I bought you underwear."

Abby's gaze shifted to the shopping bag and its familiar Walmart logo, and her face crinkled into a sneer. "I don't care where you go. I don't want Chinese. And I'm not wearing anything you bought."

Nerves tightening, Therese advanced into the room, hanging the bag from the back of the desk chair. "Has your mother shipped your other clothes yet?"

Again Abby stared at her disdainfully, but instead of answering this time, she turned her gaze back to the biology book.

A little twinge of sympathy mixed with anger shivered through Therese. She knew that look. It meant Catherine hadn't bothered to call back. Usually it took days for her to make herself available to her daughter, and too often she ignored Abby's messages and texts entirely.

The time left to change her clothes, freshen her makeup, comb her hair, and be ready for Keegan ticked off loudly in Therese's head. She was sorely tempted to inform Abby that she *would* wear what she'd bought; who did she think had bought everything for her the past four years? It might not have been her bright idea to leave her old clothes in California, but she'd gone along with it when she certainly knew better.

But Therese didn't have the energy. "You can't live with only two pairs of panties and a sports bra, unless you want to be doing laundry every night. Look at them before you decide you hate them. If you or Jacob need anything while I'm gone—"

"We won't."

"If you do—"

"We. Won't. We don't need or want anything from you." Abby shoved the earbud back into place hard enough to make Therese wince and fixed her gaze on the book. As far as she was concerned, Therese was dismissed.

Swallowing a sigh, Therese closed the door behind her and continued down the hall to her own room. She stripped off her damp pants and shirt, grabbed a pair of jeans and a lightweight sweater from the closet, and went into the bathroom to dress. For an instant, before she pulled the jeans over her hips and fastened them, she gazed at her own underwear in the mirror. A cream-colored bra, its only ornamentation a small bow between the cups, and plain pale blue bikinis. Nothing to recommend either besides comfort.

When had she stopped wearing lingerie? When had she decided function was more important than form? When had a thirteen-year-old girl outstripped her in fashion, style, and sheer sex appeal?

Laughing at the thought that the answers mattered now—the chances of anyone else seeing her undies tonight were somewhere between slim and none—she fastened the jeans and pulled the sweater over her head. She redid her lipstick, put on socks, and was lacing up a pair of water-resistant hiking boots when the doorbell rang.

Oh, God, did her heart just skip a beat?

Hastily she tied the second boot, then rushed into the hall and down the stairs. When Keegan suggested he pick her up, she hadn't thought twice about it. Now that he was here, she wished they'd agreed to meet elsewhere. All she'd told the kids was that she was going out. She hadn't said with a man. She didn't want them to know it was with a man.

She deserved a few things just for herself, didn't she?

No need to worry, it turned out. Abby didn't so much as crack her door, and Jacob was out of sight at the kitchen table. It took more than a ring of the doorbell to pull him away from food.

Like interest. Neither he nor Abby cared where Therese was going, or with whom. If she didn't come back, it would take them twelve hours or so to realize it and who knew how long for it to matter.

She opened the door, then grabbed a slicker from the closet. "Hi," she said as she shrugged into it, one arm sliding right into the sleeve, the other tangling somewhere else.

"Hey."

She felt Keegan's movement before she heard it: electricity, a quiet step, then a hand brushing her shoulder as he held her jacket. Sensation rippled through her. Murmuring thank you, she forced her mouth into an unsteady smile. "You're right on time." Inane comment, but it was his fault. If he hadn't come close, if he hadn't helped her, if he hadn't *touched* her . . .

"I always am. My father was late to his own wedding and didn't make it to the hospital for the births of any of his children until at least twenty-four hours after the fact. As a result, my mother can't stand tardiness in anyone. If you're gonna be late, you'd better have a damn good reason for it."

"I agree." She gazed past him out the open door. Streetlamps illuminated the rain falling in sheets. She looked at him again—jeans, boots, a thin slicker of his own. "Want an umbrella?"

"Nah. I don't melt."

If he touched her again, she might. After pulling the hood up over her head, she tucked her purse under her jacket. "Jacob, I'm leaving now. If you need anything, call my cell."

A garbled version of something she took for acknowledgment came from the kitchen, then she smiled at Keegan. "Shall we go?"

* * *

Walleyed Joe's was, predictably, a rustic-looking place, reminding Keegan of old fishing camps back home in Louisiana. Built so that its deck extended over the shallow water of a small lake, it looked as if it had grown right up out of the dirt, weathered and so worn that the main traffic paths through the dining room dipped an inch or two lower than the surrounding boards.

It was exactly the kind of place he preferred.

A teenage girl with orange hair and red braces led them to a table. Due to the weather, probably, there were few customers besides them. They'd barely had a chance to remove their dripping jackets before the waiter appeared to take their drink order.

The table was near the deck, with the door propped open and a cool damp breeze blowing in through the screen door. It balanced out the heavy scent of fried food and carried with it the drumming of the rain on the deck's tin roof. Definitely his kind of place on a wet evening.

He and Therese hadn't talked much on the way to the restaurant. She had folded her hands primly in her lap and gazed out the window, pretty much speaking only to give directions. He was okay with quiet. Sabrina had been a say-something-even-if-you-have-nothing-to-say sort, and her chatter had driven him crazy. Quiet was good.

To a point.

"So...Jacob is your stepson. How old is he?"

"Eleven. Looks like he's sixteen."

"And Abby is...?"

"Thirteen."

"And trying to pass for twenty. I take it that's her mother's influence."

Therese's smile was strained. "Catherine wants to be a best friend, not a mother."

At least she wanted to be *something*. That was more than he could say for Sabrina. "Can I ask why they're living with you and not her? Isn't it easier to be a best friend when you're at least in the same state?"

"Ah, but then you have to accept responsibility, and that's not Catherine's strong suit." She opened the menu, but barely glanced at it. No doubt, she'd been there often enough to know what she wanted. He didn't need to look at it, either. He'd come for catfish, and that was all that would tempt him.

As far as food went, he added to himself as he watched Therese.

She folded her hands in her lap again as the waiter brought their drinks. They ordered their meals—grilled chicken breast with a salad and roasted vegetables for her; fried catfish, coleslaw, and beans for him. The food he'd been raised on.

"Paul and I had been married four years when Catherine informed him that she needed time for herself so she was sending Abby and Jacob to stay with us. She said it was temporary, that she just needed to focus on her own needs for a while. After he died, I thought she would want them back—you know, be there for her children while they grieved for their father, but no. She wasn't ready. She couldn't deal with them. She was grieving herself. For a husband she'd been unfaithful to and had divorced when Jacob was tiny."

Selfish parents. Catherine Matheson, Sabrina, Keegan's own father. It hadn't been so bad for him—his mother and grandmother had more than made up for his father's absence—but it couldn't have been easy for Jacob and Abby. It remained to be seen what life would be like for Mariah.

"So you're raising her kids. How is that working out for you?"

Her cheeks turned pink, and she began fiddling with the paper securing silverware inside the napkin. "Like anything else, some days it's better than others."

A teenage drama princess could easily make life miserable for biological parents who'd had custody from birth. From his very brief exposure to Abby Matheson yesterday, Keegan could guess there were days she made it twice as miserable for the stepmother who'd wound up with her through no fault of her own.

He was in the same situation with Mariah, except he wasn't a step-anything. That designation didn't belong to ex-boyfriends.

"Are you married?" she asked.

She'd stopped playing with the napkin, he noticed, and the color in her face was returning to normal. Okay, so Matheson's kids were a sore point for her—or, at least, her feelings about them were. If she was having problems with them, even letting her know about Mariah's existence was pointless.

But there was still the major's family.

"Nope, never have been. I considered it a time or two…"

"But sobered up before it was too late?" she asked with a faint smile.

"More or less." He wasn't much of a drinker, mostly because his father was a hell of one, but he figured emotion could wreak as much havoc on good sense as booze could.

"No kids?"

He opened his mouth, but nothing came out. Lucky for him, the waiter brought their salads and a basket of hush puppies and Texas toast to provide a moment's distraction.

It was a simple answer. As far as he knew, he had no children. Mariah wasn't his. He owed her mother nothing, and the best he owed Mariah was a family of her own. One that had some claim on her. Since Sabrina had no family, that left her father's family by default.

When Therese repeated the question after the waiter left, he opened his mouth again, but the answer got garbled between it and his brain. "One."

Damn. His mom had been trying to get him to acknowledge Mariah as his child from the moment she met her, even knowing better, but he'd resisted. So where the hell had that come from?

"Boy or girl?"

"Girl. Nearly three years old. Mariah." Her birth certificate did list him as father. And it was easier than going into the whole explanation of how he wound up with custody of another man's daughter—especially when that man was Therese's dead husband. If the time came when there was a reason to tell her, okay. Until then...

"I take it she doesn't live with you."

"Right now she's staying with her grandmother."

"Do you mind if I ask why she's not with her own mother?"

He hadn't realized how awkward a question it was when he'd asked her. Served him right that she'd turned it back on him. "I think Sabrina and your Catherine have a lot in common."

Therese's expression wasn't shocked or even surprised. Instead, she just looked sad. "You know, there was a time when I believed becoming a parent changed you. It made you want to be a better person. It moved you from the center of your universe and put that sweet little baby there instead. It made you want to do *anything* to keep that child safe, secure, and happy."

"Some people it does. Most, probably." He'd felt some of that himself before Sabrina had told him he wasn't the baby's daddy. He'd had just enough time to imagine a baby and the responsibility and the awe and the good times and the worry. Seventeen years ago when his mom had sat him down for "the talk," she'd told him that having a baby changed everything—no option. *Get a girl pregnant, you grow up fast. You don't get to say, "But I'm still young, I'm not ready, I'm still having fun." Having a baby is the end of the world as you know it. You deal with it.*

Just as she'd done, even though Max Logan had kept running out after every kid they brought into the world. All five of them. Thank God she'd finally told him no more.

"Do you see her often?" Therese asked.

"Most days. In my job we spend some time in the field, and sometimes the hours are long. It's easier for her to be with her grandmother." Easier for him, too, but saying so would make him sound like a jerk. Even thinking it made him feel that way. "Do your stepkids get to see much of their father's family?"

She chewed a bite of lettuce before responding. "I just call them 'the kids.' I don't want to emphasize the 'step' part of the family—it sounds like we're not a real family—but I can't call them *my* kids or . . ."

Drama Princess would have a meltdown.

"Anyway, no, they don't. When Paul was alive, they saw his parents once or twice a year. Now they visit them once in the summer and talk to them on occasion. His parents are nice enough people, I suppose, but they don't have a strong sense of family. Paul was an only child. When they finished raising him, they were finished. Their focus is on each other and enjoying their retirement."

An only child. Just his luck. No aunts or uncles or grown cousins who'd want to take in their dear relative's child.

If there wasn't anyone in Matheson's family who wanted her, if Sabrina didn't come back, what would happen to Mariah? Foster care? Yeah, that had been such a success for Sabrina.

Something niggling worked down his spine, something that felt entirely too much like guilt.

For the rest of the evening, he wasn't going to think about Mariah. He wasn't going to feel guilty about her. He was going to eat dinner with a pretty woman, talk about things that didn't really matter, and put his problems out of his mind. There was time enough tomorrow to worry.

Chapter 6

Some people who had a crappy day at work went home, dumped it on their spouses, then vegged in front of the TV for the rest of the night. Some went out with their friends, focused on having a good time, and tried to forget it had ever happened. Some got stinking drunk.

Jessy had done all of the above, though in her case, instead of spouse, it was friends she unloaded on. But her favorite way of getting through the crappy evening that followed a crappy day could be summed up in one word: Serena's.

The restaurant was located in the middle of the block, just one building over from Jessy's apartment. Run by its namesake and her grandmother, Miss Patsy, it offered the kind of home cooking Jessy's mother had never done: fried chicken, chicken-fried steak, fried okra, green beans with ham hocks, and brown or cream gravy on just about everything. And the desserts were to die for—all kinds of pies, carrot cake with the cream-cheesiest frosting ever, sticky buns big enough to fill a dinner plate.

Leaving her umbrella at the bottom of the stairs, Jessy opened the door to a rush of fresh damp air, stepped outside, and locked up, then breathed deeply. The rain had started after lunch and showed no sign of stopping yet. She liked the way it smelled and the way the sidewalk and street gleamed wetly and the way it formed a halo around the streetlights and headlights. It danced along the gutter, puddled in the low spots, and spotted her clothing beneath the jacket she wore.

Rain made everything clean again.

She made the trip from home to Serena's on such a regular basis that she fancied she'd worn size six shoe prints into the concrete. It had been her go-to restaurant since her first week in Tallgrass, though the last few months instead of eating there, she'd begun taking orders home. She pretended it was because she was busy, or she wanted to catch the latest episode of her favorite reality show, or to eat in her pajamas without makeup or shoes.

Sometimes all that was even true. But mostly it was because she could have a drink or two with her meal if she took it home, and a drink or two always made dinner for one a little less lonely.

That was her intent as she breezed through the door tonight, rain dripping from her coat, her hair looking as if she'd just gotten out of the shower because she hadn't bothered to pull up the jacket's hood. By the time she'd passed through the vestibule into the restaurant proper, she was smiling broadly, as if she didn't have a care in the world beyond what culinary treats she would take home with her this evening. She knew, because she practiced that smile in the bathroom mirror every day.

"Miss Patsy, you look beautiful tonight," she said, pausing in front of the cash register.

Miss Patsy was a short, solid woman, her iron gray hair twisted into a bun that wouldn't dare release one strand until she took out the last pins. Patsy was probably somewhere past sixty, but her face was unlined, and her hair had turned gray with the birth of her first child. She came in at five every morning to bake the fabulous desserts, the flaky biscuits, and the yeast rolls, and stayed until closing every night at nine, and while she was friendly with everyone, she didn't seem to have a soft spot for anyone besides her granddaughter.

Her sharp brown gaze swept over Jessy, and her mouth settled into a disapproving line. "Why haven't you learned to cook yet?"

"I know how to cook." Sort of. Passably. But cooking for one just didn't interest her. "Besides, I'm one of your most loyal customers. If I started eating at home, think what that would do to your bottom line."

Miss Patsy rolled her eyes as she reached for an order pad. "I saved a piece of pecan pie and a slab of chocolate cake. You gonna have some real food to go with it?"

Saving desserts for her...maybe Miss Patsy did have a soft spot somewhere underneath all that grit. "If you weren't such a good baker, I wouldn't be eating all those desserts. When I'm too fat to leave my apartment, will you have one of the staff deliver them to me?"

The woman took a long look down at herself, then scanned Jessy head to foot before snorting. "What do you want?"

Jessy was checking the specials board when an arm waving across the room caught her attention. It was Lucy

Hart, one of her margarita sisters, alone at a table for four with a magazine open in front of her.

"I'll get back to you, Miss Patsy." She crossed to Lucy's table and slid into one of the empty chairs. "What are you doing out on a night like this, doll?"

"I had a craving for meat loaf."

"But you make the best meat loaf in town."

A smile creased Lucy's face. "Yeah, but if I made one, then I'd eat the whole thing. At least here, I can satisfy my craving with just one slice. Besides, my broiler broke the other day. I was finishing up a rack of ribs, and it burned a hole in the top of the blasted oven. It actually scorched the bottom of the cabinet up above."

Lucy was a cook, a baker, a nester, a maker, a mother to everybody. Though she worked for the colonel who commanded the post hospital, her passion was to make people comfortable. She'd been a great wife to Mike, who'd died in the same battle that had killed their friend Marti's husband, and would have been the best mother ever if she'd been given the chance. Sometimes she joked she would never get the chance. She barely topped five feet and had passed pleasantly plump thirty pounds ago. Sure, she had boobage, but not the perky kind guys were looking for, and along with it came broad hips, thunder thighs, and cankles.

Jessy knew too well that when Lucy joked about her shortcomings, she was anything but amused inside. She listed her flaws before anyone else could list them for her, not that the margarita girls would ever do such a thing. If they judged people on their flaws, they would have thrown Jessy out a long time ago.

"Are you getting take-out?" Lucy asked.

Was she aware of the barely noticeable hope in her

voice? "I was, but if you don't mind, I'd rather have dinner with you."

Relief, quick but fervent, crossed Lucy's face. "I've gotten used to eating out alone, but I always prefer company."

Jessy gestured, and the waitress came over to take her order for coffee and pot roast: tender beef, potatoes, carrots, and onions in thick rich gravy. It was the perfect dish for a cool rainy night. Followed by dessert, of course.

"Isn't it wonderful about Carly?" Lucy asked, cradling her own coffee cup in her hands as if she needed the warmth.

"Wonderful. And scary. And I'm jealous as hell."

"I'm so happy for her, but at the same time, I think…" Lucy's voice wobbled a bit. "What if everyone finds someone else but me? You'll all fall in love and get loved back and have homes and families and be couples, and I'll be…alone." Her eyes darkened at the thought, glistening just a little too much. Inwardly, Jessy flinched, hoping she was imagining it, seeing wetness because it surrounded them outside.

"I don't do well alone, you know?" Lucy went on. "I mean, I can handle not having Mike because I've got all you guys to lean on, but once you've all got another love—"

"We're not going anywhere, Luce. None of us." Unless they realized what a fraud Jessy was and kicked her out of the group. "Besides, you'll fall in love again long before I will. Being in love was tough enough the first time. I see no reason to give it a second shot at me. So even if everyone else marries off, I'll still be here."

Her response had the intended result—it chased the wistful sadness from Lucy's features—but it was accompanied by an unintended one as Lucy laid her hand on Jessy's arm. "Oh, don't think like that. You're so smart and pretty and funny, and you have so much to give. I know how much losing Aaron hurt, but, Jessy, you can't just shut yourself off like that. You'll move on eventually. You'll meet a guy—the right guy—and you'll be as happy as you were with Aaron."

Heat flooded through Jessy, blistering the air that a few moments ago had been cool against her skin. She shrugged out of her jacket, then pushed up her shirtsleeves. Her hands trembled with the quick gestures, so she gripped them tightly in her lap to hide it. She needed a drink, something a lot stronger than coffee, and wondered if Miss Patsy might keep a bottle hidden somewhere.

She was such a phony. Smart, pretty, funny? Not by a long shot. So much to give? Only what she gave to strange men when she'd had too much to drink. Hurting over Aaron?

Yeah, it hurt, but not for the reasons Lucy and everyone else believed. It had broken her heart that he'd died, that he'd loved her so much more than she'd loved him, that he'd wanted to come home to her and spend the rest of their lives together while she'd wanted a divorce. She'd wanted to be away from him.

And she'd gotten that. He'd had to die, but she'd gotten her wish.

God, she should have been the one to die. Aaron was so much the better person.

Summoning the breezy attitude that got her through most of her days, Jessy shrugged. "If it happens, it happens—for both of us. If it doesn't—" Hoping her hands were steadier, she lifted her coffee cup in a toast.

"We'll grow from margarita girls to margarita broads together. Deal?"

Laughing, Lucy raised her own cup for a chink of heavy-duty porcelain. "Deal."

*   *   *

Years ago Therese's parents had been fans of a TV show featuring a song about a place where everyone knew your name. Back then, that was an apt description of her hometown. She and her brother and friends couldn't do anything without word of it getting home, usually before they did. When she'd decided to move from Montana, one of her goals had been to find a place where nobody knew her.

Now one of her favorite things about Three Amigos was that they might not know her name, but everyone who worked there knew her. They asked about her, about the kids, about the other club members. They noticed who was absent one week and welcomed her back the next, or asked about her if she missed that week, too.

It was safe to say Three Amigos was one of the few places they could gather where nobody eyed them curiously. The staff and the regulars knew they were Army widows, but they treated them like any bunch of regular, raucous, and occasionally rowdy group of customers.

Normally Carly was the first to arrive, but when Miriam escorted Therese to the patio they claimed when weather allowed, the tables were empty. She chose a seat with her back to the wall, facing the parking lot. She murmured her thanks when Miriam returned with chips, salsa, and a margarita that was thick, slushy, and a delicate shade of pink.

"Johnny doesn't want you girls to get burned out on the usual," the waitress explained.

"Tell him thanks." She set the menu aside and sipped cautiously from the drink. Instead of salt rimming the glass, it was sugar, but the margarita was as sour and puckery as ever, with a tart, fruity flavor she couldn't quite identify.

Usually, by Tuesday, though the week had just begun, she was feeling pretty stressed out. This evening, she felt fine. No headache. No neck muscles straining to maintain control. No knot in her stomach or heat spreading through her without warning. She was as close to relaxed as she got these days.

Maybe it was her decision to send Abby away, even though she'd done nothing about it yet. Maybe it was the fact that Abby had been unnaturally quiet when Therese got home from dinner last night. She'd come into the living room briefly, where Jacob watched TV and Therese was settling into her favorite chair with her Bible, and she'd watched a few minutes of Jacob's show from the back of the couch. She hadn't whined, snarled, or sneered at Therese even once before leaving to nuke the leftover Chinese, and after eating, she'd rinsed her dishes and put them in the dishwasher without being told.

Abby *never* put dishes in the dishwasher without being told.

She'd been cranky again this morning, but quietly so, not the I-hate-you-you've-ruined-my-life routine Therese was used to. She hadn't even slammed the front door on her way out to catch the bus.

Or maybe Therese was relaxed because she'd spent an evening doing regular, everyday woman things—going out to dinner, sitting with a handsome man, talking the way men and women talked. Despite the rain, despite her discomfort during some of the conversation about the kids, she'd had a very good time. It had been great practice for the day when she finally went out with a man she could consider getting involved with.

She and Keegan had shared dessert with steaming cups of so-so coffee, then he'd taken her home. Even though it was still raining, he'd walked to the door with her, stood on the porch in the shadows—she'd forgotten to leave the porch light on—and waited while she unlocked the door.

She'd thanked him, and he'd said *you're welcome*, and they'd just stood there looking at each other for at least two whole minutes. She'd thought he might kiss her. Practice dates could include practice kisses, couldn't they? It had been as long since she'd kissed any man but Paul as it had since she'd dated any man but him. But she wasn't sure she wanted Keegan's kiss, or maybe she wanted it too much, and the sound of the television filtering through the door had been an uneasy reminder that Paul's kids were inside and didn't know she'd gone out with a man.

After that long look, he'd smiled—faintly, not that charming grin—and backed away before pivoting and taking the steps two at a time. He strolled to the car as if it were a clear, still night, and there he'd glanced back just for an instant. Then he'd gotten in and driven away without a word about whether she'd see him again.

The part of her that didn't always feel as if she might blow a release valve from the tension she carried inside thought she would.

The part of her that had wanted his kiss wasn't so confident.

The part of her still trying to decide about Abby and Jacob didn't know what to think or feel or want about anything.

Metal chair legs scraped on the tile floor, and she focused on the present, on the muscular form in front of her. *Think of the handsome devil*... He'd come in the low gate from the parking lot and was leaning on the chair back across from her. He wore jeans and a button-down shirt in white, the collar open at the neck, the sleeves rolled up a few times. "Are you early, or have you been stood up?"

She smiled. "I'm always a little early. Though I suppose it could happen that all fifteen to twenty of our bunch could pick the same night to stay home, it hasn't yet. There's never fewer than seven of us." She sipped her drink. "So tonight you're hungry for Mexican."

"Chips, salsa, beer...you can't get much better than that."

Had the knowledge that she'd be here influenced his decision? Before she could do more than wonder about it, he went on.

"I ran into an old buddy today. We're meeting in the bar to eat and watch the game."

"What game?"

He grinned. "Damned if I know. I heard 'Mexican' and didn't listen much to the rest." He glanced to his right as the gate squeaked and Ilena came through. His gaze went from her white-blond hair, skimmed down to her very round belly, then he smiled, pulled out the chair he was leaning against, and offered it to her. She sat, and he effortlessly slid her in to the table.

"Thank you," Ilena said, her own gaze darting from him

to Therese and back again. "Ooh, chivalry is not dead. I'll be getting up again every half hour or so in case you're available."

"Just send your friend in to the bar. I'll be there until the game is over."

Ilena made that little squeaky *ooh* again. "What game?"

"Don't know. I'm just here for the food. My friend's watching the game."

"If it's baseball and you get bored, I'll take your place for an inning or two. We're watching all the baseball we can because Hector Junior"—she patted her stomach—"is going to play and I'm going to coach."

Ilena really intended to name the baby Hector, along with a string of other names (including Juan, his father's name), but at his daddy's wish, once he made his appearance in this world, he would be called John. Still, "Hector" always gave Therese a smile. Now she laughed at the image of slim, delicate Ilena with her thin, delicate voice shouting instructions to a rampaging bunch of five-year-olds. Keegan chuckled, too, gazed at Therese a moment, then went inside the restaurant.

Ilena didn't wait for the door to swing shut before locking her attention on Therese. "Who is he?"

"His name is Keegan Logan. He's…" *A friend of Paul's,* she'd been about to say, but she wasn't sure that was entirely true. Paul had been a good man, but he'd liked the class distinctions in the Army. As a major, there'd been a buffer between him and the enlisted personnel who served under his command. Socially… well, there'd been no socializing—fraternization was the official word for it—between him and any enlisted people. If he were still alive, if Ilena's and Carly's and Jessy's husbands were still alive, no matter how close friends the women had become, Paul never would have felt comfortable with their husbands.

"He knew Paul in the war," she went on as, in the parking lot behind Ilena, Lucy and Marti got out of Marti's Suburban. Ten spaces away Carly and Fia were climbing out of their vehicles. "He didn't know…"

Ilena's nose wrinkled in an expression of sympathy. "When did you meet him?"

"Sunday."

"You seemed awfully cozy."

Therese's face heated. "Cozy? No. We were just talking about…" *About what?* Not last night, when they'd gone out on a date. Not when he'd taken her home and she'd wanted him to kiss her. *Chips, salsa, beer. That was it.* "Food. The game. His friend."

After studying her a long moment, Ilena smiled. "Okay."

Therese sighed in relief. When Ilena said okay like that, it meant end of discussion. Carly might not let things go so easily, and Jessy definitely wouldn't, but Ilena was pretty respectful of others' feelings.

By the time Therese had exhaled that bit of tension, their friends were crowding around the tables. She shifted into the empty chair nearest Ilena to save someone having to squeeze past one of them to get in, then noticed after she resettled that now she had the advantage of being able to look through the nine-paned window and across a half dozen tables into the bar.

Where she could easily see Keegan sitting with several men at one of the bar's tall round tables. Looking up, he lifted his beer in a salute. She smiled, then heard Ilena softly say, "*Oh*-kay." Therese knew what that meant, too: *this is interesting.*

It was, wasn't it?

By 6:10, the usual seven, plus Bennie Ford, were seated around the tables, with pink margaritas in front of each of them but Ilena. Her matching glass held sparkling water. Everyone had given the waitress their orders and a momentary lull fell over the group. Beside Therese, Carly took a breath, then raised her left hand. "It's official, guys."

In place of the wedding band she'd worn so long was a gold band with a lustrous pearl nestled in the center of the filigree. It was as different as could be from the sleek platinum-and-diamond ring Jeff had given her. This one was softer, more old-fashioned. It looked like the ring of a marriage that would last decades.

Squeals of delight erupted around the table as everyone leaned closer for a better look. Therese hugged Carly, then sat back to watch the others. They were happy for her, just as they'd all said they would be a few months ago when they'd discussed whether falling in love again would affect their friendship. After all, what man wanted his wife hanging out with a group that was started expressly to deal with the loss of her first husband?

Dane Clark, apparently. He was a good man, and Carly was blessed to have him.

When life was good and calm and held at least a semblance of normal, Therese would like to be blessed, too.

*   *   *

The sun had set, the light fading, as Dalton turned into the main gate at the Fort Murphy National Cemetery. There was a time the staff had been stricter about enforcing the hours, locking the gates at five in winter, seven in summer, but over the past few years, they'd relaxed their policies, trying to accommodate the families as much as possible. This evening, it appeared he was the only person making a late visit. It wouldn't take long.

The section with Sandra's grave was located toward the rear of the cemetery. The highway and businesses on either side kept it from expanding in three directions, so newer graves were to the south. The entire section he drove to— more marble markers than he wanted to count—was filled with graves of service members who'd died in the Iraqi/ Afghani conflicts.

He parked in his usual spot, picked up the yellow flowers he'd bought at the grocery store since Pansy's Posies was closed, and walked across the new-mown grass. Though all the markers were alike, the format of the inscriptions the same, he could find Sandra's grave without looking. His feet led him there automatically. Bending, he placed the flowers at the base of the stone, then touched his fingers lightly to it. It was cool, smooth. Lifeless.

Specialist Sandra Ann Jones Smith. She'd joked about trading one all-too-common name for another, but at least she hadn't had to spell it for people. She'd been twenty-seven when she died. Too damn young.

But it had been her choice. The doctors and nurses at the hospitals could have saved her. The medics in the field *had* saved her. She was the one who'd chosen to loosen the tourniquet. She was the one who'd thought bleeding to death in the desert preferable to coming home a double amputee.

She was the one who hadn't loved him enough to try.

Sometimes he hated her for it. Sometimes he hated himself. Had he said or done anything he couldn't remember to make her think he wouldn't want her that way? Hadn't her life back here meant enough to her to at least try?

Apparently not.

It was a burden, keeping a secret like that. Her parents didn't know. Dalton's own parents didn't know. No one knew she'd chosen death over them, besides Dane Clark.

More than a week had passed since Clark had come out to the ranch. They were practically strangers, but there had been something...If Dalton were a religious man, he might think bringing the soldier to his house not once but twice had been some kind of plan of God's. Clark had been keeping a secret, too, from the woman he was in love with about his war injury. He had accidentally exposed his own damaged leg that day, but telling him the truth about Sandra's death had been a conscious choice on Dalton's part.

It seemed to have helped. Clark had proposed to his girlfriend, revealing his prosthesis in front of all her friends at Three Amigos last Tuesday.

And if Dalton were honest, maybe the telling had helped him, too. Now that someone else knew about Sandra, his own knowing didn't seem so hard.

Slowly he turned away from the marker and started back to the truck. Instead of taking the shortest route, he followed a weaving path that took him to another marble stone, another set of engraved information. The fading light cast shadows, but he could make out the words. *Corporal Aaron Marlon Lawrence.* Jessy's husband. Twenty-six when he died in Afghanistan.

This was where Dalton had met her. Was that weird, meeting the only woman he'd felt any interest in since San-

dra's death in a cemetery? Noah had given him a day off
from the ranch, and Jessy had invited him for burgers and
beer at Aaron's favorite watering hole. One burger. Too
many beers.

Then she'd pretended not to recognize him the next time
he saw her. Had flirted with Noah right in front of him. And
yesterday...

Hell, he didn't want to think about yesterday. Didn't
want to think about her at all.

He climbed into his truck and headed for the cemetery
gates. A left turn put him on Main Street, and he drove past
the fort. He had all the privileges any other not-remarried
spouse/widow had: medical care at the hospital, shopping
at the commissary and PX, access to all the morale and
welfare stuff. But he'd never set foot on the post since the
day he'd kissed Sandra good-bye for her last deployment.
He'd watched her get on the bus that would take them to
Tinker Air Force Base, where they were departing from,
and he'd felt so damn empty.

Now he knew what real emptiness felt like.

His stomach growled as he pulled to a stop at a red
light. He could go home and stick something in the microwave. He bought plenty of frozen dinners and pizzas,
and every time his parents visited, Mom fixed enough
casseroles to last until their next trip. He could grab a
burger from Sonic or a sandwich from Subway or a roast
beef from Arby's...

His gaze settled on the structure that filled the middle
section of the parking lot of the Tallgrass Center. Vivid colors, bright lights, damn good food... Granted, it was Tuesday, which meant Jessy and her friends would be there—
were there; he could see the herd of women on the patio

from a hundred feet away. But they were on the patio. If he stopped, he would find a table at the dimly lit bar. She would never notice he was there.

Slowly he drove past the restaurant, his gaze scanning the women just long enough to find a head of fiery red hair. His fingers knotted, but he turned in at the next entrance anyway. He parked on the west side of the lot, in front of a liquor store that would soon close for the evening. He didn't listen for sounds of conversation as he opened the restaurant door, didn't look toward the patio at all, just followed a slender woman in a short skirt into the bar and, at his request, to a table in a dark corner.

He hadn't done more than open the menu when running shoes squeaked to a stop on the concrete floor. Looking up, he saw Dane Clark. "How're you doing?"

Dalton shrugged. Last Tuesday, Clark had been wearing shorts, had even gone down on one knee on the patio to propose to his girlfriend. Tonight he wore jeans, and no one watching him would guess that the denim covered pitifully little of his left leg.

"Things worked out pretty well last week."

Dalton was about to say *I know,* then he remembered that he'd hidden in the corner last week, too. He had come to Three Amigos to check out the support group the girlfriend belonged to. He'd thought—Clark had thought—they might have some advice that would help him, since they'd all been where he was. But after realizing that Jessy was one of them, he'd tried to fade into the background until he could pay his tab and disappear.

"Congratulations," he said instead. "So she's okay about your leg."

"Yeah. She's okay." Clark hesitated a moment, then

said, "I'm watching the game over there"—he gestured to the opposite corner—"with some friends. Why don't you come on over?"

The game. Dalton had to stop and think what season it was, what game might be on. There'd been a time when he followed football, basketball, and baseball, when he'd arranged his free time around the college schedules. Hell, he'd even played in high school, him and Dillon both. Now he doubted he'd taken an interest in any game since...

It was tedious, a line he could repeat in his sleep and apply to so many things: since Sandra died.

A week ago he'd wanted to know how to start living again. Maybe he couldn't take advantage of the support group, thanks to Jessy, but they weren't the only people who'd suffered and managed to move on.

His chair scraped back across pebbled cement, and he picked up his drink. "Sure. Why not?"

* * *

One nice thing about the Army: they might send you a hell of a lot of places, but odds were, you could find someone you knew there. If not, it wasn't hard to get to know someone.

Keegan glanced around the table. Zeke Jefferson, on his left, had been stationed at Fort Polk last year. Now he was assigned to the hospital here at Murphy. Jefferson knew the guy on his left, Dane Clark, from the hospital. Clark was with the Warrior Transition Unit and, Keegan knew from past experience, had spent enough time with medics, doctors, nurses, and therapists to last three lifetimes.

The fourth man was a friend of Clark's. Dalton Smith

was big enough to play linebacker on any professional team, but the only critters he wrestled to the ground were the cows and horses he raised. He was a quiet guy, but with Jefferson, a man who'd never met a silence he couldn't fill, it didn't matter much.

Keegan kept one eye on the game, one on the group of women on the patio. It didn't take both eyes to see that they were having a good time. Two more women had joined the original eight, one about his mother's age, the other so young he hoped she was the first woman's daughter. She couldn't be more than eighteen, too damn young to be a widow.

But so was the one his mother's age. So were they all.

He'd thought he was being pretty covert about watching Therese and her friends, but during a break in the baseball game, Jefferson said, "If you're looking for a pretty woman, our waitress tonight is single and available. Better than hooking up with any of them."

When caught, play dumb. That was Keegan's old man's motto. "Any of who?"

"The widows, man." Then he added, with a gesture toward Clark, "Well, one of 'em's about to be a bride again. But the rest of 'em…This is, like, their support group. Their grief management group."

At that moment a burst of laughter came from the patio, loud enough to be heard across the small dining room that separated the bar and patio. Clark lifted his beer with a grin. "Laughter's good medicine, right?"

"Which one's yours?" Keegan asked.

"Carly. The side closest to us, this end on the right. Burnt orange sweater."

Keegan glanced at her—light brown hair, average size,

sitting next to Therese—then back at Clark. "You a Texas fan?" According to the older of his sisters, men only grasped the nuances of colors when they matched a sports teams' colors. A regular guy might not know the difference between UT's burnt orange and the Halloween shade of Oklahoma State's orange, but football fans did.

"Born and bred," Clark replied.

"I'm partial to LSU myself. When's the wedding?"

"First weekend of June."

"Congratulations." Since Jefferson, Clark, and Smith were all still watching the women, Keegan looked back, too. Therese was leaning close to the pregnant blonde, listening intently to whatever she had to say. Had the blonde's husband known he was going to be a father? Had he suspected he might not live long enough to hold his baby? Would his kid grow up calling someone else Daddy, feeling no connection at all to the father who'd died before his birth?

If he were the blonde's husband, dead or not, he'd resent the hell out of someone replacing him in his child's life. But wasn't Mariah in the same position? She was never going to know her father, and the only resentment Keegan felt was that Sabrina had dragged him into her mess.

Besides, there was a difference: presumably the blonde's husband had every intention of coming back to her and raising his child. Therese's husband's only intent with Sabrina had been to break his marriage vows, have a little fun for the weekend, and never confess his infidelity to his wife.

They watched the women a moment longer—Clark's gaze fixed on his fiancée, Smith locked in on someone at the other end of the table, Keegan looking at Therese—

then the game came on again, and gradually each of them turned their attention back to the big screen.

It was around nine when the widows' club—damn if that name didn't suck—when the margarita club started the standing/shuffling/getting ready that signaled an end to the evening. Dalton Smith drained the last of his beer, muttered something like *nice meeting you*, clamped the cowboy hat on his head, and stalked out of the bar.

Clark finished his beer, too, and eased to his feet. "See you around, Zeke. Logan, if you're here next Tuesday, drop in."

"Wonder if he's ever been married before," Jefferson said as Clark headed toward the patio. "I'd say no. He's too eager to tie himself down to have been through it before."

Keegan's only response was a grunt. Marriage had problems; his parents were proof of that. Marriage to a woman who would likely still be married to someone else if he hadn't died must have problems of its own. But if the benefits outweighed the risks...

Jefferson yawned, then dropped his feet to the floor. "I'd better head home myself. I've got stuff to do before work in the morning. Give me a call before you leave town, man. We'll do this again."

"Yeah, see you." Keegan waited until he'd walked away a few yards before looking out again. Therese hugged the blonde, then a black woman from the other end of the table, then clasped the hand of the youngest girl in both of hers while they talked. She looked so calm, serene, the mother hen doling out affection and reassurance to her chicks.

But a good deal of the serenity was an act. Did her friends know that?

So what was he going to do? Sit here and see if she came inside? And what if she didn't? What if she just went on home?

He left the table, circling out of the bar and into the dining room, losing sight of her for a couple moments—big burly guys standing up from their table and talking instead of moving on. By the time he cleared them, the place where she'd stood was empty. He stepped out the door, scanning the parking lot where her friends were leaving in groups of two and three, but he didn't see—

"Hi."

She was standing to the left of the door, apparently waiting her turn to go inside. He would have blindly walked right past her if she hadn't spoken.

Shoving his hands in his pockets, he grinned. "Hey."

"Are you in a hurry to get back to the motel?"

I was in a hurry to catch you before you left. "Nope. You want to get a drink?" When she shook her head, he asked, "Dessert?"

Again she shook her head. "It's a nice night. You want a tour of Tallgrass's murals?"

"Sure." He recalled seeing some paintings on building walls downtown, some old and peeling, some recently touched up. He could honestly say he'd never spent time looking at old murals... but then, no one like Therese had ever asked him to.

They walked through the gate that led into the parking lot and turned right toward the street. The strip mall behind the restaurant was nothing special—the usual collection of shops, salons, and offices—but they soon left it behind.

"How was your dinner?" she asked.

"Good. How was the Tuesday Night Margarita Club?"

"Always good."

"Are any of them actually from around here?"

She thought a moment before shaking her head. "Not one of us. This was where we were when our husbands died, and this is where we've stayed."

"I just kind of figured the families would go back to wherever they were from. Home." Not exactly true. He'd never given it any thought since he'd never had a wife to widow. But he'd always figured he would go home to Natchitoches when he got out of the Army, so it made sense for a widow.

"Some do. Carly went back to Utah, but she only stayed a few months." She shrugged, looking delicate but also strong. "We're military wives. This isn't just a lifestyle for you guys. It's ours, too. We understand each other. We go through the same things. We learn to be a part of this community, and under the circumstances, sometimes it's easier to stay a part of this community."

After a moment, she softly added, "And some people don't have anything to go back to. Fia's family is a disaster. She'd be going back to nothing but trouble. Marti's parents are divorced, and they and her brothers are scattered all over the country. Jessy's family...well, I don't really know anything about them. But the fact that she's never mentioned them once in all the time I've known her says a lot."

Her steps slowed as they came to a crafts/art gallery. The emphasis seemed to be on American Indian art—paintings, metalwork, sculptures, pottery, weavings. He'd never had much interest in any kind of art for his home. All Ercella needed on her walls and tables were photographs of the family and treasures made in school by her kids and grandkids. He didn't even bother with many photographs since he had a digital collection on his computer that could cover every inch of space in his apartment twenty times over.

"I love that beaver." Therese pointed to a three-foot-tall buck-toothed piece that appeared to be carved from a single tree trunk. "Every time my dad sent my brother and me out to cut down trees for firewood, I wanted to see what kind of talent I might have with a chainsaw. So one day we left a good chunk of trunk standing, and I spent three or four hours carving and shaping that sucker. I found out that the answer to how much talent I had was none whatsoever. I'd carved it down so that it didn't look any different from the other stumps."

She gave him a sidelong look when he laughed. "Are you thinking you can't imagine me with a chainsaw?"

He tilted his head to study her. "No. I have no trouble imagining you doing whatever you want."

Her smile was small but satisfied. As she started walking again, she asked, "What about the Logan family back in Louisiana? Are you close?"

"Very." When she raised one brow in question, he went on. "There's my mom, a bunch of aunts and uncles and cousins. I have two brothers and two sisters, and the sisters have two kids each."

"Do they have interesting names like Keegan?"

"Hm. I've never thought of it as interesting. More like better than the alternative."

"What's the alternative?"

There was a new/used bookstore next to the art gallery. According to his younger sister, bookstores were the most wonderful places on earth, but he didn't read paper books if he could avoid them. Out in the field, an e-book reader was so much easier.

"My name is actually Keifer Remington Logan," he said as they moved on to an abstract and title office. "I think it was too much for my father to remember, even though he gave it to me, so he shortened it to the first syllable and the last."

"Keifer Remington. Wow. Are those family names?"

"Keifer's not. Remington might as well be. It's the name of his favorite rifle." He shoved his hands into his pockets again. "And yeah, my brothers and sisters were just as lucky. There's Ford—named after his favorite vehicle. Martha—named after his favorite cornbread mix. And the twins, Daisy and Duke."

"Named after the characters on *The Dukes of Hazzard*?"

"They wish. Nope, Daisy and Duke were his favorite huntin' dogs growing up."

For a moment she was silent, then a soft sound escaped, a breath that turned into a snort that turned into a giggle. "Why did your mother keep letting him name her babies?"

"Better question was why she kept letting him father them." Then he chuckled, too. "We've all asked her that, and she just sighs and says he was a sweet-talker and a charmer."

"Aw, that's romantic. About the most complimentary thing my mom says about my dad is he's a good provider. Though they've been married nearly forty years and still hold hands and cuddle like teenagers."

"Yeah, well, my parents have been married about thirty-five years, and my dad's actually lived with us maybe ten of those years. In addition to sweet-talking and charming, he likes to wander. He hasn't provided much of anything, and most of the cuddling he's done is with other women."

At the intersection she stopped and gestured across the street. "That's the oldest mural in Tallgrass. It's for a tobacco distributing company that used to be in that building."

He studied the painting of cowboys and Indians, sitting cross-legged on the prairie in chaps and blankets, sharing fat hand-rolled smokes. A few anorexic-looking buffalo grazed in the background underneath the block letters of the name of the company.

As she stepped off the curb, she remarked, "You don't sound hostile toward your father."

"There's no love lost, but hostile?" Keegan shrugged. "Nah. Mom says he is what he is. We can either accept it or not."

"Healthy attitude."

"It came after a lot of years of getting her heart broken."

Music drifted from a bar in the middle of the next block. Country. He'd rather have no music at all than country. What about Therese? Growing up in Montana, cattle and horse country, chopping ice, wielding a chainsaw...Crying-in-your-beer songs and two-stepping probably came naturally to her.

"Did you get your heart broken?"

Her question startled him into jerking his gaze back to her. "By my dad?"

Though she kept her gaze on the sidewalk ahead of them, she smiled. "Of course that's possible, but I was actually thinking about Mariah's mother. Was she the one you considered marrying?"

Keegan blew out his breath. "Yeah, we talked about getting married. No, she didn't break my heart." She'd cheated on him, ticked him off, saddled him with another man's daughter, and damn well infuriated him, but the sad fact was he hadn't loved her enough for his heart to break.

And that *was* sad. A man should care more about a woman he lived with. He should care more about a woman he could have kids with.

As they walked, she pointed out more murals—for a general store long since out of business, a funeral home that had moved to a new location, an oil company that had been swallowed by a bigger company, a bank that was one of the first businesses in Tallgrass. There were others that didn't serve as advertisements for anything other than a long-gone way of life: wild prairies filled with oil rigs, buffalo and mustangs, Indians and cowboys. Though there were still producing wells, she told him, as well as small herds of buffalo and wild horses, and lots of Native Americans and cowboys in the area.

They were at the intersection of Main and First when she stopped, checked the time on the illuminated bank sign, and sighed. "I should get home."

Forget about home a little while longer. The kids have been okay for three hours. They can do without you another hour. Or two. Or ten. No way he was going to say any of that, though. He wasn't even going to think it. Instead of saying anything at all, he turned, gestured back the way they'd come, and they started walking again.

A little slower this time.

Chapter 7

Therese awoke Wednesday morning, rolled over, and stretched, then opened her eyes for her first view—Paul's photograph on the nightstand. Of all the hundreds of pictures she had, it was her favorite: just Paul being Paul. That meant a devilish gleam in his eyes, a smile that stretched practically from ear to ear, and an air of anticipation that even the flat dimensions of a photo couldn't diminish.

They'd met by chance, under less-than-ideal conditions: a long, tough day at school, rush-hour traffic, her car dying in the middle of an intersection, people angrily honking. One good thing about an Army town: a person never needed help for long before it materialized in the form of young soldiers eager to lend a hand. Paul and his friends had pushed the car into a parking lot, then he'd taken the time to fix it right there, and she'd fallen in love.

If she'd known then that their time together would be so limited, if she'd had a clue how much heartache and anguish marriage to him would bring, would she still have asked him out or called a tow truck instead?

Slowly she smiled. She would have asked him out. Six years of *special* was worth all the heartache in the world.

Could she have *special* again?

An image of Keegan formed in her mind, and she hastily pushed it away. She liked him. A lot. She felt things when she was with him. But he was a soldier, a single father, and he lived elsewhere. Attraction was great, but there was zero potential between them. She wanted a man whose job description didn't include *danger*. She had a hard enough time dealing with her own stepkids; she didn't want to add anyone else's to the bunch; and when she did start looking, she would look for long-term, not long-distance.

If Keegan was anything, he was practice to get her ready for the real deal.

By the time she'd showered, dressed, and made it to the kitchen, coffee was brewing, and the air smelled of pizza. When the children had first come to live with them, she'd been determined to give them a good breakfast each day: eggs cooked to order, bacon or sausage, pancakes or French toast, even homemade hash browns. Turned out, the kids preferred cereal—milk optional—or protein bars or leftovers. Catherine hadn't been much of a cook.

Jacob was at the island with a textbook open in front of him, a pizza box beside it. With a piece of supreme pizza in his left hand and a pencil in his right, he sat hunched, scribbling the last of his homework in his notebook. He didn't look up when she came in, but he did mutter, "I made coffee."

"Suck-up." That came from Abby at the dining table, a half-eaten protein bar sharing space with her backpack and a can of pop, no glass, no ice. Therese relaxed her meal-time rules in the morning.

"Thank you, Jacob." She went to the coffeemaker, poured herself a cup, and wondered why he'd bothered. He'd never shown the slightest interest before. Some newly discovered fascination with the machine? Men were like that, wanting to play with a gadget until it lost its newness.

"I'm going over to Ryan's after school." Belatedly he added, "If that's okay."

"Ryan...which one is he?"

Abby snorted as her cell vibrated with an incoming text. "Ryan's a girl. We're not sure anyone ever told her, though. She looks like a boy, walks like a boy, talks like a boy."

Jacob hunched a little more, annoyance flushing his face as he scowled at his sister. "Shut up."

"Ooh, scathing comeback."

Therese bit the inside of her lip for thinking he could have done better herself. "Where does Ryan live?"

"A block over on the other side of the park," he mumbled.

"In that stupid purple house," Abby added. "The one that everyone looks at and says"—she did her best imitation of Catherine—"'*What* were they *thinking*?'"

This time Therese winced inside. She knew the house. In a neighborhood of houses painted white with the occasional cream or beige tossed in, the putridly violet house certainly stood out. Nothing larger than a picture frame should be painted that color.

"Maybe Ryan should come here. I haven't met her or her parents."

"Grandmother," Jacob corrected. "Her mom and dad

are deployed, so she lives with her grandmother. And she hasn't met you, either."

Good point. "I'll take you over when I get home so I can talk to her grandmother."

"Whatever." He shoved the last bit of pizza in his mouth, swiped his hand on his jeans, then stuffed his book and notebook into his backpack. "Gotta go."

She watched him charge down the hall, his hearing no doubt sharper than hers in picking out the vibrations of the approaching school bus. She sipped her coffee, which was very good, then picked up the pizza box, crumpling it until a lonely slice caught her attention. Plucking it out, she took a bite, savoring the cold meat and cheese. It had been Paul's favorite breakfast before he married her. He'd lived on delivery at night and cold leftovers in the morning.

"I have a dentist appointment at four," Abby announced. "Payton's sister is taking me."

Payton was a name Therese knew: a taller, not-quite-so-pretty clone of Abby. She was one of the few transplants to Tallgrass who had no affiliation with the Army. Her father was a surgeon who'd taken the chief of surgery position at the local hospital and brought his family along from St. Louis. Payton made it clear she would never forgive him for the upheaval in their lives and had, for a time, at least, kept a running countdown on her computer of how many days until she could leave again.

"How old is Payton's sister?"

"She just turned sixteen."

"So she got her license recently."

Abby swung her pack over one shoulder, then cocked out one hip. "Yeah, so?"

"You know the rules. No riding with new drivers." She

glanced at the calendar on the refrigerator to make sure there were no other forgotten obligations. "I'll pick you up here at three forty-five."

"But Payton's sister takes her to school every day. She picks her up after tennis, too. She takes her everywhere."

"Sorry. Your father and I both agreed on your riding with new drivers long before it became an issue." Therese shoved the bent pizza box into the trash, then carefully said, "Payton...That's traditionally a boy's name, too, isn't it?"

Naturally Abby didn't miss her point. "I promise you, no one mistakes Payton for a boy. Ryan, on the other hand..." There was nothing delicate about her shudder, or her disdain for the other girl.

"You don't like Ryan because she's not as pretty as you?"

For just an instant, pink tinted Abby's cheeks, and a rare flare of pleasure lit her brown eyes. Both softer responses disappeared in an instant, though. "Nicole says she's a geek and Payton says worse than that, she's dumb. She was in our class last fall and they had to move her back a grade because she was so dumb. I mean, like, who can't handle seventh grade?"

Therese's lips tightened. All her life she'd had a problem with anyone calling anyone else dumb. Her uncle Buddy was one of the sweetest guys a person could ever want to meet, but because he was mentally challenged, *dumb* was about all anyone ever called him. But before she could say anything to Abby, her stepdaughter gulped the last few ounces of pop, dropped the can so fast that it spun before falling onto its side, and rushed down the hall, leaving Therese to clean up the leaking liquid.

She soaked up the mess with a paper towel, then wiped it down with a bleach cloth, troubled by the last few minutes of conversation. Abby's antagonism toward her was understandable. She'd wanted her mother and father to get back together. She loved Catherine. She wanted to live with Catherine, and she blamed Therese because Catherine didn't want her.

But what about her behavior toward other kids? Speaking so scornfully about Ryan, parodying her friends' insults, possibly instigating some of her own. Had Abby surpassed Princess of Whine and gone straight to Mean Girl?

If she had, she would make the quickest U-turn on record, if Therese had anything to say about it.

She poured her coffee into a travel mug, topped it off, and grabbed a package of peanut butter and crackers from the pantry. Juggling the items with her bags, jacket, cell, and keys, she let herself out, locked up, and walked to the van.

Though a late spring snowstorm wouldn't be unheard of, she preferred to think as she breathed fresh, sweet air that spring was truly here. Bits of color showed here and there as bulbs forced their way above the mulch, and the fruit trees next door were covered with beautiful blossoms. It was time to start thinking about the yard, whether to stay safe and boring with grass and a few beds, or go all out with a brilliant display that would make their house stand out as much as Ryan's violet one did.

She drove to the end of the block, then detoured around the park that filled four square blocks. Moments later, she parked in the driveway of the violet house and climbed out, wishing she'd asked for Ryan's last name. Too late, so she climbed the steps to the porch hung with Victorian frills painted shades of red and royal purple, where the wicker chairs that flanked the door were pink and green. Whoever had chosen the colors hadn't been shy about expressing their tastes.

She rang the doorbell and listened to funereal chimes for a moment before the door swung open. She was expecting a grandmother, someone along the lines of her own mother or Paul's, but she got a surprise. Even accounting for good skin and great genes, Ryan's grandmother was much closer to Therese's age than her mom's. She was slim, wearing jeans with holes in the knees and a top that barely covered enough to be decent. A tattoo wound out from beneath the crop and stretched sinuously from one side of her rib cage to the other, wrapping around her bejeweled belly button before disappearing beneath her jeans, and her shiny black hair stood in spikes.

"Can I help you?"

Therese slammed her gaping mental mouth shut and smiled. "Hi, I'm Therese Matheson. My son goes to school with your granddaughter, Ryan." In spite of her good intentions, she asked, "Granddaughter? Really?"

"Really."

Wow. "Anyway, they'd made plans to hang out this afternoon, and I like to meet Jacob's friends' parents—or grandparents."

The woman's face wrinkled. "Aw, you've heard the rumors that people who come in this place don't come out again." Then she smiled, a white, even smile, and offered her hand for a strong shake. "I'm Prudence Nguyen."

"Nice to meet you, Prudence. We live on the far side of the park—"

Prudence waved one hand. "Redbrick with white board. Ryan has shown it to me several times when she starts her discussion on proper colors for residences. She's mentioned Jacob a time or two, which is saying a lot for her. She's usually too involved in her schoolwork or on her computer to bother with chitchat."

"Jacob, too. Sometimes it seems his entire vocabulary consists of grunts and *whatever*."

"Makes you want to smack him, doesn't it? I keep telling Ryan, God invented words for a reason, but she's not convinced." Prudence rubbed one bare foot with the other. "Would you like to come in? I've got a fresh pot of tea."

"Thanks, but I'm on my way to work."

"You're a teacher, right? Braver than me." She gestured toward an iron sculpture standing beside the door. "I only have to face torches and burning metal."

"You're an artist?"

"Depends on who you ask, though I've got a bit of a following through The Gallery on Main."

"I was admiring the work in their windows last night." She liked this woman, Therese decided. "You're okay with Jacob coming over?"

"Sure. I'll keep an eye on them with my plasma cutter in hand."

"Okay." She glanced at her watch. "Oops, I'd better get moving. It's nice to meet you, Prudence." *Okay,* she thought as she walked back to the van. Jacob now had another friend close enough to visit.

See, Paul? I haven't given up yet. I'm trying.

One of his favorite movie quotes sounded softly in her head. Yoda. *Star Wars.*

Do, or do not. There is no try.
It didn't brighten her day.

* * *

The ringing of the phone yanked Keegan from sleep at the ungodly hour of...Oh. Nine thirty. Eyes squinted, he felt around the bedside table for his cell, locating it on the fourth ring. He brought it close to his ear, grunted, and wondered if he could go back to sleep if he kept the call short.

His mother's voice destroyed all chance of that. "I realize you're on vacation and for some people that means sleeping in, but, really—" She broke off. "Never mind, it doesn't matter. That foolish brother of yours fell off a roof this morning and managed to bust himself up pretty good so I'm headed out to see him."

"Duke?" he asked groggily. Duke was always busting himself up pretty good. He was the youngest, the wildest, had the ridiculous name of Duke with a more ridiculously named twin sister, and had inherited their father's recklessness. Keegan was surprised they kept letting him set foot back on the drilling platform considering how accident prone he was.

"Not Duke, Ford. What would Duke be doing on a roof? Anyways, I'm going out to Phoenix to help out with him. That wife of his can't handle a crisis to save her life. She can't even deal with the surprise of a birthday party. She schedules everything to the minute. Probably won't even have sex with the boy unless it's written on her calendar."

Keegan pushed himself up to sit with the headboard

at his back. "I get it, Mom. Denise isn't your favorite daughter-in-law."

"No, and bless her heart, she's my only one. Poor thing. So I'm leaving in about thirty minutes and—"

A cold knot settled in his chest. "What about Mariah?"

Utter silence on the line, followed at last by a long breath. "That's why I'm calling you. I can't take her with me. Ford's in the hospital right now—intensive care, Denise said"—her voice wobbled on the words—"and that's no place for a little girl. And I can't ask Denise to take care of her. After all, he's her husband. Martha and Daisy can't take her, not with their work schedules, and Duke— Well, of course, that's out of the question, even if he wasn't out on the platform. He'd set her down somewhere and forget her. So I'm bringing her to you."

A chill rushed over Keegan, and he tugged the covers closer. The heavy drapes were blocking out the morning sun, and he'd turned the air conditioner down to 65 when he went to bed last night. That was all it was. An icy room. Not dread.

"I don't know how long I'll be gone. Pray God, not more than a week or so. You know Ford. He's tough. He'll be up and about in no time. Anyways, Mariah and I are flying to Dallas and then into Tulsa. You got paper and a pen? We'll be arriving in Tulsa at two fifteen on flight number—"

He rummaged through the night table, then found a notepad and pencil on the kitchenette counter, scribbling the information. She made him repeat it back to her, then sighed. "You're okay with this, aren't you? It'll be good for the two of you to spend some time together. She needs to know who you are."

Who I am doesn't have a damn bit of importance in her life. But he kept the retort inside. This was his mother, after all.

"Uh, yeah, I guess... You'll come back this way on your way home, right? If I'm still here?"

"Of course. I can't leave my little sweetheart for long. I'll tell Ford you send your love." She snickered. She'd spent too many years breaking up her boys' expressions of affection. "Two fifteen, okay? You'll be there, right? I'm bringing her little booster seat so you won't have to worry about that."

Keegan rubbed his forehead with his free hand. A booster seat was the least of his worries. "Yeah, Mom, I'll be there."

After hanging up, he looked around the room. It was a great room for a motel. For one person. He supposed he could make up a bed on the sofa for Mariah. There was really nothing to childproof, not that she was much of an explorer. Oh, God, he was going to have to do things for her, like bathe her and take her to the bathroom. She was potty-trained, wasn't she? And find out what she would eat and read stories to her and—

He was going to have to talk to her.

They didn't talk. Ever. He'd say hello or good-bye, at his mother's prompting, but not even Ercella could get the kid to say something back to him.

This wasn't how his trip was supposed to go. It had seemed such a good idea in the beginning: Matheson would be accommodating; so would his wife; Keegan would dispense of his only non-birth-given responsibilities to Mariah.

Matheson wasn't supposed to be dead. Therese wasn't

supposed to be so damn appealing. And Mariah was supposed to get out of his life, not dig her way in deeper.

Before leaving for Tulsa he had time to run four miles, shower, eat, and obsess for a while over where Sabrina might be and how much good it would do if he tracked her down. Would she be apologetic and happy to see her daughter again?

Probably not. She'd walked away from Mariah once already. It wouldn't be any harder the second time.

Long before he was ready, he found himself standing in the baggage area at Tulsa International. A walkway separated baggage from where passengers arrived, and he waited at the end of it, as far as unticketed passengers were allowed to go, pacing from one side to the other. When the flight arrival was announced, he stopped and pivoted, staring. After a few minutes, a flood of passengers appeared at the far end, a few strolling as they talked, most rushing with long strides, wheeled bags bumping behind them, dodging slower movers and each other.

And there, bringing up the rear, his mother and a tall, slender kid—military by the looks of his haircut and bearing. Ercella's arms were wrapped around a pink molded plastic seat, and her bulging purse hung from one shoulder. It took Keegan a moment to realize that the kid was carrying another bulging bag, done in pinks and purples, and, on one hip, Mariah.

She'd lived with him for more than a month but warmed up to a stranger on a plane while still eyeing him with obvious suspicion.

"—you so much," Ercella was saying when they came near. "You've been such an angel, Jeremy. You enjoy your time home and be careful when you get back over there.

Your mama wants you back in one piece." They stopped, and she lifted Mariah from the kid's arms and handed her to Keegan, then enveloped the boy in a hug.

"You take care, too, Mrs. L." Jeremy smiled politely as he held out the pink and purple bag, then headed off to meet his own family a few yards away.

"You never met a stranger, did you?" Keegan asked, trying subtly to give Mariah to her.

Ercella smiled, hugging him and pretending she didn't notice him pushing the girl at her. "What's the fun in that? Jeremy was a big help on the plane. He entertained Mariah from Alexandria to Dallas, then here, and carried her, too. Now, I don't have a lot of time before my flight leaves and I have to go back through security, so let's get her bag and get you on your way. You'll know it when you see it. It matches her tote."

Grudgingly he held on to Mariah. She was no happier to be there than he was to have her there. Her little body had gone stiff the moment Ercella placed her in his arms, and her smile had disappeared along with Jeremy the angel. She was holding herself rigid and glaring at him as if he'd soured her entire day. For just a moment, he was tempted to glare back. She hadn't done wonders for his past month.

You're the adult, Ercella had admonished him when discussing Mariah's failure to warm up to him. He didn't feel much like an adult.

"She's potty-trained, isn't she?"

His mother frowned as she took a place at the end of the luggage conveyor rumbling to life. "Of course she is. She's almost three years old."

"Can she feed herself?"

"Most things. You have to cut her meat and maybe mash up some potatoes or carrots."

"Can she bathe herself?"

Another frown. "Keegan, she's almost three. Could you bathe yourself when you were almost three?" She raised one hand before he could speak. "No, you couldn't. And you still needed someone to wipe your bottom. And you had to have three bedtime stories every night. And you slept with a nightlight on. And so does she, on all that. Heavens, have you not noticed anything in the past month?"

He'd noticed he was living with his mother again, which he hadn't done since he was eighteen. "What does she do?"

"She plays. She loves long walks. She watches cartoons but only on PBS. Educational stuff. She takes a nap after lunch, and she goes to bed no later than nine. She does what you did, and your brothers and your sisters, and she— Oh, there's her bag."

He stepped forward, but Ercella had already snagged the pink and purple case. She pressed the handle into his free hand, then tucked the booster seat between his arm and chest. "Okay, darlin', I've got to go now."

"Okay," Keegan and Mariah answered at the same time. She turned another scowl on him for assuming that he was his mother's darlin'. Well, he had been for thirty-one years.

"You don't have to see me to security. You just go on. The sooner you two are alone together, the sooner she'll understand." Ercella hugged him again, hugged, and made loud kissy noises with Mariah, then she started away. No long-drawn-out farewells for her.

"Call me when you know something about Ford."

"I will."

As Mariah watched his mother walk away, her tension increased until it was like trying to cradle a board. She pushed away, wriggling to get down, and when she couldn't, she kicked him hard in the thigh.

"Hey, stop that. No kicking allowed."

Her mouth puckered, she drew a breath, then unleashed a shriek that made everyone in the immediate area flinch. There was no way his mother could have not heard it, but she was still hustling down the long corridor that led to the security screening.

Oh, God, this was *not* the trip he'd planned.

* * *

The dentist was behind schedule, so it was nearly five thirty by the time Therese and Abby reached their neighborhood that afternoon. Instead of going straight home, Therese detoured past the Nguyen house, pulling into the driveway. "Run to the door and get your brother, will you?"

Abby looked horrified. "You're kidding. What if someone sees me? Triana Campbell lives right across the street, and she's the biggest gossip in school."

"I'm not asking you to take up residence. Go ring the bell and tell Jacob let's go."

They stared at each other, and Therese was starting to expect a refusal. Heaving a sigh and muttering beneath her breath, Abby got out, took a few furtive looks around, then rushed up the steps and rang the bell.

The door opened, and Jacob came out, followed by Ryan. Despite Abby's claim, she didn't look like a boy at all. She just hadn't started to develop yet. She was as tall as Jacob, board-thin, with cocoa-creamy skin, brown eyes that tilted exotically, and black hair, silky and short. She reminded Therese of a newborn colt with her long legs and arms and movements that weren't quite synced, as if she'd grown so quickly, she hadn't had time to adjust.

While the younger two talked, Abby turned and flounced down the steps. As she reached the sidewalk, someone called her name from across the street. Triana, Therese guessed by the sudden flush reddening Abby's face, her ducked head, and her accelerated pace back to the car.

She threw herself into the backseat, slamming the door. Jacob's entry into the front passenger seat was practically silent in contrast. Therese backed out, grateful it was such a short drive home.

As they turned at the corner, Abby straightened from her slouch. "Oh, God, you are going to ruin my life. Triana will tell everyone I was at Ryan's house, and people will think I like her. I. Don't. Like. Her." She thumped Jacob on the back of the head. "This is all your fault."

"Hey," Therese said sharply. "No hitting."

Jacob smirked over his shoulder. "Yeah, well, Ryan doesn't want people thinking you're friends any more than you do."

"Ha! She should be so lucky to have me for a friend. People adore me. They admire me. They just think she's a joke."

"She's not a joke!" Jacob snapped. After a moment he glanced at Therese. "She's not a joke. She's really smart. She just…" At a loss for words, he shrugged and turned away.

"I'm sure she's very nice." Therese turned into their drive, and the instant the van stopped, Abby jumped out and rushed inside, using her own key.

"Jacob." Therese faced him on the sidewalk. "Does Abby have friends besides Nicole and Payton and those girls?"

"I don't know."

"Is she mean to other kids?"

He shrugged again, with his head ducked and his gaze on the ground. Paul had done that when he didn't want to talk about something. After a moment, he walked off. By the time she got inside, he was in the kitchen, looking for a snack.

Therese put her purse down, then went upstairs. The temptation to pass Abby's room and go straight to her own was strong, but after a moment she stopped and knocked at the door. Naturally Abby didn't invite her in; naturally that didn't keep her out.

Her stepdaughter lay on the bed, her backpack tossed on the floor and her phone in front of her. Her hands were tucked under her chin, and she was staring at the phone as if willing it to ring. "What do you want?"

Therese walked past a pile of dirty clothes. Jacob managed to get his discards in the hamper every day, though she suspected it was more the fun of making the shot from across the room than any desire for neatness. Abby seemed to think the laundry faerie would blink hers to the laundry room.

Pulling the chair out from the desk, Therese moved a stack of DVDs, then sat down. Every conversation she'd had with Abby in recent memory had been loaded with her hostility and Therese's own pathetic attempts at patience, discipline, and understanding. She didn't expect this one to be any different. "Why don't you like Ryan?"

Abby scowled harder at the phone. If it would ring, she

would have an excuse to shove Therese out the door and delay or avoid the conversation entirely. The sad thing was, Therese would welcome the delay and/or avoidance just as much as Abby would.

"What's so awful about her?" Therese waited until Abby was about to speak, then added, "Your own opinion. Not Nicole's. Not Payton's."

"My opinion *is* their opinion. I agree with them a hundred percent. She's a geek. She's dumb. She looks like a boy. She's weird."

"How well did you get to know her before she was transferred? Did you talk to her? Have lunch with her? Work on any projects with her?"

"Duh. I hang out with the cool kids."

"By 'cool,' you mean lacking compassion, kindness, empathy, and common courtesy."

Abby rolled into a sitting position, knees bent, ankles crossed, as graceful as a dancer. "You weren't one of the cool kids, were you?" Her chin tilted. "You can't tell me who to be friends with. I'm not a loser like Ryan. I've got friends."

"Friends who admire you." The earlier pronouncement had been so arrogant coming from a girl barely in her teens. Therese would have rolled her eyes and snorted if it hadn't made her worry instead.

Abby's response was underwhelming. "What can I say?"

"Obviously, I don't know Ryan. Apparently, you don't, either. But I'm guessing, with both her parents deployed, leaving her friends, and moving here, she's had some tough times. I'd hope that, having been through what you have, you would have some empathy for her. Life is full of heartaches, Abby. The only good thing about that is we can learn from them. We can be kinder. More understanding. More accepting. Or what's the point?"

Before Abby could counter her argument, Therese stood and walked to the door, then turned back. "I hope you'll reconsider the way you feel about Ryan. If she and your brother are going to be friends, she'll be spending time here. It would be easier without your hostility. But I expect you to change the way you talk about her. If you can't say something nice, don't say anything at all. No more insults. Understood?"

For a long time, she thought the only response she would get was the angry glower, but after a moment, Abby curtly nodded.

Therese closed the door quietly behind her and listened for a response. No shrieking, no slamming, no throwing. Nothing but stillness. She doubted a single word she'd said had penetrated, but at least she'd said them.

It was up to Abby to hear them.

Chapter 8

It was the end of another stiff, uncomfortable dinner—grudging hand-holding for the blessing, grudging responses to Therese's attempts at conversation—when shrieking sounded down the hall at the front door, startling her. It sounded remarkably like Abby, though of course it wasn't. She and Jacob were both staring in that direction, and they both got to their feet as Therese did. Before she'd taken more than a few steps from the table, the doorbell rang.

Hurrying down the hall, she opened the door and blinked. Keegan stood on the porch, a very unhappy bundle of pink held forcibly in his arms. Her hair was blond and stood on end, her face was screwed up and red, and her volume was somewhere around ear-shattering.

Without waiting for an invitation, he stepped inside and shoved the girl into Therese's arms. "She's been doing this for five hours, less the seven minutes she fell asleep in the car coming back from Tulsa. My ears haven't stopped ringing, and I'm afraid my neighbors at the motel are going to call the police. Do something, please."

The little girl's hair and skin were damp, but few tears fell from her eyes. She was angry, Therese recognized, not heartbroken as her sobs indicated. She held herself stiff even after Keegan backed away—in fact, even managed to go a little stiffer when Therese spoke. "Well, hello, Mariah. Don't you make a sweet first impression?"

Mariah paused in the middle of a breath and narrowed her gaze on Therese. She must look like an angel when her skin wasn't all splotchy and her hair corkscrewing like drunken snakes. She had a lovely peaches-and-cream complexion, a rosebud mouth, and wore an adorable girly-girl dress with lace and ribbons and pink-and-white sandals.

The girl took another breath to shriek, but when Therese laid her finger gently against her lips and said, "*No,*" she cut it off, still staring but with less of a frown. Then movement down the hall caught her attention, and she studied Abby and Jacob as they approached. For a two-year-old, she looked for all the world as if she were plotting something sinister.

"What is that awful noise—" Abby's voice faded away as she reached them and scowled. She recognized Keegan— her attitude confirmed that—but her gaze locked in on Mariah. She eyed the girl as warily as Mariah eyed the rest of them. When she got even with Therese, Mariah gave a kick and extended her arms, very nearly escaping Therese's grip before Abby had hold of her.

Keegan closed the door and leaned against it, drawing Therese's attention back to him. If he'd had much hair, it would have been standing on end. As it was, he wore a variety of stains on his shirt and a panicked look in his eyes, only slightly offset by the amazement that Mariah was currently silent. A big, strong man—a fireman, a paramedic, an Army combat medic, for heaven's sake—and it appeared he might not survive an evening with his daughter with his sanity intact.

For the first time all evening, Therese felt the urge to smile. "I didn't know Mariah would be joining you on the trip."

"I didn't, either, until today. My brother had an accident, and Mom had to fly out to Arizona to be with him. My sisters couldn't take her, and my other brother isn't exactly responsible, so Mom stopped in Tulsa and brought her to me."

"I hope your brother's all right."

"They'll know after his surgery tomorrow. I didn't mean to interrupt. I didn't know where else to go."

"Apparently you came to the right place." Therese gazed at Mariah, contentedly settled into Abby's arms. "Have you really been screaming for five hours, sweetie?"

With the pink fading from her cheeks, Mariah smiled, revealing a few unevenly spaced teeth. She shared the smile with Therese, Abby, and Jacob, then frowned at Keegan.

"She really doesn't like you," Abby said flatly. "Are you mean to her?"

Keegan straightened defensively. "Of course not. We just don't really know each other."

"And she doesn't like you." Stepping around Jacob, Abby headed back toward the kitchen. "Mariah, huh. I'm Abby. You need some milk, don't you? It takes a lot of energy to be a long-term screamer. We've got some food, too, and maybe..." Her voice trailed away.

Therese was surprised. Abby had never shown interest in any kid younger than her besides Jacob, and that was always temporary. Even when Nicole had started babysitting, Abby wasn't the least bit tempted. Change diapers, wipe butts, and stuff food in a moving target for slave wages? No. Way.

The novelty faded quickly for Jacob. "Can I have some cake?"

"Sure. I'll be in in a minute." Therese waited for his footsteps to fade, then folded her arms over her middle. "Does this poor child know you at all?"

"Yes. I see her practically every day," Keegan said, then reluctantly added, "she just doesn't like me very much."

"Well, if you're going to be caring for her until your mother gets back, you'd better make her like you. Are you hungry? I recognize ketchup and mustard on your shirt. And—" She sniffed. "Juice? I don't recall you being such a sloppy eater."

He snorted. "I tried taking her to McDonald's. It's supposed to be her favorite place, but she started throwing her Happy Meal before I could even sit down. People were looking at us funny, so... Yeah, I'm hungry, but you don't have to feed me. Just give me a few minutes of peace."

Therese laughed. "Come on back to the kitchen. If Abby's replenishing Mariah's strength, you need to replenish your own."

As she walked down the hall, warmth seeped through her. It was the welcome distraction from the usual strained evening in the Matheson household, she told herself. The surprise of meeting Mariah. But honesty forced her to admit, it was mostly the sheer pleasure of seeing Keegan again.

Despite Jacob's request for cake, all he'd done was remove it from the bakery box and set it on the island, along with a stack of plates and forks. He was rooting inside the refrigerator, a jug of milk in one hand, a bowl of grapes, and a carton of strawberry yogurt in the other. "What else do you want?"

"Some carrot sticks," Abby replied. "That should be enough." She sat at the breakfast table, Mariah in her lap. Other than the red-rimmed eyes, there was little of the temper tantrum still visible on her little round face. Abby had combed her hair with her fingers and cleaned her face with a damp cloth—the Princess of Tantrums knew how to clean up after—and was bouncing the girl on her knee.

She was paying such careful attention to Mariah that Therese felt guilty for the princess comment, even if it was only in her head. Abby had calmed a child who'd spent the better part of the day in hysterics. It was a good sign.

Some days good signs were all a person could hope for.

*   *   *

"I used to have a baby doll who looked just like you," the sullen teenager Keegan had met Sunday afternoon crooned to the smiling child who had just about broken him today. He had a headache, his neck muscles were in spasm, his ears really were ringing, and his patience was shot.

You used to be *a baby doll who looked just like her.* He wondered when Therese would see the resemblance. No doubt her husband or his ex-wife would have noticed right away, but they'd had the advantage of knowing Abby when she was tiny. Therese hadn't.

Jacob carried the food he'd gathered to the table, still

bearing the dishes from their dinner. The smart kid included a sports bottle with a lid for the milk. His sister might like being the one to bring calm to Mariah, but Keegan bet she'd like it a lot less if she was wearing a glass full of milk.

"How about a sandwich? I have turkey and ham."

Keegan slowly pulled his gaze from Mariah and Abby to find Therese now rummaging through the refrigerator, taking out the makings for sandwiches. He should say no, thanks, a few minutes of quiet were all he wanted, but he hadn't eaten dinner, either, since his quarter-pounder and fries had been the next things to fly once Mariah had emptied her Happy Meal on the floor.

He walked over to the island. "You don't have to fix…"

Jacob snorted as he laid a loaf of bread and two plates on the countertop. "She's not fixing. She's Smurfing." After a glance at him, he explained, "Gathering. Smurfs are gatherers. You have to make your own sandwich." Which he then proceeded to do for himself.

"You just ate dinner, Jacob," Therese said, but there was no scolding in it.

"I'm growing."

"You won't have room for cake."

The kid snorted again. It was a good-natured sound, though. No derision intended.

Keegan fixed himself a ham sandwich, then followed Jacob to the table while Therese hastily cleared the dishes. He started to sit in the chair at a right angle to Abby's, then moved to the opposite side. Mariah's long-distance aim might need some work, but up close she was deadly accurate.

After a moment, Therese and Jacob joined them. She

brought a glass of iced tea for Keegan and a cup of coffee for herself. Keegan felt bad for coming over unexpectedly, but he was glad she'd invited him in. It was the first time since his mother's phone call this morning that he'd felt containable. One more hour of Mariah's screaming, and he might have just come apart at the seams. Securing her in her car seat, then watching from a distance had seemed the best bet, even if it was illegal.

"How well did you know my dad?" Abby asked.

He froze for a moment, then slowly chewed the food filling his mouth. Her gaze never left him while she waited, though she continued to spoon yogurt into Mariah's mouth like a mama bird feeding her baby. After swallowing hard, he glanced at Therese, whose expression was impassive, then back at Abby. "Not very well."

"Figures," she muttered with a pointed look at Mariah. "Why did you come here to see him if you didn't know him well?"

"Abby—"

Keegan stopped Therese with a shake of his head. "I wanted to talk to him about some things that happened."

"Good things? Bad things?"

"Some things can be both good and bad."

"Is this one of them?"

He thought of Mariah, having no family without him, and Therese, attracting him a hell of a lot more than any woman in years, and smiled ruefully. "That remains to be seen."

Abby studied him a moment, so exactly the way Mariah did, then lowered her gaze. "Mariah, do you need to go potty?"

Mariah's curls bounced with her nod, and Abby immediately turned sideways in her chair. "Here, Therese, you take her."

Therese's brows arched with surprise. Remembering the way the girl had screeched *Tuh-reese* Sunday, he figured it must be rare for her to pronounce her stepmother's name properly.

From across the table, Jacob laughed. "You brought it up, you get to take her."

"I brought it up because she just sucked down a glass of milk and I don't want her peeing on me. I don't have a lot of clothes to start with." The last was said defiantly in Therese's direction. "Besides, I've never taken a little kid to the bathroom. I wouldn't know what to do."

Jacob laughed again. "Crap, even I know that."

Abby gave him a threatening smile. "Then you take her."

Keegan understood how she felt. Some things just weren't dignified. Still, he stuck the last bit of sandwich into his mouth and started to slide his chair back.

"I'll do it," Therese said. "I got an A in Potty-time one-oh-one in college. Come on, Mariah."

An instant after the bathroom door clicked shut down the hall, Abby sat back, crossed her legs, and folded her arms. "Where's her mother?"

Interrogation by a thirteen-year-old. Fun. But a thirteen-year-old who'd gotten Mariah to be quiet. "I don't know."

"You mean, you just took your daughter and left?"

"No. I mean she just left her daughter and left. She dropped her off at day care on her way to work and drove away. Never showed up for work. Never came back."

That earned him attention from both of the kids. "At least our mom left us with our dad," Jacob said.

"Mariah's with her dad," Abby pointed out, and Keegan winced inside.

"Yeah, but Mom planned it. She told us. She told Dad. She didn't just drop us off somewhere and hope he found us." Though Jacob spoke matter-of-factly, his words sparked a flash of hurt in his sister's eyes.

The sandwich that had tasted so good turned leaden in Keegan's stomach. What was it with parents abandoning their kids? Wasn't there supposed to be some built-in parental instinct that made caring for their babies as necessary as eating and breathing? How could Sabrina have walked away from Mariah? How could Catherine Matheson have decided unilaterally that life was better without her kids in it? How the hell could neither of them have not cared about the impact on those kids?

The hurt gone, Abby locked gazes with him again. "Well, you're gonna have to do better than you did today. She can't cry herself silly every day."

She had a talent for stating the obvious. Probably from experience, Keegan knew, which didn't change the fact that she was giving him fathering instructions. "I know. I guess we haven't done as much of playing and reading together and stuff as we should have."

She raised one brow in a gesture that reminded him of Therese. If Abby realized she'd mimicked her stepmother, she would probably shave the brow off. "Well, since you're the grown-up, that's your failure, isn't it?"

"Yeah, my failure." He hadn't wanted to get involved, and barring that, he damn well hadn't wanted to get attached. What if he grew to care about Mariah and Sabrina came back? It would be like losing his own kid. Hell.

Granted, he'd made that decision when the social

worker had brought Mariah to him. More than a month, with no word from Sabrina. She was likely gone for good. So was Matheson. Mariah deserved a good home. If he got attached...if he lost her...

He was the grown-up, as Abby had pointed out. He would cope.

Mariah's shoes slapped the floor as she raced into the room. A grin split her face ear to ear, and her eyes brightened as she made a beeline for Abby. "I went potty. I want cake."

A few feet behind her, Therese detoured to the island. "Is she allowed to have sweets this close to bedtime?"

Damned if he knew. He might have lived the past month with her, but her care had been entirely Ercella's domain. "Sure, why not?"

Therese's look was dry. "Small children plus high levels of sugar sometimes equal a tad bit of hyperactivity. Though maybe not tonight. She's had a big day."

Yeah, if *big* meant *traumatic*. Her first plane ride, yanked from one place to another for the second time in five days, watching the only security in her life walk away from her in the airport, being stuck with Keegan, who obviously didn't count as stable...

If it was true that adversity made a person stronger, Mariah was well on her way to superhuman strength.

Fate and Sabrina had made it his responsibility to ensure, one way or another, that she didn't need to be that strong.

He just wished the choices were better.

* * *

By the time the dessert plates were empty, Mariah was drowsing in Abby's arms. Therese was truly surprised.

Who ever would have guessed that Abby could nurture and cuddle as well as she threw tantrums? She wanted to freeze this moment in her mind: Abby's tenderness with Mariah, Jacob shaking off the sullenness she knew so well to talk with Keegan, Keegan treating both her children with respect, albeit tinged with wariness in regard to Abby, Therese herself feeling relaxed. Contented.

For this moment, it was almost like being a family. Whole. Normal.

She swallowed hard as the clock chimed. "Abby, Jacob, you should get ready for bed."

Jacob scraped his chair back, picked up his dishes, then gathered everyone else's, too, and carried them to the sink. When he came back, he paused. "We didn't clean up from dinner."

That had been one of Therese's rules from the day the kids moved in: they set and cleared the table, put away leftovers, and loaded the dishwasher. They'd never had chores at home, and even after nearly four years, they still fussed about them. She'd heard enough versions of *Our mother never made us . . .* to last a lifetime.

But tonight had been a departure from their usual evening at home, and there were no leftovers to put away, just dishes to rinse and stack. "I'll get it later."

Both kids looked surprised. Abby had often accused her of only knowing how to dirty dishes, not clean them. But both were too smart to question the suspension of a rule, even one time. Jacob grunted and left the room. Abby carefully got to her feet, shushing Mariah when she stirred, and circled to Keegan. "You need to hold her."

Her tone was accusatory, but Therese didn't chastise

her. If Keegan was sole caretaker of his daughter for the time being, he did need the practice.

Mariah stirred again when they made the transfer, then sank against Keegan with a soft sigh, her lashes fluttering shut. She seemed so peaceful, though that would probably change if she opened those big brown eyes and saw whose arms cradled her.

With a *Good night* directed to the room in general, Abby went down the hall. For the first time in a long time, she took the stairs quietly. No stomping, no rattling the pictures on the wall, no slamming the bedroom door. It was heavenly.

Therese lifted her coffee cup, realized it was empty, and set it down again. It was too late for more caffeine. She pushed the cup away, then leaned back in the seat. "What is Sabrina's story? Did she need *me* time, too?"

The question increased Keegan's uneasiness. It couldn't be easy having a casual conversation about the woman who'd abandoned his daughter. Though Paul had been thrilled to have his kids living with him again, he'd never gotten over wanting to strangle Catherine for hurting them like that.

"I don't know," Keegan said at last. "I haven't seen her in a long time. Right after she told me she was pregnant, she moved out. Moved on. Then a month ago, a social worker contacted me. Said she'd dropped off Mariah at day care and never came back. I was listed as Mariah's emergency contact, so..."

So Sabrina had been fine with Keegan before the pregnancy but had moved out after. Had she had an affair? Suspected the baby wasn't his? Or had she decided he was fine for a fling but not father or family material?

Despite his awkwardness, he was clearly both father and family material. Considering Mariah hadn't been in his life long, and had entered it under stressful circumstances, he wasn't doing badly. He was learning.

Though it meant nothing, Therese saw no resemblance between the two. His hair was much darker, his eyes blue, his jaw squarer, his nose stronger. Not a single feature suggested they were related. Had he noticed that? Did he wonder?

"She's a beautiful girl."

"When she's not screaming."

"Even when. Abby put on the ugliest face this morning, and I thought, 'Darn, she's gorgeous even when she's trying to be ugly.'" Therese chuckled. "They both look like angels. Maybe their halos are a little crooked, but still angels."

Keegan gazed at Mariah for a moment, then looked up again. Some of the stress that had lined his face when she'd opened the door had eased. It warmed her that simply being there could make an evening easier for someone else.

Following his lead, she studied Mariah, too, and some bit of longing eased out of the dark places she hid it. She'd always wanted kids—had loved the idea of getting pregnant, her body changing, nurturing another life inside her that would mean more to her than her own life. She'd anticipated all the milestones: the positive test. The first ultrasound. Labor. Birth. One-month, two-month, three-month birthdays. First Easter, Halloween, Christmas, first day at school...

Paul had shared her desire. He'd loved Abby and Jacob so much and wanted two more, maybe even four. But they'd waited. Waited for his deployment to Iraq to end, waited to get settled at his new duty station, waited for the kids to adjust to the idea of living with them, waited for the deployment to Afghanistan to end.

Waited too long, it had turned out.

Too long for *them.* Not too long for her. She was only thirty-four. Even if she gave up the notion of sending the kids back to Catherine, she would still be young enough to get pregnant once Abby had gone to college. If she was lucky.

"I missed the baby parts," she said wistfully. "Jacob was two and Abby four when Paul and I got married. They'd already outgrown sleepers and diapers and cribs and cuddlies and rocking to sleep and bottles and pacifiers."

With her cupid's bow mouth slightly opened, Mariah made a soft, steady sound that didn't quite qualify for snoring. Keegan smoothed a curl back from her face with one fingertip, and Therese watched, fascinated by the gesture, so sweet, so touching.

"It'd be easier if we'd met when she was born, I guess," he said.

"Or with her mama there to smooth the way." Therese waited a long time, then took a breath and asked, "Are you going to keep her at some point or let your mother raise her?"

He stroked that curl again a time or two before finally meeting her gaze. "I don't know."

It was a simple, honest answer, and it made perfect sense. He was single. In the Army. Worked long hours. Was likely to get orders back to the desert or wherever the next conflict broke out. Could be moved anywhere in the world at the Army's whim.

Raising a child in that environment was a job for two

people. There would be times when he couldn't be home for Mariah no matter how hard he tried. He needed his mother's help.

Unless he married. Unless he found a woman who didn't mind raising another woman's child, with a family who could welcome that child wholeheartedly. Therese's own parents were sweet and affectionate with Abby and Jacob, but they didn't love them the way they would if she had given birth to them. They didn't feel that blood-of-their-blood bond with them.

How could they when Therese had never quite been able to form it herself?

Just one more way that stupid dream of a happy, loving, blended family had failed her.

One more way she'd failed the kids.

"I think it's time to go. You've got dishes to do, and my arm's going to sleep."

She smiled, though she was willing to sit there a few more hours in exchange for the peace—and Keegan's company. "Take my advice," she said as she stood up. "If she doesn't wake up on the way to the motel, just let her sleep. Change her clothes and bathe her in the morning."

He eased to his feet, his grimace making the movement appear awkward. "Yeah, I kind of figured that. Tonight's not the night for new experiences of the Mariah sort."

A soft laugh escaped Therese. "Which have you never done—bathed her or changed her clothes?"

"Neither."

"Oh, Daddy, you are in so much trouble."

"I don't suppose you'd have time before school..." He looked so hopeful as they walked down the hall that she couldn't help laughing again.

"Only if I brought a video camera to tape it."

When he turned at the door, he was scowling good-naturedly. He would do fine with Mariah. It might take a few days, and he'd probably lose more than one battle, but eventually...

"I'm glad you came over." She bent close to brush a kiss to Mariah's cheek and whispered, "Good night, sweetie."

When she straightened, she was closer to Keegan than she realized. Close enough that she wouldn't have to lean more than an inch or two to brush a kiss to his cheek. Close enough to do a whole lot more than that.

Primly she backed away and opened the door, keeping the solid wood between them. "If you survive tomorrow, why don't you come over for dinner?"

"Thanks for the boost of confidence."

"I don't boost confidence, but I do make delicious baby back ribs, baked beans, and sweet corn salad."

"I make the best baby back ribs in the entire history of the Logan-Dupree families. Just saying."

She followed him out onto the porch, where the night breeze sent a cooling rush through her. "I doubt they meet the standards of the Matheson-Wheeler families, but I'll loan you my kitchen and/or grill sometime, and we can find out."

"What time should I come, and what should I bring?"

"Six. Yourself and Mariah."

"It's a date." He carried Mariah down the steps and past Therese's van to his car, bending on the passenger side to fasten her into the child seat in the rear. When he came back around to the driver's side, he waved.

She returned the wave, then went inside. She wouldn't stand on the porch like a lovesick teenager and watch until he'd driven out of sight. And no matter what he said, to-morrow's dinner wasn't a date. It was two friends getting together with their families for dinner because that was what friends did. Two friends with a boy and two very loud girls between them was as far from a date as possible.

Still, as she began loading dishes into the dishwasher, she found herself softly repeating, "It's a date."

* * *

When Jessy's alarm went off Thursday morning, it was louder and more obnoxious than usual. Mumbling curses—Thursdays always came too soon in the week for her—she blindly felt for it on the nightstand, stabbed the button to silence it, and was just sinking back into the pillows when the noise sounded again.

It wasn't the alarm, but the damn cell phone. God, who knew a ringtone could destroy her brain as effectively as a dozen bulldozers? Eyes still closed, she fumbled until she found it, propping it against her ear. "H'lo."

"Jessy, where are you?" a woman's voice whispered loudly. "Mrs. Dauterive is looking for you because you're *an hour late*!"

It was Julia. From the bank. And she was whispering be-cause that old hag of a supervisor was somewhere around causing trouble. But why was Julia at work so early in the morning? And why was she—

"An hour late?" Jessy's eyes opened wide and she rolled to her side to see the clock. It was 9:08. The sight made her pop up as if on springs. Her alarm should have gone off at a quarter to seven; she should have left the apartment an hour later. Lord, what was she doing still in bed?

"Get over here fast as you can!" Julia hissed, then abruptly her tone turned sweet. "Not a problem, Mrs. Hitchens. I'm happy I could help."

As the line went dead, Jessy dropped her phone on the bed, swung her feet to the floor, and stood...and immediately swayed with a bout of nausea. She clamped her hand to her mouth and took a cautious step toward the bathroom, then another.

The reflection in the mirror wasn't too horrible. A sniff test showed she could skip the shower, the upright tufts of her hair could be tamed with a dunk under the faucet, and a good scrubbing would take care of the roadkill taste in her mouth. As far as covering the shadows under her eyes, well, she usually spent a good chunk of each paycheck on cosmetics that worked wonders for the under-rested and hung-over.

Too bad they couldn't remind her of what she'd done last night. A few drinks—that was a given. But where? When? With whom? Nothing in the apartment gave her a clue, and her brain...Even as it came slowly to life, thanks to blood flow, sticking her head in cold water, and downing a cup of strong java, the place where last night's memories were stored remained one big blank.

She worried the thought as she hustled down the stairs and along the sidewalk, swilling her second cup of coffee faster than she was taking in breath. She remembered getting off work at five. She'd laughed with Julia on their way out, then she'd headed toward the apartment. She had been tempted into a detour, though, walking the extra blocks to CaraCakes Bakery, carrying home the distinctive pink-and-black box filled with a variety of single-serving desserts. And then...

Then nothing. But there'd been no sign of the CaraCakes box in the kitchen when she'd made coffee.

She was through the first set of glass doors before she turned her thoughts to Mrs. Dauterive. The woman loved displays of authority, and she never believed anyone's explanations for why they were late. At least, not Jessy's. Granted, Jessy's were usually lies. Still, should she build on the tale from Monday about a sick father and a worried mother?

Inside she bypassed her desk and went straight to the boss's office. It was one thing to behave casually when she was a few minutes late, but more than an hour required remorse.

She tapped lightly at the open door, then stepped inside. "Hi. I know." She raised one hand to stave off the woman's usual *You're late.* "I am so sorry. I've been having trouble sleeping, so I took something last night and slept right through my alarm." It was true on the surface: either she'd eaten herself into a CaraCakes stupor or she'd drunk herself into a Patrón stupor. Either way, she really had slept through the alarm.

Mrs. Dauterive stared at her so long that she fidgeted. The woman's expression was severe, but there was something in it, something...searching. Like she knew Jessy hadn't told her everything and if she just looked hard enough, she could find the truth.

Finally she broke the silence. "Perhaps you should get some help for your...sleeping problem."

That hesitation tightened the muscles in Jessy's neck. Mrs. Dauterive couldn't possibly know about her personal problems. They never saw each other outside the bank. They didn't have any friends in common. All she could do was doubt the veracity of her excuses.

Jessy swallowed, forced a smile, and said, "You're right. I should. It won't happen again."

Keeping the smile in place by sheer force of will, she went to her desk and logged on to the computer. But the smile on the outside couldn't keep the worries quiet inside. There was a name for when a person lost a whole chunk of time—blackouts—and it wasn't a good sign.

How could she go about discovering her movements for the previous evening? Call friends, hint at whether she'd been with them? Stop in at CaraCakes at lunch and see if she'd mentioned anything to the clerk about her plans for the evening? Call the bars around town?

Silently she snorted. Oh, yeah, there was an easy task. She could start with Bubba's out on the edge of town, her most frequent hangout. Buddy Watson's was just a few blocks from the bank. TwoSteps, Jammerz, and Yellow Moon were all within walking distance of her apartment. Then there were all the restaurants that served liquor, dives she wouldn't be caught dead in—assuming she knew what she was doing—and liquor stores every few blocks.

Hell, she could have met some stranger on the street and gone home with him, or shared a bottle with someone in the front seat of his car. She could have been anywhere, doing anything. Including in her own damn apartment drinking from her own damn bottle.

So she'd lost a few hours of her evening. It'd been Wednesday. Nothing important ever happened on Wednesday. It was no big deal. She was just overreacting.

But the nerves knotted in her stomach showed no sign of easing anytime soon.

Chapter 9

Keegan had followed Therese's advice, putting Mariah to bed on the sofa without changing her into pajamas. He'd tucked a stuffed alligator into her arms, then covered her with a quilt his mom had sewn for her, and then he'd sat, all the lights off but one, and watched her sleep for two hours before finally crawling into his own bed.

Now she stood beside the bed, hair sticking straight up on the left side, two fingers stuck in her mouth, and watched him as intently as he'd watched her last night. He pushed himself up to sit with the headboard against his back and said, "Hey."

"Potty," she said, or at least that was what he guessed. The fingers made the sounds hard to distinguish.

Hell. As he shoved back the covers, last night's conversation replayed in his head. Abby: *I wouldn't know what to do.*

Jacob's laugh. *Crap, even I know that.*

Keegan had never taken a little kid to the bathroom before. It had to be easier with a girl than a boy: just set her on the commode, right? Nothing to aim. In the years since joining the Army, he'd learned to do all kinds of things he'd never imagined before.

When he was standing, he started to pick up Mariah, but she backpedaled out of his reach, spun, and walked into the bathroom on her own. He switched on the light, then looked at her. Okay, at least she was wearing a dress, so no need to remove that. Just lift it and pull her underwear down, set her on the seat, wait…He could do it.

He set her on the commode, then took a few steps to the bathtub, intending to turn the water on to heat for her bath, but a splash sounded before he'd even reached the knob, and a wail filled the room.

He turned back to find Mariah wedged partway through the toilet seat, her face scrunched up, her fingers clenching the rim, her feet in the air. Along with the tears, to say nothing of the shock of having her butt plunged into cold water, she was giving him a look that could kill.

"Sorry, Mariah. I'm sorry. I didn't realize—" Grabbing her under the arms, he jerked her up, then, unsure what to do with her, set her on her feet in the sink.

She continued to cry, adding to the mix hiccups and a mournful sound. "Celly, Celly, Celly." It was her name for his mother, since he hadn't wanted her calling Ercella any version of grandmother. He'd thought it would somehow be harder on Ercella when Mariah left, but he knew now it couldn't get any harder.

He turned on the bath, shoved the plug in, then began undoing the ridiculously small buttons on the back of her dress. "Celly's not here, Mariah. Shh. There's no need to get louder. I'm gonna give you a bath and put some clean clothes on, then we'll get something to eat, okay, and everything will be better, I promise. Just—just don't scream."

Of course she screamed.

His mother always acted like bath time was fun time, playtime, but it'd been a lie. Mariah fought him on getting her dress off. She kicked him when he picked up her naked little body and set her in the tub. She climbed out when he turned to get the shampoo and body wash Ercella had sent. She screamed so loud it made the small enclosure vibrate and sliced a sharp wedge into his brain. When shampoo got in her eyes, she screamed even louder, and when he was soaked to the skin and she was clean and relatively free of suds, she leaned forward, lowered her head, and puked in the water.

God help him.

He drained the tub and started the process again, and she didn't like it any better the second time around. The only good thing was she skipped the vomiting.

After wrapping her in towels that seemed skimpy for the job, he carried her into the bedroom in time to hear his cell ring.

"They just took your brother to surgery," Ercella said before he could even say hello. "They think he's going to be okay, though he took an awful hard hit to the head."

"It's an awful hard head." Keegan felt a moment of shame. He'd been so stirred up about Mariah for the past twenty-four hours that he'd hardly had a thought to spare for Ford.

"Ain't that the truth. Now...how are you and Mariah doing?"

He related the bathroom experience, and Ercella didn't know whether to laugh or cry. She settled for chastising him. "You've seen that skinny little butt of hers. You can't just set her on a toilet and expect her to balance all on her own. Lord, Keegan, you've traumatized her. She'll probably revert back to diapers and I'll have to potty train her again when I get back."

"She's been traumatized since you walked off and left us alone with each other yesterday. If it weren't for Therese and—" Too late he broke off.

"Who's Therese, and what did she do?"

He sighed. "She's Matheson's widow."

"You're calling her by her first name now."

He didn't respond to that. "When Mariah and I got back yesterday, she wouldn't stop screaming or eat or anything. I was desperate, so I went over to Therese's, and it turns out the kindergarten teacher is good with little kids. So is her daughter."

Ercella caught her breath. "Mariah met her half sister."

"And half brother. She really liked Abby."

"Do they look anything alike?"

"I don't know how any of them missed the resemblance." But that was easy for him to say. He knew the one thing the family didn't: that they *were* family.

"Is she going to see them again?"

Should he tell her they were having dinner tonight? Would she think the idea was good, bad, stupid? Would she suspect he had ulterior motives, like hoping maybe, just maybe, Mariah would wiggle her way into her stepmother's heart and, eventually, out of his life?

"Keegan?" Ercella's voice raised. "Are you there?"

"Celly?" Shucking the towels and standing naked in front of him, Mariah grabbed the phone, pressing it to her ear. "Celly, I wanna go home. Now."

His mother's tone changed from matter-of-fact to a croon while she, presumably, explained yet again why she was gone and Mariah was stuck with him. Ercella could tell her a thousand times, and the kid still wouldn't accept it. He didn't blame her.

After a few minutes, lip stuck out, Mariah dropped the phone, went to the couch, and grabbed the gator to tuck it beneath her chin. Fingers in her mouth again, she stared mutinously at him.

"Poor baby," Ercella said when Keegan got back on the phone. "She just doesn't understand...Maybe I should have brought her with me."

Aw, man, his mother never second-guessed herself. Him, his brothers and sisters, the entire rest of the world, sure, but never herself. "Mom, she'll be fine. We'll be fine. Just concentrate on Ford, okay?"

It took a couple minutes to convince her of his words. Finally, he used Mariah's naked state as an excuse to go.

Ercella's laugh was part amused, part tearful. "I dress her, fold clothes, and cook breakfast all at the same time."

"You also don't dunk her in the toilet. I need both hands and all my attention. Call me when you have news about Ford. I love you."

After he ended the call, he went to the dresser and opened the top drawer, pulling out the first set of clothing he came to, a blue shirt and denim shorts, plus a pair of rabbit-covered underwear. "Come on, Mariah, let's get dressed."

"No."

"Aren't you hungry?"

"No."

"I'm hungry." He wanted to get dressed himself, brush

his teeth, and get some breakfast. A gallon of coffee and a handful of aspirin tablets would be a good start.

She swiped a hank of hair from her face. "Pink."

With a shrug, he traded the shirt for a pink one. "Okay, come on."

She shook her head.

"Look, it's pink, see?"

She wasn't impressed.

Keegan bunched up the clothes in his hand and gazed at the door. Maybe he could leave her just long enough to go to QuikTrip on the corner and pick up breakfast there. He didn't make a habit of buying hot food from convenience stores/gas stations, but judging by the wide selection, a lot of people did. How much trouble could she get into alone for five minutes? Not even Ercella required line-of-sight on her every single minute.

Sighing heavily, he went to the couch, lifted her onto the cushions, then reached for one leg to slide into the underwear. She pulled and twisted, but he succeeded with that foot, reached for the other, and she slid the first one out again. "Come on, Mariah," he cajoled. "You can't run around naked all day, and I know you've got to be hungry. Maybe after breakfast, we can find a park to play."

"No, no, no, *no!*" She jerked free, scrambled to the other end of the couch, then jumped off and headed for the bed.

His patience evaporated. "Mariah!"

She froze, her back to him. Any minute now, she was going to let out a shriek that would do both her and Abby proud. He steeled himself, waiting for the assault on his ears and his headache, but it didn't come. Slowly she turned, came back, pulled the panties from his hand and primly said, "I do it my own self."

It took her a while, though nowhere near as long as it had taken him, and she was actually wearing the underwear when she was done. A smile split her face at the accomplishment, then disappeared the minute she saw him watching. Next she grabbed the shirt, put it on backward, pulled her arms loose, twisted it so the picture of the princess was on the front, then spent another few minutes getting the shorts on, all but baring her teeth when he tried to help.

Relieved at the progress, Keegan got clean clothes for himself, pushed the bathroom door almost closed, then changed in record time. When he went in, Mariah was considering the long row of shoes he'd lined up beside the dresser. When he came out, dressed and having brushed his teeth, she was still crouched in front of them. With a dismissive look for him, she finally picked a pair of flip-flops with an elastic band around the heel, put them on the wrong feet, then trotted to the door.

"I want pancakes. Hurry, let's go."

"You've got your shoes on the wrong—" Aw, hell. Considering how long it had taken them to get to this point, if she didn't mind, why should he?

* * *

For the second time in two weeks—and only the second time in four years—Dalton knocked off work early. There was more he could do. With horses and cattle and buildings to maintain, there was always more, but the necessary jobs were done, the stock taken care of. The world wasn't going to end if he didn't check off a few more entries on his never-ending to-do list.

After a shower and a change of clothes, he drove into town, a stack of bill payments to mail and the grocery list tossed in the passenger seat. Like the chores, both of those could wait until tomorrow, too. There was just something about him this evening that couldn't wait. He needed to go somewhere. Do something. See someone. Anyone.

He thought on the way in about calling Noah and asking if they could meet for dinner. Stillwater wasn't much of a drive, and he hadn't been there in years. But his brother would be home in another twenty-four hours, and frankly, he wasn't the company Dalton was looking for.

He considered calling Dane Clark. Dane was about the closest thing he had to a friend around Tallgrass—four years of ignoring people was hard on a friendship—but he probably already had plans with his fiancée. If he didn't, he'd be wishing he did.

From the day he'd met Sandra, Dalton had wished. For years, he'd had everything he could have wanted…other than knowing whether Dillon was dead or alive, and he'd lived with that question for so long it had become nothing more than an occasional thought.

But Sandra…he'd wanted to spend every minute with her from the day they'd met in the feed store. She'd been looking for a trellis and tape to support the lone tomato plant on the balcony outside her apartment. She had asked questions about the feed and medications he was buying, confessed to loving horses more than anything in the world, and wrangled an invitation to see his.

Ten days later they'd flown to Las Vegas and gotten married. Their mothers had cried, both because they were happy for them and because there hadn't been a wedding. His folks had been surprised. Dillon was the impulsive twin, the one who acted first and thought later, while Dalton had always been responsible.

But he'd never regretted it.

Until he'd found out the truth about Sandra's death.

When he passed the flower shop just inside the city limits, he focused on where to go. Almost all of his rare meals out were at Serena's, but he wasn't hungry for home cooking. What he really wanted was a fat, greasy burger with onions and jalapeños cooked right into the patty and fries so crispy they were almost charred. While there were several places that could supply the burger, only one had the fries.

Bubba's had started life during the log-cabin craze back in the early eighties, both home and showroom for a contracting company. The location might have been okay for living, but it was bad for a business, and with log cabins not being a novelty in Oklahoma the way they were elsewhere, it hadn't taken long for the contractor to close up shop and move out of the area. Bubba Watson, on the outs with Buddy, his brother and partner in a bar downtown, had bought the place and turned it into what Dalton's father called a good old-fashioned honky-tonk.

Every guy Dalton knew back in school had had his first bar fight at Bubba's and gotten his first drunk on there three years before they were of legal age. Dalton and Dillon had been thrown out too often to count, and after a go-round with Bubba's younger sister at the newly built motel across the parking lot, Dillon had been banned from the place for life. No one knew if Bubba would have held his ground, since Dillon had left town soon after.

Stubbornly ignoring memories of the last time he had come to the bar—resulting in his only time at the motel—

Dalton parked at the end of a long line of pickup trucks on the east side. The music was loud, even through the thick log walls, and the aroma of fried onions and beef drifted on the air. With the customers primarily working cowboys or oil-field hands, odds were he'd find an old friend inside. If not, well, he wasn't a stranger to eating or drinking alone.

But damned if the first familiar face he saw wasn't exactly the one he'd rather never see again.

Jessy Lawrence sat on a stool at the end of the bar, wearing a dress and high skinny heels that couldn't disguise the fact she was maybe three inches over five feet. A bag big enough to double as an overnighter sat on the empty stool beside her. Saving it for a friend or using it to keep guys away?

She'd told him that day at the cemetery that Bubba's had been her husband's favorite bar, and it had been her suggestion they come here together. Tonight she didn't look particularly happy to be here. A drink sat untouched in front of her, her arms rested on the polished wood, and she stared at the thick beams behind the bar as if they were the most fascinating thing she'd seen all day.

He was trying to cut wide around her on his way to a booth in a dimly lit corner when a waitress dodging a grabby customer lost her grip on the tray she carried and a dozen empty bottles crashed to the floor. Three of them spun to a stop right between Dalton's boots. Everyone in the place turned to look, with a couple of cheers for the spill, more for the punch the waitress landed on the offending cowboy's shoulder, and Dalton found his gaze locked with Jessy's.

This was the point where he should say *what the hell,* turn around, and walk out. God couldn't possibly mean for him to run into her twice in four days. It was a sign that he was better off at home and working, that maybe he wasn't ready for anything else yet.

But he didn't say *what the hell*. Didn't turn around or walk out. For a long time he didn't do anything but stare at Jessy, and she stared back. He didn't break contact with her until the flushed waitress retrieved the bottles at his feet, then flashed him a smile. "If you know what you want, honey, I'll get it to you soon as I can."

"Burger, fries, Bud." He stepped back to let her pass, took one more look at Jessy, then continued to the table farthest from where she sat.

Why was he surprised? He knew she liked this place. He'd known, whether he acknowledged it, that there was a chance of seeing her here. Hell, subconsciously, had that been why he'd come? Because he wanted more than what he had? Because she did like this place? Because she was the first woman he'd looked twice at since Sandra?

Because he'd done more than look twice at Jessy?

Nah. Seeing her again was just bad luck. Coincidence. Tallgrass wasn't so large that a man could avoid a woman forever.

He sat down, his back to the bar, and cracked open a peanut from the pail in the center of the table. Though discarded shells littered the floor, he left his in a neat pile out of habit. After eating a dozen, he was thinking a swallow of ice-cold beer would be good to wash away the salt when Jessy walked up to his table.

"I come bearing gifts."

He looked at her, raising his brow, and she smiled uneasily, stepping forward to set his beer on the table, stepping back in the same smooth movement.

"Lora's got her hands full with the boys, so I offered to

deliver it." Another flash of uncomfortable smile. "Can you tell I used to be a waitress?"

He picked up the beer, took a drink, and set it down without looking away. Her dress was not too tight, not too short, not revealing at all, but she still managed to look more dressed up than any other woman in the place. The electric blue somehow made her eyes even greener and looked just right with her fiery hair.

Damn, she was pretty.

And awkward. She hadn't been awkward at all the day they'd met.

"Do you mind...?" She gestured toward the empty chair across from him, and he wondered what she would do if he said he did. Because his mother didn't raise him to be any ruder than he'd already been, he shrugged.

She slid into the chair and set her huge bag on the table with a thunk. He realized she'd left her own drink at the bar. Didn't she know better than that? There were a lot of guys who wouldn't hesitate to put something in it if they thought it would get them a little time in her bed.

She picked out a fat peanut and popped it open. "Any more trouble with your brother's account?"

"No." Then, because that sounded so abrupt, he added, "Not that I know of. And if there had been, I would have heard."

The waitress breezed over to drop off a thick stack of napkins and a bottle of ketchup, along with a bottled water. "Thanks for bringing that, Jess. Your food will be out any minute."

"No problem, Lora."

Dalton took another swig of beer as Jessy unscrewed the cap on the water. "You come here a lot."

Tilting her head, she studied him a moment. "Is that a question, a statement, or an accusation?"

All of the above. His neck grew warm, and he shoved his rolled-up shirt sleeves higher on his forearms. "A question."

After another moment, she smiled, but it didn't touch her eyes. "Not a lot. Often enough. I told you, this was Aaron's favorite place."

So she did remember inviting him here and what went on afterward. Why had she pretended not to recognize him the following week at Serena's, when she'd been laying the charm thick and heavy on Noah?

Before he could bluntly ask her, Lora set a plate of steaming food in front of him. "Can I get you anything else?"

He shook his head, and she took off again. Waiting tables at Bubba's wasn't for the slow. He cut his burger in half, then squirted a big blob of ketchup into the fries. "You're not eating?"

Jessy's gaze slid to the food, and her nose wrinkled delicately. "Not tonight." She had a bit of a queasy look as she said it, but it didn't stop her from cracking open another peanut.

"So you're not eating. Not drinking. Not dancing. Not flirting. What are you doing in a bar?"

She sat back, folding her arms beneath her breasts, and gave him an unhappy smile. "That's a good question, isn't it?"

* * *

Therese was taking the baby back ribs from the oven when the doorbell rang. Automatically she looked at the clock.

Keegan and Mariah were ten minutes early, but that was okay. The ribs had spent the day in the slow-cooker, going to the oven only for a quick blast of heat to caramelize the sauce. The baked beans were warm in the microwave, dishes of potato salad and corn salad shared island space, and a pan of brownies cooled on the stove. It was her favorite meal in the entire world, and she was looking forward to sharing it with Keegan.

Looking forward to spending time with him.

From down the hall she heard Abby's voice. "Therese is in the kitchen." Then, in a softer, sweeter voice, "I like your outfit, Mariah. Is pink your favorite color?"

Was the child a novelty to Abby that would lose interest soon? Did she recognize a kindred drama-princess spirit? Maybe she related to Mariah deep down on the abandoned-by-her-mother level. Whatever the reason, Therese was grateful to learn her stepdaughter could show compassion and kindness. She hadn't really been sure before last night.

Keegan's footsteps sounded a moment before he came into the room. "Hey."

He wore snug-fitting jeans and a polo shirt and looked good enough to make her smile for no reason besides the pure pleasure of seeing him. "Hi. How did it go today?"

Instead of taking a seat at the bar, he leaned against the counter a few feet away. She smelled his cologne as she moved near to take a serving platter from a cabinet beneath the island. If she didn't know better, she might think it was what made her mouth water and not the delicious food around them.

"We're both clean. We're both fully dressed, though she's insisted on wearing her shoes on the wrong feet all day. Don't mention it to her, okay? It just annoys her."

"And you don't like to annoy her? Or you're afraid someone will call the cops on you?"

"Both." He grinned. "Besides, I have an image to uphold. I am Army. I am strong."

"Yet a two-year-old child can break you with one wail." She liked that about him. Tough guys were sexy. Tough guys wrapped around a toddler's little finger were ten times sexier. "You are mush."

"Can I help with anything?"

She glanced around. The kids had set the dining table earlier, with slightly less grumbling and sigh-heaving than usual. Jacob had filled four glasses with ice and put them on the table, and a newly purchased sippy cup full of milk was waiting in the refrigerator. "If you can take this plate into the dining room…" She braced one salad bowl in the crook of her elbow, picked up the other serving dishes, and led the way.

"Abby, Jacob, Mariah, dinner's ready!"

While the kids gathered and settled in, Therese returned to the kitchen for drinks. When she came back, Keegan and Jacob were seated on one side of the table, Abby and Mariah on the other, the little one sitting atop a pile of cushions so she could reach. Therese slid into her own chair, laid her napkin on her lap, then automatically extended both hands. "We say the blessing."

"*She* does," Abby muttered. Heaven forbid that anyone think she had something in her life to be grateful for.

Therese ignored her comment, as she always did, then belatedly realized she would be holding Keegan's hand. Something fluttered through her. Anticipation, pleasure. She tamped it down. She wasn't starved for human contact. She held hands, patted shoulders, and gave out hugs every day. And this was for a prayer, for heaven's sake. It was no more personal than a handshake.

On her left, Mariah readily took Therese's hand. Little ones were generally good about that. On her right, Keegan was a little slower, his hand a lot bigger, rougher, stronger, his fingers wrapping around hers in a manner that was way more personal than a handshake.

Her insides fluttered again.

She bowed her head and was about to pray when Mariah piped up. "Bless this food. Amen. Let's eat."

Jacob snickered. Abby giggled. "My mother was lucky to get all five of us at the table at one time, so she had to get the prayer out fast," Keegan said apologetically.

Therese smiled at Mariah, beaming with pride for her blessing that had earned a laugh. "That was a good job, sweetie." But it was harder to release Keegan's hand than it should have been.

Once the dishes had been passed and everyone's plate was full—if the single rib and tablespoon each of side dishes on Abby's plate could be considered that—Therese asked, "How is your brother?"

Keegan speared a grape tomato in the corn salad. "The surgery went well. He was awake and talking this afternoon."

"What was wrong with him?" Abby asked.

"He fell off a roof and hit his head."

"Why was he on a roof?"

"Because he's a roofer. That's what he does."

She wrinkled her nose distastefully. "What? He can't do any kind of normal job?"

"Don't mind her." Jacob grinned at his sister. "She's been dropped on her head a bunch of times."

"Jerk," she said.

"Freak." His taunt was followed by a commotion that ended with him grunting and Abby smirking.

"No more kicking under the table," Therese warned. "Behave."

Abby smirked again, but this time Jacob mirrored it. She might have struck first, but he would get back at her. He'd learned patience from his father. He would wait for an opportune time, meaning when Therese wasn't around and his sister was least expecting it.

The skirmish didn't deter Abby. "If your brother had surgery, why are you here and not there?"

Before Therese could admonish her again, Jacob did. "Because, of course, you love me so much, you can't imagine not giving up everything, anything, to be with me, can you?"

"Oh, gross." Abby leaned closer to Mariah. "You are so lucky to be an only child. Brothers are nothing but trouble."

Mariah's only response was a big grin before she shoved another fistful of rib meat into her mouth.

When the meal was done, Mariah appeared to be wearing as much food as she'd eaten. Barbecue sauce ringed her mouth and coated her fingers, and both her shirt and napkin were heavily stained. Even her curls on one side were crimson. As Abby stood up, the girl grabbed for her, toppling the cushions and leaving Abby only two choices: catching her or letting her fall.

Therese gave silent thanks that Abby opted to catch her, stickiness and all, but stiffened, waiting for her outburst. She wasn't the only one. Keegan's chair scraped as he started to rise, his protective-father instincts surfacing, and Jacob looked apprehensive. Even Mariah was still, legs dangling in the air, her fat little lip starting to tremble, not sure what she'd done but aware it was wrong.

For one endless moment the very air seemed to vibrate while Abby stared at the stains newly transferred to her white souvenir shirt from a Hollywood movie studio tour. Finally, her sharp intake of air broke the tension. "Eww, gross. You need a bath and your hair shampooed."

Mariah's gaze darted toward Keegan, her hair swinging. "No bath. No shampoo. No no no *no*."

"Lucky for you, I don't do kid baths. Come on, we'll clean up upstairs. And by the time we're finished, Jacob will have already cleared the table and loaded the dishwasher"—starting toward the door, she stuck her tongue out at her brother—"and all we'll have to do is eat brownies."

When they left the room, Therese unloosed a slow breath. "Wow."

"Yeah," Jacob agreed. Then he shrugged, and some of his usual sullenness returned. "Of course she skips out on chores again."

Keegan sat down again as Jacob stood. The boy grabbed two handfuls of dishes and headed for the kitchen.

Therese bent to retrieve the napkin that had fallen from Keegan's lap and laid it on the table, set her own napkin on top of it, then, as if a miracle hadn't just occurred, narrowed her gaze on him. "What's behind the 'no bath, no shampoo'?"

Chapter 10

Keegan's nerves were slow to settle. He hadn't over-reacted in expecting a major tantrum from Abby. The people who knew her best had, as well. If she'd yelled at Mariah or swatted or shaken her, he would have...He wasn't sure what he would have done, but he would have done something. It wasn't like Mariah had deliberately gotten herself or Abby dirty. Everyone had known after watching her eat cake last night that she was enthusiastic about food and feeding herself.

But Abby had responded with so much more restraint than anyone gave her credit for. The shirt looked brand new, but she'd blown it off. She might be ticked off inside, but if that was the case, he appreciated her keeping it there.

Absently he stacked the remaining plates, gathering the silverware onto the top dish. "I gave her a bath this morning. That's what you do with kids, you know. Bathe them. Sometimes twice in a row."

Without further prompting, he recounted the morning's

experience, puking and all, and Therese laughed. "This is shampoo your mom packed for her?"

He nodded.

"Didn't you realize baby shampoo doesn't burn or sting?"

"How am I supposed to know? I haven't been a baby in a lot of years, and she was screaming like I'd gouged her eyes out with a dull spoon."

"She was tweaking you. Kids do that. As long as you give her the response she wants, she'll keep doing it."

He shifted his gaze upward, where the sound of running water sounded distantly. "Yeah, older kids do that, too." Her faint grimace showed that she'd gotten his message. "I think Mariah's goal for this trip is to make me feel incompetent. I've faced raging fires, combat, and injuries you wouldn't want to imagine. I've saved lives when people were trying to take mine. And this thirty-pound pink and purple mess of blond curls can make me quake in my boots."

Maybe it would have been different if she really was his daughter, or if Sabrina had let him believe she was. He would have been there from the beginning; he would have felt an emotional bond; he wouldn't have been trying to keep his distance.

Therese's smile was sweet and a little dreamy. "Yeah. Isn't it wonderful?"

She'd missed the baby parts, she'd said last night, and she hadn't just meant she wasn't physically there for Abby's and Jacob's infant/toddler years. She'd been denied the whole experience, with her stepchildren, with children of her own. The fun part, the anticipation, the cute and cuddly stages, the bonding ages.

Before Keegan responded to her last comment, Jacob came in for another load of dishes. "I made coffee and cut the brownies and put them on a plate," he said as he loaded up again.

"Thanks." Therese was too busy scenting the rich caffeine in the air to notice the crumb of chocolate in the corner of the kid's mouth.

Keegan pantomimed wiping his own mouth, and Jacob grinned, swiping his on his shoulder before he left.

"I saw that." Therese stood, then neatly scooted her chair under the table. "I may just be a stepmother, but I know real mother things. Jacob puts the brownies on a plate to hide the fact that he's already sampled them. Abby hides her shampoo and pretends she's out because she likes mine better, and neither of them has ever, ever used the last square of toilet paper in the bathroom. It disappears magically, spills happen spontaneously, empty milk cartons march themselves back into the refrigerator, and food disappears without being eaten."

Keegan pushed his own chair in, then did the same with the kids'. "But they do dishes, he makes coffee, and she keeps Mariah happy. What more could you ask?"

Her smile was agreeable but strained.

In the kitchen, she poured two cups of coffee, then he circled the counter, standing beside her while she stirred cream and sugar into hers. The space between the island and the counter hadn't seemed so cramped before dinner, but they'd been the only two in the entire room. Jacob took up twice the space his physical size accounted for as he rinsed plates, scraped leftovers into storage containers, and loaded the dishwasher. It forced Keegan and Therese into close quarters around the coffeemaker.

Close was fine with him.

"It's a nice night. Let's sit outside," she suggested. She placed a saucer with a half dozen brownies on top of her coffee mug, grabbed a handful of paper napkins, and headed toward the French door. "Jacob, will you tell Abby she can send Mariah out here if she wants?"

He grunted in response.

Keegan followed Therese onto a patio that was unimpressive compared to the rest of the house. A gas grill occupied one corner, hidden beneath a dusty cover, and wood chairs with bright yellow cushions filled the rest of the space. It looked an awful lot like the patio off his apartment, which was nothing special, either, except her chairs were a lot nicer.

The grass was a little shaggy, and the flowerbeds were empty except for decaying mulch. His mother would have already planted enough flowers for any five yards. Before the major's death, he suspected Therese would have had these planted as soon as the frost danger was past.

"My uninspired yard." Her voice was soft in the dim evening, calm and soothing. It was a good voice for reading bedtime stories to children. For telling bedtime stories to their father. It was sweet, mellow, her native accent diffused by her years in Georgia and Oklahoma. If he hadn't known she was from Montana, it wouldn't have been among his first five guesses.

"You should see my friend Carly's yard. She planted a truckload of flowers a week or two ago, and it's so bright and colorful. Now they're putting in a fountain. I'm jealous."

He sat in the chair beside her and took one of the brownies from the plate resting on the arm of her chair. "You have plenty of room for a fountain."

"I don't actually want one. I'm just jealous that she's getting stuff done. Painting her house, rearranging things, getting ready..."

Getting married and moving on with her life, Keegan added silently. And not dealing with stepchildren who didn't adore her.

"Not that she doesn't deserve every bit of happiness she's found," Therese went on. "God knows, she's earned it. I'm just...jealous."

What was he supposed to say to that? *Things will get better? Your stepkids will learn to love you or grow up and move out eventually? You'll move on with your life?* It would be at least seven years before she could reasonably expect both kids to move out. Maybe once they were in college and needed a home only for weekends and breaks, their mother would feel like being a mother again.

No matter how old they got, they would always need a home for more than just weekends and breaks.

"What is it you want to get done?"

She slid farther down in the chair, her long legs stretched out in front of her, and cradled her coffee in both hands as she stared across the yard. A moment or two passed with no sound but their even breathing and the occasional snuffle from a neighbor's dog, hidden from view by the wood fence.

Finally she sighed. "I want things settled with the kids. I want..." Another sigh, and her voice softened. "I don't know what I want."

What things needed settling with Abby and Jacob? He couldn't see much changing there. Abby would mature as she got older, but she was always going to be a drama princess who wouldn't appreciate all Therese had done for her until she was grown and a mother herself. Jacob was ahead of his sister on that. He didn't cut his own mother as much slack as Abby had. But he was still a kid, with all the fun of middle and high school ahead of him.

Behind them, the door opened, and Mariah dashed across the patio, passing so close that Keegan smelled her shampoo. Her skin had been scrubbed clean, and in place of her dirty clothes, she wore a T-shirt with a glittery crown on the front. The hem had been tied into a knot to keep it from dragging the ground, and a ribbon looped through the sleeves and flopping in a bow at her neck stopped it from sliding off her shoulders, and she clearly loved it.

Her mother had left her, her father was dead, and nobody else wanted her, but she was thrilled to be wearing one of Abby's shirts. How long would she be so easy to please?

Abby and Jacob followed her out, Jacob sprawling into the chair on Keegan's right, Abby going to stand in the grass beside Mariah. "I put our clothes in the laundry room," she said with a look that made clear she had no faith in Keegan's ability to properly do laundry.

It was no easier being found wanting by a thirteen-year-old than a two-year-old.

"If you tell me where you got your shirt, I'll replace it," he said evenly.

She opened her mouth, drew a breath, then closed it again. "It doesn't matter."

Keegan glanced from her to Therese, who was watching Abby with a bemused expression. *My stepdaughter spent spring break in California with her mother*, she'd told him when they'd met in Walmart. Abby must have gotten the shirt on-site, a keepsake to remember the visit with Catherine. It wasn't something he could just replace, and that made him feel worse about it.

"I'm a kindergarten teacher," Therese remarked. "I'm the queen of stain removal."

"My mom might arm-wrestle you for that title."

She looked at him, one brow arched, but her lips twitched with a smile. "First you think your ribs are better than mine, now you think your mother can remove stains better than me. You're awfully full of yourself, aren't you?"

He grinned. "Five kids, remember? Three of them boys. And I concede to you on the ribs. Mine are still the Logan family's best, but yours are better."

"Thank you," she said primly. "Tiffany Wheeler didn't raise any slackers."

"Tiffany? Your mother's name is Tiffany?"

"Grandma Tiffany and Grandpa Clyde." That came from Jacob, with a snort from Abby.

Therese's smile was gentle, softening everything about her. "That name has been the bane of her existence. She'd go by her middle name, except she doesn't have one. Gran said she couldn't find another name she liked that sounded good with it, but Mom's convinced she wanted to be positive Mom was stuck with Tiffany."

"It's not a bad name," Keegan said. "I've known a half dozen Tiffanys."

"Over the age of sixty?"

"No," he admitted. "But it could have been worse."

Her smile faded a little, and she sighed softly. "Yeah, things could always be worse."

Silence settled around them, uncomfortable, as if everyone was considering what would constitute "worse" for them. They had already been through so much that it was a scary thought. Therese might not have even a small part of her husband left without the kids, though it didn't take a genius to see that they weren't holding together the way a family should. Abby could fall out of favor with the popular kids at school, since Keegan had no doubt a girl as pretty and confident as she was did hang out with the cool kids. Jacob...well, he wasn't sure what Jacob would hate to lose about his life. His video games? His height and brawn? His sports skills?

Keegan was lucky. He'd seen some horrible things in war. He'd lost friends. He'd had someone else's child dropped into his care. But he liked his job. He loved his family. He didn't regret his past, was okay with his present, and looked forward to the future. He had a good life.

The moment was broken by Mariah tugging at Abby's hand. "Play with me, Abby."

"What do you want to play?"

Mariah wrinkled her face as if it was a tough decision. "Hide-and-seek."

Jacob scoffed. "Even Abby can win at that. There's no place to hide."

Abby kicked his foot.

"The baby doesn't need great places to hide." Therese's tone held a note of warning.

"Neither does Abby. If she can't see you, she thinks you can't see her, either."

Abby started to kick him again but instead straightened her shoulders and sniffed. "You're such a moron. Come on, Mariah."

"Idiot," Jacob replied under his breath, but before they'd gone ten feet, he shoved himself out of the chair and trailed after them into the shadows.

"Did you call your siblings names all the times?" Therese asked when they were barely visible in the dim light.

"Jerk, idiot, moron, stupid, pig, nerd, fish-face, shrimp." Keegan glanced her way. "Didn't you?"

"No. My brother and I always treated each other with great respect." The quaver in her voice belied the claim before her laugh escaped. "He called me Grace because I was the clumsiest kid in school. And Worm because I read a lot. And Bowlegs just because."

He let his gaze slide down to her legs, still stretched out. She wore jeans, faded and clinging snugly to slim thighs and nicely muscled calves. "Aw, you're not bowlegged."

She raised first one foot into the air, turning her leg to study it, then the other. "No, I'm not. Though with as much time as I spent on horseback..."

"You were a real cowgirl, huh."

"If you'd called me that when I was fifteen, I would have roped you and left you tied to the nearest tree. I loved the ranch and wouldn't trade the way I grew up for anything, but I always knew I wanted something different."

How close did her life at this moment come to what she'd wanted?

Not close enough. He couldn't shake the memory of that yearning in her voice earlier. *I don't know what I want.*

He'd come to Tallgrass knowing exactly what he wanted.

Now, only five days later, he wasn't so sure anymore himself.

* * *

After work Friday, Therese stopped at QuikTrip to fill up the gas tank, then followed the lure of the frozen cappuccino machine inside. She limited herself to a twelve-ounce kids' cup, bypassed the machine that would squirt thick whipped cream on top, and was standing in line to pay when a wistful voice spoke behind her.

"Man, I miss caffeine."

Her mouth automatically curving into a smile, she turned to face Ilena. "Hey, baby mama. What are you doing off work early?"

"I'm spending the weekend with Juan's family, so I took off at noon. I meant to leave right after lunch, but Hector needed a nap, and who am I to stand in his way?" Smiling, she patted her belly.

"Aw, all Hector does all day long is sleep."

"Yeah, and he practices kicks all night long. This boy's gonna be a martial arts expert, like his daddy."

Therese marveled that only the faintest hint of sorrow darkened Ilena's eyes when she talked about Juan. She grieved for her husband; Therese had no doubt of that. But, more than any of them, she also celebrated him. She didn't fixate on him like some women did, and she didn't avoid mentioning him like others. He had been and always would be a huge part of her life, and while she may have wanted to crawl into the casket with him, she continued to live life, to move forward and embrace the future.

Maybe it was because of little Hector, who would be making his appearance in six or seven weeks, or because Juan's very large family lived only ninety minutes away and loved Ilena, with her white-blond hair and blue eyes, as if she were theirs by birth and not merely marriage. Maybe it was just her nature.

Whatever, sometimes Therese envied her.

Thinking of her comments about Carly the night before,

she smiled ruefully. It seemed she'd been doing a lot of envying lately.

"Since you plan to coach his baseball team, are you going to learn martial arts, too?"

Ilena went into a chop-chop karate pose and emitted a tiny grunt. "What do you think?"

"Fierce. I'm shaking." Therese moved up to the counter, paid for her coffee, then hugged her. "Have fun with the family. And be safe."

"Everyone always coddles me on these visits. I put my feet up, and they wait on me like I'm a *princesa*." She grinned. "That's what Mamá and Papá call me. Can you believe it?"

"We all need someone in our lives who thinks we're princesses." In a good way. Not the way Therese called Abby that.

She waved good-bye and was headed for the door when Ilena called, "Hey, the friend of Paul's you were so cozy with Tuesday... have you seen him again?"

Therese's face warmed, and she blamed it on the fan right above the double doors. "Uh, yeah, a time or two."

"Good. When I'm ready to start dating again, I'll need some pointers."

"And a babysitter. You can count on me for both."

Therese took a long appreciative drink of her coffee as she dodged cars across the parking lot. Tallgrass had plenty of traffic and bad drivers—all bad drivers eventually wound up in Oklahoma, Paul used to tease—but she deemed this lot a tough one. Small space, lots of customers, short tempers.

But she made it out, van and good mood intact, and headed home. Jacob was going to a Drillers game in Tulsa with his best friend, Liam, and his family, and Abby and Liam's sister, Nicole, were sleeping over at Payton's. An entire evening stretched out ahead, with no plans besides watching TV, maybe getting a jump on the weekend's chores of vacuuming and laundry...and daydreaming about Keegan.

She'd had a lovely time last night. It hadn't been a date, of course, or at least not a traditional one. People didn't usually have their kids along on dates, and they usually got at least a good-night kiss, didn't they?

She and Keegan had come close when he and Mariah left. She'd carried the girl, half-asleep and still wearing Abby's shirt, to the door, and he'd leaned in close to take her. They'd been bumping arms and elbows, noses and heads, and in the middle of it, their gazes had locked for a long, long moment. She loved blue eyes, she'd thought, going a little dreamy even now with the memory. Her first real boyfriend had had eyes like Keegan's—blue, clear, full of decency, honesty.

Close but no smooch. He hadn't kissed her, and she hadn't kissed him. She'd been married so long that she sometimes forgot that was an option. Instead, with Mariah all settled, he finally stepped back, and so had she. She opened the door for him, and he'd said *See you*, and she had repeated the words to him.

Tonight would be a good time.

When she pulled into the driveway, Jacob was loping across the yard, a backpack over his shoulder. He slowed near the van as she got out. "What time will you be home?"

He shrugged. "When the game's over. I'm staying at Liam's since it might be late."

"Okay. Do you need some money?"

"Nope. I'm using Nicole's ticket, and Mr. McRae always pays for food."

A couple houses down the street, a car horn sounded, and he glanced that way. "Gotta go." He took a few steps, then came back and looked at her, frowning. "It's okay if I spend the night, isn't it? I know I didn't say anything sooner, but—"

She cleared her own expression. "No, it's fine. Have fun." Impulsively she laid her hand on his arm, squeezing. He didn't flinch, pull away, or act as if she'd zapped a million volts into him.

As the horn honked again, he broke into a trot, calling over his shoulder, "We will."

Therese's fingers tingled, and her palm warmed. It was rare she could touch Jacob without him making clear he didn't welcome it, and impossible to touch Abby. Just as well, since what she usually itched to do with Abby was thump a little courtesy and respect into her.

But she missed touching them. They'd never been overly affectionate, but at least when Paul was still with them, she'd been able to straighten clothing, comb hair, or hold hands without every muscle in the kids' bodies going taut. Cuddling with Mariah was sweet. Giving Jacob or Abby a hug would be sweeter. Them hugging her back...

Might happen with Jacob. Never would with Abby, no matter how improved her behavior since Mariah came into her life.

The front door was unlocked, so Therese slid her keys into her bag as she went inside. The television was on in the living room, but Abby's voice came from the kitchen. Therese was surprised to find her home. Abby had taken a bag with her to school, intending to catch a ride to Payton's with Nicole's mother.

"Abby?" she said as she walked into the kitchen. "Change of plans?"

Pacing the length of the kitchen, Abby turned to look at her. "Hold on," she muttered into her cell. "I need a ride to Payton's."

"Okay. You have her address?"

She spoke to the person on the phone, stopped at the island, and scribbled on the shopping list before ripping the page free. "I'll be there soon."

"I thought you were getting a ride from Mrs. McRae."

"Yeah, I did, too, but something came up. She said Nicole could ride with Payton's sister, and you said I can't so I took the bus home. I've been waiting for you."

Therese didn't know what to say. Abby had not only listened to her but actually obeyed her. She could have so easily climbed into Payton's sister's car, and since Therese rarely indulged in more than a chat with Nicole's mom, she likely would have never known.

But Abby had come home. Had missed out on time with her best friends. Had followed the rules even though it put a crimp in her plans.

"Thank you," she said at last. "I appreciate it. Are you ready now?"

In answer, Abby slung her bag over her shoulder, tucked the phone in her pocket, and headed for the door.

The address she'd scrawled was on the southeast side of town. Unlike their own neighborhood of nice old homes on oversized lots, this one was filled with mini-mansions, each set on its own acreage. The homes were grand, spacious, and all bore a similar stamp: same architect, same builder, same materials. Not one of them showed any personality, though Therese imagined the homeowners' association would put them firmly in their place if they tried.

"Payton has a swimming pool," Abby commented as she looked for the number. "And Aubrey—that's her sister—got a brand-new Mustang for her birthday. Payton said she's getting a Challenger when she turns sixteen, or maybe a Camaro."

Inwardly Therese shuddered at the idea of a brand-new driver with a brand-new vehicle of any model, but on the outside, she just smiled. "Cutting people open must pay a lot better than teaching."

"Just about anything pays better than teaching." Abruptly Abby pointed. "There it is. The yellow Mustang out front."

Therese slowed and turned into the driveway that wound past a lawn big enough for a nine-hole golf course and a fountain with a massive stone piece rising out of the center. Art, she supposed, though it looked exactly like the big chunks of rock a person could find all over this part of Oklahoma.

"Wow." She gave voice to what Abby was clearly thinking. "So this is the home Payton's so desperate to leave for St. Louis."

"Yeah."

"It's lovely." In a massive brick-and-stone sort of way.

She expected envious agreement from Abby, but after gazing at the house a moment, her stepdaughter said, "Yeah. Can you imagine having to clean it?"

Abby got out of the van, swung her bag over her shoulder, then glanced back. "Nicole's mom is supposed to pick us up, but...if she bails..."

"Call me."

With a nod, Abby headed toward the house. The double doors swung open as she approached, and Nicole and Payton grabbed her, dragging her inside with squeals of welcome. In the moment before the doors closed, Therese caught a glimpse of marble flooring, a chandelier, a grand staircase. Some part of her was impressed, as she was meant to be, but she was happy to return to her own cozier house.

It didn't take long to travel from the land of the rich back to middle-class-comfortable. She was driving past the park, her windows down to enjoy the warm afternoon, when shrieks of delight drew her gaze to a head of blond curls. Mariah was hugging the center post of the old-fashioned merry-go-round as Keegan spun it in circles.

Her heart warmed at the sight and the sound. Last night the girl had given her father fewer wary looks than before, but there'd been little ease between them. For at least this moment, she'd put that aside to be nothing more than a little girl enjoying playtime with Daddy.

Therese drove to her house, parked in the driveway, then hesitated on the porch. She could go inside, though there was nothing calling her: no homework to push, no dinner to fix for the kids.

Or she could walk back to the park. She'd done it two hundred times since moving into the house. She didn't think she'd be intruding. There were other parks in Tallgrass; Keegan had found City Park on Mariah's first full day in town, with its much more elaborate playground, just a few blocks from his motel. If he'd wanted private time, he would have taken her there instead of to the park a half block from Therese's house.

"You're so easy to persuade," she murmured as she left her purse on the kitchen counter. She stuck her cell phone in her pocket, hesitated, then went upstairs, pulled her hair back, and changed clothes. At least she wasn't needy enough to freshen her makeup or spray on perfume.

Or was she just too school-girl anxious to get to the park before Keegan left?

*   *   *

Keegan gave the merry-go-round one last push and watched its wood planks, each painted a different shade, spin in a kaleidoscope before it slowly came to a stop.

Mariah let go of the rail, tottered a step or two, then jumped to the ground. "Now I swing." She ignored the kids' swings, though, with their yellow plastic safety seats, and headed for the swings of his youth: flexible seats, heavy-duty chains, long legs anchored in concrete. The kind she could fly into the sky on … and crash right back to the ground.

"How about this one?" he called, gesturing toward the smaller version.

She didn't even look. "No. No no no. I want this one."

"Do you get the feeling you're going to be hearing, 'No no no, I want this one' the rest of your life? About school, clothes, boys, cars, jobs…"

Keegan turned to Therese, and automatically he smiled. He couldn't have stopped it if he'd wanted to. She was dressed more casually than he'd seen her: faded denim shorts that revealed a lot of leg, a T-shirt that clung to every curve, flip-flops that showed bright pink toenails and a silver ring curled around her second toe. Her hair was pulled back in a ponytail, and she looked...relaxed. Pleased.

"Hey, you."

She fell in step with him as he headed toward the swing set where Mariah was trying to climb, belly first, onto a webbed seat. "It's a beautiful day for playing in the park."

"And yet we're the only ones here. Where do you hide your kids?"

She gave the surrounding blocks a cursory look. "The little ones are at day care, the older ones watching TV or on their computers. Pretty much all the parents I know work. There will be kids here tomorrow. They play soccer and baseball"—she motioned to the big grassy area in the middle—"and the mothers will walk and talk while the dads watch the kids."

"You bring yours here?"

A look flashed through her eyes, making him remember their first dinner, when she'd said she didn't call them step-kids or claim them as her own. But she didn't remind him. "We used to come at least a couple times a week. Abby sat with her friends, Paul taught Jacob to throw and catch a baseball, and I walked with my friends. We always finished on the swings. The Matheson family were good swingers."

As she finished, she called Mariah's name and crouched as the girl spun, grinned, and ran to her. They hugged tightly, then Mariah stepped back and looked around. "Where's Abby?"

"She's spending the night with a friend."

"Where's Jacob?"

"He's staying with a friend, too."

Mariah's disappointment showed on her face. Keegan wondered if his pleasure showed on his. No kids around tonight but Mariah, and with luck, she would be asleep before nine. He and Therese could be alone, for all practical purposes.

Assuming she didn't have other plans, didn't want to just luxuriate in the peace of an empty house, wasn't tired of other people's kids filling her life, wasn't tired of him.

"Will you swing with me?" Mariah asked.

Therese straightened again and took her hand. "Sure. You want me to push you or do you want to sit on my lap?"

"Sit on your lap."

Kicking off her shoes, Therese walked across the spongy ground covering to sit on the middle swing. Mariah kicked off her own sandals and followed, holding her arms up for a boost.

Therese turned Mariah to face her, little legs wrapped around her waist, and linked her arms outside the chains to provide extra protection, then she pushed back until she was standing, kicked, and stretched out her legs for the glide forward.

Sitting in the swing beside them, Keegan twisted the chain until he faced them. For a while he was mesmerized by the sight of Therese's legs, muscles flexing as she pushed off, stretching straight out, lengthening as she strove for the highest bit of air she could reach, then pumping. The skin was tanned and smooth but for a scar on this calf, a bruise on that ankle, and he wondered how those muscles would feel stretching and tightening against him.

He was following that thought in his head, out of the park, and into her bedroom, imagining his hands exploring those legs, stroking from her slender ankles over her calves, tickling the backs of her knees, reaching her thighs

and the barrier of her clothing and going still farther,
discovering—

"Kee—you—Celly's boy!" On Therese's lap, Mariah
looked torn between pleasure and frustration.

A knot formed in his gut at the realization that this child
who was living with him, who was in his care for the fore-
seeable future, had no name to call him.

Satisfied she had his attention, she laid her cheek against
Therese's and beamed. "Look at us. We're flying."

But Therese had stopped pushing and pumping, and
they were gradually coming to a stop, the swing twisting
side to side before she planted her feet. Mariah frowned. "I
want to fly more."

"Over here." Therese carried her to the end of the set,
next to the steel poles, and deposited her in a kiddy seat,
warned her to hold on, pulled her back, and let go.

He picked up their shoes and slowly followed them,
leaning against a post.

"She doesn't call you Daddy."

He shook his head. He'd been adamant about that with
Ercella. "Daddy" meant something. It was reserved for her
real father.

"Is Celly your mother?"

"Ercella. Mariah can't quite get the whole thing out."

"So your daughter calls you 'Celly's boy'?"

His face grew hot, and he knew from past experience
that his ears had turned candy-apple red. "She . . . she hasn't
been with us long. She never talked to me. She never liked
me enough to say anything besides 'no no no.' I just never
thought . . ."

Therese gave her a harder push, sending her high
enough to make her squeal. "If you're not going to let her

call you Daddy or Father or Pop, you should at least teach her your name."

He wondered if she would leave it at that, but in the next breath, she asked, "Why can't she call you Daddy or Father or Pop?"

His ears were probably starting to glow by now. He scuffed one foot over the rubber. It would please his mother to know that he pretty much always told the truth, but that wasn't an option here. If he said, *Because I'm not her father,* then Therese would have more questions, starting with, *Who is?*

That was a conversation he didn't want to have right now.

"I—I'm not comfortable with it," he said lamely.

"When it involves a child, it's not your comfort that counts."

He could let Mariah call him Daddy, for a while at least. She'd never had a father figure in her life, and she was too young to understand the complexity of the title. It would just be another name to her, like Celly, Abby, or Jacob. And it wasn't like her real father was going to return from the grave to protest.

But Keegan understood the complexity of it. Calling him Daddy might mean no more to her than calling him Manny, Caillou, or Sid, her favorite cartoon characters, but it would mean a whole world of things to him. It would mean losing something when she left.

"It's not my business," Therese went on, "so here's my last comment. Whether she lives with you or your mother, whether she goes back to her own mother, she needs something to call you for those times when 'hey, you' and 'Celly's boy' just don't cut it."

Keegan nodded. Of course she was right. Damned if he liked any of the options, though. His sisters' kids called him Uncle Keegan. His grandmother called him Keifer. Everyone else used Keegan, Logan, or Sergeant. None of them felt right for Mariah, and Daddy wasn't open for discussion.

After a couple minutes went by in silence, he deliberately changed the subject. "I tried to get her to swing on the kids' swings, and all she'd say was no no no."

"I heard." Therese caught hold of the seat and bent close. "You want to go really high?"

Mariah bobbed her head.

"Okay, hold on." She backed up, lifting the seat until she stood on tiptoe, then she gave a great shove. The motion pulled her shirt above her belly button, and the bend that ended her follow-through tugged her shorts tight over the curve of her butt.

Keegan's mouth went a little dry. Man, if the guys back home knew what sights awaited in a park, there would be traffic jams at the gates of every one.

"Your mistake was that you asked her. Did you notice that I didn't ask? I just put her in the swing."

"Yeah, well, if I'd done that, she'd've kicked and screamed."

"Considering she doesn't even know your name..."

He scowled at her. "I thought you'd made your last comment on the subject."

"Yeah, I fibbed."

Mariah began squirming in the seat. "I want to slide now, Trace."

Therese stopped the swing in one smooth movement and lifted her to the ground. The kid shot off as if her life depended on reaching the jungle gym and its big red slide in the next five seconds. If she noticed the prickle of the grass on her bare feet, she gave no sign of it.

He handed Therese's shoes to her, and she brushed the soles of her feet primly before putting them on. As they started after Mariah, she said, "If you'd gone to City Park, you could have staked out a prime spot for the kick-off of the spring concert series this evening."

"I know. I saw the sign. But what are the odds I would have seen you there?"

Her cheeks turned pink. "Pretty slim. Tonight is country music, and I'd rather hear fingernails on blackboards. Not that we have blackboards in the classroom anymore."

"I figured a cowgirl—" At the sharp look she cut him, he rephrased. "A ranch girl from Montana would love country music."

"Heard enough of it in Montana to last me a lifetime. So…" They walked through a gate in the brightly painted fence that surrounded the jungle gym, and she chose a bench with a good view of all the exits. "Were you going to come by the house when you finished here?"

"Already been there once. No one was home."

She didn't look at him, but the words made her smile, just the tiniest bit. She sat, ankles together, spine straight, hands folded in her lap. He sprawled a few feet away, close enough to smell the faint scent of flowers—perfume, shampoo, laundry soap, he didn't know. Just something that smelled like her.

"I had to take Abby to her friend's house. She actually listened to me when I said she couldn't ride with the sixteen-year-old newly licensed sister."

The comment hung between them for a while before he

asked the obvious question. "Does she usually not listen?"

Therese's sigh was softer than the breeze in the leaves. "Her ears are very sensitive to the sound of my voice. Something about it sends her on a rampage."

"She's a teenager. She lost her dad—"

She laid one gentle hand on his arm. "I know all the reasons. I've been excusing her behavior with them for more than three years."

Keegan's gaze went automatically to her hand. Like her toes, her fingernails were pink, but not the same electric, hot-summer-days shade. This pink was softer, paler, subtler, only a few shades off from white. Her fingers were long and strong—riding horses, chopping firewood—but still too delicate for the diamond ring on her fourth finger. He doubted she'd picked out the honking big stone. More likely, Matheson had bought it, thinking to impress both his bride-to-be and everyone who saw the ring. Something smaller that took its dazzle factor from the cut or color or intricate setting would better suit her.

What would persuade her to take off the chunky diamond?

More than he wanted to consider at the moment.

"When Paul told me Catherine was sending the children to live with us, I envisioned the perfect blended family," she went on, withdrawing her hand though he could still feel the warmth of it against his skin. "We were going to be the exception to the rule. Love and sunshine and happy endings. Instead, we were the very stereotype I wanted to avoid: the daughter who hates her evil stepmother and the mother who just wants the spoiled brat out of her life."

Keegan stilled as her words penetrated the haze her simple touch had stirred. The heat dissipated with a breath, and chill dread lodged somewhere in his chest as he slowly lifted his gaze to hers.

Her smile was faint and vulnerable and helpless. "Does that make me an awful person?"

Chapter 11

Hank Williams—the original, not the son—played in the background while Jessy curled into the chair fronting the desk in the living room, feet tucked into the seat, arms wrapped around her legs. The computer was on, a slideshow of her own photographs filling the screen. Chin resting on her knees, she watched them with a photographer's eye, noting composition, color, contrast, ignoring the memories of when she'd taken each shot, where, whether she was alone, whether there was anything memorable about it.

She'd been fourteen when she'd asked for a camera for Christmas. Already her life was unsettled, but something about looking at the world through a lens offered her solace. Distance. She'd taken the camera with her everywhere—still did most times, tucked inside oversized purses to accommodate it and the things a woman normally carried.

Few people saw her photos—pretty much only the

friends who were comfortable enough to drop in on her. The margarita girls. Ilena had called them majestic and haunting. Jessy liked the descriptions. She liked that she could make someone feel something from seeing a scene the way she saw it.

The slide show progressed chronologically, now beginning what she jokingly called her Tallgrass period. Images of the murals, the buildings, the ranchland and woodlands and prairies all around. There were shots of horse heads—part of the mechanism of oil pump jacks—lighted and wreathed for Christmas, along with pictures of real horses grazing in green pastures. There was sunshine and snow and lightning streaking across a storm-darkened sky, trees whipped by the wind, even a tornado hovering above the ground.

With the exception of the margarita club, she rarely included people in her photographs. When she did, it was always from a perspective that revealed little, if anything, of their faces. Faces and emotions cluttered the shot.

Maybe that was because emotions cluttered her life.

A series of photos detailing the dignified transfer of Juan Gomez's remains came on the screen: a sunny day, American flags whipping in the breeze, hundreds of people thronging the route, the Patriot Guard motorcyclists, the long line of police cars from the city, the county, and the highway patrol. A viewer could have mistaken it for a parade except for the sorrow that filled the very air.

She'd never shown the photos to Ilena. She hadn't known her at the time, and once they'd met, at the third meeting of the Tuesday Night Margarita Club, it had never seemed appropriate to say, "I took pictures of the second or third saddest day of your life. Wanna see them?"

She did remember praying one of her rare prayers between shots. *God, give her the strength to get through this.*

Who knew Jessy could be part of the answer to a prayer?

Her own saddest days were easy to list: worst, the day she'd gotten the casualty notification call. Second, the day Aaron's body had arrived home for burial. Third, the day of the funeral. Fourth, practically every day since then.

Why hadn't she loved him as much as he'd loved her? What was wrong with her? Was she damaged goods, as her father had claimed? Selfish and caring only about herself, as her mother said?

Her only comfort was that Aaron had never known. No one knew she'd planned to file for divorce. No one knew she'd been happier without him than she ever would have been with him.

The ring of her cell phone came during a lull in the music, startling a small jump out of her. Letting her feet slide to the floor, she pulled the phone from her pocket, drew a breath, and with the best show of fake cheer for the day said, "You've reached Jessy, who has nothing to do this Friday evening, so please have something fun to suggest."

After a moment of silence, a laugh sounded over the line. "Do you always answer the phone like that?" It was Fia Thomas, the youngest of their group in years if not burdens.

"Only when I'm bored. Do you have something fun to suggest?"

"Not unless they've redefined the word. I—I have a favor to ask."

Jessy's brows arched. That was unusual. Fia was fierce

in her independence. That was what happened when a girl pretty much raised herself. "Yes."

"You haven't even heard it."

"I don't need to hear it. Yes, I'll do it. You know I love you more than my apartment."

Fia laughed, as Jessy had intended. All the margarita girls knew her attachment to these four walls and the space they protected. "It's nothing drastic. I just…I need a ride home."

"Car trouble?"

"Um, no. The car's fine."

"Are you okay?"

"Yeah. I'm just…I don't think I should be driving."

Every nerve in Jessy's body went on alert. She'd never seen Fia drink a lot, and on recent Tuesdays, she'd hardly touched her margaritas. Granted, that didn't mean she wasn't drinking in private—how well Jessy knew that—but she figured one drinker could recognize a kindred spirit in another.

Drinker, she emphasized for her own benefit. Not drunk. Not alcoholic.

"No problem. You know I never get to drive enough, not with working down the block and all the restaurants in walking distance. Where are you?"

"At the gym." There was a hint of relief in Fia's voice. "I'll meet you out front."

"I'll be there in five." Jessy hung up, shoved her feet into sandals, slung her purse over her shoulder, and headed downstairs. It was only a few feet to the alley, then halfway down the alley to the tiny parking lot behind the building where her car pretty much stayed.

Had Fia's voice been a little slurred? Not really, but she

had sounded...off. No way she was using drugs. She was a personal trainer, and she was in better shape than ninety percent of the soldiers on post whose lives depended on physical conditioning. She wouldn't work so hard to get in such good shape only to put poison in her system.

She was coming down with something. Jessy was sure it was nothing more than that.

The gym was located on East Main, across from the main gate onto the fort. It was open twenty-four/seven, but Fia generally finished her day about seven except on Tuesdays. She really must be feeling bad to cancel her last couple appointments and call for a ride.

Even that thought didn't prepare Jessy for the surprise when Fia walked out the door. It wasn't just her limp; strains and sprains were part of the territory for her. It wasn't the lines of pain etched around her eyes and mouth. There was an air about her of...Jessy didn't even know how to describe it. Frailty. Wrongness.

Fia tossed her gym bag in the backseat before climbing into the front. "I really appreciate it."

"What's wrong, doll? You look like hell."

With an unsteady smile, Fia brushed her off. "I have the queen bitch of all headaches. My mom used to call them sick headaches. I didn't know what she meant until I had my own."

"Nauseated, queasy, God-just-shoot-me-now." Jessy nodded. She'd had more than a few of those, but hers were usually preceded by a night with too much booze. She waited until Fia was settled with her seat belt fastened, then pulled back onto Main.

Fia laid her head back, closed her eyes, and sighed.

"You want to go to the hospital? They should be able to

give you a shot or a pill or something to stick where things shouldn't be stuck and make you feel all better."

"Nah. I just need to lie still in a dark room for a while. I'll be fine."

"Have you eaten anything?"

"Ugh. Not for a while. I'm pretty sure it would just come back up."

She fell silent, and Jessy was fine with that. She did wonder, though, as she turned onto the street that wound through a business complex before reaching the apartment complex where Fia lived, why her friend had called her. Jessy wasn't the first one to come to anyone's mind, even her own, when they thought motherly, nurturing, caregiving.

Process of elimination. Carly was with Dane. Therese was waging yet another battle with the demon children. Ilena was visiting Juan's family, and Lucy and Marti were probably out shopping for Lucy's new oven.

And Jessy was fine with that, too. She loved her girls, but it was better for everyone if they didn't count on her too much. Hell, she still didn't know where she'd been or what she'd done Wednesday night. If she couldn't even be responsible for herself, how could she ever be there for anyone else?

*   *   *

Therese had shocked Keegan with her admission about Abby. Oh, he'd assured her that saying she wanted to be free of Paul's problem child didn't make her a horrible person, but she'd seen the widening of his eyes. Had felt in the air the stillness that had spread through him so quickly.

She shouldn't have told him. No one knew but the margarita club, LoLo, the JAG officer she'd spoken to, and the chaplain. She hadn't even discussed it with her own pastor, because she hadn't wanted anyone who saw Abby regularly to know. There was no reason to tell Keegan except that he was easy to talk to and he was in a similar situation with Mariah, and she...Well, she thought people who were more or less dating, even if it was temporary because one of them lived four hundred miles away, even if it was really just a practice relationship for when the real thing came along, should be honest about things.

Too late for regrets now, wasn't it?

The growl of motors cut through the early evening quiet. Someone was mowing nearby. Someone else was using a weed trimmer. Barely audible over that was the mournful wail of the basset hound who lived a block over from her, along with the barks of a half dozen other dogs. Growing up, she'd always had dogs of her own, along with chickens, calves, and horses. They would teach her responsibility, her dad always said.

Cleaning up after them, worrying about them, doctoring their ills, and handling their middle-of-the-night feedings would prepare her for motherhood, her mother said with a smirk.

A herd of the most recalcitrant calves that ever lived had nothing on Abby.

Oh, how Abby would loathe being compared to bovine babies.

Because conversation had lagged in the past half hour since her revelation, she picked a subject that came to mind from time to time, only to be pushed away by something more important. "Why are you still in Tallgrass?"

Keegan was leaning forward now, elbows resting on his knees, hands loosely clasped and dangling. He looked just as relaxed as he had earlier when he'd sprawled bonelessly on the bench, pre-giving-up-Abby bomb. He tilted his head to look at her, but the grin she'd come to expect wasn't there. "I'm pretty sure the Chamber of Commerce thinks it's a destination in and of itself."

"Yeah, they get paid to think that. It's been nearly a week since you came to talk to Paul. He's gone, but you're still here. Why?" She had asked him once before, and his answer had been simple. *I'm on leave. I'm just taking things as they come.* But there were so many different places to see, especially now that he had Mariah. He could go to Tulsa or Oklahoma City, with their zoos and children's museums and family activities. He could go to Arizona and be near his brother during his recuperation, or stop off in Dallas with its big-city fun things to do.

He watched Mariah for a moment, but that was a delaying tactic. The girl wasn't timid by any means, but neither was she adventurous. She didn't get stuck in the twisty slide, afraid to let go, or try to climb to the ground on top of it instead of inside it. She wasn't huddling on the rope bridge, too scared to run to the secure end, or testing a hypothesis that she could fly if she just got to the highest point of the playground and leaped.

Finally Keegan shifted his gaze to Therese, and the faintest hint of that charming grin appeared. "Haven't you figured it out yet?"

She shook her head.

"You. You're the reason I'm still here."

It took a moment for his meaning to sink in. Still,

cautiously, she clarified, "Because the children who can stop Mariah's tears as easily as turning off a faucet live with me?"

He shook his head.

"Because you might decide that talking to me is the next best thing to talking to Paul?"

"No." Something unidentifiable flashed through his eyes.

The sensation curling through her was sweet, warm, pleasurable, and it reminded her of how much she'd loved Paul, how long he'd been gone, and how alive she still was. It made her feel not like a widow, a stepmother, an anxious mass of sorrows and indecision, but like a woman, and she hadn't felt like a woman in such a long time.

"Because my ribs are better than yours?" she teased.

He took the opportunity to slide his gaze from her face: over her breasts, her rib cage, her hips, and all the way down her legs to her ridiculously painted toes. By the time he met her eyes again, the warmth had turned to heat, simmering just beneath the surface of her skin, and it seemed to reach out to him, adding a touch of crimson to his cheeks and neck.

"Honey, your everything is better," he said, sounding as if he needed to clear his throat.

Wow. For a moment, that was all she could hear in the rushing that filled her ears and her head. The man she'd thought would make a great practice boyfriend was actually interested in that, too. *Wow.*

At least, in the boyfriend part. She didn't know his feelings on the temporary nature that seemed inevitable to her. Time to find out, right?

"You live in another state," she pointed out.

"I know. But I can be here at least another week, and I can probably extend it a week beyond that."

But even after a few more weeks, he would still go home to Louisiana. It wasn't as if he could decide to move to Tallgrass to give their relationship its best·chance. The Army got final say on where he lived.

"Planes and highways travel both ways," he added.

She pressed the palms of her hands together between her knees and felt the bite of her engagement diamond against her flesh. "You're a soldier."

She didn't need to say more. He acknowledged it with a nod. "Until the end of my enlistment. Then I can stay a soldier, or I can go back to being a firefighter or a paramedic. I can do whatever I want, Therese. I'm not bound to any particular job."

Things were fluttering inside her: not panic, but emotions, pleasure, serious affection. How had that happened in less than a week? Serious affection was supposed to take time, to grow slowly, to be built on shared experiences and goals and a deep understanding of who the other person was.

But within a few hours of meeting Paul, she'd been in bed with him, and by the end of that first meeting, she'd known she was in love. Months of sharing experiences, goals, and understanding had done nothing but strengthen it.

The fluttering intensified. "We've got kids. Jacob and Abby don't even like me most of the time, and their loyalty to their father's memory is intense. On top of that, I don't even know if Abby will still be here in a few weeks, and I don't know whether that would be a good thing or a really bad one."

Keegan paced a few yards away, then turned back and dragged his hand through his hair. "Look, Therese, about the only answer I have is to the question you asked me. Why am I still here. I'm here because of you. What comes of that, whether anything comes of it, I don't know. But we're adults, and acknowledging something has to be better than not acknowledging it." Then he grinned, the slow, sweet grin she was sure he'd inherited from his charmer of a father. "You wouldn't want to send me back to Polk without exploring this thing between us, would you? For all you know, this could be fate."

"Or a disaster."

His grin broadened. "At worst, we'll have some fun."

No, at worst, she could get her heart broken. Falling in love with a soldier who was raising a two-year-old daughter on his own…another child abandoned by her mother…Lord, if things went horribly wrong, she could find herself raising a third child who wasn't hers, with all the responsibilities of being a mother and none of the pleasures of being a mom.

And never having babies of her own.

As if reading her mind, he shoved his hands in his hip pockets. "At least I can promise you'd never have to be responsible for Mariah. My mom thinks she's the best gift since her last grandchild. She's more than willing to raise her."

A grandparent who loved being a grandparent. That was a novelty in her life lately.

But practicing a relationship with Keegan was one thing. Any mistakes made in practice wouldn't haunt her forever. All she'd planned to do with him was get herself accustomed to being single and available and looking again. A date, sure. Dinner, some kisses, naturally. Sex? Judging by how much she'd wanted him to kiss her the night before, almost a guarantee.

But a real relationship, risking her heart, risking the already fragile situation in her home...

"It's kind of scary, isn't it?" His chuckle was rueful. "Believe me, I didn't come here intending to get involved with anyone. But things happen when they happen. You accept it and take advantage of it, or you don't. And if you don't..."

She would wonder. Always wonder. And regret.

With a shriek of delight, Mariah charged across the sand, curls bobbing, and climbed onto the bench beside Therese. She smelled like a sweaty, happy little puppy. "I'm hungry. Can we eat supper?"

Moving on automatic pilot, Therese picked up the girl's sandals, brushed her feet, then slid them on. "What are you hungry for?"

"Monkey toes!"

"Monkey toes?" She directed that at Keegan, and he shrugged sheepishly.

"Monkey bread. My nephews used to climb like crazy when they were tiny. As long as their feet were bare, they could grab hold of anything, like monkeys. It became a family nickname for all four of them and somehow became the name of the bread, too."

"Much better than fish-face or jerk." Taking Mariah's hand, Therese helped her from the bench and started toward the gate. Once they cleared it, Keegan moved beside her and, as if he'd done it a hundred times, took her other hand. The flush of warmth that spread through her was almost indecent. "I think we can manage monkey toes for dessert, but you have to eat regular food first, sweetie. Would you eat fried liver?"

Mariah's nose wrinkled, and she hopefully said, "I like fried chicken."

"Fried skunk?"

"No, Trace, fried chicken. You know, *er-er-er-ooo!*"

Therese laughed at the free hand tucked into Mariah's armpit to mimic a wing, the bobbing head, and exaggerated high steps she took. "Okay, fried chicken. What do you want with it? Cauliflower, broccoli, Brussels sprouts?"

The hopefulness remained in the little girl's face. "Celly makes mashed 'taters and gravy and biscuits, and I eat the drumsticks. *Only* the drumsticks."

"Okay." Therese looked at Keegan. "Is fried chicken all right with you?"

"And monkey toes for 'zert," Mariah reminded her.

"Fried chicken's fine."

Fine. It was an overused, underrated word, but this warm Friday evening, with the fragrance of spring in the air, the kids happily preoccupied elsewhere, and Keegan's big, strong hand holding hers, Therese thought it just might be the best word possible.

* * *

Dinner was over, the dishwasher humming, and a freshly bathed Mariah was kneeling on a tall stool at the kitchen island, watching with a gleam in her brown eyes as Therese laid out the stuff for monkey bread. She wore another T-shirt, this one Therese's, tied and knotted the same way as the night before, and her hair was still damp from the bath she'd required after spilling gravy from somewhere around her upper lip all the way down to her toes.

Keegan sat on the stool next to her, making a mental note to pack some of her clothes in a bag to keep in the car. He'd never noticed at home that she tended to wear as much food as she ate.

He'd made a point of not noticing.

Therese set two cans of biscuits on the island, put butter in a saucepan to melt, and mixed sugar and cinnamon in a bowl. There was nothing special about the way she did things—quickly, efficiently—but he liked watching her move. She was graceful in the same way his mother was. The kitchen was Ercella's domain, and like her, Therese hardly seemed to think but simply did.

"Is your mother the only grandparent in Mariah's life?" Therese peeled the paper from one biscuit can, popped it open, then repeated the process with the second.

"Yeah. Sabrina grew up in the foster-care system. Her father was in prison, her mother had drug problems and lost custody when she was nine. She was in three or four homes, plus a group home, but she never felt like she belonged, like she was wanted. She took off on her own when she was fifteen."

Therese's brow wrinkled, and her eyes darkened. Thinking about all the unfortunate kids with parent issues? Or her desire to give up on her stepkids after everyone else had already done the same? Keegan had no doubt she saw it as one more abandonment and probably thought he did, too, after his surprise when she'd told him.

It wasn't. He understood. She wasn't the sort to walk away from responsibilities and obligations, and she hated seeing her husband's kids as either of those things. If she felt she had no choice but to give them up, she really had no choice.

He'd just been...*Disappointed* seemed as good a word as any. Some part of him had still been nursing the hope, however unreasonable and unlikely, that he would be able to pass off Mariah to her father's family, after all. Stupid, he knew. Why would any woman agree to raise the illegitimate daughter from her dead husband's affair when she was already saddled with two legitimate children from his previous marriage? Yes, she was maternal; yes, she was responsible; yes, she'd loved Matheson...though maybe not so much if she ever found out about the affair.

But there were limits to what a maternal, responsible woman could do.

And, truthfully, he hadn't realized things were quite so bad between her and the kids. Sure, he'd seen Abby being snotty, but wasn't that part of being a teenager? Hadn't her behavior reminded him of his own sisters at her age? Though, for all their drama, neither Martha nor Daisy had ever been disrespectful to their mother.

There must be a lot going on that he knew nothing about to drive Therese to even consider such a decision.

She laid out the biscuit rounds on a plastic cutting mat, then pulled a rectangular piece of metal from a drawer, offering it by its plastic handle to Mariah. "You want to cut the biscuits?"

Mariah drew back, hands folded together. "No knives. Celly says."

"It's called a chop and scoop. It's not sharp, see? It won't cut you, but it'll cut the dough." She pressed it against her own skin, then used it to neatly quarter one of the biscuits.

Mariah darted a look at Keegan, then gingerly took the tool. After running her finger along the edge, she grinned and made two crooked cuts in a biscuit. With a nod of encouragement from Therese, she attacked the rest.

"I know a tremendous number of wonderful parents," Therese remarked as she watched, "and some who are so-so. But bad parents..."

He didn't need to hear the sadness in her voice to know she was including herself, at least a little, in that last group. He was grateful, given what she knew of his relationship with Mariah, she didn't include him, as well.

The beep of his cell phone signaling a text came as a welcome interruption. He read the screen, then grinned. "Mom's fixing jambalaya and cornbread for Ford tomorrow. If he's not already feeling better, he will be after that."

"Good for what ails you, huh?"

From beside him came a tuneless line. "Jambalaya, crawfish pie-uh..." Apparently those were the only words of the song Mariah knew. She trailed off and sucked her lower lip between her teeth as she concentrated on her task.

"I bet you make the best jambalaya in the Logan family," Therese said. "After your mother, of course."

"Mine's not even close, but it's pretty darn good. Give me your kitchen tomorrow or Sunday, and I'll show you."

"How about Sunday evening?" Her look was challenging. Doubting his cooking ability?

"It's a deal."

For the next few minutes she ignored him while she and Mariah coated the biscuit pieces in cinnamon sugar, then dropped them into a baking dish. She added brown sugar to the melted butter, poured it over the biscuits, put the pan in the oven, and set the timer. "Twenty to twenty-five minutes until the monkey toes are done. Now what do we do?"

Keegan could think of plenty of things, but the question was directed to Mariah, who gave it a lot of thought if her wrinkled forehead was anything to go by. "Where are the toys?"

"Oh, honey, Abby and Jacob don't have any toys. Not the kind you mean."

That didn't faze the kid. "We play in Abby's room."

"Um, no. Abby doesn't like her things disturbed."

"Read me a story?"

"I don't think we have any little kids' books, sweetie." She glanced at Keegan. "I can't believe I'm going to say this, but...You want to watch TV? We have On Demand. I'm sure we can find something you like there."

"On Demand! Yay!" Mariah grabbed his arm, using it to balance herself as she slid to the floor, then took off for the living room at the only speed she had: fast. Long after she let go, he felt the imprint of her tiny hands.

A bad mother, a dead father, grandparents who didn't know of—and likely wouldn't care about—her existence, and no other family to care...The poor kid hadn't gotten the best shot at life. But it didn't have to matter. It didn't have to mean that she'd grow up to be like Sabrina or Matheson's ex-wife. She could still be happy and loved, and if things worked out between him and Therese, she could know her half sister and half brother, even if she couldn't know their true relationship. She could have a normal life.

All he had to do was accept her. Stop trying to find a way to unload her on someone else. Stop trying to protect himself.

If he could. If he could keep the secret of her parentage. If he could take the risk of loving her. And losing her.

Wasn't that a risk everyone faced? There were no guarantees when it came to caring about someone. People died, they went missing, they became complete strangers and never found their way back to the people who loved them.

You're the adult, his mother had told him more than once. *You're the grown-up,* thirteen-year-old Abby had snootily informed him the night they met. He had coping skills, family, and friends to fall back on.

It was up to him to make sure Mariah had the same things.

* * *

Cooking breakfast was a Saturday-morning tradition in Therese's house. The rest of the week, they made do with cold cereal, instant oatmeal, or energy bars, but on Saturdays she made eggs, bacon, pancakes, hash browns, whatever struck their fancy. Okay, so *made* wasn't entirely accurate. Once a month she mixed the dry ingredients for pancakes and stored them in the pantry, and though she added her own touches, the hash browns started with frozen potato shreds. Still, it was a tradition.

One that held absolutely no appeal when she was the only one in the house. Silence ruled, broken only by the occasional hum of the refrigerator motor or the hot water heater kicking on in the utility closet. No muted sounds of virtual-reality combat drifting from Jacob's room, no slamming drawers or stomps from Abby's room. Just quiet that was somehow a little more peaceful than it had been a week ago.

Sliding onto a stool at the island, she picked off a chunk of leftover monkey bread—*monkey toes,* she could hear Mariah insisting—and stuffed it into her mouth. It was a little stale on the outside, but a swallow of coffee helped it go down.

After forty-five minutes of cartoons, the girl had beamed when they returned to the kitchen to fill their plates with warm, sticky bread. Keegan had lifted her onto this same stool—Therese made a mental note to check her clothes for sugar/butter stains when she got up—and after giving him the shyest of smiles, Mariah had gobbled three pieces before proclaiming them the best monkey toes she'd ever eaten.

Then she'd leaned close to Keegan and whispered, "But Celly's are better."

Therese smiled now as she'd done then. Sweets baked by a grandmother always tasted better than those made by a woman the child hardly knew. Mariah didn't have a clue about Therese's role in her life. She might be momentarily bereft when they went home, though the promise of Celly waiting for her at the end of the trip would negate that, but in two weeks, two months, two years, she would have completely forgotten Therese, Abby, and Jacob.

The likelihood made Therese's heart hurt.

Unless something came of this trial relationship.

"Am I a fool for wanting something to come of it?"

Of course there was no answer. The house was more than just quiet. It was empty. This was the way it would be if Abby and Jacob went to live elsewhere. She would come home to emptiness. She would wake up to it. She would have only her schedule to worry about, only her laundry to do, only her meals to prepare, only her messes to clean.

A few weeks ago, that had sounded like heaven. At this very moment, it felt like loneliness.

Sliding to her feet, she peeled the wrapper from an energy bar, took a big bite, then found her cell phone next to the coffeemaker. Like for most working women, Saturdays for Carly were usually catch-up days, when she cleaned house, ran errands, and took care of her yard. That might have changed since her engagement, but it couldn't hurt to ask if she had a little time.

"Hey, sweetie, can you spare an hour for an old friend?" she asked when Carly answered on the third ring.

"Of course I can. Should I get comfy in the recliner with a cup of coffee or make an effort to be at least somewhat presentable so you won't be embarrassed to be seen with me?"

"Doesn't matter," Therese automatically replied, then corrected herself. "I'd like some face-to-face time if Dane doesn't mind. Want to take a walk with me?"

"A walk." Carly said the words as if they were significant. Truthfully, they were. Everyone in the margarita club knew she could work for hours in her yard without a word of complaint, but her place of choice for walking was in a store. She insisted that was why she couldn't lose the pounds she'd gained after Jeff's death—that, and the sinful chocolate-covered caramels she ate for breakfast every day—but everyone else knew she'd needed the extra weight. Having a spouse in a combat zone was stressful. Some people ate to quiet their fear; some starved theirs.

"I'll head your way. Meet on Cimarron?" Carly's house was three blocks south and three blocks east of Therese's.

"I'll be there. Should I bring Mojos?" That was significant, too, offering to bring her Mags' Mojos. Sharing her caramels with Dane, she joked, was how she'd known she'd fallen in love with him.

Therese laughed. "No, the situation's not dire. I just need to talk to my bestie."

"Okay. See you soon."

Other than her after-dinner meander with Keegan on Tuesday, it had been too long since Therese had walked for the pure pleasure of it. Back in Montana, she'd never needed exercise. Her daily life had been active enough. Though Paul had loved to run, she hadn't thought her body deserved that kind of punishment. Walking, though...they'd taken a lot of long strolls wherever they'd been. It had been their time to catch up on each other's lives, to reconnect.

Every neighborhood in Tallgrass had sidewalks, a throwback to long-ago times when strolls had been more common. It took the caution out of walking—no need to deal with traffic except at intersections, no cause to watch her steps. She could let her mind wander, and it did.

Straight to Keegan. Again, Mariah had been more asleep than awake when they'd left the night before. Again, they'd come within an inch of kissing and, again, neither of them closed that inch. She had wanted to. He had wanted to. She'd seen it in his eyes. But when he'd taken the first step back, he gave her a smile filled with such knowing and promise and desire that she shivered even now at the memory of it.

Tomorrow, he'd whispered before shifting Mariah to lie against his shoulder and heading to his car.

Tomorrow was here, and they were going on a picnic at Tall Grass Lake, maybe just the three of them, maybe all five. It would be nice to have a private picnic with him or a private dinner, but they were parents. Privacy was hard to come by.

She caught sight of Carly when they were still a block apart. She returned Carly's big wave, then lengthened her stride until they came close enough to speak without yelling.

"Which way do you want to go?" Carly asked.

Therese glanced around. If they headed south, they would be on Main Street within minutes. East or west would take them back toward their respective homes, so she gestured to the north and they turned that way. "How's Dane?"

"Perfect." It was a word Carly used a lot, a concept that had given Dane some trouble. He'd taken the word on its surface and felt so *im*perfect with his amputated leg and his trouble adjusting to the loss. But Carly had known exactly what she was talking about. He truly was perfect to her.

"How are the kids?"

Therese shrugged. "They were both gone last night. Abby had a sleepover and Jacob stayed at Liam's."

"So you were alone all night. Was it as nice as you remember?"

They came to a chalk drawing on the sidewalk, pastel colors, lots of fuzzy circles, and both of them automatically moved into the grass to avoid stepping on it. When the concrete was beneath her feet again, she said, "Not exactly alone. I had company for dinner." An oddly formal way to describe Keegan and Mariah, but it was better than just blurting that in the six days since she'd told Carly about him, she'd decided to get involved with him. To explore the possibilities.

To risk getting her heart broken.

Carly gave her a shrewd look. "Does this company have a name?"

"Keegan Logan. I told you about him."

"The medic from Fort Polk who knew Paul in Afghanistan. The very handsome medic. I remember." Carly tapped one finger against her lower lip as if pondering an unfathomable question. "Gee, he's been in town about a week, hasn't he? He didn't go home after finding out Paul had passed? What could possibly be keeping him here?"

"I asked him that yesterday."

"And did he say, 'Why, you, of course'?"

"Sort of." Therese's face warmed when Carly did a double-take, her eyes dancing with delight. "I mean, he didn't say 'why' or 'of course,' but he said 'you.' Me. He wants to see what—" She had to stop to take a breath, to fill lungs that had suddenly gone empty like an excited teenage girl with her first boyfriend. "What's between us."

As they stopped at the intersection to wait for three kids to race across on their bikes, Carly slugged her on the arm. "Aw, man, you've been holding out on me! Last I heard, you'd met the guy, talked for a few minutes, realized he was sexy and you were alive, and that was it. Now you've got something between you? Just how many times have you seen him since then?"

Therese started to do a mental count, then gave it up. "We've had dinner every night but Tuesday, and he was at Three Amigos then, and we went for a walk after you guys left."

"He went to Three Amigos because he knew you'd be there? Oh, my gosh, Dane did the same thing! Therese, I can't believe you haven't been on the phone with me every night or hanging outside my classroom every single day, keeping me updated!" Carly stopped short in the middle of the street. "He hasn't been staying the night, has he?"

"No, he hasn't. And I haven't said anything because ... I hardly know him, Carly, but ... I want to. Really well." Therese sighed. "But there's these little obstacles. He's in the Army. He lives in another state. He has a two-year-old daughter whose mother pulled a Catherine with her, only Sabrina totally disappeared. Keegan's got custody of her."

Therese started walking again, and so did Carly, giving her a sidelong look. "This Army thing ... you know it's just an excuse."

It took Therese a moment of scuffing her feet before she huffed out a sigh. "I know." Being a soldier hadn't killed Paul. He could have just as easily died in a car crash on his way to work, been in the line of fire when a wacko with a gun started shooting at the local grocery store, or simply gone to sleep and not woken up. The world wasn't safe, and there were no guarantees. When it was time to die, it was time.

Things happen when they happen. Keegan's words from yesterday fell completely in line with her own beliefs. But sometimes it was easier to think that her husband— and Carly's, Ilena's, Jessy's, all the margarita club's husbands—had died because they were soldiers than to accept that God had planned from the beginning to cut their lives short.

"And the long-distance thing," Carly went on. "You know it can work. Look at us. We probably spent more time waiting for Jeff and Paul to come back from somewhere than we did actually with them."

"Yeah." All those days, weeks, years. All those bittersweet good-byes and just plain sweet reunions.

"And as far as his daughter—she's here in Tallgrass with him?"

Therese told her about his mother's trip.

"Has he met Abby and Jacob?"

A nod.

"And he's still coming around. Wow. I'm not sure you get to use his kid as an excuse if he's willing to accept yours. No offense, but Abby takes a *lot* of acceptance."

"She hasn't been so bad this week." The words surprised Therese—not that she'd said them. She had defended Abby and made excuses for her for the better part of four years, but this time she actually meant them. "You should see her with Mariah. She's so good. She seems to have a really soft spot for her."

"I'll take your word for it."

Therese couldn't blame Carly for sounding skeptical. She'd been on the receiving end of Abby's scorn and drama-princess behavior ever since they'd met. "I think she relates to Mariah. Two girls abandoned by their mothers."

"It's good to know that Abby's capable of compassion."

Nudging a soccer ball sitting forlornly off the sidewalk and into the grass, Therese nodded. She'd been relieved by that discovery, too. How sad it was that this was truly the first sign of the quality she'd seen in Abby in over three years. Was Abby really so self-absorbed? God knows, she'd been in situations before that called for compassion. Had she simply never felt it? Hadn't known how to show it?

So many months living together, and so much Therese didn't know about Paul's daughter.

And yet she was on the verge of giving up on her. Had, in some ways, given up on her the day Abby slapped her.

How different a person would Abby have been if she hadn't had to face so much adversity so young? If Paul and Catherine had stayed happily married, if motherhood hadn't lost its allure for Catherine, if Paul hadn't died. Each one was a major trauma in itself. Dump all three on any preteen girl, and the results weren't going to be pretty. Add in Abby's natural flair for drama...

"Okay, you're thinking hard thoughts and not cutting yourself any slack in them. I can tell by the lines between your eyes. You always scrunch up when you're blaming yourself for something."

They'd reached the end of the street, a cul-de-sac with houses on two sides and the empty lot in the middle turned into a tiny park. A red-white-and-blue sign designated it as the Private First Class Shan Walker Memorial. He and his wife had lived in the house on the left, and he'd been the first casualty in Iraq from Fort Murphy so many years ago. The town had built and dedicated the park a few months after his death, but his widow and children had long since moved on.

If they'd built a park to memorialize every soldier who'd died since, practically every block would have green space.

Without speaking, Therese and Carly both headed automatically toward the central pavilion, just big enough to shelter a picnic table from the sun. Therese sat on one bench. Carly took a seat on the table, feet resting on the bench.

"Have you made any decisions about the kids?"

Therese sighed. "It was nice last night, having Keegan over for dinner, no one but Mariah to interrupt us, and she's very good at playing by herself. I woke up this morning thinking I finally had the house to myself. No bad moods, no grunting, no dagger-eyed glares, just doing what I want when I want. And you know what?"

"Instead of quiet and peaceful, it was lonely."

Of course Carly knew that. She'd been waking up to an empty house for a long time before Dane. "I think I actually missed them, Carly. Even though Abby drives me crazy and my blood pressure spikes whenever she's around, and sometimes when Jacob does his caveman imitation I just want to smack him on the back of the head. There was no one to cook breakfast for. No one to glare at me. No one whining about doing their chores.

"There was no one breathing in there but me."

"But you weren't being driven crazy and your blood pressure wasn't spiking and you didn't want to smack anyone." Carly fingered her engagement ring. "You just spent five days without them. Didn't the place feel lonely then?"

It hadn't. Therese had spent part of that time meeting with people about giving up custody and the rest of it thinking about it, wanting to do it, hating to, giving herself headaches and stomachaches and pains around her heart.

"I knew they'd be back after the visit."

"They'll be back today. Their friends' parents haven't taken them to raise."

"I know." She seemed to be saying or thinking that a lot, when the reality on this particular subject was the total opposite. It was such a huge decision with such lasting impact—on the kids, on herself, on every aspect of their lives.

She didn't know what to do about Abby and Jacob.

Chapter 12

"You can take off today if you want. I'll handle things around here."

Dalton looked up, a biscuit dripping butter and jelly halfway to his mouth. That was the second time in less than a month Noah had offered to step in for him—only the third in his whole lifetime. Not that the kid was lazy. He always helped out when he was home, but shouldering all the responsibility himself, even for just a day...

Something that felt like pride swelled inside Dalton. He'd done his share of helping raise Noah, especially after their parents had moved, but he'd never try to take credit for his being a good kid. People made their own decisions and sometimes forgot all their raising, like Dillon. But Dalton was proud of Noah.

He took a bite of biscuit, not like the thick flaky ones his mom made but a decent substitution considering it came from a can, and gave the offer some thought. His first impulse was to say not only no, but hell no. The last time he'd had a free day, he'd gone into town, had too much to drink, ended up in bed with Jessy Lawrence, and couldn't get it—or her—out of his mind.

But not working didn't have to mean having a drink, seeing anyone, or even leaving the ranch. He could watch a game on TV. Read a book. Hike through the woods with Oz, the dog he'd finally named. Lie on the couch and be too lazy to do more than roll over once in a while. Little things. Nothing things. Things he hadn't taken time to do in more years than he could remember.

"Why the offer?" he asked.

"'Cause you look like hell. An old man needs a break every now and then."

"Yeah, this old man can still kick your ass."

Noah laughed. "You never kicked my ass. The physical stuff was all between you and Dillon. Mom would have kicked *your* ass if you'd laid a hand on me."

Dalton's nerves went tight the way they always did at the mention or thought of their brother, but not as bad as usual. Most times Dillon came up in conversation, Dalton lost his appetite or his patience and turned stone-faced. This time he was still for a moment, then he stuffed the rest of the biscuit in his mouth. "You always were a mama's boy."

"I had to be. You guys pestered me all the time, and all Dad ever said was, 'Don't let 'em catch you, son.'" Noah did a credible imitation of their father's deeper voice. "Hell, I spent half my life running and hiding from you two."

Dalton didn't remember it quite that way. Yeah, they'd been obnoxious big brothers, but they'd also done a lot of stuff with Noah, not to him. Besides, he'd been an obnoxious little brother. He'd deserved some of the tricks and teasing he'd gotten.

Rising from the table, Noah folded the last two slices of bacon to fit inside a biscuit, gulped the rest of his coffee, and headed toward the door. "I'll see you later. And you're welcome for the day off."

"You're welcome for the college education," Dalton retorted before the door shut.

He dredged another piece of biscuit through the yolk of his eggs-over-easy, looked at it, then offered it to the dog. Oz took it delicately, dropped it into his food dish across the room, then settled down to eat it at his leisure.

Dalton cleared the dishes from the table, rinsed and loaded them in the dishwasher, and wondered what to do with this gift of a free day. The first thing he ruled out was visiting Sandra's grave. Sometimes the visits helped— actually made him feel a little…Not better. He would never feel better about her final choice. But going there, brightening the plot with the yellow flowers she'd loved, maintained some sort of connection.

But since meeting Jessy there weeks ago, the visits made him think of her, too. As if he wasn't already uncomfortable enough inside those gates.

The time he'd spent with Jessy Thursday evening at Bubba's had been odd. He was still harboring a lot of resentment, and he guessed she sensed it even though he tried to be civil, because she'd been unsettled the whole time. She hadn't said much and had looked as if she'd rather be anywhere else and with anyone else in the world.

But if that was the case, why had she come over in the first place? Why had she asked if she could sit with him?

About the time he'd finished his burger, she'd mumbled something about getting home, grabbed her purse, and left. A couple of guys had called to her on the way out, one of them even blocking her way, but she'd just detoured around him as smooth as if she'd done it a hundred times and gone on out the door.

Shaking his head to clear her from it—yeah, what were the odds of that?—he wiped down the dining table, then glanced at the dog. "Well, Oz, what do you want to do?"

The mutt held his gaze a long time before blinking, then trotted into the living room. A moment later came the sound of nails on leather, then a whoosh as he settled himself in the recliner. Dalton knew from a week's experience that the dog's eyes were already closed and in a minute or two, he'd be snoring.

Sounded like a good idea for him, too.

* * *

"So the town Tallgrass is one word, but the lake is two," Keegan commented as Therese turned onto a blacktop road flanked by wooden signs carved with the lake's name. It was past noon, the food he'd picked up from a downtown restaurant smelled almost as good as his mother's cooking, and he was looking forward to his first picnic in more years than he could remember.

Anticipating a picnic. It was almost too juvenile. His buddies back home would be snickering and calling him names.

Though that would stop once they got a look at Therese.

"Yeah," Abby said from the back. "No consistency." She tossed her hair with a teenager's disdain, a gesture that would have had a lot more impact with more hair and one that Mariah had been imitating the last few days.

There were a lot of things Mariah could learn from her half sister, but dramatic flair wasn't one of them. Her nearly three-year-old tantrums could put Abby's to shame. She'd had one just this morning after deciding she wanted to wear an outfit from the to-launder pile instead of the dresser. It had taken the threat of canceling the picnic to stop her, but ten minutes later she'd been all sweetness and smiles.

Women, he silently sighed, thinking of Mariah and Abby, Sabrina and his sisters. Then he gave Therese a sidelong look. He would bet she'd never thrown a tantrum in her life. Maybe it would help ease some of her stress if she did.

Maybe she would let him ease some of her stress.

Though at the moment, with her hair in a ponytail that blew in the breeze through the open windows and dark glasses hiding her eyes, she didn't look tense at all. Add in shorts, a T-shirt, and flip-flops decorated with sparkly gems and big yellow daisies that had made Mariah's eyes light up greedily, she looked damn near carefree. Pretty. Hot.

Desire stirred way down low, and he was grateful for his own dark glasses that hid his eye-roll. It was the middle of the day, they had three kids with them, and they weren't likely to get even two minutes of privacy.

But two minutes was a start.

Breaks in the heavy woods that lined the road showed occasional glimpses of the lake, until a tight curve and suddenly there it was: big, blue, rocky shores broken up by small beaches. The water level was lower than normal, he could see from the marks on the rocks, but that didn't stop the boaters and fishermen from enjoying it.

"The southeast section of the lake butts up to the fort," Therese said as she took another tight turn. "They have several areas out here for camping and picnicking."

"You should have gotten a boat," Jacob said from the third-row seat. The kid had earbuds in and was immersed in a video game, but he had a talent for tracking the conversation around him when he wanted to.

"And they have boats for rent," Therese said with a glance in the rearview mirror, "but I didn't think about seeing if they had any available. I started driving my dad's two-ton truck when I was twelve and moved on to the tractor when I was thirteen, but I've never tried a boat."

"You're deprived. I used to take out my uncles' fishing boats when I was way younger than Jacob," Keegan teased. "You did have picnics up there in Montana, didn't you?"

She gave him a dry look. "Sure. It was called a lunch break."

"Toted out to the fields in a pail with a Mason jar full of cold water from the creek?"

His comment was rewarded with two snorts from the rear seats, followed by Mariah's effort at one. It made her cough.

Therese pulled into a space beside an empty table, shut off the engine, then pushed her glasses up on her head to give him the full effect of her chastising look. "Yeah. Like you ate crawfish, danced to the fiddle on the bayou, went shoeless until you were full-grown, and called everyone *cher.*"

Keegan gave her his best offended look. "My mama

bought us new shoes every August when school started. But the rest of it…" He shrugged.

"What are crawfish?" Abby asked, unfastening her seat belt before freeing Mariah from hers.

"Crawdads. Mudbugs."

She shuddered. "You ate bugs? That's disgusting. You're not putting them in our dinner tomorrow, are you?"

Therese started to speak, but he beat her to it. "You don't know what they are, so you won't know whether you're eating them. Just think of them as a low-calorie protein source."

She jumped out with another shudder, lifted Mariah to the ground, and headed for the table nearby. As Jacob climbed out from the back, he grinned and gave Keegan a thumbs-up. "Mudbugs. Cool."

Therese just shook her head. When they met at the back of the van to unload the food, she said, "Now she probably won't eat the jambalaya."

"Jacob and I can eat her share. Not that she appears to eat more than a few bites of anything."

As Therese picked up a bag from the restaurant, she gave him a sidelong look, trying to be casual, and asked, "Will there really be crawfish in it?"

He hefted the ice chest, then deliberately bumped her. "Like I said, *cher,* think of it as protein." He was pretty sure as he walked to the table that he wasn't supposed to hear her murmur.

"We're going to eat bugs. Oh, boy."

Grinning, he set the ice chest on the concrete bench, then helped Jacob spread a plastic cloth over the table. They secured it at each end with rocks someone had stacked underneath the nearest tree, then Jacob wandered to the water's edge where Abby crouched beside Mariah, watching as she pitched stones in and giggled at the splashes.

"Did the kids come willingly?" he asked as he helped Therese set out the food. When she'd called a few hours earlier to set a time, she hadn't known whether either kid would be with her. She'd given them a choice, and it was usually to not spend time with her.

Even if she wanted to give them back to their mother, their behavior had to hurt.

"Actually, they did. Since we're so close to the house, I told them they could stay home if they wanted, but when I got ready to leave, they were both ready, too."

"Too bad we couldn't have left Mariah with them and come alone. Or sent the three of them out and stayed home ourselves."

She darted a look at him. "Gee, you, me, alone in the house. Whatever would we have done?"

"So obvious it's not even worth a guess."

For a moment he thought she was going to come back with something teasingly smug, but all she did was blush and gesture to the dishes spread across the table. "You did well."

Changing the subject. That was all right. Soon enough they would manage some time alone. One way or another.

"You're not the only Smurf around, you know. I don't cook a lot since I live alone, but I know my way around restaurants and deli sections." He'd chosen a chunk of barbecued bologna, a warm slab of ham, boiled shrimp, sweet pea and macaroni salads, and—even though they'd had them just a few nights before—baked beans and potato salad. How could they have a picnic without them?

The only thing left to unpack was the plastic tote she'd brought. He took a can of pop from the cooler and leaned against the tree while she laid out sturdy plastic plates that she could toss in the dishwasher just as easily as the trash. A heavy clay pot held disposable forks and spoons, and she'd brought a handful of real utensils—serving spoons, butter knives, and one wicked-looking butcher knife. A roughly made wooden contraption went in the center of the table, dispensing napkins while keeping the rest from blowing away.

"That is—"

"Jacob's project from summer camp the first year we lived here."

"—handy," he finished, as if he hadn't been about to say *butt-ugly* instead.

The smile she gave him, both knowing and appreciative, was worth the catch. "You want to call the kids, and we'll eat."

Pushing away from the tree, he went to stand beside her. "Abby, Jacob, Mariah, come and eat!"

Wincing at his shout, Therese shook her head. "I bet people used to call you incorrigible when you were little."

"Used to?" He grinned and thickened his Southern accent. "Honey, they still do."

* * *

"Six o'clock is kind of early for a dinner date, isn't it?"

Therese met Abby's gaze in the dresser mirror as she chose a pair of shimmery gold dangles from the jewelry box. It was right here that things had fallen apart between them. Only their positions were reversed: Therese had been standing in the open doorway and Abby had been rummaging through the jewelry box. Therese had told her she couldn't borrow her earrings, and Abby had reacted in anger, knocking everything off the dresser, breaking the jewelry box, scattering pieces over the carpet. She'd shoved Therese, then slapped her, and something inside Therese had broken.

That was the moment she'd decided she was done with Paul's daughter.

Easier to say than to do.

"It's not exactly a date," Therese said as Abby came into the room. "It's just friends having dinner."

"A man friend and a woman friend." The girl stopped beside the bed, and in the mirror Therese saw her gaze slide to the photograph of Paul on the nightstand. "I don't want a stepfather."

Of course she didn't. Therese had been as sure of that as she was that the sun rose in the east, but hearing it aloud in such unequivocal terms made her gut clench. She swallowed hard and forced her hands to steady so she could slide first one wire, then the other, into her earlobes. "Keegan and I are a long, long way from getting married."

"But you're thinking about it."

Another swallow. Lord, she couldn't believe she was having this conversation. If anything developed between her and Keegan—between her and any man—she wanted it to come so naturally that it was a done deal before Abby even had a chance to realize what was happening. "Any time you invest yourself in a relationship, you have to open yourself to the possibilities, or what's the point?"

"God, that sounds so Dr. Phil." Abby plopped onto the bed hard enough to bounce. "My mom has relationships all the time, but she swears she's never getting married again."

Her mom had affairs, and she hadn't waited until divorcing Paul to start. But Abby didn't need to know that, not now, not ever. "Most relationships don't lead to marriage. Most people you date turn out to be just that—people you date, then say good-bye to. That's probably the case with Keegan and me."

Abby snorted. Oh, how Therese hated snorts. "Yeah, right. You spend more time with him than you do with anyone else, even Carly. And he doesn't even live here. What are you going to do when he goes home? Sell the house and move to Louisiana? Gross."

After spraying on perfume, Therese hesitantly sat at the foot of the bed. "If I fall in love with and marry someone whose job requires moving, yes, I'll sell the house and move with him. That's what I did with your father."

"And Jacob and me don't even have a choice. You'd ruin our whole lives so that you could be happy. Why do you have to be so selfish?" Abby's lower lip quivered, and tears glistened in her eyes. She insisted she was grown up and tried so hard to make it true, but in that moment she reminded Therese of no one so much as little Mariah.

"Abby . . ." Therese forced down a sigh. She sighed so often that she was starting to hate them as much as she did snorts and grunts. "If your father hadn't died, we would have already moved from Tallgrass. Moves are part of Army life. I know it would be hard for you and Jacob. It would be hard for me, too, leaving my friends and my job and this house. But it's part of what we do."

She waited for Abby's outburst, but when the girl spoke, her voice was little more than a whisper, full of heartache. "I didn't ask to be born into a stupid Army family."

At that moment, Therese wanted more than anything in the world to wrap her arms around Paul's daughter, to hold her close and ease her fears and make certain she knew that someone cared, someone wanted her to be happy, someone loved her. But she knew too well what would happen: Abby would stiffen, jerk away, be angry that she'd dared touch her, and deep down inside, it would hurt.

"I know you didn't." *Sweetie.* She should end the sentence with that. She called kids at school sweetie and honey and babe all the time. She'd called Mariah sweetie the first time she'd ever spoken to her. Abby was so much more than a student or a friend's daughter, yet Therese couldn't remember the last time she'd called this child who lived with her an endearment, if ever.

The doorbell pealed downstairs, and Therese's glance slid to the clock. Keegan was right on time, expecting to leave Mariah there in Abby and Jacob's care, expecting dinner for two, adult conversation, and so much more. Therese, who wore her sexiest lingerie beneath her summer dress, had shared those expectations, but she dismissed them as she rose from the bed and summoned a smile. "Why don't we all go out to dinner tonight?"

Abby considered it a moment, then sniffed as she stood up. "I'd rather have pizza. Besides, I promised Mariah we'd watch every Shrek movie ever made."

"You're sure you'll be okay with her?"

Now a hint of the old Abby returned, with a roll of her eyes and a toss of her hair. "She's nearly three, and she adores me, and Nicole's mom is down the street. Why wouldn't we be okay?"

"Therese!" Jacob yelled, Mariah's slightly softer,

"Trace!" echoing his. An instant later, she added, "Abby, where are you?"

"I'm coming," Abby called back. She looked at Therese as if she didn't know what else to say, shrugged, and left the room.

After picking up a delicate sweater that matched her dress, Therese checked her image in the mirror once more, noting the heightened color in her cheeks, a side effect of the knot in her gut. She closed her eyes a moment, whispered a silent prayer for guidance and strength, then headed downstairs.

They were gathered in the foyer, Mariah with a pink-and-purple pack strapped to her back. She would bring DVDs, she'd said excitedly on the way back from the lake, and clothes and pajamas. Just in case.

Keegan looked up when Therese was halfway down the stairs, and appreciation darkened his eyes, sending a shiver of warmth through her. He wore jeans, faded and snug, and a rich blue shirt, the color somewhere between navy and turquoise. The cuffs were rolled back a few times, exposing his muscular forearms, and the tail was untucked. He was incredibly handsome in a charming, incorrigible sort of way.

His smile formed slowly, and her stomach flip-flopped. She was glad she'd chosen the dress with its swaths of pastel colors and fitted cut and hem that was almost too short, that she'd taken extra time with the curling iron to put waves in her hair, that she'd picked the pretty, skimpy bra and panties of pale green satin and lace that left little to the imagination.

Not that she imagined Keegan would actually pay attention to them in the process of removing them.

Hoping no one noticed the huskiness in her voice, she started to repeat the instructions to the kids. Abby stared at the ceiling as if bored, and Jacob interrupted when she paused for breath.

"We got it the first three times, Therese. Keep the doors locked, eat the pizza Keegan brought, watch out for the cookie monster"—he pointed to Mariah, and she beamed—"and call you if we need to. Right?"

She breathed. "Right. And no company. No—"

"Blah blah. Good-bye." Abby took Mariah's hand. "Come on, let's see what kind of pizza your dad brought."

Predictably Jacob followed them down the hall to the kitchen. Nearer, Keegan chuckled, handed her purse to her from the hall table, then steered her to the door. "Okay, Mom. Can we go now?"

"Abby and Jacob have never babysat before—"

"They'll be fine."

"I know." Mariah did adore Abby and would do whatever she said, and Abby obviously adored her right back. Jacob was always responsible, and she was only worrying about them because it kept her from thinking too much about herself and the step she was going to take tonight and the man she was going to take it with.

A step she wanted to take. A man she wanted. More than she'd let herself admit.

On the short drive downtown, Keegan asked her to choose a restaurant, and she opted for Luca's, the best Italian place in Tallgrass. They had to park nearly two blocks away, but the air was still warm and it was too early in the evening for the heels that showed her legs to such advantage to pinch.

Keegan didn't open the car door for her—she'd always

felt foolish sitting inside as if helpless—but when he met her on the sidewalk, he took her left hand, twining his fingers with hers. It put the tiniest bit of pressure on her wedding and engagement rings, making them bite just the littlest bit, and for the first time since Paul had put them there, she wondered if it was time to remove them.

The bittersweet thought made her breath catch and a small lump form in her throat.

"You're a beautiful woman, Therese."

Her breath caught again, the lump growing. "Thank you. And you're a sweet-talker and a charmer like your daddy."

"Thank you," he retorted smugly. "There's one big difference between us, though: I understand the importance of commitment."

She understood his message. He wasn't taking anything that happened here lightly. He really wanted to see what this thing between them could become. He really thought their getting together might be fated.

Was he destined to break her heart, too?

Things happen when they happen. You take advantage or you don't.

She had enough regrets for things that had happened. She didn't want regrets for things she'd never given a chance.

"Abby seemed upset," he commented as they crossed the street. "Is everything okay?"

Therese marveled that he'd even noticed. So many people wouldn't have felt the faint tension radiating from the girl or seen the tiny signs of distress on her face. Catherine wouldn't have. Paul wouldn't have. "Not upset so much as concerned."

"About you and me?"

"About things changing." She gazed at the sidewalk ahead, cracked and buckled where the roots of a hundred-year-old oak pushed against it. "I realized while talking to her that I don't make as much effort with her as I do with kids I don't even know. All this time I've thought I was so noble and patient for putting up with her tantrums and her drama. I reason with her. I punish her. But I don't try to comfort her or show her affection."

"You've tried before."

"Sure, when they first came to live with us, when Paul deployed, when he died."

"You get rejected enough times, it's natural to stop trying."

"I'm not sure, as a parent, you get to stop trying. How many times have I criticized Catherine for that? How many bad thoughts have I had about other parents, like Sabrina, who put themselves ahead of their kids?" She shook her head grimly, grateful for the warmth and comfort of his hand holding hers. When was the last time Abby had that sort of physical, nonjudgmental comfort? "I may be just a stepparent, Keegan, but I'm the only parent Abby's got. And apparently I've got no room to criticize Catherine. I'm no better a mother than she is."

* * *

Keegan wasn't even a stepparent, but he was the closest thing to a parent Mariah had. Sometimes, he was learning, it didn't have anything to do with a blood tie. Sometimes an emotional tie was just as strong. Even stronger.

Like him, Therese was discovering just how strong her emotional tie to Matheson's kids was.

He stopped underneath the oak in front of the restaurant, where the massive trunk shielded them from view of the people inside, and turned to face her. She really was beautiful, whether in this pretty girly dress and heels or shorts and T-shirts and flip-flops, whether her hair was down and curling back from her face and tempting him to touch or in a ponytail. Solemn eyes, delicate bones, full lips that were flattened now in an unhappy line that matched the look in her eyes.

Raising his free hand, he brushed his palm lightly over her hair. "Do you know how few women would have allowed their husband's kids from a former marriage to live with them? Would have kept them while he deployed? Would have let them stay after he died? Especially when their mother was alive and well and loving the single life in another state?"

She dropped his gaze for a moment as if she didn't want to agree with him but couldn't quite bring herself to disagree. Her situation was unusual, and they both knew it.

"Things have been tough. You've lived with a lot of anger and grief and conflict, and no one could blame you for wanting to end it. You've tried with Abby. You know that."

"But I gave up too easily."

"You haven't given up."

She shook her head, dislodging his hand to her shoulder. "I went to JAG to find out how to get her out of my house and my life."

"Wow, you asked some questions of a lawyer. You're a horrible mom. But, Therese, she's still there. You haven't taken JAG's advice. You haven't called her mother or her grandparents. You haven't done a thing to start the process.

You haven't told her to pack her bags. Not that she has a lot of clothes to start with." He grinned as he repeated Abby's comment from the night they'd met, and so did Therese, easing the bleakness in her eyes.

Momentarily. "But—"

Since she wasn't going to give up easily on blaming herself, he leaned forward and kissed her. Her protest stopped immediately, and her lips softened against his. She gave what he thought might have been a little sigh and seemed to sink against him and opened her mouth so his tongue could slide inside.

A kiss is just a kiss, the song said, but whoever wrote it had obviously never kissed Therese. It was sweet and simple and complicated and hungry and sent a rush of heat through his body like an inexperienced boy getting his first kiss from the homecoming queen. A kiss could be just a kiss, but it could promise so much more, and this kiss was definitely going to lead to more.

Aroused, shaken, and in need of oxygen, Keegan ended the kiss, but didn't draw away. Her eyes fluttered open, and they stared at each other, so close, not close enough. But soon.

She raised her hand to his face, laying her palm lightly against his jaw. He couldn't see the big diamond, but he felt where the cool gold bands touched his skin, or imagined he did. What would it take to persuade her to remove the rings? Putting a ring of his own there?

He could see himself doing that.

The thought both surprised him and felt as natural as if he'd planned it forever. They hadn't known each other long enough. He was still keeping the secret of Mariah's real father. But it wasn't the length of time that was important. It was the quality. Whether two people clicked. Whether they were meant to be together.

As for Mariah's secret…He didn't have to think about that right now, did he?

"Luca's gnocchi is calling my name," she said with a little smile. "Let's continue this later."

Definitely the kiss had held a promise.

The restaurant occupied an old house, the graceful kind with big porches, wide arched doorways, high ceilings, and cozy rooms. Therese requested a table near the garden, and the hostess led them down a long, broad hallway and through the rear door onto another porch. Only one of the half dozen tables was taken, at the far end from their own table.

As Therese shrugged into her sweater, she gazed toward the garden, taking a deep breath. "I'm not sure which smells better here—the flowers or the food."

In Keegan's opinion, the food won, hands down, but he didn't say so. His mama hadn't raised any fools, though Duke came close. "You should plant some," he said as he opened the menu.

"I know. I will. If I don't, I'll regret it come June."

Neither of them wanted regrets come June.

When their waiter came, Keegan ordered the pasta combination platter and tea. Therese asked for gnocchi and a glass of wine. It came in a tall glass, deep in color, hints of red showing when it sat on the table, looking purple when she lifted it for a sip. A faint lip print remained on the rim of the glass when she set it down again, which he found insanely sexy.

In an effort to distract himself, he asked, "What do you and the kids do in summer when school's out?"

She rolled her eyes in a good impression of Abby. The voice was pretty dead-on, too. "'Oh, God, it's so boring. I'd rather go to school year-round than stay home all day with you.'" Ruefully she sipped the wine again, as if she regretted mimicking her stepdaughter, especially after faulting herself for not trying hard enough with her.

"Jacob does basketball, football, baseball, and soccer camps, and Abby goes to swimming, science, computer, and cheer camps. They also do a week of camp with the church youth group, and they spend a week with Paul's parents. Last summer they stayed five days with my parents, but the ranch didn't rate among their favorite places. Mom and Dad expected them to do chores." Making a face, she shuddered.

"I wouldn't have pegged Abby for science or computer camps." Cheer, hell, yeah. She looked exactly like every cheerleader/homecoming queen/prom queen he'd ever known: slender, pretty, blond, tanned, graceful.

"She actually prefers those two, I think. She does the other two because her friends do. It's cooler to look good in a swimsuit and to do cheers than it is to be a geek. But she dropped out of gymnastics after she sprained her ankle six months ago, and she hasn't kept up with the swimming since last summer. I haven't said anything about either one because, frankly, I think kids are way overscheduled. Back in my summers, once my chores were done, the rest of the day was mine to do what I wanted. Of course, I had horses, two thousand acres to roam, and didn't hate my mother."

"Abby doesn't hate you."

"She sounds pretty convincing when she says it."

"All kids say that."

"I never did."

Neither did he, he acknowledged. It would have been sacrilege in his home. If the thought had even flickered through his brain, someone—God or Ercella—would have smacked it right back out. "I know I brought it up, but let's make a deal. No more talk about the kids for now, okay?"

Her smile took a minute to form, and it was tenuous at best, but she nodded.

Reaching across the table, he took her hand, studying her slender fingers and pale pink nails with white tips. He turned it over, tracing her palm with his fingertip. "Hard to believe these hands broke horses, drove heavy equipment, and herded cattle."

"It's been a while. And I wore gloves and have invested a small fortune in the baby-lotion industry since." Her muscles tightened as he touched a particularly sensitive place on her palm, so he did it again. Such a light caress to evoke such a sensuous shudder.

Their salads arrived, along with a basket of warm bread, and she reluctantly tugged free. He reluctantly let her.

She primly spread the linen napkin on her lap and picked up her fork. "I'm looking forward to tomorrow's dinner. Authentic Louisiana food cooked by an authentic Louisiana charmer."

"Sometimes the charm is questionable, but the recipe's my mom's, so it's always good."

"Aw, you're always charming. Even when you're not." After taking a bite, she asked, "When you joined the Army, how did she feel about your leaving one dangerous job for another?"

"First she cried. Not because she was worried but because she was proud. All the Dupree men have done their service, all the way back to the Civil War." He shrugged, and a thousand memories of Ercella doing it exactly the same way flashed in his head. "Life is dangerous. She knows that. She says you're born and you die, and hopefully between those times, you do something you enjoy and love someone who loves you back."

For the first time that evening, Therese's smile was genuine pleasure—no stress, no worries, no regrets. "I would like your mother."

It was easy to envision Ercella meeting Therese and the kids. She would know in that mother-to-all way of hers that Abby needed extra welcome and affection and would give it with her embrace, and would charm Jacob into turning off the games and tuning in to her one hundred percent. She would recognize in Therese a woman very much like herself, would see immediately why Keegan was so certain he wanted a chance with her after only a week.

"You would. And she would adore you."

"I'd like that. It's been a long time since I've been adored," Therese replied breezily.

"Aw, your margarita friends adore you."

She nodded. "They do."

"And all your little kindergarten students who hug you every day and leave their sticky little prints on everything and compete for your attention."

"Them, too." She smiled smugly.

"And me."

For a moment, the smile wavered and he thought it might slip away, but instead it widened, lightening her whole expression, making her look younger and happier and carefree and so damn beautiful. "Good. I'm finding that I adore you, too."

Chapter 13

Jessy prowled her apartment, feeling like a lion she'd once watched in a zoo. She'd been seven or eight, and she'd felt for the animal, pacing in a cage when he should have been running free. Before her mother had drawn her to the next enclosure, she'd gripped the bars of the fence and leaned close, though twenty feet and a deep chasm separated them, and whispered, *I'm sorry.*

So many years, and nothing had changed. She was still sorry.

When she reached the glass door that led to her tiny balcony this time, she stopped instead of pivoting, opened the door, and stepped outside. The air held just a bit of a chill, not enough to need a jacket if she was moving. The sun was out of sight, leaving only a beautiful palette of blues and purples and smoky grays in the western sky.

The balcony had been an afterthought to the apartment, a small rectangle of wood that had turned silvery with age. It held two cheap plastic chairs and a tiny gas grill, the kind meant for tailgating or picnics, and it looked over the one-story rooftops of the buildings behind hers. She and Aaron had sat out here when he got home from work, sharing a beer and their day while he'd tended brats, burgers, or steaks on the grill.

She could count on one hand the number of times she'd been out here since he'd deployed. The day of his funeral. The day she'd packed his things. The early hours of the morning when she'd come home from her first bout of meaningless sex with someone she'd picked up in a bar. The time—

God, she couldn't do this. Couldn't think about Aaron. Couldn't face her regrets.

So what else could she focus on? She'd taken lunch to Fia and found her looking better but not right. Fia had insisted she was fine, it had just been a headache, but Jessy wasn't convinced. Something was wrong with her friend, and the thought made her gut clench.

Something else. What else? She still didn't know where she'd been or what she'd done Wednesday night, and she couldn't begin to forget what she'd done Thursday night. What in the world had made her offer to deliver Dalton's beer to his table? At least he'd been sociable—more than she'd been able to muster after asking if she could join him. The man had seen her at her worst; he knew her for what she really was. There was a reason she engaged in anonymous sex: so she wouldn't have to face the guy when she was sober. Why in God's name make Dalton Smith the exception to her rule?

Damn, there must be something she could think about that wouldn't dig her deeper into the dark hole she was already living in. Something she could do...

Only one thing helped her cope, made her forget, and it was no more than fifteen feet away, in a kitchen cabinet. Waiting for her, offering comfort and peace and oblivion. Just the thought of it made her mouth water, made her hands unsteady.

She hadn't had a drink since Thursday night, when she'd taken a few small sips of beer before Dalton had come into Bubba's, just to steady her nerves, to give the appearance that everything was all right and not rouse anyone's suspicions. That was some kind of record for her. Surely it was all right to have one tonight. Just one, to steady her nerves. To give her peace. To keep her from falling apart.

Her breathing shallow, she went inside and turned into the kitchen. Opened the cabinet. Took out a glass. Poured a small amount, no more than an ounce. Sipped. And sighed.

She would make it.

At least one more night.

* * *

Dinner was over, dessert just a memory, and the pleasure of the entire evening left Therese feeling more comfortable and happy and content than she'd been in years. She could sit there on Luca's porch nursing her second glass of wine for another few hours if it weren't for the flutters in her chest and stomach. Not panicky flutters, but anticipation. Desire. Heat.

Keegan had paid the check, and the waiter returned his card and receipt with two delectable handmade filled chocolates, their version of the mints other restaurants provided but oh, so much more. She picked up the gold foil cup nearest her and lifted out the candy. The fillings were liqueur-flavored, amaretto or brandy or hazelnut, and each piece was two tiny bites of heaven.

"Umm," she sighed as the first bite melted over her tongue. Her favorite. She closed her eyes for a moment of pure pleasure overload, letting the flavors of chocolate, butter, and hazelnut wash through her, re-creating the sensation with the second bite. When she opened her eyes with another sweet sigh, she found Keegan watching her.

His gaze was intense, his features stark, his face a shade paler—or was that warmer?—than it had been before. The knowledge that he was aroused sent an even headier sensation through her. She had never been classically pretty like Marti, sexy like Jessy, delicate like Ilena, or gorgeous like Abby. She was a schoolteacher, a widow, a failed stepmother, a woman who'd hardly noticed—or been noticed by—a man in a long time, but she'd turned on the hottest guy around by doing nothing more than eating a piece of candy.

She felt powerful. Womanly. Wanted.

She gestured toward the other chocolate. "Try it. It's incredible."

"I'd rather watch you eat it." His voice was husky, dark, wrapping around her with the heat of a soft blanket on a cold night.

Her hand surprisingly steady, she slid the tray to him. "Try it. And take your time. Good candy is meant to be savored."

He took the remaining chocolate, bit it in half, chewed, and slowly swallowed. Surprise sparked in his eyes. He had expected it to be good, just not that good. He finished the piece, then pushed his chair back and extended his hand.

It was time to go. Time to start. Time to take that big step she'd been looking forward to.

She laid her hand in his, rose, and walked with him along the porch, past empty tables, into the restaurant and out front. They turned toward his car, strolling as if they had nowhere to be and all the time in the world to get there. Neither of them spoke until they reached it.

"I'd ask if we could walk all the way," she remarked as he beeped the locks, then opened her door, "but I'm afraid these shoes would kill me."

In the white glow of the streetlamp, he made a show of checking out her shoes. "They make your legs look incredible."

She looked, too. "They do, don't they?"

"Granted, your legs look incredible anyway."

God, she loved blunt-spoken compliments.

It took them all of three minutes to drive to his motel. The room was dimly lit by a table lamp, barely enough to make out the furniture, and smelled of cinnamon and sugar, little girl, and the masculine fragrance of exotic, musky cologne. The scent of a man was one of the many little things she missed in her daily life.

The instant he closed the door and locked it, Therese's nerves tightened and her stomach flipped. They were here. Now what? Small talk? Coffee? How did they go from the awkwardness of standing there, fully clothed, to naked and passionate in bed? Heavens, it had been so long since she—

Keegan stopped behind her, slid the purse strap from her shoulder, let it drop on the chair, and touched his mouth to her neck in the softest of kisses. Goose bumps danced along her skin, her nerves tightened for an entirely different reason, and her stomach settled. There was no awkwardness. He adored her, and she adored him, and they both knew that was a simpler way of saying so much more. Their present was definitely together, and their future...

They had a future. She couldn't say anything else with certainty, about that or any other aspect of life. But it was enough.

Her head tilted to one side on its own, giving him better access, and he trailed kisses along the skin where a necklace would be if she'd worn one while his hands slid slowly from her shoulders to her wrists. He folded her arms across her middle and held her against the hard muscled strength of his body as his kisses teased and promised, never paying any particular bit of skin the attention it craved but moving on.

Sensation didn't hum through her. It burned. Each place he touched her, her muscles tensed and her nerves rippled with a rush of raw, electric pleasure. The tiniest contact, even his breath on her skin, stoked the need building inside her. Her own breathing was nothing but shallow gasps, her chest too tight to allow anything more, and she was quivering deep in her gut when he brushed his mouth across her ear.

She jumped, as much as she could in the confines of his embrace, and a sound part giggle, part shriek, escaped her. "That tickles."

"Ah, good to know. Does this tickle?" Freeing his hands, he slowly pulled the tab of the dress zipper down her back, pushing aside hair and fabric, and he kissed her at the base of her neck, his tongue bathing the skin, giving a tiny nip before laving it again.

"N-no." For such a short word, it sounded dragged out

of her in a voice so thick and raspy she hardly recognized it.

"How about this?" His powerful hands were gentle as he pushed the dress off her arms, touching her far too much for such a simple task, not nearly enough. When her arms were free, when the dress was bunched around her waist, he lost interest in it and turned his attention to her breasts instead.

Therese closed her eyes and let her head fall back against Keegan's shoulder. It was just too much effort to keep them open, too much strength to hold it up, when she needed all her will to not collapse at his feet. She'd been so alone for so long, craving intimacy the way she craved oxygen but refusing to recognize it. Every part of her body, even her hair, was burning, sensitized to his touch, wanting more, needing it.

He traced the lace edges of her bra, stroked across the slick satin, one moment so light she barely felt it, the next with the pressure she craved. When he finally closed his fingertips around her nipples, sweet pain rocketed through her, intense and breath-stealing, and she pivoted in his arms, clasping her hands to his cheeks, kissing him, tasting him, stroking his tongue with hers.

When he pushed her back too soon, she whimpered, but he shushed her. "We've got time," he murmured, but judging by the strained look on his face—and the straining of his body against her pelvis—he wasn't any steadier than she was. Maybe she should push him over the edge and jump with him.

"Time," she repeated with a nod. She took a step back, then another, putting a few feet between them before sliding her hands beneath the fabric at her waist and slowly pushing the dress over her hips, giving a little shimmy to help it in its fall to the floor. Still wearing the killer heels, she stepped out of the pile of soft color, then turned in a slow circle. "What do you think?"

"Green is definitely your color." His voice was unsteady, and his gaze burned. So much heat radiated from him that she was surprised he didn't glow in the dark. She was just as surprised that she hadn't self-combusted.

He reached for her, but she backed away, bending to retrieve the dress, shaking it out, laying it on the couch. The kids might guess what she and Keegan had done, but no need to help them reach that conclusion.

Then she walked to the bed, folded back the covers, and lay down on her side, propped on one elbow, one leg stretched out straight, the other bent at the knee. "Time," she repeated. "Let's not waste any of it. Good candy's not the only thing meant to be savored."

* * *

Savor might be his new favorite word, Keegan thought some time later, once his heart rate had dropped below a hundred beats a second and his muscles had finally stopped twitching and his breaths were easier to come by. He'd savored every moment, every touch, every taste, every kiss, and by the time they'd finished, he was sure of one thing.

He owed Major Matheson a hell of a debt for bringing Therese and his kids into his life.

He'd disposed of the condom in the bathroom, then returned to the bed where she lay on her back, her long pale body gleaming in the pitiful illumination. He wanted to turn on every light in the room, to banish every shadow and see every inch of her, but when he'd reached for the bedside lamp, she'd paralyzed him with an intimate caress, and he'd forgotten everything but her.

The bedspread and blanket lay in a jumble on the floor, along with her bra, panties, those sexy shoes, and his clothes. He lay next to her, facing her, head on his hand, and studied her—hair tumbled across the pillow, flushed cheeks, moist lips—intently enough to make her laugh self-consciously. "What are you doing?"

"Looking. Just looking." He wanted to remember everything about this moment. The faint fragrance of her perfume. The exact taste of her mouth—rich chocolate, hazelnut, and wine. The sweet, lazy, well-pleasured look in her eyes. The earring dangling drunkenly to the side, catching in her hair. And the way he felt. The satisfaction. The still-there desire. The possessiveness. The sense of absolute rightness.

"What do you see?" Did she hear the wistful uncertainty in her voice?

"The beautiful woman who has been waiting a long time for me even if she didn't know it."

Her smile came slowly, the one that made her look like the most important woman ever in his life, and she raised her hand to his jaw, cupping it gently as she whispered, "I knew it somewhere."

She kissed him then, pushing him onto his back, rising up over him. Kissing was sweet and innocent and fun. It was serious fun when she settled over him, her legs flanking his thighs, her breasts rubbing against his chest, her hands sending tingles of electricity through him with every stroke. His body was quick to respond. Ten seconds into the kiss, he was hard again, as if he hadn't fiercely come less than ten minutes before.

He was damn near sizzling when she stretched away long enough to reach a condom on the nightstand, and he damn near came when she deliberately fumbled it into place. Only sheer determination held him together as she slid deeply, fully over him, and then the heat of her, the tightness of her, took what little control he had.

It was fast and hard and primal, and neither of them lasted more than moments, her cries mixed with the guttural groan that was all he could form. She collapsed against him, her skin as slick with sweat as his, her breathing as ragged. Her hair, damp and smelling of something sweet, drifted against his skin, silken and soft, losing its waves fast.

He liked the wild-abandon look about her and told her so two hours later when they finally, reluctantly left the bed and dressed.

"Wild abandon," she repeated, amusement dancing in her eyes. "I don't think anyone's ever called me wild before. Most people see"—she zipped her dress and gestured toward herself with a flourish—"a thirty-something mother, teacher, churchgoer, widow."

"That's okay. I'd rather they not see you this way." He nodded toward the bed as he finished buttoning his shirt, then lifted the covers from the floor. By the time he turned again, she was wiggling into her heels and combing her fingers through her hair. She picked up her purse, slung the strap over her shoulder, and faced him. "Well, do we look presentable enough for our kids?"

He slid his arms around her waist and pulled her near, nuzzling her throat. "Mariah's going to be asleep, Jacob wouldn't notice if we walked in wearing each other's clothes, and if Abby suspects anything, she'll just roll her eyes and go, 'Eww, that's disgusting.'"

Therese laughed, rested her forehead against his for a moment, then pulled back. "Let's face the lions."

The clock outside Tallgrass National Bank showed it was 10:37. Probably the earliest end to a date since he was fifteen, but Therese hadn't been comfortable about leaving the kids alone any later. Besides, there was always tomorrow... and the next day and the next ten thousand days.

The neighborhood was quiet when he turned onto Cheyenne Street. Since moving out of his mom's house, Keegan had always lived in apartment complexes or barracks, where Saturday nights were rarely quiet. A peaceful family neighborhood was something he could get used to.

At the Matheson house, lights shone through the living room windows and from one bedroom upstairs. The television was on when they went inside, and Abby was curled at the end of the sofa, her head pillowed on the arm, while Mariah occupied the other two-thirds, snoring softly.

Looking up, Abby muted the television and straightened as they came into the room. "Wow. Four and a half hours. That's a long time for dinner."

Keegan was amused to see a faint blush color Therese's cheeks, which she tried to hide by sitting in an armchair and bending to remove her shoes. "We took a walk, and we had dinner on the porch at Luca's."

Abby rolled her eyes. "It's a restaurant. The idea is to eat and leave, not take up residence." To Keegan, she added, "She and her margarita friends think one meal makes the table theirs for the rest of the night."

"Well, good food and good company are meant to be savored." He restrained a grin and went on to cover the sound of Therese's choking cough. "Did Mariah behave?"

"Better for me than she does for you."

"She likes you more than she does me."

Something flitted through Abby's eyes—surprise, maybe a little pleasure at the thought. Gazing at her, he saw that Therese had been right earlier: the girl needed affection. She tried hard to act like she didn't care about anything, but she was thirteen. Caring too much defined thirteen-year-old girls. So did acting out.

She shrugged, and the emotion, whatever it was, disappeared. "She ate two pieces of pizza, a bunch of grapes, some yogurt, and four cookies." A shudder rocketed through her. "Then, because she was wearing pizza, yogurt, and chocolate chips, I gave her a bath, and she fell asleep while her hair was still damp. That means you'll have to wet it in the morning to make it behave. Not wash it. Just spray it a bit."

He knew that. He hadn't worn a high-and-tight forever. But since so many other things about Mariah were a mystery, he appreciated her telling him. Still, he couldn't resist teasing her a bit. "Will the sprayer in the kitchen sink work?"

And there were the eye roll and the heaving sigh. "I figured you'd be clueless, so I put a spray bottle in her bag. What was your mother thinking? How could she trust you all on your own with a little girl?"

"Hey, I'm not totally clueless," he said as she passed on her way out.

She turned back in the doorway, one hand on her hip, one brow arched. "You let her fall in the toilet and puke in the bathtub."

From behind him came Therese's soft voice. "She's got you there, Keegan."

"Yeah, well, that first morning with her wasn't my best."

"Neither was the night before," Abby added helpfully.

He rubbed his jaw as they regarded him with similar expressions of amusement mixed with pity. "Yeah," he said again. Even if he'd disagreed with them, he knew better than to argue with two females. "But I'm learning. Thanks, Abby."

Once more, surprise flashed across her face. She moved as if to turn away, so he spoke again quickly. "You're a sweetheart."

This time she went still. Her mouth worked, but nothing came out. Then abruptly she turned and all but ran up the stairs. Seconds later came the click, not a slam, of her bedroom door.

Therese swore quietly and fluidly, words he hadn't heard her say before. He stared at the stairs a moment longer, then went to sit on the footstool that matched her chair. "Hey. You kiss me with that mouth."

Her hands covered her face. "No matter how much she tests me, I'm the grown-up here. I should have managed better. This is my failure."

He pried one hand away, then the other. "It's not a failure, Therese. She's old enough to know that behaviors have consequence. And you both went through some tough times. Neither of you was quite ready to deal with each other." And most importantly . . . "It's nothing that can't be undone. My mom has spent her entire life mothering kids, and she honestly believes there isn't any problem that can't be solved with enough love and affection and respect."

And the respect went both ways. Therese deserved it for no other reason than taking in and keeping Abby, but Abby deserved it, too. Just as it was tough for Therese to keep trying when all she got for her efforts was rejection, it was hard for Abby to try at all when she knew the only person who would have her around did it out of obligation and responsibility and not because she actually wanted her.

Therese's fingers curled tightly around his. "Your mom's a good woman, and she's raised a good son."

"She would be the first to agree with you." He stood and used his grip to pull her to her feet. "I'd better take the cookie monster and go." But he didn't let go of her right away. Without the heels, her head came about to his shoulder, and when he pulled her up snug against him, they touched in different places than he'd become accustomed to. Exploring those differences seemed a great way to spend an hour or two, but not with Mariah snoozing a few feet away.

"Don't beat yourself up about Abby. Give both you and her another chance." He meant the words seriously, for her sake, for Abby's sake, but there was also something selfish underlying them. It was unfair for Mariah to meet her half sister, then lose her if Abby went to live elsewhere.

He kissed Therese, intending a quick, good-night-her-kids-were-upstairs kiss, but instantly his blood turned hot, and want and bone-deep need shot through him. If it hadn't been for a thump somewhere above them, there was no telling where they would have stopped.

Though he would draw a line at sneaking into and out of her bedroom.

When he scooped up Mariah, her body was warm and limp, her hair flat on one side, the curls wiry and kinked on the other. She opened her eyes only for a moment, smiled sweetly at him, then snuggled close. Curling her hand around his shirt between two buttons, she sighed contentedly, and emotion swelled until he couldn't breathe, couldn't swallow.

"You're lucky," Therese murmured. "Not many men can pinpoint the exact moment they fell in love with their child."

His glance was dazed, and his mouth opened to automatically protest, but it closed again. It was a major concept, something he'd been determined to avoid from the moment he'd gotten custody of Mariah. Hell, he'd avoided anything to do with her for a month because he didn't want to care about her. He didn't want to put himself on the hook for raising another man's kid. He didn't want to risk getting involved in case Sabrina changed her mind and came back to reclaim her.

But he was on the hook and he was involved and Sabrina coming back didn't automatically mean he'd lose her. Not if he'd made a good home for her, provided her with family who loved her, given her stability.

Not if he loved her, too.

Therese was smiling at him, those dark eyes of hers smug, and he couldn't think of anything to say. No admission, no denial, no dancing around the facts. He needed a little time to process things. He'd come to Tallgrass to get Mariah out of his life and into the family where she belonged. Instead, he'd found a family where they both belonged.

This trip wasn't turning out at all the way he'd planned.

He was incredibly lucky for that.

* * *

When Therese arrived at Three Amigos Tuesday evening, Carly had already staked out a seat at the patio tables shoved together and sat with a margarita that hadn't been touched and a travel magazine open in front of her.

"Ooh, honeymoon planning." Therese slid into the chair beside her.

A full, lovely, in-love smile bloomed across Carly's face. "A trip to celebrate our wedding, since we jumped ahead to the honeymoon part about an hour after the proposal."

"What's in the running?" Therese knew Carly loved the beach, but how comfortable would Dane, still adjusting to the fact that his leg was gone, feel about a tropical destination?

"No cruise. That was what Jeff and I did. We're actually thinking about Italy. He was stationed there for a while, and he says I'd love it."

"What's not to love? The food, the wine, the history, the gorgeous men. Oh, wait, you're taking your own gorgeous man with you."

"It sounds incredible, doesn't it? Though, frankly, I'd be happy renting a cabin at the lake. I'm getting Dane. Everything else is just icing on the wedding cake." Carly closed the magazine, sat back, and narrowed her gaze. "You look different. I've always thought you seemed serene, even when you were simmering inside, but now you look really serene, both inside and out."

Therese blushed, and Carly's mouth and eyes both rounded. Even her voice took on a rounded tone. "Have you been getting down and dirty with Keegan?"

Pleasure spread through Therese, the way it had for three days now, sweet and warm, though sometimes it had a needy edge that made her feel desirable and feminine and alive again. "We're doing our best. Do you know how hard it is to find privacy with three kids, one of whom can't be left alone for five minutes?" Though they'd managed a few hours alone on Sunday afternoon while the kids went to a movie. And another dinner out Monday evening— fast food, then a few hours in bed—while Abby and Jacob watched Mariah.

"Hey, Dane and I are always available to babysit. Since we threw away the condoms the first night, it'd be practice for us."

Momentarily distracted, Therese blinked. "You're going to get pregnant right away?"

"We're doing our part. Now, if God smiles on us…" Carly's smile faded, her expression turning serious in a blink. "I waited with Jeff—for me to finish school, for us to settle into marriage, for his deployments to slack off. You waited with Paul while his kids adjusted to being here, while he was gone to Iraq and then to Afghanistan. Look where waiting got us.

"Every day with Dane is a gift, and every day with our kids will be, too. Oh, sure, I'll be threatening to pack them off to Aunt Therese's at least once a week, but…I'll never get to hold Jeff's babies, Therese. I damn well don't intend to miss out on holding Dane's."

Therese gazed at the margarita, the heavy glass bearing a faint tinge of green, the drink itself vivid blue tonight. She'd missed the baby parts, she'd told Keegan with more than a little wistfulness. She had always thought she and Paul had plenty of time. When she'd kissed him good-bye the day of his departure for Afghanistan, she'd never dreamed it was already too late for her to have his baby.

She'd never dreamed he would die.

But she still had the chance to hold his babies. Maybe Abby and Jacob had long outgrown the cuddly phase, but they were Paul's children, and even grown kids needed a cuddle now and then. And they'd both come around a little since their trip to visit Catherine. Jacob spoke more often than he grunted. Abby's tantrums were smaller, her anger less palpable. She was really good with Mariah, and she'd lost most of her disdain for Keegan and even some of it for Therese. It might be temporary, but Therese would take what she could get.

Just like this thing with Keegan might be temporary.

That possibility squeezed around her heart, making her grateful for new arrivals to distract her. Lucy and Marti sat across from them, and a moment later Ilena joined them. "Okay, guys, I officially cannot see my feet anymore."

"Another couple pounds, and your tiny little feet will be officially unable to support you," Marti teased.

Lucy made a face. "At least she has an excuse and it's temporary. Another couple pounds, and I will be officially as big as a house." She helped herself to a chip with a big scoop of salsa.

"Oh, honey, you will not," Ilena chastised her. "You're beautiful, Lucy. Men like curves, you know."

"Dane likes curves," Carly confirmed, and Therese and Marti both nodded. Of their close-knit group's spouses, Fia's husband, Scott, had had a serious appreciation for her muscles, but all the rest of them were softer, rounder, curvier, and their husbands had adored them.

Keegan adored her.

Lucy smiled, but Therese wasn't convinced their assurances had lightened her mood. She still seemed down when Jessy and Fia arrived, followed by a few of the other semi-regulars.

They had their usual fun, talking and teasing, I-hate-my-job stories from Jessy and tales from Marti about her thrice-married mother's latest engagement. Lucy described her new oven with the same loving detail another woman might have given a designer outfit, and everyone had advice to offer Carly about her honeymoon.

Therese always enjoyed their evenings, but tonight it was even more of a pleasure. These women were her best friends, her support, her sisters in sorrow but also in joy. She loved them.

She loved a lot of people and had the capacity to love more, whether they wanted her to or not.

Whether they loved her back or not.

*   *   *

When the party broke up and she'd said her good-byes, she went home to a quiet house. Jacob was helping himself to a snack while he did homework with books and papers spread across the island. "Everything okay?" she asked as she took a bottle of water from the refrigerator.

"Yeah." He set his plate next to his books, then met her gaze. "Real quiet without the cookie monster around. How is it little girls can make so much noise?"

"Little boys aren't known for their soft ways, either."

"Huh." He took a bite of sandwich and flipped open a book. His hair fell over his forehead, the same shade of brown as his dad's, though she'd never seen Paul's hair so shaggy. He'd been spit-and-polish when they met and never relaxed his standards, shaving on his days off and as squared-away in jeans and a T-shirt as he was in uniform.

Still, there was so much of him in Jacob. The eyes, the coloring, the gestures, the focus. He was his father's son.

"What?"

Even his voice sounded like Paul's. Realizing she'd been staring, she said, "Nothing," then opened the fridge again, grabbed two small bunches of grapes, and headed toward the hall. She took the long way around, though, circling the island, passing behind him, and patting his arm on the way.

Not even so much as a single muscle twitched away from the contact. It was a marvel.

Before she could reconsider her actions, she climbed the stairs and stopped outside Abby's room, drew a breath, then knocked. The response—a flat *What?*—was neither an invitation nor encouragement, but Therese opened the door anyway and went inside. "Everything go okay tonight?"

Sprawled on her bed with a textbook open and her cell phone beside her so she could respond instantly to her next text message, Abby looked surprised. Surely this wasn't the first time Therese had asked about their evening. She hadn't missed a Tuesday night at Three Amigos in more than a year. She distinctly remembered, in the beginning, questioning the kids when she got home.

But she couldn't remember doing it in a long time since then. *My failure.*

"Fine," Abby said at last. "We ate dinner, watched TV, and now we're finishing our homework. Why?"

"Just curious." Therese offered her a handful of grapes. When Abby sat up, cross-legged, Therese sat at the foot of her bed. "Jacob said it was awfully quiet around here without Mariah."

An unexpected smile lighted Abby's face. She looked a lot like her dad, too, but what was entirely masculine on him and Jacob was delicately beautiful on her. Perfect bone structure, silky hair, huge eyes.

"She's so sweet, but she's awful needy. 'Abby, I sit with you. Abby, read to me. Abby, play with me. Abby, I go potty.' "

"Well, she is only two. Besides, you've heard her scream. The needy adoration is a big improvement, isn't it?"

"I guess." She popped a grape into her mouth, concentrated on chewing it, then lowered her gaze to her cell as if willing it to ring or vibrate and demand her attention. When that didn't happen, she fingered the grapes uneasily, finally plucking one, then turning it over and over instead of eating it. "Why do you think her mom just left her like that? Did she think Mariah was that much trouble? Didn't she love her? Moms are supposed to love their kids."

The grape Therese had just swallowed swelled to the size of a golf ball on its way down, leaving an ache from her throat all the way to the pit of her stomach. She'd suspected from the start that, Mariah's cuddliness and obvious affection aside, Abby related to the girl on a more basic level: they'd both been abandoned by their mothers. But Therese hadn't thought to use that as a conversation starter. *Failure.*

"Your mom loves you and Jacob," she said gently, and the girl's response was immediate.

"I know that." Her tone was sharp, snotty. "Mom had reasons for sending us here. She needed time for herself.

The divorce changed things for her, and she had to figure out who she was once she was no longer Daddy's wife."

She parroted the words as if she wanted very much to believe them. The truth was simpler, and she and Jacob both knew it. It was Catherine's problem, her flaw, and it had nothing to do with either of them. But all the reasons in the world couldn't lessen the impact that their mother had no longer wanted the everyday bother of being their mother.

"I assume Mariah's mother had reasons for what she did, too. Maybe Sabrina did the best she could but knew it wasn't enough. Maybe leaving her with Keegan was best for Mariah. Maybe she knew he and his mother would give Mariah the kind of family she deserved."

Shoving her book aside, Abby drew her knees to her chest and hugged them. "But she's just a little girl, and her mom took her to the babysitter like every other day and never came back. She never said good-bye. How could she walk away from her own kid like that?"

There was such bewilderment in her voice, on her face, that Therese's heart hurt with the desire to hold her and soothe it away. She even reached out, but caught herself before the movement was noticeable. Keegan was right. She'd been rejected so many times that it was hard to offer comfort. Baby steps. Even having this conversation was a big step. Physical contact could come later.

"The sad truth, Abby, is that some people aren't cut out to be parents."

"Yeah, well, the time to learn that is before you have kids," Abby retorted, tossing her head in that oh-so-familiar defiance. The momentary flare faded, though, and she grudgingly added, "You said so. I heard you."

Therese's smile was tiny and tremulous. "I didn't know you ever listened to anything I said."

"Yeah. Well. I do. Sometimes. Especially if you're talking to Carly and I'm not supposed to hear." She rubbed her nose with one hand, then clasped her fingers together again. "If Mariah's mom doesn't come back, when she's grown, she won't even remember her. She'll be a total stranger."

That was sad, Therese acknowledged, but Mariah would be so well-loved that she wouldn't miss a stranger she couldn't remember. Giving birth didn't make a woman a good mother, just as a good mother didn't have to give birth to love a child.

Therese had always wanted to be a good mother, and she did feel something for Abby and Jacob, something far beyond obligation, beyond the fact that Paul's blood ran through their veins. Something that had very nearly gotten lost in the anxiety, hostility, and resentment they'd lived with so long.

"But when you think about it, not remembering the woman who dumped you probably isn't a bad thing," Abby commented. Balancing her feet on her heels, she wiggled her toes, then studied the pedicure she'd gotten while with Catherine. Faux gems studded two toes on each foot, with a spot of glue showing where another had fallen off.

Staring as if the pedicure were the most fascinating thing in the world, she finally spoke, her voice little more than a mumble. "She never called me back."

Therese swallowed hard. No need to ask who she was referring to. Only the lack of calls from one person could make her so glum.

"We've been back a week and a half, and I called her

eleven times and texted her twenty-three times. I told her we got back okay. I asked her to send my clothes to me if she still had them. I told her all the girls at school were jealous of my hair and my tan." Her voice lowered even more. "I told her I wanted to come back and live with her. And she never answered. Not even to say no."

"I'm sorry, Abby. I wish…" Tears clogged Therese's throat and dimmed her vision. She didn't need to see, though, to reach out and squeeze both of her stepdaughter's feet.

Abby went very still, barely breathing, and so did Therese. She steeled herself for yet another rejection, for a sharp voice, a snide order not to touch her, but it didn't come. In fact, after a moment, Abby sighed heavily. "A foot rub. After five days of wearing those heels, I still need one. I'm never wearing high heels again."

The fervent words startled a laugh from Therese, then she began a real massage of Abby's slender feet. "Trust me, you'll wear them again. You'll be praying for the moment when you can take them off, but you'll wear them because they make your legs look so—"

"Freaking sexy. That's what Mom said."

Therese shuddered at the notion that Catherine had wanted her barely teenaged daughter to look sexy. "I wouldn't have said 'freaking.'"

"You wouldn't have said 'sexy,' either. Not to me. Not for at least ten more years."

"You're right." She gave Abby's feet one last squeeze, then stood. "Get back to your homework, then get ready for bed. I'll be doing the same."

She was walking through the doorway when Abby softly spoke. "Good night, Therese."

"Good night." Therese pulled the door shut, then leaned against it. That was the first time Abby had ever told her good night. In the beginning, Paul had done the bed-checks, tucked the blankets, and gotten the kisses. After he'd deployed, both kids had made it clear they didn't need good nights from anyone else.

How could two little words mean so much?

Chapter 14

Ercella didn't believe in sitting idle, and Keegan was his mother's son. He had nearly two months' leave on the books because he'd taken only enough over the years to keep from losing accumulated days. A few days to take his mom to Nashville for her birthday, a few days in Shreveport at Christmas with his sisters' families, long weekend trips to New Orleans or the nearest beach with Sabrina— those were the extent of his times off. This was the longest stretch he'd gone without working in his life, and he missed it.

And yet he'd called his first sergeant and asked to extend his leave by another week. If his request wasn't approved...well, the drive from Leesville to Tallgrass wasn't so bad, and flights between Alexandria and Tulsa weren't too expensive. He'd already checked. And he had only seven months left on this enlistment. He could tolerate anything for seven months.

It was Wednesday afternoon, and they were at Tallgrass's biggest nursery. Therese liked flowers but hadn't persuaded herself to plant any yet, and he needed some activity that resembled work, so he'd decided to help out. He was buying just enough flowers to fill a couple of large pots on the patio. If she was okay with that, he'd move on to the beds. If she wasn't... well, what woman didn't welcome men bearing flowers?

Forced out of the shopping cart by the flats of flowers he'd picked, Mariah toddled to a wooden stand filled with four-inch pots, picked one up in her pudgy hands, and held it for inspection. "For Celly."

He crouched beside her. "Celly would like that." He wasn't sure of the variety, but the pale purplish shade was his mother's favorite. It was a sharp contrast to the bold colors he'd selected—hot orange, red, deep pink, and purple. Therese wasn't a pale person. "Let's put it in the cart." And hope they could keep it alive long enough to get it back to Louisiana.

"Celly loves labender." Mariah watched him place it on the flat shelf of the cart, then stopped still, cocking her head, listening intently for a moment before rocketing off along the aisles. Because he was in no hurry—Therese wouldn't be home from school for an hour—Keegan followed her past displays of succulents and shade plants to a small area shielded by trellises covered with flowering vines. The centerpiece was a rock fountain, easily seven feet high, water splashing over large stones into a pool below.

While she knelt on the ground to trail her hand in the water, Keegan sat on one of the three benches that flanked the area. The place smelled sweet, even for a nursery, and the repetitive splashing was calming. No wonder Therese's friend wanted a fountain in her yard.

Mariah fished a leaf from the water and brought it to him. "Hey, Celly's boy, look what I found."

Though no one was around to hear, Keegan winced. It was so wrong that she had nothing else to call him—and past time to take care of that. "It's a maple leaf," he said. "It came from that tree over there." He pointed, and she looked and nodded, though odds were low she'd recognized it in the small forest of trees. "Come up here, Mariah. We need to talk."

He started to lift her, but she shrugged away. "I climb my own self." She crawled onto the bench, then sat beside him, legs dangling. Her toenails were polished purple, courtesy of Abby Monday night, and a good match to the clear purple sandals she wore.

How to start? Simply.

"You know what a daddy is, Mariah?"

She bobbed her head. A week ago he would have taken her at her word, but he'd learned a little since then. "Can you tell me?"

After thinking it over, she swiped a strand of curls from her face. "I don't know."

"Daddy is another name for father. Do you know what that means?"

She shook her head.

He could hear his mother's voice in his head. *You're making it too complicated. She's not even three yet.* "You want a name to call me instead of Celly's boy?" As she nodded, he took a deep breath, part of him not at all sure this was a good idea, but the rest of him knew it was too late. If Sabrina returned, if he lost Mariah, what she called him wouldn't make a difference in the way he felt. "Call me Daddy."

She swung her feet as if pondering the words, then with a shrug, said, "Okay. Can I go to the water again?"

Disappointment welled in him. "You want to try it? Daddy?"

After lolling her head to one side for a moment, she shook it, bouncing her curls. "I wanna find another leaf."

"Okay, go on." As she went to lean on the rock ledge that supported the pool, he ruefully shook his head. It wasn't a big moment for her. Daddy was just a name to her, like Fluffy, Muffy, and Tuffy in one of the books Ercella had sent with her. The concept behind it, the significance, was way outside her grasp.

But not his. And she would learn in time.

Mariah had rescued seven leaves from the water by the time he called her away. She insisted on helping him push the cart to the checkout, more of a hindrance as he had to watch that he didn't run into her, then he buckled her into the booster seat before loading the car.

"Now we're gonna see Abby," she announced when he started the engine.

"We are. You like Abby and Jacob and Therese?" In the rearview mirror he saw her head bob.

A few blocks had passed in silence when she unexpectedly asked, "You like Abby and Jacob and Trace?"

He grinned. "I do."

"I do, too. And Celly. And basketti and meatballs. I *love* basketti and meatballs. Can we have it?"

"We'll have to see." He wasn't sure he could bear another night at Luca's unless they managed a way to ditch the kids afterward. Pasta, wine, and chocolate were going to be major turn-ons for him for a long time. Did that make him weird or what?

Therese's minivan was parked in the driveway, and Jacob was walking across the yard from the school bus stopped one house down. When Keegan pulled into the driveway, the kid tugged out his earbuds, letting them dangle around his neck, and lifted one hand in a wave. Dropping his backpack at the steps, he came to the car and opened the rear passenger door to unbuckle Mariah. "Hey, Keegan. Hey, cookie monster."

"We got flowers!"

"Cool. Therese likes flowers. You want to ride or help carry?"

"Ride." She wrapped her arms around his neck, then, when he straightened, wiggled around until she was on his back. She made the transfer as if she'd done it a dozen times before. Considering the amount of time she'd spent with him and Abby, maybe she had.

"Hold on." He bent, grabbed a large bag of potting soil from the floorboard with one hand, then headed for the gate that led to the backyard.

Keegan watched a moment, wishing he'd been taking pictures the past week. It was an important thing, getting to know her brother and sister, even if none of them ever knew their relationship. The best he could do was get some shots later with his cell phone, something simple enough, common enough, that neither the subjects nor Therese would wonder why he was photographing them.

As he carried three large pots with a flat of flowers balanced on top onto the patio, the back door opened and Therese stepped out. She always greeted him with a smile, but this time it grew a little brighter when she saw what he had. "I adore a man who brings flowers."

"Hey, Trace!" Letting go of Jacob's neck, Mariah leaned far to the side to swing into Therese's arms, giving her a kiss once she was settled. "I brung flowers, too."

"Hi, sweetie. I adore little girls with flowers, too. And big guys with potting soil."

She smoothed Jacob's hair where Mariah had messed it up, the movement not quite natural. Going still, Keegan watched the boy for a reaction, but he didn't give one. If he welcomed the touch, didn't want it, or even noticed, it didn't show on his face. He just shrugged his shoulders as if relaxing them and asked, "Is there more?"

"A couple of flats, more soil, and a bag of mulch in the trunk."

"You get the flowers," Jacob said as they headed back to the car. "I only do heavy lifting."

"The only jobs I've ever had have required occasionally carrying people who weigh twice what you do. I'm happy to take the flowers."

The boy gave him an appraising glance. "You're a medic, right? What else?"

"I was a firefighter before I joined the Army."

"Huh. A medic's kind of like a doctor, isn't it?"

"Sometimes better than."

"Medics and doctors couldn't save my dad."

Though his tone was matter-of-fact, Keegan's gut knotted. Jacob rarely brought up his father's death with Therese. Maybe he thought it would be too hard for her to discuss; maybe he felt, as the man in the family, he didn't have the right to burden anyone else or there just wasn't anyone to listen. In his years as a paramedic, then a medic, Keegan had learned there were times when all he could do was listen.

"Yeah, I know," he said quietly. "But they did their best, Jacob. It's just sometimes your best isn't good enough."

They stopped at the back of the car, Jacob staring hard across the street, his cheeks pink, his eyes narrowed. "My dad always said your best was all anyone could ask. If it's not good enough, why bother?"

"Because that's what we do. We try. We try really hard. And usually it *is* enough. I'm sorry it wasn't for your dad."

After staring a moment longer, Jacob turned and met his gaze head-on. "Did anyone you took care of ever die? Even though you tried really hard?"

Keegan swallowed. "Yeah. I will always remember every one of them and wish it could have been different. But I also remember the ones I did help, the lives we did save, the ones who survived to come home to their families because of us."

"I wish my dad had been one of them." Jacob's whisper was almost lost in the rumble of another school bus stopping in the middle of the street.

"So do I, buddy." And he meant it. But what a difference it would have made in his life. Therese would still have been happily married, grateful to have her husband back from war whole and healthy. Jacob and Abby would have been happier, too, better adjusted, feeling less abandoned. They would have been a perfect little family, Therese would have dealt with Paul's infidelity, and they would have welcomed Mariah into their lives.

And Keegan never would have known what he'd missed.

Abby climbed off the bus, the skirt of her school uniform already rolled a time or two at the waist to shorten it, her head cocked to the side while she listened to the tall, slender girl with her. They talked a moment, then the other girl headed down the street while Abby turned her attention to Jacob and Keegan. Her gaze slid to the open trunk, the soil her brother was hefting onto his shoulder, and the flowers, and she shook her head. "I hope you're not expecting me to help with that because I'm telling you now, I don't do manual labor."

"No one's expecting you to do anything, Princess Whine," Jacob retorted, then snorted at his own words, sounding very much like a pig. "Princess Swine. Get it?"

Abby drew herself up to every inch of her not-so-impressive height and gave her brother a steely gaze. "You are such a child."

"Jerk-face."

"Moron." Nose in air, she passed the car and headed for the steps, where she gave Jacob's backpack a not-so-delicate nudge off the sidewalk.

Keegan set the flowers on the ground, lifted the mulch from the trunk, then closed it. The lock beeped automatically. "She's not so bad for a big sister, is she?"

"Nah. Kinda like a heart attack's not so bad if the alternative is cancer."

They delivered the bags to the patio, then returned for the flowers. When they got back, Therese was kneeling beside the pots, using a screwdriver to enlarge the drainage holes. Abby had already changed into shorts and a T-shirt, gotten grapes and a can of pop from the refrigerator, and was sharing one of the lawn chairs dragged into the late-afternoon sun with Mariah. Both their heads were tilted back, eyes closed, arms and legs stretched out to gain maximum exposure.

Jacob gave another coarse pig snort, which Abby pretended not to hear, then grinned. "I'm gonna change, then get something to eat. Want something?"

"Nah," Keegan said. "I'll wait until dinner."

"He'd be in heaven on a cruise," Therese commented as the door closed. "He'd be present for every seating of every meal, then would hang out by the buffet tables the rest of the day."

"He's a human garbage disposal," Abby said archly. "And if he calls me Princess Swine again, I'm going to unleash my minions in his room. You my minion, Riah?"

"Uh-huh. What's a meanion?"

Tuning out Abby's answer, Keegan hunkered down beside Therese, pulled out a pocketknife, and slit open the first bag of soil, then the mulch. "So . . . the colors work for you?"

"They're gorgeous. Exactly what I would have chosen." Her smile was sweet and a little sly. "My father told me to beware of men bearing gifts."

"Isn't that supposed to be Trojans?"

"It's supposed to be Greeks. The Trojans were the ones taken in by the gift." Her forehead wrinkled for a moment in thought, then she said, a little softer so the girls couldn't hear, "I'm positive he would tell me to beware of men bearing Trojans."

Her reference to condoms surprised a laugh from him. "These days you have to be more wary of men who don't have them. All kinds of things can go wrong."

"Or maybe right." She sighed as her gaze flitted to Mariah. Having a little kid around had reawakened her maternal instincts. Having *her* around had awakened his version of the same.

"I told Mariah to call me Daddy," he admitted as she spread a layer of mulch in the bottoms of the pots. "She was, like, yeah, whatever, can I go play in the fountain?"

"Disappointed?"

He shrugged.

"She'll do it. And you won't regret it."

"Promise? Because I see a lot of years before us of butting heads, slamming doors, temper tantrums, and her saying *no no no, I do my own self.*"

"Now it's dressing and feeding herself. In two years it'll be school, and in ten years it'll be boys."

"Oh, no. Not before she's twenty."

Not bothering with gloves—Ercella said they took the pleasure from digging in dirt—he and Therese scooped handfuls of potting soil into the first pot. "Poor guy. So naïve. I'd almost feel sorry for you if I didn't envy you."

Help me raise her. Marry me, make a family with me, let me help you with Abby and Jacob, and you help me with Mariah. The words almost slipped out, though any rational person would say it was way too soon to be so damned serious.

But if there was one thing Logans didn't worry about, it was being rational, especially when it came to their love lives. *Things happen when they happen.* That was their family motto. That was why Ercella had four more kids with his father after it became obvious Max wasn't father material. Why Martha and Daisy had married right out of high school. Why Ford had moved to Arizona to be with a woman he hadn't yet had a single date with.

Things happen when they happen.

And sometime in the last week and a half, he'd fallen in love with Therese Matheson.

* * *

Though Mariah had requested spaghetti for dinner, Therese offered a compromise with a ziti, mozzarella, and pepperoni casserole from the freezer, a salad, toasted Italian bread, and spread made from garlic cloves simmered in olive oil. It was Abby's favorite dinner, and one Jacob, aka the human disposal, liked as well. They ate in the kitchen, an extra chair squeezed into the table for four, and it was fun. Normal. The way a family dinner should be.

Not that they were technically a family, a snide voice inside reminded her. Someday they might be.

Or maybe not.

From her chair, Therese could see the three pots, planted with bright flowers, lining the edge of the patio, and the sight made her smile. Who else would have thought to bring her flowers, everything needed to plant them, and to help with the planting? They meant more to her than any other gift Keegan could have offered. They touched her heart and in a good way, all happiness, no sorrow.

When the doorbell rang, Jacob was already on his way to the island to refill his plate, so he said, "I'll get it," and headed that way. A moment later a soft female voice filtered down the hallway, not Carly's, not Nicole's, and a moment after that, he returned to the kitchen, his face set in a stark scowl. As he veered toward the table, second helping forgotten, Therese saw the woman, so petite his broad shoulders had hidden her from view, and her heart stopped.

"Baby!" Catherine exclaimed, opening both arms wide. "I've come to take you home!"

Abby's shriek split the air, and her chair tumbled back as she jumped to her feet and raced into her mother's arms.

Keegan caught the chair and set it down again, his gaze moving from the tearful reunion to Therese, then back again. She was too numb to move, too stunned to breathe.

Catherine wanted Abby back. Therese's prayers had been answered.

And all she could think was *No no no!*

"Oh, Mom, I've been hoping and hoping, but it's been so long and I thought— This is the best surprise ever! Ooh, it's so perfect!" Abby's voice broke, and she hid her face in her mother's shoulder.

Cold emptiness spread through Therese. She was aware of Jacob sliding his chair a little closer to hers, of Keegan reaching under the table to take her hand, but only in a distant way. She couldn't reach out to Jacob—who clearly wasn't the *baby* his mother had missed so much—or return the squeeze of Keegan's hand. She could hardly register the bewildered look Mariah wore, clearly aware of the sudden tension in the room. The girl slid out of her chair, knocking her cushions to the floor, and circled the table to Keegan, climbing into his lap, whispering, "Daddy."

See? she wanted to say. *I told you she'd call you Daddy.*

Too soon—for Abby's sake, at least—Catherine pushed her back, slid her arm around her shoulders, and beamed a smile at the rest of them. "Hello, Therese."

"Catherine."

Abby gestured. "That's Keegan and his daughter, Mariah, and this is my mom, Catherine Matheson." There was such pride in her voice, such joy in her smile. She looked like a little girl who'd never seen a holiday getting a lifetime of Christmases and birthdays all at once.

Catherine's interest in the Logans was somewhere between nil and none. Keegan was obviously a soldier, and she'd hated the Army, and she didn't even glance at Mariah. When she could ignore her own children for months at a time, why would she notice someone else's?

"I probably should have called," Catherine said, "but I really wanted to surprise Abs. So I took a few days off, packed my bags, and here I am."

"Sit down, Mom," Abby encouraged, taking the pillows Mariah had sat on to a counter stool and pushing Catherine toward the chair. "Are you hungry? We have pasta and salad and garlic bread."

"You know I don't eat pasta or bread. All those carbs. Besides, I had a late lunch."

All those carbs. Therese studied her as she primly sat in the chair and crossed her legs. They'd met face to face fewer than a dozen times in the years they'd known each other, usually for less than ten minutes. Still, the changes were striking. She was thin, with surgically enhanced boobs that had apparently been part of finding herself. Her dark hair was bleached to a silvery-white blond that didn't exist in nature, her brown eyes were now brilliant sapphire, and her forehead was so smooth that Therese would bet she couldn't show surprise if she wanted to, thanks to the miracle of Botox.

"So when do we leave?" Abby asked. "Have you already found a new place to live? Is it a house or another apartment? Do you know what school we'll be going to? Maybe I can meet some kids on Facebook who go there so I won't be totally new on my first day."

Catherine patted her leg. "We're going to stay in the apartment I have for now."

Abby's nose wrinkled. "But it's only two bedrooms. That means Jacob will have to sleep on the couch."

Jacob snorted, then went still as a look came over Catherine's face. Discomfort. Awkwardness. She tried to disguise it by smiling at her son, but it was so obviously phony that even Mariah could see through it.

"Well, baby, I thought... You know I love you, Jacob, but... right now it would just be you and me, Abs. Jacob's got his school and his sports and his friends, and..." Catherine shrugged helplessly.

Had Therese thought she'd turned cold before? Now she was absolutely icy inside. Catherine wanted only Abby, not Jacob. She'd already abandoned him once, and now she was rejecting him again, displaying such incredible self-ishness that Therese wanted to smack her. She wanted to throw her out of the house, to magically erase the last five minutes from everyone's memories.

"I've got school and friends, too," Abby said, sounding confused. "I'll go to a new school and make new friends. So will Jacob. Of course he's got to go with us. You can't— We can't—"

"That's okay," Jacob said flatly. "I didn't like California. I'd rather stay here." Scowling hard, he pushed out of his chair. "I've got homework to do." On the way from the room, he grabbed a handful of cookies from the platter on the island, then stalked off.

Therese's heart ached, but she couldn't move to go after him. She was barely managing to suck air into her lungs. Keegan gave her hand another squeeze. "We'll go up-stairs," he murmured. Grateful, she nodded, and he and Mariah left the kitchen. A moment later, his treads sounded softly on the stairs.

"Well, that wasn't the best way to break the news, was it?" Catherine brushed at her shoulder, surreptitiously checking for any stains Abby might have transferred in her hug—she couldn't fool a kindergarten teacher—then sighed, reminding Therese where Abby got her flair for drama. "But then, there's no best way to tell him he's got to stay here a while longer, is there?"

A lot of the thrill had gone from Abby's face. She'd dreamed about moving back with Catherine from the time she'd been sent away, but she'd always dreamed Jacob would be going with her. They were sister and brother, a team that mostly ignored or called each other names, but still a team. "I don't understand why he can't come, too."

Catherine's perfectly glossed lips curved into a perfectly phony smile. "It's not forever, baby. I just think you and I need some girl time. Remember how he spent spring break? Playing that stupid video game, grumbling along behind us while we shopped, not interested in anything we did except when he was going to eat again."

"Well, Mom, we didn't do anything any boy would have liked besides eat. It was all pretty much about you and me."

Catherine's smile somehow got more perfect. God help her, the woman didn't realize she'd just been subtly chastised by her daughter. "Exactly. So you and I will get our girl time out of the way, and soon we'll send for Jacob."

"Soon." Abby repeated the word quietly, as if she was trying to encourage herself to believe it. She must have done a decent job because the confusion gave way to sheer excitement again. "I'm so glad to see you, Mom, this is so cool! When will we be leaving for California?"

With a slender hand bearing more rings, possibly, than Therese owned, Catherine smoothed a strand of Abby's hair. "I'm not sure, Abs. There are a few things I need to settle with Therese first. But I'm staying in town. I've found a quaint little bed-and-breakfast that's almost like a real hotel, and I'd like for you to stay there with me."

"Wow! Can I, Therese?"

Tiny lines marred the corners of Catherine's mouth. "Of course you can, baby. I'm your mother."

Bitch. Traitorous, coldhearted, selfish, manipulative— Therese interrupted her thoughts and forced a smile for Abby, still looking at her expectantly. "Sure, you can. Just be sure you're not late for school in the morning."

Why was it an excited shriek was so much less painful to the ears than an infuriated one when the pitch was the same? Abby jumped from her chair, gave Catherine a hug, then raced toward the stairs. "You guys settle, and I'll get packed!"

The only thing to settle in the wake of her going was silence, cold and uncomfortable.

* * *

Jacob stood at the window, shoulders hunched, staring out. He'd been facedown on the bed when Keegan and Mariah came in, then had sat up rapidly, swiped his hand over his face, and gone to the window. They hadn't caught a glimpse of his face since then, and he'd said nothing beyond his initial *Go away* when they knocked.

No eleven-year-old boy liked an audience for his tears.

Keegan was sitting in a straight-backed desk chair, and Mariah stood between his knees, backed up close to him. He liked that he was her safe place in a moment of doubt and wished he could be the same for her brother.

"I remember one time when my dad left," he said at last. "He'd been living with us for about eight months, which was some kind of record with him. Long enough for me to get used to having him there. I was fifteen, and it was kind of a big time for me. School was letting out for the summer, I was getting this big award that was really a big deal, I was turning sixteen and getting my driver's license and starting my first job, all in a couple of days. My mom had a big party planned with the entire family, even the second cousins of second cousins we hardly knew."

Jacob was so still it was impossible to tell if he was listening or practicing his talent for tuning people out. Too bad he couldn't tune out his disaster of a mother.

"I got home from school the day before the party, and Dad was packing his bags. I couldn't believe he was leaving like that, sneaking out before Mom got home from work, skipping out on my birthday. He shrugged and said, 'I don't question the itch. When it's time to go, I go.' The itch was what he called his desire to move on to another place. He didn't say congratulations or happy birthday. He didn't even say good-bye. He just finished packing and walked out. We didn't see him again for four years."

A long heavy moment passed before Jacob asked, "Do you hate him?"

"No. But for a long time I wouldn't have pissed on him if he was on fire."

His response choked a laugh from Jacob. He sniffled loudly, then wiped his nose again as he sprawled onto the bed. "The stupid thing is, I don't even want to live in California. It was boring, and my friends and my coaches are here, and—and Therese would be all alone if Abby and I both left. It's just…"

It would warm Therese's breaking heart to know that, even when he was hurting, Jacob was thinking of her.

She'd felt hopeless for so long, but clearly she was doing something right.

Throwing Catherine out would be the right thing, too, but he hadn't heard the bounce of a plastic-surgery-enhanced body hitting the front sidewalk yet.

But right now he had to focus on Jacob. "It's hard when you're not invited even when you don't want to go."

"Yeah."

"Your mom didn't mean to hurt you. She just wasn't thinking."

"Oh, she was thinking. She was thinking of herself and her BFF Abby. The whole time we were there, she acted like she was her sister instead of her mom. It was like I wasn't even there." Silence. "My dad said she had issues."

Mother issues, responsibility issues, self-esteem issues. And being Abs's new best friend wasn't going to help. If Abby was gorgeous at thirteen, she was going to be incredible at eighteen and amazing at twenty-five, while Catherine was going to continue to age. Now she could take pride in a beautiful daughter, but in a few years, she wouldn't appreciate finding herself in Abby's shadow.

"Abby always wanted Dad and Mom to get back together, even after he married Therese. But I didn't. All they did was fight and slam doors and not speak to each other. He was a lot happier with Therese."

And yet he'd still been unfaithful to her. A drunken mistake? A lapse in judgment? Maybe. Not that there was enough booze in the world to make Keegan turn to another woman if Therese were waiting at home for him.

Though without that infidelity, Mariah wouldn't be here, resting her elbows on Keegan's legs, swaying side to side. Every cloud had its silver lining, Granny Dupree used to say.

In this case, Mariah was his.

* * *

"Could I trouble you for a cup of coffee? I've been to four places since getting into town, and not one of them makes a decent cup."

Mouth pressed in a line, Therese left the table and went to the coffeemaker. As soon as the brew was started, she began clearing dishes from the table. When she set the second stack down so hard on the counter that they should have broken, she knotted her fingers and turned to face Catherine. "You should have called me instead of just coming here."

Catherine moved from the chair to a stool at the island. "She's my daughter."

"I have legal custody." *Remember? Because you didn't want them anymore.*

Her shrug was elegant, her bleached hair rippling in waves around her shoulders. "She doesn't want to live with you. And a girl belongs with her mother."

Especially a young one. Especially one who'd lost her father. But *that* girl required effort, work, patience, dealing with. A new haircut, a manicure, or new clothes weren't going to ease that trauma. "What about a boy? Doesn't he belong with his mother, too?"

"Jacob's doing fine here." Catherine's tone was so dismissive that Therese's fingers curled tighter. If only it was her throat they were gripping.

Therese forced a deep breath, then another. It was quiet

upstairs. Keegan was taking care of Jacob, and Abby was no doubt on the phone with Nicole, telling her about this fabulous turn of events. She was so excited. She must be feeling as if every dream she ever wanted had come true.

And wasn't this what Therese had wanted, too? Hadn't she prayed for Catherine to step up? Hadn't she been willing to keep Jacob if only she could send Abby elsewhere? Was she no better than Catherine?

She had prayed...but she wasn't sure...she didn't think...

God, what do I do now? Is this Your will? Is this best for Abby? Will Catherine be any sort of mother to her, or is she looking for someone to adore her, someone she can shape in her silicone image?

"I talked to a lawyer," Catherine said. "All you have to do is sign a few papers, and Abby and I will head back to California. Though...there is one other thing."

The hairs on Therese's nape stood on end, and her stomach clenched. Catherine already assumed she could just swoop in and take back her daughter without any problem. What else could she possibly want?

The woman rested her hands on the countertop, gold and diamonds catching the light from above, and tapped her bloodred fake nails. "Raising a teenager isn't cheap, and it's different in California. Abby will be adapting to a more sophisticated lifestyle. She'll need things."

Therese stared. Dimly she registered that her mouth was open, but she couldn't bypass the shock to give her brain the command to close it. Catherine was asking for *money*? She'd finally decided to live up to her responsibilities as a mother, but she wanted Therese to pay her for it? Oh, no. Oh, hell, no.

"It's only fair," Catherine said defensively. "Paul's life insurance was meant to provide for the three of you. If I'm taking care of Abby, then I deserve a third of the money."

"Fair?" The word squeaked out, barely able to form since Therese's chest was so tight she couldn't get a breath in. "Deserve?"

Steps sounded on the stairs, and Catherine darted a look that way, then slid to her feet. Quickly, softly, she said, "I know what she's like. It's a small price to be rid of her."

Then she put on her phoniest smile and, in an unnaturally loud voice, went on. "You know what? Forget about the coffee. I've had enough caffeine for the day. I've got all the paperwork in my car. I'll bring it by tomorrow after I get my baby off to school, and you can set up an appointment with your attorney."

Therese didn't point out that she went to school, too. She didn't scream at Catherine to get the hell out of her house and never come back. She didn't slap that fraud of a smile off her face. She didn't do anything but watch as the bitch glided down the hall, intercepting Abby on her way to the kitchen, turned her around, hooked her arm through Abby's, and strolled out the door.

But once the faint rev of an engine faded away, Therese sank to the floor, right there against the cabinets, and hugged herself tightly. That was where Keegan, Jacob, and Mariah found her some while later. Keegan didn't try to coax her to her feet, to move her someplace better suited for falling apart, but all three of them joined her, Keegan on one side, Jacob on the other, Mariah curling up on Jacob's lap and periodically patting Therese's arm. "It's okay, sweetie," she murmured.

Though her eyes were swimming with tears, Therese smiled at her. "Is that what Celly says?"

She nodded vigorously and patted again. "Celly knows."

After a long time, Jacob asked, "Are you gonna let her go?"

Comforted by the feel of Keegan's arm around her waist, Therese slid her left arm around Jacob's waist and pulled him closer. "I may not have a choice."

"The law says you do. When she gave us up, she gave up all her rights, too."

"But Abby's thirteen. A judge would consider what she wants. And can you imagine how unhappy we're all going to be if she's disappointed?"

But a little voice in Therese's head argued. *She's thirteen—still a child. And Catherine as much as admitted she wanted her for the money. What if you refuse to give it to her? Will she still take Abby?*

"This is my fault," Jacob muttered. "If we hadn't gone out there on spring break...and that was my idea."

"It's not your fault." It was the first time Keegan had spoken since joining Therese on the floor. "You're not responsible for decisions made by adults, Jacob."

"Still..." The boy sighed, then rested his head on Therese's shoulder.

Life without Abby. It was what she'd wanted...or so she'd thought. But even after speaking to the lawyer at JAG and the chaplain, she hadn't been able to bring herself to take any action. She'd prayed for guidance, talked to her friends, confided in Keegan, but she hadn't called Catherine or Paul's parents. She hadn't broached the issue with anyone who could actually do something.

And Abby had been so much easier. She'd lost so much of the snottiness. She'd let down her guard. They'd begun building a relationship. *Lord, am I supposed to just let go of that? Let a woman I wouldn't trust with a kitten waltz away with Paul's daughter? Buy my freedom and forget about Abby and what's best for her?*

Her only answer in that moment was the aching in her own heart.

Chapter 15

Thursday morning always came too soon.

Jessy squinted at the clock, but the numbers were blurry, dancing before her grit-filled eyes. Her mouth tasted like grit, too, and her head was pounding. Again. The sunlight creeping into the room at the edges of the window blinds seemed brighter than it should have been for six forty-five a.m. Shoving her fingers through her hair, she sat up in bed and checked the clock again.

Holy crap, it was 7:53. She launched out of bed and nearly lost her balance, her legs wobbling, her arms windmilling. Before the wave of nausea had passed, she was moving again, grabbing a dress from the closet, clean underwear from the dresser, yanking her pajamas off as she stumbled into the bathroom.

It was the quickest put-together she'd ever done: clothes, shoes, makeup, hair, teeth brushed, in five minutes. She didn't have time for a cup of coffee, but she could mainline the stuff at work, and food would have to wait until her midmorning break. Grabbing her purse, she sailed out the door and down the steps, then practically ran to the bank.

Mrs. Dauterive gave her one of those looks, all prim and pruny, even though she reached her desk at exactly eight o'clock. Jessy flashed her a bright smile, stuffed her bag in the bottom desk drawer, then headed to the break room for coffee.

"You barely made it," Julia murmured as she stirred sweetener into her own mug.

"Yeah, but it counts." Jessy filled her own mug, added real cream and too much sugar. She could use the calories since she'd missed breakfast.

"You look like hell, girlfriend. You coming down with something?"

Heat warmed Jessy's face, but she pretended otherwise. "Trouble sleeping." It wasn't necessarily a lie. She couldn't remember actually going to bed last night. She did remember getting takeout at Serena's—a slice of sweet potato pie, one of pecan, and one of coconut cream, and sipping a glass of wine while she indulged.

Everything after that was a little fuzzy.

She felt like one of her own photography subjects in the camera viewfinder in that instant before she pressed the shutter release and brought everything into clear focus. She hadn't had any clear focus in her life for a long time.

Grimly she returned to her desk, uncomfortably aware of Mrs. Dauterive's beady stare. She was grateful when the first customer of the morning took a seat in front of her desk. She smiled her fake smile, greeted the old lady in her fake-friendly-professional voice, and forced her attention to the opening of a new account.

By the time her break came, she was starved. She'd already drunk enough bad coffee to make her jittery, but she took advantage of the free minutes to go across and down the street to Java Dave's for real coffee and a pastry. The woman in front of her took forever to decide about her order, leaving Jessy to waste half of her break waiting. "For God's sake, hon, it's coffee," she muttered under her breath.

Her blond hair swinging, the woman turned to give her a piercing look, the blue of her eyes as fake as the green of Jessy's was real. Slowly she faced the counter and the patient barista again and ordered.

The moment the blonde walked away, Jessy rattled off her own order, then glanced over her shoulder. The woman might be slow, but she wore a pair of killer heels that would look so much better on Jessy, and the casual-chic outfit would be more flattering on Jessy, too. She had on too much jewelry, and the silvery tint to her hair left a lot to be desired, and—

And she was meeting Therese. At ten o'clock on a Thursday morning. When Therese should be in school surrounded by all her little rug rats. What the hell? Therese never missed work unless she was on her deathbed, and she had the constitution of a horse. She never had the sniffles, colds, or even menstrual cramps.

So why was she off today, who was the woman, and why was the air around them icy enough to produce August snow on the Oklahoma prairie?

The barista cleared her throat, and Jessy turned back to pay for her order. She'd intended to eat at one of the small tables before heading back to Mrs. Dauterive's snotty glare, but not now. Not with one of her best friends engaged in frosty conversation with a stranger just across the room. She'd much rather sit in the gazebo on the court-house's back lawn.

Feeling furtive, she put extra effort into leaving the cof-fee shop unnoticed. As she took one last look at Therese at the door, a thought occurred to her: this meeting must be about Abby. Was she making good on her threat to send the girl away?

God, Jessy hoped not. She knew Abby was a brat. She'd never been timid about sharing that with Therese. But she also knew that sometimes being bratty was a cover for how lost and unhappy and unwanted a kid felt. Therese was the best thing to ever happen to Abby, and if she gave up on her, what chance did the girl have?

Jessy knew a few things about kids parents had given up on. She wouldn't wish that on anyone, not even a snotty thirteen-year-old who'd slapped her stepmother.

Not even Abby deserved to grow up and become Jessy.

* * *

Keegan sat on the stoop in front of his motel room, check-ing the time on his cell phone every minute or so. Therese had called earlier to tell him she'd taken the day off to meet with Catherine and would let him know when she was done. He hadn't tried to influence her either way, not this morning or last night. She had to make her own decision.

But, God, he hoped she said no. Every instinct he pos-sessed said Catherine Matheson was the worst possible choice for Abby. She was self-centered and as shallow as the dewdrops that had formed on the grass this morning. Had about as much permanency, too.

At least that call had been followed with good news:

his request to extend his leave another week had been approved. He had more time with Therese, which they would both need if she let Catherine take Abby right away the way the woman wanted.

At the bottom of the steps, Mariah sat on her haunches, intently watching an ant crawl from one chunk of gravel to the next. "When is Celly coming back?"

Her question didn't surprise him. She asked at least once a day, usually his cue to call his mom and let them talk a bit. "In a few days." Not that she had much concept of time. Her entire life had consisted of just a few days, as far as she was concerned. No past to remember, no future to worry about, nothing but today. He envied her, but then, her *todays* were, for the most part, good days.

Finally she stood, tottered a moment, then climbed the steps. "Tell me a story."

"Your books are inside. Grab one and—"

Stubbornly she shook her head. "Not read, tell. Celly tells stories."

"But—"

"Abby tells stories. Jacob tells stories."

"Yeah, I get it, everyone tells stories." He lifted her onto his lap, trying to remember any of the hundred stories his mom had told when he was a kid. There had been one about a muskrat, a bunch with alligators, lots with dogs and cats and brave little boys who looked a lot like him in his imagination, but he couldn't recall enough details to make a coherent tale. "Okay…"

"Once upon a time," she supplied helpfully.

Sure, that worked for him. "Once upon a time, in a far, faraway land, there lived a princess named—"

"Mariah!"

"—and she lived in a big castle and had a pet—"

"Alligator!"

"A pet alligator named Chompers." Pulling her hand to his mouth, he pretended to munch on her fingers, and she giggled with delight. The moment hit him hard: the little girl who'd cried at the sight of him a week and a half ago was now giggling in his lap. How cool was that?

He went on, his voice husky. "Mariah and Chompers liked to go on adventures in the bayou around the castle. One day—"

The ring and vibration of his phone in his free hand jerked his gaze to the screen. Disappointment rose when he realized it was his mother instead of Therese. He held the phone to Mariah's ear and said, "Say hello to Celly."

"Hey, Celly!" She slid to her feet and tugged the phone from his hand. "I hold it my own self. Guess what, Celly?" She wandered around the stoop, barely breathing, launching into new topics before she finished the old ones. She talked about Abby, Jacob, and Therese, and just as Keegan was about to tune her out, she mentioned him. "Celly, Daddy's telling me a story about a princess named Mariah and a pet 'gator."

Even from across the small porch, he heard his mother's voice rise with pleasure. "Daddy?"

"Uh-huh." After rambling another couple minutes, Mariah said, "We got you a pretty labender flower for when you get back and— Ooh, kitty!" She set the phone on Keegan's leg, skipped down the steps, and followed from a distance as a cat stalked along the back wall of the motel office, headed for the Dumpster.

Drawing a breath, he raised the phone to his ear. "Hey, Mom."

"Daddy, huh? Oh, darlin', I'm so glad you finally came to your senses. I know you were worried about getting hurt and all, but you can't give away the child who calls you Daddy, now can you?"

"No," he agreed quietly. He expected his gut to knot a little—after all, Mariah still wasn't his daughter—but it didn't come. Only the same sense of rightness he'd felt practically from the beginning with Therese. "How is Ford?"

"He's doing fine. Getting up and about, even talking about going back to work, but Denise isn't going to let that happen one moment too soon. You know, I might have been wrong about her. She's handled this pretty well, considering. Right now I'm thinking I'll head home Sunday, maybe Monday. What about you guys? Should I book a seat for Mariah from Tulsa to Alexandria?"

He could say yes. God knows, Mariah would be thrilled to see her again, and he would have a little privacy, time to go for a run, to savor some quiet. But the thought of sending her off, of not hearing her snores at night or her laughter during the day, of not shaping his time and activities around her, held zero appeal. Somewhere down the line, sure, but not when this was all so new.

"Nah, Mom. I extended my leave for another week. I'll bring her back with me."

"Oh." An interested note came into her voice. "Does this have to do with Therese?"

"Yeah."

"Ohhh. Well, if you don't need me back right away, I might stay a little longer. Ford hasn't been able to do much talking so far. Now that he's getting stronger, I'd like to spend a bit more time with him. You give Mariah lots of hugs and kisses from me, and send me a picture of this girl Therese. I want to get an idea what my next grandchild might look like."

Before he could respond to that, she laughed and rushed out, "Love you, darlin'. You take care."

"Love you, too." He hung up and double-checked to make sure he hadn't missed a call-waiting signal.

It sounded like a hokey line from a song, but waiting really was the hardest part.

* * *

The meeting with Catherine hadn't gone well, not that Therese had expected it to. She'd been awake most of the night, asking hard questions of herself and today of Catherine, and still wasn't satisfied that she had any answers.

Paul's ex had shown up at the coffee shop with the papers in a large envelope, and Therese had scanned them. There were no surprises in the documents. In exchange for one-third of the proceeds of Paul's life insurance, Catherine would take back custody of Abby. Simple. Easy.

Except it was neither.

After Catherine left Java Dave's in a huff, Therese went home. The house was quiet, welcoming, not the place she'd dreaded for so long. Letting her purse slide to the floor, she walked into the living room and straight to the fireplace and the large photo of Paul. "What do I do?" she whispered. "She's your little girl. I promised you I would take care of her, and we're getting to the point that I believe I can do it right. But Catherine's her mother. That means so much to Abby. But she's not a very interested mother, and I worry...Oh, Paul, I worry."

Sadly, she got no response.

She wandered the room, looking at photographs, keepsakes, mementos that lined the shelves. She was about to sink into her favorite chair when a stack of boxes on one shelf caught her eye. They were heavy-duty, gaily striped, so much prettier than the shoe boxes Paul had stored his pictures in when she met him. She picked up the top one, sat down, and lifted the lid.

There was no order to the photos inside. Organizing them was a job he'd been saving for someday, when he would scan them onto the computer, label them, and file them chronologically. The top handful she removed were mostly snapshots taken in the few years before the kids came to live with them, with a few early school photos added.

Abby and Jacob got progressively younger the deeper she dug into the box: preschool, with wispy blond curls, big brown eyes, missing teeth, big grins. She shuffled through them, smiling at moments she'd missed, back when the original Matheson family was intact and looked so happy. They'd been a beautiful family, the kids small, perfect images of their father, their mother holding them as if she wouldn't grow tired of them in a few years. The happiness, the sheer perfection, of the family was so real, so alive in those moments captured in time.

But Therese knew it was a lie. Catherine had had affairs, Paul had delivered ultimatums, and, as Jacob clearly remembered, they'd fought all the time. The happiness and perfection had lasted for the blink of the camera's eye.

She'd browsed through most of the box when she came to a photograph that made her go still. A little girl wearing a ribbons-and-lace dress, her curls untamed, her smile so bright a person couldn't help smiling back. What was a picture of Mariah doing in this box of Matheson family photos? Had Abby taken it and printed a copy on her computer?

No, Therese had never seen Mariah in that dress. It was far frillier than anything she'd worn since arriving here, a special-occasion dress, Easter or birthday or Christmas.

Had Abby seen it in Keegan's wallet and asked for it? Presumptive action, but one she could see Abby taking. When she wanted something, she wanted it.

But Therese had seen inside Keegan's wallet when he'd paid for various meals. The card slots held his driver's license, his military ID, a credit card, and nothing else.

Besides, the paper was too old, the dress too frilly for current styles.

Slowly she put everything else back in the box, closed it, and set it aside, then she turned the picture over. In Catherine's graceful hand on back was written: *Abby, age three*.

Therese's gut knotted, and fluttering started in her chest, like a trapped butterfly frantic to beat its way free. Her hands trembled so badly that she wrinkled one corner of the paper from gripping it so tightly. Otherwise, it would have fluttered, too.

Why did Abby, age three, look so much like Mariah, nearly age three? Coincidence? It must be. What else would explain it? Little girls, blond hair, brown eyes, all chubby cheeks and cute and cuddly—of course they looked alike. Their faces hadn't yet developed the distinctive features that would separate them as adults. They had too much in common not to resemble each other.

But this was more than a resemblance. This was...It was...

You knew Paul through the Army? she'd asked the first time she and Keegan met.

I was in Iraq and Afghanistan, he'd replied. Not *Yes, I did.* Not *We served together in Iraq and Afghanistan.*

The cold that had enveloped her from the moment she'd recognized Catherine in her kitchen last night threatened to turn her blood to ice. Why hadn't she noticed that he'd avoided giving an answer?

Because she'd just had to tell a stranger that her husband was dead and she'd been more than a little shaken by it.

Keegan had gone on to say, *I'm at Fort Polk now,* and she'd commented that Paul had gone there several times for training. The last had been shortly before his final deployment. That had been . . . She did the math easily in her head, but it was hard, so damn hard, to give the answer: about three and a half years ago.

About the time Mariah was conceived.

No. No no no. Sure, when the battalions went away, some of the men did play, but not Paul. He knew what it was like to be cheated on. He kept his word, honored his marriage vows. He never would have inflicted that kind of hurt—that kind of insult—on her.

But if he had, if he'd been tempted, if he'd fallen, he would have taken the secret to Afghanistan—to the grave—with him. One infidelity in the years they'd been married, one weak moment? Not enough to risk their marriage, he would have thought, especially if she never knew. And she never would have known if the woman—Sabrina—Keegan's girlfriend—hadn't gotten pregnant. If she hadn't abandoned her daughter with the next best thing to a father. If he hadn't come looking for Mariah's real father.

While her head found the scenario entirely plausible,

her heart rebelled. Paul had loved her. She'd trusted him. She wouldn't—couldn't—believe he'd been unfaithful to her. Dear God, surely she was wrong.

But there was one way to find out.

Not trusting her voice to hold steady, she texted Keegan, asking him to come to the house. He replied with an affirmative answer in less than a minute. Rising from the chair, still clutching the photo of Abby, she paced through the house, front to back, through every room, remembering Paul in every place she looked. How blessed she'd been to have a loving, faithful husband. He'd understood the sanctity of love and trust and marriage, same as she had.

But while he and Therese had waited for the right time to expand their family, he'd had a daughter with another woman. She didn't want to believe it, but it was hard to deny when the truth was staring her in the face.

When the doorbell rang, she was in the kitchen. She walked down the hall with measured steps, delaying the moment when she would have no choice but to ask Keegan, when he would have no choice but to answer, when her heart would break all over again. Finally she opened the door.

Mariah was sitting on his shoulders, his hands securely holding her thighs, her own hands clutching his forehead. He ducked and she bent forward to clear the door frame, then she leaned down as far as she could to smooch Therese. "Hey, Trace. Where's Abby?"

Therese stared at her. How had she missed it? Granted, she hadn't known Abby when she was this age; by the time they'd met, Abby's curls had given way to sleek, fine hair, and her happy smile had disappeared, too. But now that she knew to look, she saw Paul in every one of Mariah's features, just like she did with her own kids.

After a moment, she stirred. "Abby and Jacob are at school, sweetie."

Keegan lifted Mariah to the floor, then wrapped his arms around Therese. For just an instant, she let herself relax as much as she could in his embrace. Then she remembered—Paul, Mariah, Sabrina, and Keegan, who'd known—and she stepped back. Looking away quickly from the concern in his eyes, she turned. "Let's go out back. Mariah can play, and we can talk."

* * *

We can talk was always a bad sign, Keegan thought as he followed Therese and Mariah down the hall. Therese stopped at the refrigerator to grab a juice box and two bottles of water, then opened the door for Mariah, who skipped onto the patio and went straight to the first pot of flowers, circling around it while sniffing each bloom.

"Have you made a decision?" Keegan finally asked, unable to stand the quiet any longer. He accepted the water from her and settled in a chair while she stripped plastic from a straw and stabbed it into the juice box.

"Not yet." Before she sat down, she slipped something from her pocket, then handed it to him.

It was a photograph, the paper yellowed on the edges, the colors slightly faded. Except for that, a person could be forgiven for thinking it was a picture of Mariah. The extent of the resemblance was a surprise to him, even though he knew the relationship. He hadn't imagined that Abby's hair had been curly when she was little, or her cheeks so fat, or that two girls who shared only a father could look damn near like twins at the same age.

The paper shook, and he realized his hand was trembling. He rested it on his leg to help stop the tremors. The knots in his gut he'd expected earlier, in the call with his mother, came now, hard cramps of fear, dread, regret, and just a little relief. Some part of him wanted Therese to know—not that her husband had been unfaithful. Never that. But to know Mariah for who she really was. Didn't the kid deserve that?

When he gathered the courage to look at Therese, she was watching him. She was working hard to maintain control, to show no emotion, but she couldn't keep the betrayal from her eyes. Who did she feel betrayed by? Paul? Him? Or both?

God, he'd never wanted to see her hurt. Damn well never wanted to be the one who hurt her.

He took a long swallow of water, then a deep breath to force out the words. "I was finishing up a short deployment to Afghanistan—only six months—the last time Paul went to Fort Polk for training." His voice was hoarse, and he couldn't seem to raise it to a normal level. But that was okay. Therese could hear him, and Mariah, who'd been drawn to the fence by the snuffle of the dog next door, couldn't.

"I got home a month later, and a few weeks after that, Sabrina told me she was pregnant. I wasn't thrilled. I didn't want to marry her. I didn't want to have a family yet. I loved her, but not enough." Not the way he loved Therese. "But if I was going to be a father, I intended to be a good one. Then she told me I wasn't the father. She'd met a man while I was gone—a major. Quite a step up for someone living with a specialist at the time. He was stationed at Fort Murphy, at Polk for training before heading to the desert. They met in a club, she took him home..."

He didn't need to say more. The color draining from Therese's face and the muscle twitching in her jaw were proof of that.

Damn, he hated this.

"We broke up, she moved out, and I didn't see her again for a couple years, until I ran into her outside another club in Leesville. Mariah was about one and a half at the time. Sabrina told me she'd tried to contact the major—Paul— but he never answered her e-mails so she'd given up on the idea of him being a part of Mariah's life." Sabrina had been disillusioned, as she so often was, and he'd felt sorry for her, but she'd brought it on herself. She'd been involved. The major had been married. Why hadn't either of them thought, *This is wrong,* and put a stop to it before it was too late?

"I never saw her again. I never met Mariah until five, six weeks ago. Social services called me, said Sabrina had abandoned her and they wanted me to take her since I was her father. Turned out, she put me on the birth certificate. I don't know why, unless she was just hurt or pissed that the father didn't want anything to do with them or because we were together when she got pregnant or if she thought, I don't know, that I would step up if needed. Whatever the reason, as far as the state was concerned, I was Mariah's father, and if I didn't take her, they would put her in foster care. I couldn't...I thought maybe I could persuade her real father...It just didn't seem right to make Mariah go into foster care. Not after the experiences Sabrina had there."

Therese clutched the water bottle so tightly that her fingers were splotched red and white. "So you came here to tell Paul that he had another daughter."

Keegan nodded. "I had no idea he was..."

Therese nodded, too, her head bobbing without thought like Mariah's. "Of course not. How could you know? How could Sabrina? I didn't know to contact his—his one-night stand—" Her voice broke on the word, a strangled sob escaping her. She regained control quickly, though, one hand pressed to her mouth, her eyes blinking rapidly to clear the tears.

He set the picture on the ground beneath her chair, placed the two bottles beside it, pulled her hand from her mouth, and drew her out of the chair and into his lap, wrapping his arms around her. "I'm sorry, Therese. I never wanted you to find out. I know it hurts—"

"I'm not hurt!" she cried, pressing her face to his shoulder, tears soaking his shirt. "I'm furious! He knew how this felt, he lived through it over and over with Catherine, and he still did it. For what? One night of sex? He couldn't wait a week or two until he got back home to me? What the hell was he thinking?"

"I don't know, babe. I don't know." He stroked her hair, rubbed her shoulder, patted her back, and slowly the stiffness seeped away, her body relaxing against his. She might claim she wasn't hurting, but he knew better. She'd loved and trusted Matheson—had been faithful to him through much longer absences than his short stint at Polk. Not only had he betrayed her, he'd tarnished his memory for her.

"Oh, my God," she whispered, the pain in her voice slicing through Keegan. "That means—Mariah is my stepdaughter." Abruptly, she pulled out of his arms, balancing precariously on his knees, her gaze narrowed on him. "Is that why you stayed? Why you brought her here? To find a new home for her even if her father was dead? So I'd fall in love with her? Did you think because I accepted custody of Paul's other children, I might take her, too?"

He could lie and make her believe it. Hadn't he been willing to hide the truth for the rest of their lives to protect Therese? But that was the coward's way out. Though he'd been willing to do it, he wasn't a coward.

"I brought her here because Mom had to go to Arizona. There was no one else to take care of her. But...yeah, I thought maybe the major had some other family, or maybe you'd be willing to take her since she's Abby and Jacob's sister. I thought that for about a day." He grabbed her hands when she would have gotten to her feet. "For about a day, Therese. That's all. I stayed because of you. Because I've never met a woman like you. Because I felt something for you right from the start. Because I liked you and respected you and wanted to know you better. Because—"

He had to swallow over the lump in his throat, and it made his voice huskier. "Because I was falling in love with you."

For a long time she stared at him, her eyes damp, round and wide and aching...and disbelieving. That stirred his own ache. "How convenient." The snideness in her voice echoed Abby in a bad moment. "If you're going to fall in love, it might as well be with the stepmother of the child you got saddled with. I'm sorry—that your *mother* got saddled with."

This time when she pulled away, he let her go. Her actions jerky and graceless, she stalked to the edge of the patio and stood with her back to him, spine straight, shoulders erect. He stood, too, and walked to the opposite end of the patio, staring out into the yard as she was. "Maybe I was wrong to put all her care on Mom. Maybe I was wrong to even take her, I don't know. But legally she's mine, and I'm not giving her up. Not to her mother, not to her grandmother, not to her stepmother."

"Well, good, because I don't—" She cut off the words, and heat flooded her face.

I don't want her. That was what she'd meant to say. That was okay. He and his family could take care of Mariah. They could give her everything she needed. Just as he hadn't missed his father's presence in his life, Mariah wouldn't miss having a mother.

Though, God help him, he wasn't sure *he* could live without Therese.

Slowly he turned to face her. The three flowerpots stood between them, like giant hurdles they couldn't find their way around. Was it only yesterday afternoon that they'd planted them? That life had seemed so good and perfect?

"Therese, I'm sorry." He raked his fingers through his hair, then practically had to pry the next words from his mouth. "I think Mariah and I should go. Give you some time to think." He barely breathed, hoping she would say, *No, we need to talk this out*, but she didn't respond other than to fold her arms over her middle. Deep inside he hurt with disappointment.

"Mariah, come on, monster. Time to go."

She was kneeling next to the fence, her fingers wriggled into the space between two boards, and talking softly to the dog on the other side. "I gotta go," she said before climbing to her feet and running across the yard. She headed for Therese instead of him, and though he could have intercepted her, he didn't. Therese might not want to raise Mariah, but she could use a hug from her.

"Are we going to lunch?" Mariah jumped, and Therese automatically reached to swing her up. The faith that child had in other people's ability and willingness to catch her amazed Keegan every time. "Can we go to McDonald's?"

Therese hugged her a moment, tightly enough to make her squirm. "Honey, I'm not hungry, but I bet Daddy will take you wherever you want."

Mariah's little face screwed up, her lip trembling. "But I want you to come, Trace. Please?"

"Not this time."

Therese set her on the ground and gave her a nudge in Keegan's direction. He met Mariah halfway, took her hand, and walked inside the house. Before closing the door, though, he looked back. "Don't mistake my leaving for giving up. This isn't over, Therese."

Her gaze darted his way, and for an instant he was sure he saw hope in it. Just as quickly, she turned away again. With Mariah chattering about the possibility of getting a puppy all her own, they walked through the house and out the front door. Though a dull, empty ache filled him, he felt a bit of hope, too.

He would be back. They would make this thing right.

They had to.

Chapter 16

Therese didn't know how long she stood there, shut down, but finally she forced herself to move, picking up the bottles and the picture, going inside, setting everything on the island. She was blessedly numb inside, though she didn't expect it to last, because two facts kept pounding through her brain.

She'd loved Paul dearly, and he'd betrayed her.

She loved Keegan, and he'd hidden the truth from her.

And a third fact: she still had to decide what to do about Abby.

Dear God, how had her life gotten so screwed up? Twenty-four hours ago she'd been blissfully happy. Now she just wanted to curl into a dark corner and weep, but damned if she would. She was strong. But she had to do something before she covered her ears and started shrieking like Abby and Mariah on a really bad day, because if she started, she might never stop.

The ticking clock pulled her gaze to the wall, and she

realized it was almost Carly's lunch period. Fumbling with her cell phone, she sent her friend a text: *Bringing lunch. Meet me in parking lot.* Then she jerked open the refrigerator, gathered ingredients, and slapped together a ham and cheese sandwich. Leaving the island a mess, she shoved the sandwich into a plastic zippered bag, grabbed bottles of water, and headed for the door.

By the time she pulled into a space in the parking lot shared by the post schools, Carly was already striding over to the van. She slid into the passenger seat, then treated Therese to a somber study. "What happened?"

Aiming for an unaffected manner, Therese gave a quick rundown of recent events. She thought she'd pulled it off fairly well—no catches in her voice, no tears in her eyes— but when she finished, Carly leaned across the console and hugged her tightly. "Poor baby."

With a lump in her throat and tears suddenly back in her eyes, Therese took comfort from the embrace. No matter how good she felt in Keegan's arms, sometimes what a woman really needed was a hug and a *poor baby* or two from her best friend.

"I don't even know where to start," Carly murmured. "Catherine, Abby, an affair, a baby..." She pushed Therese back and surprised her by smiling. "Keegan's in love with you. Aw, honey, isn't it incredible?"

"He only stayed around because he wanted me to take Mariah off his hands."

Carly waved that away. "The thought occurred to him. Men entertain stupid thoughts all the time. Look at Dane, thinking I wouldn't want him if I knew he'd lost his leg. Trust me, Keegan isn't looking to take on responsibility for a teenage girl and a boy who's almost a teenager just to get someone to help him with his daughter. From what you say, his mama was already doing everything for her."

That was true. And things had changed between Keegan and Mariah since the first evening he'd brought her to their house. He'd gotten comfortable with her. He was over his fear. He'd fallen in love with her, too.

"I'm so sorry about Paul. Oh, my God, if I found out that Jeff had—" Pressing her lips together, Carly broke off and shook her head.

It would have broken her heart. It should have broken Therese's heart, too, but she critically examined her emotions. She was hurt. She was angry. She was disappointed in Paul. She was bitter that Sabrina had his child while *she* had waited and lost out. But was she brokenhearted?

She wouldn't describe it that way. Did she love him any less? No. Did she respect him less? Yes, no doubt. Could she forgive him since his affair had brought Keegan and Mariah into her life?

Yes. Maybe not right this minute, but when the hurt eased, when the shock was past, when she'd had time to get used to the idea.

Settling back in her seat, Carly spied the sandwich, opened it, and took a bite. "And Catherine showing up like that, without calling or anything...I don't know how you kept from snatching her hair out."

"As over-bleached as it is, it probably would have broken off in my hands." At the image of a stubby-haired Catherine, a laugh bubbled inside Therese. "And she's so thin, I could heave her like a bale of hay, though if she landed on her boobs, all that silicone would make her bounce."

Carly laughed, too. "It's hard to imagine the two of you

appealing to the same man. You're so normal, and she's so odd."

"Apparently, he wasn't that choosy." The next laugh sounded strangled, and Therese pressed her hand to her mouth. "Oh, God, Carly, what if Sabrina wasn't the only one? What if there are more women? More kids?"

"You have nothing to suggest it happened more than once."

"I have nothing to suggest it didn't." She sighed sadly, wistfully. "I never worried about him being unfaithful. From the very beginning, we were both insistent on an exclusive relationship. I never imagined he would— *Why? Why?* Why would he do that?"

Carly took another bite of her sandwich and chewed it before shrugging. "You'll drive yourself crazy asking why, because you'll never know. I doubt even Paul could tell you. It could be as simple as he had too much to drink or as complicated as he had to be unfaithful in order to bring you and Keegan together. Things happen for a reason, sweetie. You've heard enough sermons to know that. If God intended you and Keegan and Paul's three kids to be together at this point in your lives, then He had to get you all here somehow."

"I can think of easier ways," Therese muttered, but Carly shook her head.

"If Paul hadn't slept with Keegan's girlfriend, you probably never would have met Keegan, and Mariah wouldn't even exist. Whatever problems they caused, they made a beautiful little girl whom her family adores. Whom Abby adores—and how many people can you say that about? God didn't promise us easy, sweetie. He just promised He'd help us through."

Therese blew out her breath heavily. She'd had a good life: loving parents, a stable home, a good education, the ability to take care of herself, the best friends in the world. She'd had a husband who loved her but had betrayed her at least once, and another man who loved her who had hidden the truth of Paul's betrayal. Before now, Paul's death and dealing with the kids were the only traumas she'd ever gone through.

And she'd gotten through them, with God's help, her family's, her friends'.

The warning bell rang, and Carly stuffed the crusts of her sandwich in the plastic bag and picked up her water. "I wish I could take off, stock up at CaraCakes, and join you for a pity party, but the boss would have a fit. Are you going to be okay?"

Therese nodded. "Sure. I always am."

Carly hugged her again. "I'm so sorry all this hit at once, but it's going to work out. I promise."

"I'll hold you to that." Therese watched her climb out, then cross the lot in long strides, reaching the door just before the second bell sounded. For a long time, though, she didn't start the engine. She just sat there, gazing into the distance.

What would have happened if Paul hadn't died? He would have responded to Sabrina's e-mails. Therese had no doubt. He would have confessed his affair and done whatever was necessary to be a part of Mariah's life. He would have asked Therese to forgive him, and she would have. She would have felt all the same emotions she did now, but she would have weighed one mistake, serious as it was, against their love, their marriage, their family. Sabrina wouldn't have resorted to putting another man's name on the birth certificate, and Therese never would have met Keegan.

She could bear Paul's infidelity.

She wasn't sure she could bear a life without Keegan.

Which led to the next big question: could she bear a life without Abby?

She didn't have an answer to that one yet, but at least she felt better when she left the school than when she'd arrived. Her stomach wasn't churning. The butterflies weren't battering her chest. Though her tears were still far too close to the surface, the sharp edge was gone from her anger. She would never forget, but she could forgive.

She made one stop before going home. Sitting in the driveway, she texted Catherine to come to the house at four.

Can't. N Tlsa shppng. Wl try 2 make it by 5.

Abby gets out of school at 3:30, Therese reminded her.

Tld hr 2 take bus 2 ur house. Wl pick hr up there.

Already ducking out on time she could be spending with her kids, and she had the nerve to end the message with a smiley face. Witch.

After a moment's hesitation, Therese sent a text to Keegan, asking him to come at five. He agreed.

A few hours, and this mess her life had become would straighten out or tangle inextricably. They would all know what their immediate future looked like—and if it would get worse before it got better.

Please, God, give me an answer before then.

* * *

It had turned into the day from hell for Jessy. *I hate my job* kept echoing through her head, the words occasionally interrupted by a chorus of *You can't fix stupid.* Every moronic customer she'd ever had came into the bank, never sitting down at Julia's desk but always at Jessy's, and they asked every moronic question in the book. By midafternoon, she had a pounding headache, her stomach was queasy, and the only thing that would help was the sweet oblivion of a drink.

My job is driving me to drink, she'd often joked. Today her mouth watered at the thought.

An eighteen-year-old girl sat across from her, long bronzed legs crossed, fingers twirling a gold curl, as beautiful as she was empty-headed. She listened while Jessy explained yet again that to spend money from her account, she had to have money *in* the account. Seeing no sign of understanding on the girl's face, Jessy rubbed her temple to ease the pain.

"But my daddy will cover it," the girl replied yet again, clearly bored with the conversation. "He always does. So give back my debit card."

"Sundrae—" Jessy covertly checked the computer screen to make sure she had the girl's name right. What the hell kind of name was Sundrae? "Your debit card was retained by the ATM at a gas station in Stillwater. We don't have it here."

"So get me a new one."

"That'll take two to four weeks."

Sundrae looked appalled. "What the hell am I supposed to do for money the next two weeks?"

"The next two to four weeks. Use cash or checks. After you've deposited funds into your account."

The girl snorted, reminding Jessy of Therese's stepdaughter. This was what Abby would be like in five years if she went back to live with her mother. Snide, derisive, and shallow, though Jessy was pretty sure Abby's IQ was currently about a hundred points higher than Sundrae's. The brat was probably releasing brain cells into the atmosphere every time she tugged on that perfectly colored, perfectly spiraled curl. "Nobody uses cash or checks. I don't even have any checks."

"We have forms at the service counter you can use. Would you like me to show you how to fill them out?"

"No. I'd like you to get off your ass and get me a new debit card, and if you're too stupid to manage that, then get me someone who can."

Jessy's fingers curled tightly, her nails biting into her palms. "Excuse me?" she asked, frigidly polite.

Sundrae leaned forward in one sinuous movement, meant to be threatening, but it was hard to feel threatened by a spoiled, snot-nosed teenage brat with the intellect of a slug. "My daddy has all his business and personal accounts here. He's on the board of your freaking bank. He's your boss. Get me a new debit card now, or I'll have your job."

"You couldn't do my job." If Jessy weren't feeling so crappy, it would have amused her to watch the slug try to process her response. But she'd had her fill of rude, stupid, and/or demanding people. "Now if you don't mind getting off *your* ass, I've got other customers to help."

Sundrae's jaw dropped so low, Jessy was surprised it didn't hit the desk. Her nostrils flared, her heavily mascaraed eyes widened practically enough to pop out her contact lenses, then her mouth started working fishlike as she tried to form words. Finally, with an outraged gasp, she rose to her full five-foot-ten-inch height and stalked away.

Not to the exit, of course. Jessy couldn't be that lucky,

not on this Thursday from hell. No, Sundrae's heels—
another set of killer high-dollar shoes that would look
damn good on Jessy—were tapping along the wide swath
of marble that led to the executive offices. This wasn't going to be pretty. While being stupid would certainly be
an acceptable excuse for Sundrae's behavior in the boss's
opinion, it wasn't acceptable for Jessy's. She would definitely get counseled for this.

God, she hated this job.

And that was probably a good thing. Thirty minutes
later, after Mrs. Dauterive had been summoned to the president's office and while Sundrae watched with a smug, ma-
licious smile, for the first time in her life, Jessy Lawrence
got fired.

* * *

Keegan arrived right on time. Therese wasn't surprised;
most soldiers had a keen sense of punctuality. They'd
hardly had a chance to even look at each other, much less
speak—though she registered the concern in his eyes, the
regret, the love—when Catherine's rental car glided to the
curb out front. What a surprise that she could pull herself
away from buying new pretties for herself just to take care
of a pesky bit of family business.

"Is Abby home from school?" Mariah asked, peering
through the door, drawing Therese's attention to her. Paul's
daughter. Keegan's daughter. She would never know her
father-by-birth, but she would always know the love of her
father-by-choice. That was a more than fair trade.

"She is, sweetie. Upstairs in her room."

Mariah dashed inside, her little legs making short work

of the stairs. Therese watched until she turned the corner, then looked back at Catherine. She'd changed outfits since that morning, wearing a dress so crisp and fresh, it shrieked, *Brand new!* So did the leopard-print sandals with heels far beyond practical or even sexy, and she sported an entirely different set of rings, earrings, bangles, and necklaces that were approximately four times as numerous as one person should wear at a time.

Therese didn't look her best, knew it, and didn't care. The stop she'd made on her way home was at the nursery, and she'd spent the afternoon loosening and amending soil, planting bloom after bloom, mulching and watering. She had dirt stains on her shorts and T-shirt, her hair was blown half out of its ponytail, and her skin showed the signs of a few hours in the warm sun. She still had a lot of work to do, but the beds nearest the patio were vibrant and fragrant and made her happy just to look at them.

So did Keegan. So did Mariah.

Too bad she had to look at Catherine, too, at least one more time.

"You decided?" Keegan asked as they watched Catherine sashay from the street, taking her sweet time because the teenage boys across the street were salivating over the show.

"I did." She couldn't say anything else, not with Catherine now climbing the steps, but blindly she felt for his hand and gave it a tight squeeze. His relieved sigh was almost lost in Catherine's greeting, but the squeeze he returned said it all.

"I don't know how women around here survive. No wonder all of Abby's clothes are so tacky. The first place I went, I couldn't find a thing to buy. Thank God a woman directed me to Utica Square." Catherine's gaze shifted from Therese to Keegan. "What are you doing here again?"

"I asked him to come," Therese replied. "This involves him, too."

"Oh, God, you're *dating*? Paul hasn't been dead even three years."

"Excuse me if I don't take relationship advice from a woman who began dating again four years *before* her divorce." Therese went inside, leaving them to follow. The heavy waft of expensive perfume indicated Keegan had allowed Catherine to enter first.

Therese didn't take them into the living room and didn't stop in the kitchen, but went outside onto the patio. She didn't offer anything to drink, either. She wasn't feeling that hospitable toward Catherine, and hopefully Keegan and Mariah would join her and the kids for dinner.

Catherine looked at each of the chairs, touched one with cautious fingertips, then checked for dirt. Gingerly she perched on the edge of the cushion while Keegan and Therese settled in their own chairs. "I don't think I like the idea of a strange man coming around my children."

Married, Therese wanted to remind her. *Affairs, four years.* "As long as I have custody of them and I'm not doing anything inappropriate, that's none of your business."

"But that's about to change. The custody part. With Abby, at least."

Catherine smiled such a pretty smile, her head tilted just so, gazing up through her thick lashes, so feminine, so confident. For a moment, Therese could see why Paul had fallen for her. In the beginning, at least, she'd promised him everything with nothing more than that look.

And she could see just as clearly that the woman had

zero effect on Keegan. Maybe it was petty, but the fact made her heart swell.

"I've given this a lot of thought," Therese said, folding her hands in her lap. "I've considered what you want, what I want, what Abby and Jacob want, and what's best for them. But first let me answer your second request, for a portion of Paul's life insurance."

Catherine leaned forward, greed taking the shine off all that pretty femininity.

"That answer is simple. No. Paul didn't make the kids his beneficiary. He didn't need to because he knew I would provide for them until they're able to take care of themselves. He didn't make you his beneficiary because you weren't married anymore, you didn't have custody of the kids, and frankly, he didn't want you to have the money. Neither do I." Therese took a breath even as Catherine gasped for one.

"But—but—that's not fair!"

"No, Catherine, being unfaithful to your husband wasn't fair. Giving up your kids wasn't fair. Asking Abby to live with you and telling Jacob you didn't want him damn sure wasn't fair, and trying to profit now from their father's death isn't fair."

"But how am I supposed to provide Abby with the lifestyle we need without Paul's money?"

Therese breathed deeply. "Abby doesn't need a 'lifestyle.' She needs to be with family who love her. She needs friends and security and stability, and she's got all that right here."

Once more she heard a relieved sigh from Keegan. He hadn't wanted her to give up on Abby, but he hadn't known what she would do. She hadn't been absolutely sure herself until she'd been on her knees earlier, digging holes in the soil, thinking about how the seedlings she was planting would grow into huge, thriving plants as long as they had strong roots and plenty of nurturing.

Abby hadn't had enough of either, and that was in part Therese's failure. One she intended to rectify.

Catherine popped to her feet, quite a marvel considering the tightness of her dress and the height of her heels. "I'll fight you on this. Abby's old enough to decide for herself, and she'll choose me. She'll always choose me over you."

Therese stood, too, and faced her. "Go ahead. Take it to court. Abby can give her opinion, but it's the judge's decision, and it'll be based on a lot more than what a thirteen-year-old girl says. Think about it carefully, Catherine. Do you really want the kids to know you cheated on their dad? That you offered to take Abby off my hands in exchange for money? That you actually said, 'I know what she's like. It's a small price to be rid of her'? Do you have any idea how deeply that would hurt both of them?"

Something flashed through Catherine's eyes—the anger Therese expected, but more. Fear. Did losing her kids' respect and affection actually mean something to her? Or was it seeing the easy payday she'd expected slip out of her grasp that frightened her?

In the next instant, Catherine's jaw jutted out. "So give me the money and Abby, and they never have to know."

It probably seemed a logical solution to her, and Therese had even considered it. But whatever share of Paul's life insurance Catherine got would run out sooner rather than later, and then what would she do? Discard

Abby again? Send her back to Therese or, worse, put her
out on her own?

And Abby would know. She would try to convince herself that her mother truly loved and wanted her, but in her
heart she would know she wasn't as important to Catherine
as a daughter should be. It would break her heart all over
again.

Therese slowly, firmly shook her head as she walked the
few feet to the kitchen door and opened it. "I'd appreciate
it if you would leave before Abby or Jacob realize you're
here. Don't worry. I'll make your excuses to Abby."

"She'll hate you." Catherine's face was splotched beneath her flawless makeup, and a muscle near her left eye
twitched. Unlike her daughter, she couldn't pull off anger
and beauty at the same time. "I'll make sure of that."

"You do what you have to do, Catherine, and I'll do
what I have to to protect my family." *My family.* The words
sent a shiver of bone-deep pleasure through her. Jacob and
Abby were her family, and Mariah, and soon Keegan and
all those Logan relatives he loved so much. A bit of sadness washed through her that Catherine didn't understand
how important family was. She probably never would.

She half expected Catherine to shriek, stomp, and
scream for her daughter. The woman inhaled deeply, but all
that came out was a sputter as she crossed the threshold.
She strode through the kitchen and down the hall, Therese
a few feet behind her, ready to catch the door before she
could slam it. Catherine stopped there and faced Therese.
"This isn't over."

When Keegan had said the same words a few hours earlier, they'd been reassuring, a warm promise. Catherine's
might or might not be a promise. She might slink back to

California without the money she'd come for and go back to her neglectful, self-centered life, or she might turn her full charm on Abby, tempting her, coaxing her, luring her away just to punish Therese.

One thing was sure, though: Therese would fight, too, and she'd pit her skills against Catherine's any time.

Lifting her head haughtily, Catherine walked out, leaving the door open, taking the time despite her anger to put on a display for the boys across the street. Preening for men, displaying her body to its most advantageous, appeared to be the only thing that came naturally to her.

Therese's relief was so strong as the rental car drove away that her knees went weak and she sagged against the door frame. An instant later, strong arms went around her from behind, and Keegan pulled her against his body. "I'm so proud of you."

"I don't know if I could have done this without you." She folded her hands over his where they rested on her middle. They were so strong, like him. They made her feel safe and protected and loved.

"You could have. You would have. It's best for Abby and for you."

"I've prayed about it so long, and I believe it is, too." She sighed heavily. "I just hope she comes to the same conclusion sometime before we're old and gray."

"She will. Though I think we should both cover our ears when you tell her."

He intended to stay while she broke the news. Warmth flooded through her. She could do it—could play the evil stepmother, could bear Abby's tears and tantrums, could handle her overwrought emotions. She could do anything with Keegan at her side.

Therese laid her head against his shoulder, absorbing the heat and strength of his body, finding the only moment of peace she'd had in twenty-four hours. For that moment, she wasn't hurting or afraid. She wasn't feeling betrayed. Her lungs weren't starved for air, her stomach wasn't turning acid-laced flips, and her nerves weren't braced for the next bad flare.

"You told Mom no, didn't you?"

Abby's voice, stiff and accusing, came from the hallway behind them. Therese and Keegan turned to face her where she stood halfway between them and the kitchen, a box of crackers and a jar of peanut butter clenched in her hands. She must have been in the pantry getting a snack when Therese opened the door and asked Catherine to leave. Was that all she heard?

Please, Lord, don't let her have heard her mom ask for money or me repeating what Catherine said about her.

Her expression was stark, jaw clenched, eyes so like her brother's and sister's, wide with unidentifiable emotion. She wasn't vibrating with rage, though, or acting out in any other way. She simply stood there, still, waiting, looking...confused.

Therese moved from Keegan's embrace and took a few steps toward her, steeling herself for an outburst of teenage angst. "I did."

The outburst didn't come. Abby stared at her a long time, then tossed her hair. "Okay."

Unable to stop herself, Therese repeated, *"Okay?"*

Abby moved a few steps herself, then stared at the floor as she shifted from one bare foot to the other. "She lives in a tiny apartment. I mean, it's really expensive and gorgeous, but it's tiny and there are no kids around. And she wanted to leave Jacob behind. Sure, he's a moron and a jerk, but he's my brother. I couldn't just go off and leave him like that. And Nicole cried when I told her I was leaving, and I would've missed her and Payton and school and geek camp and the cookie monster and—and—"

She stopped abruptly, breathed deeply, and into the silence came a call from her room. "Abby! I don't want crackers. Can I have blue yogurt?"

"Yeah, Riah," she called back. "Just a minute." After another moment of shuffling, she went on. "When we got to the bed-and-breakfast last night, she spent the whole night on the phone with her friends. They talked about dates and where to get their nails and hair done and who's got the best clothes. Every time she hung up, I tried to talk to her, but then someone else would call and she'd say, 'Oh, sorry, Abs, I've got to take this.' And it would be more of the same. And she never even mentioned me. She never said, 'Guess what? My daughter's here with me.' It was just all clothes and men and...you know. Unimportant stuff."

Therese hid a smile at the last remark. Clothes and men unimportant? Were they sure she was Catherine's daughter?

"Today I wanted her to pick me up at school so Nicole and Payton could meet her. I guess I kinda wanted to show her off. But she wanted to go shopping. That's what she does all the time at home. Couldn't she have skipped it just once to spend some time with me?" The pleading in her voice was echoed in her eyes when she looked at Therese.

"Sweetie, I'm sorry." Taking a couple more steps, Therese reached out, resting her hand on Abby's shoulder. When the girl didn't shrug her off, she pulled her closer and wrapped one arm around her. "I wish..."

She wished Catherine were a better mother. She wished *she'd* been a better mother. She wished neither Abby nor Jacob would ever suffer a moment's pain or disappointment again.

For one sweet moment, Abby rested her head on Therese's shoulder. Almost immediately, though, she lifted it and met her gaze. "You called us family. Are we your family, me and Jacob?"

"Yes. Not by birth but by choice." Like Keegan and Mariah.

Abby considered the words a moment, then nodded. "I'd better get the monster her yogurt." She pivoted and walked back to the kitchen, then stopped to face her once more. "I don't hate you." With another toss of her hair, she disappeared down the hall.

*   *   *

I love you couldn't have had more impact, Keegan thought as a smile bloomed across Therese's face, erasing every bit of tension, every line, every worry she'd ever had. Taking his hand, she said with something close to awe, "She doesn't hate me."

"I heard. For what it's worth, neither does Jacob or Mariah, and neither do I. In fact..." He pulled her closer and wrapped his arms around her. "I meant what I said earlier."

She scrunched up her face as if trying to recall. "That you adore me?"

He shook his head. "I do, of course, but the other."

Her step forward removed the scant distance between them, her breasts brushing his chest, her hips against his, her thighs, long and lean and golden in his memories, touching his. "That you stayed in town because of me?"

"And?" He nuzzled her neck, and every breath he took smelled entirely of her. Perfume and, fainter, shampoo, fresh earth, flowers, and sun.

"That you never met a woman like me?"

"God knows, that's true."

She raised her palms to his face, and though he saw in the movement the light overhead reflecting in the sparkle of her engagement ring, he couldn't feel it; he wasn't hypersensitive to it the way he had been before. It pleased him somewhere deep inside that she hadn't removed it in a fit of anger over Paul's affair. Hurt, confused, and angry she might be, but she wouldn't throw out the thousands of good memories of him in punishment.

Cradling his face in her hands, looking serious but in a good, burden-lifted sort of way, she studied him a long time before the tiniest smile curved the corners of nicely kissable lips. "That you love me."

He stared back. "I love you." He'd said the words before—too easily in high school, too often afterward—but he'd never said them to Therese. He'd even meant them before but not like this. These words were a promise, a commitment, forever, not just now, not something he might one day stop doing, any more than he might stop needing oxygen or blood.

He wanted to marry her. Spend the rest of his life with her. Help her raise Paul's and Sabrina's kids. Trudge through the hard times together and celebrate the good times the same way. To make love with her and make a family with her and make them all feel whole and wanted and safe. To tell her how much he adored her tonight and every night for sixty years to come. To protect her, to be strong for her, to have her to lean on when it was her turn to be strong.

He wanted nothing but her and these kids and this life.

He wanted everything.

And with three words, with her hands trembling, her voice soft as a whisper, her heat enough to set him ablaze, she gave him everything. "I love you."

Then she kissed him. It was hungry and yearning and sweet and intimate and promised untold pleasure, and it sent her fire into his blood, licking through his body, arousing him, calming him, tantalizing him, tormenting him, making him greedier than any man had ever been. Within seconds, all rational thought had fled. All he could think was *more* and *where* and *need* when a young disgusted voice sounded behind them.

"Eww, gross. There are innocent kids in this house." Clutching spoons and napkins in one hand and carrying three containers of yogurt between her arm and rib cage, Abby shielded her face from them with the other hand on her way to the stairs. At the top of the stairs, she stopped but didn't look back. "Me and Jacob are teaching Riah how to play video games. We decided we'd like to have pizza for dinner, and we'd like to eat around seven, so you can go make out some more until then. Just not where the little ones can see, okay?"

A moment later the bedroom door clicked shut. Keegan loosened his hold on Therese, but kept her close. "What do you think? You want to go make out some more?"

"I'd love to." Her gaze strayed to the clock on the living room wall. "They didn't give us much time."

Claiming her hand, he led her down the hall, through the

kitchen, and onto the patio, where he settled on the chaise longue, then pulled her down with him. With a sound part laugh, part contented sigh, she sank against him, head on his shoulder, hands clasping his so his arms enclosed her.

"Aw, *cher,* we've got plenty of time. The rest of our lives. Just you, me, and three little monsters."

"And we'll all live happily ever after?"

"Absolutely."

The pronouncement was suitably profound, he thought, until she slanted him an amused look.

"You've been reading Mariah's fairy tales, haven't you?"

He settled her snugly against him and replied, "I don't need fairy tales, darlin'. I have you."

Since she lost her husband, Jessy Lawrence
struggled with her own guilt over his death.
After his wife's passing, Dalton Smith
became alienated from his family and friends.
When these two wounded souls meet,
they spark a fiery passion. But can love heal
old scars—or will the demons of the past
pull them apart forever?

Please turn this page for a preview of

A Love to Call Her Own.

Chapter 1

Monday mornings came too damn soon.

Jessy Lawrence rolled onto her back and opened her eyes just enough to stare at the shadows the sun cast across the bedroom ceiling. It was high in the sky. Ten o'clock, maybe eleven. In the four weeks since she'd lost her job, she'd been sleeping in late. Why not, with no more annoying alarm clock beeping at six forty-five? No more dressing up, putting on makeup, smiling for customers who annoyed her so much that she wanted to smack them. No more caring whether she was late or if she looked more ragged than she should or if anyone noticed—like that nosy hag, Mrs. Dauterive—she was having a tough day.

It should have been heaven.

If possible, she was more miserable than before.

After her eyes became accustomed to the sun's glare, or what there was of it peeping around the edges of the blinds, she turned her head carefully to the nightstand and bit back a groan. It was 12:21. Officially afternoon. She'd slept away the whole morning.

She should shower. Brush that god-awful taste from her mouth. Put some drops in her eyes so they didn't feel so puffy. Get something to eat—proteins, vegetables, carbs, fruit. She'd been subsisting on junk food and booze so long that she couldn't remember the last time she'd had a real meal.

She should get dressed, too, walk down the street, buy a copy of the Tallgrass newspaper, and check out the help-wanted section. She needed a job. A sense of purpose. A reason to get out of bed in the morning...or afternoon, as the case may be. She didn't need the money. Bless Aaron and the United States Army, his life insurance would cover her expenses for the next few decades even if she did nothing but loll on the couch.

What she did need was a reason for living. It was two years and eight months too late to crawl into Aaron's grave with him, and she didn't deserve to be there anyway. He could have done so much better than her if he'd survived his last two weeks in Afghanistan.

But he hadn't survived, and she had, and here she was, wasting her life. It was shameful.

She sat up, her head pounding, and slowly eased to her feet. The shuffle to the bathroom jarred every pain sensor in her head and made her stomach do a queasy tumble. Once inside, she peed, turned the shower to hot, then faced herself in the mirror. She wasn't a pretty sight.

Her red hair stood straight up on top, a counter to the flattened frizz that cradled the sides of her head. At some point in the last day or two, she'd put on makeup, then failed to remove it before crawling into bed. Shadow smeared and mascara smudged, giving her eyes a hollow, exaggerated look. Deep circles underneath emphasized their emptiness. Indentations from the pillow marked her cheek and forehead, and her usual healthy glow had gone gray and pasty.

It was a wonder small children didn't run away at the sight of her.

Only because small children didn't frequent the places she did.

Steam was forming on the mirror when she sighed, turned away, and stripped off her tank and shorts. She took a long shower, scrubbing herself once, twice, closing her eyes, and letting the stinging water pound into her face. By the time she was ready to get out, it had turned cold, bringing shivers and making her teeth chatter.

Nearly four weeks since she'd been fired—all because some snotty teenage brat with a sense of entitlement could dish it out but couldn't take it—and she hadn't told anyone yet. Not that there were many people to tell, just the margarita girls, her best friends. None of them banked at Tallgrass National. Like her, they were all Army widows, and like her, they kept their accounts at the Fort Murphy Federal Credit Union.

She should have told them at their first Tuesday-night dinner after it happened. She liked to think she would have, except they were all preoccupied with other, mostly happier stuff. Carly was planning her wedding to Dane Clark, scheduled for the first weekend of June, and Therese was in the early throes of mad love and lust with Keegan Logan, who made the long drive up from Fort Polk, Louisiana, with his daughter, Mariah, to spend weekends with Therese and her kids, Abby and Jacob.

Ilena was thirty-some weeks pregnant, due to deliver Hector Junior the week after Carly's wedding, and Fia...Poor Fia was...off. That was the only way Jessy could describe their youngest friend lately. She wasn't drinking. Jessy could recognize another drunk from a mile away. She didn't believe it was drugs, either. Fia worked too hard as a personal trainer. She wouldn't poison herself. Something was wrong, but like Jessy, Fia wasn't sharing.

That left Lucy and Marti, the last two who formed the core of the Tuesday Night Margarita Club, also known as the Fort Murphy Widows' Club. Nothing earthshaking was happening in their lives. They were as everyday normal as any of them could be. Jessy didn't want either of them—any of them—to know what a colossal loser she was. If they knew all her failings, they would lose respect for her, and she would lose the six most important people in her life. Better that she keep her secrets.

God, how she wished she could talk to someone who wouldn't hold them against her.

For the first time in years, she wanted—needed—a closer relationship with her family. They lived in Atlanta: mother, father, two sisters with husbands and children who got regular gifts from their aunt Jessy but wouldn't recognize her if she break-danced in front of them. She couldn't recall the last time she'd gotten an affectionate hug from her mom or a word of advice from her father. She'd been such a disappointment that she was pretty sure, if asked, Prescott and Nathalie Wilkes didn't even acknowledge the existence of their middle daughter.

She got dressed, finger-combed her hair, then wandered through the empty apartment with its high ceilings and tall windows to the kitchen. A quick look in the refrigerator and freezer showed nothing but a few bottles of water, condiments, and some frozen dinners, age unknown. The pantry held staples: rice, pasta, flour, sugar, plus a lonely can of pinto beans and some packets of instant mashed potatoes. The cabinets were empty, as well, except for a box of oatmeal and another of instant pudding. As in the childhood poem, her cupboards were bare.

Except for the one below and to the left of the sink. *Out of sight, out of mind,* the old saying went, but the bottles in that cabinet were never far from her mind. That was her problem.

She needed food, real food, healthy food. Though she wasn't much of a cook, she could learn. She could fill a few of her empty days with taking care of herself: eating properly, exercising, cleaning, detoxing herself. It was a momentous project, but she was worth the effort, right? And what else did she have to do?

She would start with shopping, she decided, grabbing her purse and keys and heading toward the door before she could talk herself out of it. She was a champion shopper, though she preferred to look for killer heels and cute outfits and Bobbi Brown makeup. She could handle a sweep through Walmart, maybe even grab a burger at the McDonald's just inside the door, and at this time of day, she wouldn't risk running into any of her margarita sisters.

After locking up, she took the stairs to the street level, stepped out into the warm May afternoon, and stopped immediately to rummage in her purse for a pair of dark glasses. Cars passed on Main Street, a few steps ahead, and a few shoppers moved past, running errands on their lunch breaks or grabbing a meal at one of the nearby restaurants. Jessy loved living right in the heart of downtown Tallgrass, on the second floor of a sandstone building that dated back to Oklahoma's statehood. She loved the busyness of the area during the day and the quiet at night, her only neighbors few and far between in other converted spaces.

Her car was parked down the alley in a tiny lot shared by the owners of Serena's Sweets next door and a couple other businesses. She drove to First Street, then headed south to Walmart, stoically ignoring the bank at the intersection of First and Main as she passed. They'd replaced her with ease—people with the skills to be customer account reps weren't hard to come by, else Jessy couldn't have done the job—and after electronically sending her final paycheck, they were done with her. Not even Julia, the account rep she'd known best, had bothered to contact her.

Walmart was always busy, even in a military town where service members and their families had the option of the post exchange and the commissary. She parked at the far west end of the lot, figuring she could use the exercise and a little fresh air, since among the many things she couldn't remember was the last time she'd seen daylight. She felt a tad like a vampire. Had looked like one, too, in the mirror before her shower.

Determination got her into the store and all the way to the back, where she started with bottled water. Municipal water in Tallgrass tasted like it came from one of those shallow ponds that the cattle stood in on hot summer days. She added milk, two percent, though she wasn't sure for what. But healthy diets included dairy products, right? She tossed in a twelve-pack of Greek yogurt and added fake egg blend, turkey bacon, whole-grain bread—whatever caught her attention as she trolled the aisles.

She was standing in front of the jarred pasta sauces, remembering the spaghetti sauce Aaron had taught her to make—ground beef, tomatoes, mushrooms, onions, and just a bit of sugar—when a crash jerked her attention to a woman fifteen feet away. A jar of pizza sauce lay splattered on the floor around her, its bright red spotting her jeans like blood, and she was clenching her cell phone tightly to her ear.

Such a look on her face.

Jessy went hot inside, then a chill spread through her. She knew that look. Dear God, she'd *lived* that look. She still wore it in her nightmares, still saw it at times in her mirror. That awful, heart-stopping, can't-breathe, can't-bear-it look of shock and pain and anger and grief and pure, bitter sorrow.

The nearest shopper edged her cart away from the woman while sneaking looks. Other customers and a few stock boys barely old enough to shave stared at her outright as she sank, as if in slow motion, to the floor, a wail rising out of her, growing with anguish until it scraped Jessy's skin, uncovering her own barely scabbed-over anguish.

This shouldn't be happening here, and it damn well shouldn't be happening with Jessy. Therese—she was motherly, loving, kind. Carly, too. Ilena could empathize and offer comfort with the best of them. Marti, Lucy, Fia—any of them could handle something like this better than Jessy. Jessy didn't comfort. She didn't reach out. She didn't get involved in strangers' emotional messes.

But no one was helping the woman. No one was trying to move her off the glass-shard-littered floor, giving her any assistance or, barring that, any privacy. Jessy knew too well what it was like to grieve alone. She'd done it for eighteen months before she'd met her margarita sisters.

She knew in her heart that this woman had just found out she could be a margarita sister, too.

Her first step was tentative, her stomach knotted, her chest struggling for air. Too soon she was beside the woman, though, sobbing amid the broken glass and splattered sauce as if she, too, were broken. She was older, probably in her fifties, gray roots just starting to show in her brown hair. Her clothes were casual but well made: faded jeans in the hundred-dollar price range, a cotton shirt whose quality shone in its very simplicity, stylish leather sandals. Dior clouded the air around her, mixing with the scent of tomatoes and basil, and the gems on the fingers that still clenched the cell phone were tastefully impressive.

Jessy noticed all those things to delay that first touch, that first word. What did you say to a person whose world had just shifted so dramatically that it might never be normal again?

Trying to channel Therese, Carly, or Ilena, Jessy crouched beside the woman, touched her, and said, "I'm so sorry." Three totally inadequate words that made her feel almost as low as the jerks gawking from both ends of the aisles.

"Patricia? Patricia, are you there?" The tinny question came from the cell phone.

Gently Jessy pried the phone free and raised it to her ear. "Hello?"

"Who is this?"

"A friend of Patricia's. What did you tell her?"

"Oh. I thought she was alone. At least, she was when she left her house." The voice belonged to a man, old, smug, with a touch of whine. It brought back long-ago memories of visits from Nathalie's parents, a hateful old woman and a spiteful old man. "I told her there's two Army officers all dressed up in their finest lookin' for her. I bet it's about her husband, George. He's in the war, you know. Over in—"

Jessy disconnected and pocketed the phone. Despite the Army's best intentions, things sometimes went wrong with casualty notification calls: no one home but kids who called their parent in a panic; nosy neighbors who couldn't resist being the first to pass on bad news. She'd received her call at work, just about this time of day on a Wednesday, back from lunch and summoned into the bank president's office to face a weary chaplain and a solemn notification officer. *We regret to inform you...*

Army wives knew that soldiers on their doorsteps never brought good news, especially during wartime. Just the sight of that official government-tagged vehicle in the driveway, those dress uniforms, those somber expressions, was enough to break their hearts before they started beating again, slowly, dully, barely enough to sustain life, or pounding madly until it felt like they might explode.

Everyone in the margarita club had been through their own notification, and every one remembered two things about it: the unbearable grief and those five words. *We regret to inform you...*

"Come on, Patricia," she said quietly, wrapping her arm around the woman's shoulders. "Let's get you off the floor. Let's find someplace quiet."

Unexpected help came from one of the young stockers. "The manager's office," he volunteered, taking hold of Patricia's arm and lifting her to her feet. "It's up at the front of the store."

Jessy paused to take the woman's purse from her cart—

her own bag hung messenger-style over her head and shoulder—then the three of them moved haltingly down the aisle. By the time they reached the end, a heavyset guy in a shirt and tie was hurrying toward them, a dark-haired woman on his heels. The manager, she presumed, and likely an assistant. Maybe she could turn Patricia over into their care and get back to her shopping. Get those awful memories back into the darkest corners of her mind.

But Patricia was holding on to her like they were best friends, turning a stricken look on her. "Please don't go... You know... don't you?"

She could recognize a drunk from a mile away, Jessy had thought an hour earlier. Could a newly widowed woman recognize someone who'd been through it before?

Her smile was a grimace, really, but she patted Patricia's hand, feeling like the biggest fraud that ever lived. "I know," she admitted. "I'll stay."

* * *

Benjamin Noble was dictating notes in the small workspace outside the exam rooms that made up his pod of the clinic when the office manager came around the corner. He paused, wasting a moment trying to decipher the look on her face. Luann was competent, capable, and faced crises on a regular basis without so much as a frown, but this afternoon the smallest frown narrowed the space between her eyes.

"Dr. Noble, you got a call from a Jessy Lawrence. She asked you to call your mother. Said it's urgent."

She offered him a pink message that he hesitated to take. His cell phone was on vibrate, as it always was while he saw patients, but he'd felt it go off three times in the last half hour. Jessy Lawrence's name had shown up on caller ID, but since he didn't know anyone by that name and she'd left no voice mails, he'd ignored it.

"Urgent" messages from Patricia were common enough, given their relationship, that this one didn't concern him. It could mean she wanted a diagnosis of her cough over the phone or information about hormone replacement therapy, despite his polite reminders that he was an orthopedic surgeon. It could mean she'd made the acquaintance of a friend's children or grandchildren and wondered about her own or that she'd had a little too much wine and was feeling a rare moment of remorse.

Remorse that had come way too late to mean anything to him.

"Thanks, Luann. I'll take care of it when I get a chance." He pocketed the number, breathed deeply to clear his head, then picked up the dictation where he'd left off. He had a patient in room one awaiting an injection in her knee, another in two for a post-op follow-up, one in three with a fractured wrist, and one in four with a fractured ankle, and he could only guess how many were still in the waiting room. Clinic days were never good days for dealing with his mother.

Honestly, he couldn't imagine a good day for dealing with his mother.

Twenty years ago she'd walked out on the family. She hadn't just left his father for another man. She'd left all of them—Dad, him, his sisters. Ben had been fifteen, old enough and busy enough with school to not be overly affected, but Brianne and Sara, eleven and nine, had missed her more than either Ben or his father could handle.

Not the time to think about it. He put on a smile and went into room one. "Mrs. Carter, how'd you do with that last shot?" Picking up the needle his nurse had waiting, he sat on the stool and rolled over in front of the patient on the table. She was fifty-five—his mother's age—and had severe osteoarthritis in her right knee, bone grating on bone. The injections weren't a cure but were helping delay the inevitable surgery. Though she'd recovered beautifully from the total knee replacement on her left, she was hoping to put off a repeat of the brutal rehab as long as she could. He didn't blame her.

He positioned the needle, deftly pushing it in, and was depressing the plunger when his cell phone vibrated again. His hand remained steady. Whether giving shots, inserting appliances to strengthen badly fractured bones, or sawing through the femur or tibia to remove a diseased knee, his hands were always steady.

The nurse blotted Mrs. Carter's knee and applied a Band-Aid while they exchanged the usual chatter—*Don't stress the joint for twenty-four hours, call me if you have any problems, see you in six months if you don't*—then he returned to the workspace to dictate notes again. There he pulled out the cell and looked at it a moment.

He routinely told his patients to call him if they had any problems, but he didn't want to speak to his mother no matter what her problem might be. Granted, his patients didn't abuse the privilege—most of them, at least. There were a few for whom hand-holding was part of his job, but when Patricia was needy, she did it to extremes.

Besides, none of his patients had contributed to his father's death.

He was still looking at the phone when it began to vibrate. Jessy Lawrence again. He might ignore her, but she apparently had no intention of remaining ignored. Since he had no intention of being stalked around his office by a stranger on a smartphone, he grimly answered. "This is Benjamin Noble."

There was that instant of silence, when someone was surprised to get an answer after repeatedly being sent to voice mail; then a husky, Southern-accented voice said, "Hey, my name is Jessy Lawrence. I'm a—a friend of your mother's over here in Tallgrass."

He'd heard of the town, only an hour or so from Tulsa, but he couldn't remember ever actually having been there. "I didn't know she was back in the state."

Another moment's silence. She must have thought it odd that he didn't know where his mother was living. When Patricia had left them, she hadn't made much effort to stay in touch except when guilt or selfishness pushed her, and he'd learned not to care.

"She is," Jessy said at last. "If you've got a pen, I'll give you her address. Ready? It's 321 West Comanche—"

"What is this about, Ms. Lawrence?"

"I'm sorry, Benjamin—Dr. Noble. There's no easy way to say this. Your stepfather was killed in Afghanistan. Your mother just found out. She needs you."

Ben stared at the five-foot-tall skeleton on a stand beside the counter. He'd met George Sanderson twice—no, three times: when Patricia had brought him to his high school graduation, then to Brianne's, then Sara's. The bastard hadn't had the nerve to attend Ben's father's funeral with her—a good thing, since they would have thrown him out. As it was, neither Ben nor the girls had wanted Patricia there, either.

What he knew about George was sketchy: the man had had no qualms about an affair with a married woman or breaking up a family. He'd been married once before, had no kids, and had been in the Army a long time. Yet Patricia expected him to mourn the man's death? To drop everything and rush to her side to be with her?

Yeah, that wasn't going to happen.

"Give her my condolences, Ms. Lawrence. If you'll excuse me, I've got patients waiting."

"But—"

He hung up, returned the phone to his pocket, then on second thought laid it on the counter, beneath a stack of charts, before heading to room three where the fractured wrist waited.

* * *

Dalton Smith gave the palomino colt one last assuring pat, then headed toward the house. The animals were all cared for, including the colt who'd somehow opened a laceration on his leg, so now it was time to feed himself before he went to work on the tractor sitting uselessly inside the shed. The hunk of machinery was as cantankerous as its owner and broke down a lot more. He ought to give in and buy a new one, or at least new to him.

But in this economy, ranchers didn't pay the bills by giving in, not without giving a hell of a fight first.

When he cleared the barn, the first thing he noticed was Oz, the stray who'd adopted him, stretched out in a patch of lush grass. He lay on his back, head tilted, tongue lolling out, all four legs in the air, letting the May sunshine warm his belly. The shepherd had been painfully scrawny, covered with fleas and ticks, when he'd shown up. Five weeks of regular meals had turned him into a new dog. His coat was thick and shiny, his ribs no longing showing through his skin. He had suckered Dalton into giving him a cushy new home, and he was making the most of it.

The second thing Dalton saw was the dusty RV parked behind his truck. He groaned, and Oz opened one eye to look at him. "Some watchdog you are," he muttered as he passed the dog. "You could've at least barked."

Nimbly Oz jumped to his feet and fell into step with him, heading for the back door. As Dalton pried his boots off on the top step, he scowled at the dog. "You're gonna wish you'd warned me. Mom doesn't allow animals in the house." He might have bought the house from his folks six years ago when they retired and moved to south Texas, but that didn't make it any less David and Ramona's house.

The first thing he noticed when he walked inside was the smells. The house never stank; he wasn't that bad a housekeeper. It just sometimes smelled a little musty from the dust accumulated everywhere. At that moment, though, it smelled of beef, onions, jalapeño peppers, grease, sugar, and cinnamon, and it made his mouth water. How many hundreds of times in his life had he come home to the scents of hamburgers, Spanish fries, and cinnamon cookies in the oven? Thousands.

Dad was sitting at the kitchen table, reading glasses balanced on the end of his nose, the Tallgrass newspaper open in front of him, and Mom stood in front of the stove, prodding the sliced potatoes, onions, and peppers in a pan filled with hot Crisco. She looked up, smiling brightly. "Sweetheart! I thought I was going to have to send your father looking for you. I hope you haven't eaten lunch yet because there's way too much food here for just your dad and me."

Before Dalton could do more than hug her, her gaze shifted lower. "Didn't I already tell you once that you couldn't come in?"

As Oz stared back, Dad spoke up. "Ramona, you're the queen of the house on wheels parked out there, not this one. If Dalton doesn't mind having him in here, then you don't get to mind, either." He folded the paper and laid it aside as he stood. Tall, lanky, his face weathered from years working in the sun and wind and cold, he looked the way Dalton expected to look in thirty years. "How are you, son?"

No handshakes for David. He was a hugger. It used to drive Dillon, Dalton's twin, crazy, being twelve, sixteen, eighteen, and getting hugged by his dad in front of everyone. Knowing that was half the reason Dad did it was enough to make it bearable for Dalton. Noah, the baby, never minded it at all. He was more touchy-feely than the rest of the family combined.

"Good," Dalton replied as Oz defiantly pushed past Ramona and went to his water dish. "I wasn't expecting you guys."

"Don't worry, we're just passing through." Mom spooned the batch of potatoes, onions, and peppers onto paper towels to drain, then tossed a second batch in. "Our friend Barb Watson—do you remember her? She and her husband Trey stopped by here with us a few years back. Anyway, Barb died yesterday, so we're heading home for the funeral."

"Sorry." Dalton went to the sink to scrub his hands.

"It's such a shame. She was only eighty-three, you

know, and she got around as well as I do. She was too young to die—"

In an instant, everyone went still in the room, even Oz. Mom's face turned red, and her hands fluttered as if she could wave away the words. "Oh, honey...I didn't mean..."

To remind him of his wife's death. No one in the family talked about Sandra, not because they hadn't loved her or didn't miss her, but because it had always been so hard for him. It had been four years this past January—four miserable years that his grief and anger had made tougher than they had to be.

She'd been a soldier, a medic, on her second combat tour when she'd died. Twenty-seven years old, way younger than his parents' friend Barb, way too young to bleed out in the desert thousands of miles from home. Losing her had been hard enough. Knowing she'd died in war had made it worse. Finding out she'd chosen to die had damn near killed him.

Reaching for a dish towel, he dried his hands, surprised they weren't shaking or knotted into fists. His gut wasn't knotted like it usually was, either.

Sandra was dead. He'd loved her more than anything, but she hadn't loved him back the same. She hadn't trusted him enough to come home to him. Being pissed off at her and the world and making everyone tiptoe around any subject that might bring her to mind weren't going to change that.

He hung up the towel again, then slipped his arm around his mother's shoulders. "It's okay, Mom. I know what you meant. Oz and I are starving. Are those burgers about ready?"

* * *

Jessy stared at her cell long after Benjamin Noble hung up on her. She was no stranger to cold people, but he'd been able to give her a chill long-distance. When the screen went dark, she slid the phone into her pocket, then turned her attention to the coffeemaker, the glass carafe slowly filling with strong black brew.

Patricia, she'd learned in the past hour, was Patricia Sanderson, wife—now widow—of Colonel George Sanderson. He'd been in the Army twenty-nine years and would have been promoted to general or retired by the end of thirty. Patricia had been in favor of retiring. She'd grown tired of traveling from assignment to assignment and never wanted to face a moving van and a stack of cartons again.

And she had a bastard of a son.

Immediately Jessy regretted that thought. She was proof that not all parent/adult-child relationships were healthy. She hadn't spoken to her own parents in years, had had LoLo Baxter, the casualty notification officer, inform them of Aaron's death. They hadn't called, come to Tallgrass for the funeral, sent flowers or even a damn card. That didn't make her a bitch of a daughter.

It had just made her sorry.

"Is that coffee about ready?" LoLo came into the kitchen, bumping against Jessy deliberately on her way to choose a cup from the wooden tree. The major had the toughest job in the Army: telling people their loved ones had died. The first time—delivering tragic news, watching the surviving spouse collapse, getting dragged into the grief—would have destroyed Jessy, but LoLo had done it countless times with grace, professionalism, and great empathy.

She'd made the worst time of Jessy's life a little easier to bear, and Jessy loved her for it.

"I talked to the son," Jessy said as LoLo poured the coffee, then sipped it and sighed. "He said, and I quote, 'Give her my condolences.'"

LoLo wasn't surprised. She'd seen families at their best and their worst. *The stories I could tell,* she'd once said. Of course, she hadn't told them. Was there someone she did share with? Someone who helped eased her burden and made it possible for her to continue doing her job?

Jessy didn't know. Though all the margarita sisters knew LoLo, none of them knew anything about her personal life. She was compassionate, kind, supportive, and a mystery.

"Any other kids?"

"Two daughters, both in Tulsa. She doesn't have their phone numbers." Jessy fixed her own coffee, with lots of sugar and creamer, then peeled an orange from a bowl on the counter. She hadn't gotten anything to eat yet, and her stomach was grumbling. She glanced toward the doorway. Down the hall in the living room, Patricia was sitting with the chaplain, their low voices punctuated time to time by a sob. She lowered her own voice. "Her son didn't know she was living in Oklahoma."

"Any other family?"

"No one on George's side besides some nieces and nephews she doesn't really know. Her sister lives in Vermont, her brother in Florida. They'll both be in sometime tomorrow. And some nieces and nephews of her own. Her sister's going to contact them."

LoLo leaned against the counter, cradling the coffee cup, and studied Jessy. "You know her from the bank?"

"No. Never met her before today."

"So you picked a stranger up off the floor, dusted her off, and brought her home. That's a tough thing to do, Jessy."

With someone else, Jessy could have been flippant. *Tougher than you know.* Or *Not tough at all; I am Superwoman.* But LoLo did know. She'd done way more than her share of picking people up off the floor. Instead of saying anything, Jessy focused on sectioning the orange.

"I was at the bank yesterday," LoLo said.

Heat flooded Jessy's face, and her gut clenched. "I thought you banked on post."

"I do. I went there with one of my wives." Always supportive, doing anything she could to help the women whose tragedies brought them into her life. "Someone else's nameplate was on your desk. So were his things."

"Yeah." She mumbled around a piece of orange, sweet and juicy.

"You making a career change?"

Reaching deep inside, Jessy summoned the strength to meet her gaze, to smile brashly. "Yeah. I always hated that job."

"You have any plans?"

Besides falling apart? "I'm thinking about it." She thought about a lot of things. She just never found the energy to actually do anything. Going to get groceries today had been a big deal—and look how that had bitten her on the ass. Two hours now she'd been tied up with Patricia Sanderson, and she didn't know how to extricate herself. She'd hoped the son would head this way as soon as he got the news, but she might as well have told him there were clouds in the sky for all the concern he'd shown.

As long as LoLo and the chaplain were there, she could leave, she told herself. Even knowing that eventually they would both have to leave, too. Knowing that eventually Patricia would have to be alone in her house, surrounded by memories of her husband, drowning in her grief. Eventually everyone had to be alone.

But not yet. Jessy could cope a while longer. It wasn't like anyone else in the entire world needed her.

"Maybe this time you'll find a job you like." LoLo drained the last of her coffee and squared her shoulders. "I should get back in there."

Jessy watched her go, figuring that in a few minutes the chaplain would come in for coffee and a break. Kind of a tag-team comforting. With her stomach still too empty, she opened the refrigerator, located a couple packages of deli meat, mayo and mustard, some pickles and cheese. Sooner or later, Patricia's friends would start showing up with casseroles, fried and rotisserie chicken, sweets from CaraCakes, pop and doughnuts and disposable dishes, but in the meantime, a sandwich or two would stave off hunger for her, LoLo, and Lieutenant Graham. If Patricia was like Jessy, she wouldn't eat for days. If she was like Therese, she would be sensible and eat even though she had no appetite, and if she was like Lucy, bless her heart, she would stuff herself with food to numb the pain.

Sure enough, about the time she finished putting together the fourth ham-and-turkey sandwich, Lieutenant Graham came into the kitchen. He wasn't as experienced as LoLo; his lean solemn face showed the bleakness of his burden.

Chaplains made Jessy uncomfortable. She hadn't been raised in church and had never found a reason to start attending as an adult. Aaron's services had been held at the chapel on Fort Murphy, and the memory didn't make her eager to return. Besides, chaplains were good people. Earnest. They didn't make the mistakes Jessy couldn't seem to escape.

"We didn't get lunch. This looks good," the lieutenant said as he accepted a plate. "We called one of her neighbors, who's coming over as soon as she can get away from the office. I think she's asked about as many questions as she's capable of processing at the moment."

"She'll think of more." Jessy's first questions had been simple: how had Aaron died, and why. The how had been understandable: he'd been shot by a sniper. She still struggled with the why.

There had been more questions, of course. When would he get home? What did she have to do? How did one arrange a funeral? Where could she bury him?

And more: had he died instantly? Had they tried to save him? Did he suffer? How did they know he didn't suffer?

Would she be able to see him, touch him, kiss once more when he got home?

Could she tell him how very, very sorry she was?

The chaplain took a seat at the breakfast table, ate a bite or two, then gazed at Jessy. "LoLo says you've been through this."

Her hands tightened around the coffee mug. She forced her fingers to loosen, to pick up a plate, to join him at the table and take a bite to settle her stomach. "Two and a half years ago," she said at last.

"I'm sorry."

Why did the words sound so much more sincere coming from him than they did from her? Because he was a chaplain. He'd probably never let anyone down. Never failed to live up to others' expectations. He was a man of God.

She was just a woman.

With way too many flaws. Way too many regrets.

THE DISH

♥ ♥ ♥ ♥ ♥ ♥ ♥ ♥ ♥ ♥ ♥ ♥ ♥ ♥ ♥ ♥ ♥

From the desk of Marilyn Pappano

Dear Reader,

One of the pluses of writing the Tallgrass series was one I didn't anticipate until I was neck-deep in the process, but it's been a great one: unearthing old memories. Our Navy career was filled with laugh-out-loud moments, but there were also plenty of the laugh-or-you'll-cry moments, too. We did a lot of laughing. Most of our tears were reserved for later.

Like our very first move to South Carolina, when the movers lost our furniture for weeks, and the day after it was finally delivered, my husband got orders to Alabama. On our second move, the delivery guys perfected their truck-unloading routine: three boxes into the apartment, one box into the front of their truck. (Fortunately, Bob had perfected his watch-the-unloaders routine and recovered it all.)

For our first apartment move-out inspection, we had scrubbed ourselves to nubbins all through the night. The manager did the walk-through, commented on how impeccably clean everything was, and offered me the paperwork to sign. I signed it, turned around to hand it to her, and walked into the low-hanging chandelier where the dining table used to sit, breaking a bulb with my head. Silently she took back the papers, thumbed through to the deduction sheet, and charged us sixty cents for a new bulb.

There's something about being told my Oklahoma accent is funny by multi-generation Americans with accents so heavy that I just guessed at the context of our conversations. Or hearing our two-year-old Oklahoma-born son, home for Christmas, proudly singing, "Jaaan-gle baaaa-ulllz! Jaaan-gle baaaa-ulllz! Jaaan-gle *alllll* the waaay-uh!"

Bob and I still trade stories. *Remember when we did that self-move to San Diego and the brakes went out on the rental truck in 5:00 traffic in Memphis at the start of a holiday weekend? Remember that pumpkin pie on the first Thanksgiving we couldn't go home—the one I forgot to put the spices in? Remember dropping the kiddo off at the base day care while we got groceries and having to pay the grand sum of fifty cents two hours later? How about when you had to report to the commanding general for joint-service duty at Fort Gordon and we couldn't find your Dixie cup anywhere in the truck crammed with boxes—and at an Army post, no less, that didn't stock Navy uniforms?*

Sea life was great. We watched ships leaving and, months later, come home again. On one homecoming, the kiddo and I watched Daddy's ship run aground. We learned that all sailors look alike when they're dressed in the same uniform and seen from a distance. We spied submarines stealthing out of their bases and toured warships—American, British, French, Canadian—and even got to board one of our own nuclear subs for a private look around.

The Navy gave us a lot to remember and a lot to learn. (Example: all those birthdays and anniversaries

Bob missed didn't mean a thing. It was the fact that he came home that mattered.) I still have a few dried petals from the flowers given to me by the command each time Bob reenlisted, as well the ones I got when he retired. We have a flag, like the one each of the widows in Tallgrass received, and a display box of medals and ribbons, but filled with much happier memories.

I can't wait to see which old *remember when* the next book in this series brings us! I hope you love reading A MAN TO ON HOLD TO as much as I loved writing it.

Sincerely,

Marilyn Pappano

MarilynPappano.com
Twitter @MarilynPappano
Facebook.com/MarilynPappanoFanPage

♥ ♥ ♥ ♥ ♥ ♥ ♥ ♥ ♥ ♥ ♥ ♥ ♥ ♥ ♥ ♥

From the desk of Jaime Rush

Dear Reader,

Much has been written about angels. When I realized that angels would be part of my mythology and hidden world, I knew I needed to make mine different. I didn't want to use the religious mythos or pair them with demons. Many authors have done a fantastic job of this already.

In fact, I felt this way about my world in general. I started with the concept that a confluence of nature and the energy in the Bermuda Triangle had allowed gods and angels to take human form. They procreated with the humans living on the island and were eventually sent back to their plane of existence. But I didn't want to draw on Greek, Roman, or Atlantean mythology, so I made up my own pantheon of gods. I narrowed them down to three different types: Dragons, sorcerers, and angels. Their progeny continue to live in the area of the Triangle, tethered there by their need to be near their energy source.

My angels come from this pantheon, without the constraints of traditional religious roles. They were sent down to the island to police the wayward gods, but succumbed to human temptation. And their progeny pay the price. I'm afraid my angels' descendents, called Caidos, suffer terribly for their fathers' sins. This was not something I contrived; these concepts often just come to me as the truths of my stories.

Caidos are preternaturally beautiful, drawing the desire of those who see them. But desire, their own and others', causes them physical pain. As do the emotions of all but their own kind. They guard their secret, for their lives depend on it. To keep pain at bay, they isolate themselves from the world and shut down their sexuality. Which, of course, makes it all the more fun when they are thrown together with women they find attractive. Pleasure and pain is a fine line, and Kasabian treads it in a different way than other Caidos. Then again, he is different, harboring a dark secret that compounds his sense of isolation.

Perhaps it was slightly sadistic to pair him with a woman who holds the essence of the goddess of sensuality.

Kye is his greatest temptation, but she may also be his salvation. He needs to form a bond with the woman who can release his dark shadow. I don't make it easy on Kye, either. She must lose everything to find her soul. I love to dig deep into my characters' psyches and mine their darkest shadows. Only then can they come into the light.

And isn't that something we all can learn? To face our shadows so that we can walk in the light? That's what I love most about writing: that readers, too, can take the journey of self discovery, self love, right along with my characters. They face their demons and come out on the other end having survived.

We all have magic in our imaginations. Mine has always contained murder, mayhem, and romance. Feel free to wander through the madness of my mind any time. A good place to start is my website, www.jaimerush .com, or that of my romantic suspense alter ego, www .tinawainscott.com.

Jaime Rush

♥ ♥ ♥ ♥ ♥ ♥ ♥ ♥ ♥ ♥ ♥ ♥ ♥ ♥ ♥ ♥

From the desk of Kate Brady

Dear Reader,

People ask me all the time, "What do you like about writing romantic suspense?" It's a great question, and it always seems like sort of a copout to say, "Everything!" But it's true. Writing novels is the greatest job in the world. And romantic suspense, in particular, allows my favorite elements to exist in a single story: adventure, danger, thrills, chills, romance, and the gratifying knowledge that good will triumph over evil and love will win the day.

Weaving all those elements together is, for me, a labor of love. I love being able to work with something straight from my own mind, without having to footnote and document sources all the time. (In my other career—academia—they frown upon letting the voices in my head do the writing!) I love the flexibility of where and when I can indulge myself in a story—the deck, the kitchen island, the car, the beach, and any number of recliners are my favorite "offices." I love seeing the stories unfold, being surprised by the twists and turns they take, and ultimately coming across them in their finished forms on the bookstore shelves. I love hearing from readers and being privy to their take on the story line or a character. I love meeting other writers and hobnobbing with the huge network of readers and writers out there who still love romantic suspense.

And I *love* getting to know new characters. I don't create these people; they already exist when a story begins and it becomes my job to reveal them. I just go along for the ride as they play out their roles, and I'm repeatedly surprised and delighted by what they prove to be. And it never fails: I always fall in love.

Luke Mann, the hero in WHERE EVIL WAITS, was one of the most intriguing characters I have met and he turned out to be one of my all-time favorites. He first appeared in his brother's book, *Where Angels Rest*, so I knew his hometown, his upbringing, his parents, and his siblings. But Luke himself came to me shrouded in shadows. I couldn't wait to write his story; he was dark and fascinating and intense (not to mention gorgeous) and I knew from the start that his adventure would be a whirlwind ride. When I put him in an alley with his soon-to-be heroine, Kara Chandler—who shocked both Luke and me with a boldness I hadn't expected—I fell in love with both of them. From that point on, WHERE EVIL WAITS was off and running, as Luke and Kara tried to elude and capture a killer as twisted and dangerous as the barbed wire that was his trademark.

The time Luke and Kara spend together is brief, but jam-packed with action, heat, and, ultimately, affection. I hope you enjoy reading their story as much as I enjoyed writing it!

Happy Reading!

Kate Brady

♥ ♥ ♥ ♥ ♥ ♥ ♥ ♥ ♥ ♥ ♥ ♥ ♥ ♥

From the desk of Amanda Scott

Dear Reader,

The plot of THE WARRIOR'S BRIDE, set in the fourteenth-century Scottish Highlands near Loch Lomond, grew from a law pertaining to abduction that must have seemed logical to its ancient Celtic lawmakers.

I have little doubt that they intended that law to protect women.

However, I grew up in a family descended from a long line of lawyers, including my father, my grandfather, and two of the latter's great-grandfathers, one of whom was the first Supreme Court justice for the state of Arkansas (an arrangement made by his brother, the first senator from Missouri, who also named Arkansas—so just a little nepotism there). My brother is a judge. His son and one of our cousins are defense attorneys. So, as you might imagine, laws and the history of law have stirred many a dinner-table conversation throughout my life.

When I was young, I spent countless summer hours traveling with my paternal grandmother and grandfather in their car, listening to him tell stories as he drove. Once, when I pointed out brown cows on a hillside, he said, "Well, they're brown on this side, anyhow."

That was my first lesson in looking at both sides of any argument, and it has served me well in my profession. This is by no means the first time I've met a law that sowed the seeds for an entire book.

Women, as we all know, are unpredictable creatures who have often taken matters into their own hands in ways of which men—especially in olden times—have disapproved. Thanks to our unpredictability, many laws that men have made to "protect" us have had the opposite effect.

The heroine of THE WARRIOR'S BRIDE is the lady Muriella MacFarlan, whose father, Andrew, is the rightful chief of Clan Farlan. A traitorous cousin has usurped Andrew's chiefdom and murdered his sons, so Andrew means to win his chiefdom back by marrying his daughters to warriors from powerful clans, who will help him.

Muriella, however, intends *never* to marry. I based her character on Clotho, youngest of the three Fates and the one who is responsible for spinning the thread of life. So Murie is a spinner of threads, yarns... and stories.

Blessed with a flawless memory, Muriella aspires to be a *seanachie*, responsible for passing the tales of Highland folklore and history on to future generations. She has already developed a reputation for her storytelling and takes that responsibility seriously.

She seeks truth in her tales of historical events. However, in her personal life, Murie enjoys a more flexible notion of truth. She doesn't lie, exactly. She spins.

Enter blunt-spoken warrior Robert MacAulay, a man of honor with a clear sense of honor, duty, and truth. Rob also has a vision that, at least for the near future, does not include marriage. Nor does he approve of truth-spinning.

Consequently, sparks fly between the two of them even *before* Murie runs afoul of the crazy law. I think you will enjoy THE WARRIOR'S BRIDE.

Meantime, *Suas Alba!*

Sincerely,

Amanda Scott

www.amandascottauthor.com

❤ ❤ ❤ ❤ ❤ ❤ ❤ ❤ ❤ ❤ ❤ ❤ ❤ ❤ ❤ ❤

From the desk of Mimi Jean Pamfiloff

Dear People Pets—Oops, sorry—I meant, Dear Readers,

Ever wonder what's like to be God of the Sun, Ruler of the House of Gods, and the only deity against procreation with humans (an act against nature)?

Nah. Me neither. I want to know what it's like to be his girlfriend. After all, how many guys house the power of the sun inside their seven-foot frames? And that hair. Long thick ribbons of sun-streaked caramel. And those muscles. Not an ounce of fat to be found on that insanely ripped body. As for the...eh-hem, the *performance* part, well, I'd like to know all about that, too.

Actually, so would Penelope. Especially after spending the evening with him, sipping champagne in his hotel room, and then waking up buck naked. Yes. In his bed. And yes, he's naked, too. Yeah, she'd love to remember what happened. He wouldn't mind, either.

But it seems that the only one who might know anything is Cimil, Goddess of the Underworld, instigator of all things naughty, and she's nowhere to be found. I guess Kinich and Penelope will have to figure this out for themselves. So what will be the consequence of breaking these "rules" of nature Kinich fears so much? Perhaps the price will be Penelope's life. But perhaps, just maybe, the price will be his...

Happy Reading!

♥ ♥ ♥ ♥ ♥ ♥ ♥ ♥ ♥ ♥ ♥ ♥ ♥ ♥ ♥

From the desk of Shannon Richard

Dear Reader,

I knew how Brendan and Paige were going to meet from the very start. It was the first scene that played out in my mind. Paige was going to be having a very bad day on top of a very bad couple of months. Her Jeep breaks down in the middle of nowhere Florida, during a sweltering day, and she was to call someone for help. It's when she's at her lowest that she meets the love of her life; she just doesn't know it at the time. As for Brendan, he isn't expecting anyone like Paige to come along. Not now, not ever. But he knows pretty quickly that he has feelings for her, and that they're serious feelings.

Paige can be a little sassy, and Brendan can be a little cocky, so during their first encounter sparks are flying all over the place. Things start to get hot quickly, and it has very little to do with summer in the South (which is hot and miserable, I can tell you from over twenty years of experience). But at the end of the day, and no matter the confrontation, Brendan is Paige's white knight. He comes to her rescue in more ways than one.

The inspiration behind Brendan is a very laid-back Southern guy. He's easygoing (for the most part) and charming. He hasn't been one for long-term serious relationships, but when it comes to Paige he jumps right on in. There's just something about a guy who knows exactly what he wants, who meets the girl and doesn't hesitate. Yeah, it makes me swoon more than just a little. I hoped that readers would appreciate that aspect of him. The diving in headfirst and not looking back, and Brendan doesn't look back.

As for Paige, she's dealing with a lot and is more than a little scared about getting involved with another guy. Her wounds are too fresh and deep from her recent heartbreak. Brendan knows all about pain and suffering. Instead of turning his back on her, he steps up to the plate. He helps Paige heal, helps her get a job and friends, helps her find a place in the little town of Mirabelle. It just so happens that her place is right next to his.

So yes, Brendan is this big, tough, alpha man who comes to the rescue of the damsel in distress. But Paige isn't exactly a weak little thing. No, she's pretty strong herself. It's part of that strength that Brendan is so drawn to. He loves her passion and how fierce she is. But really, he just loves her.

I'm a fan of the happily ever after. Always have been, always will be. I love my characters; they're part of me. They might exist in black and white on the page, but to me they're real. At the end of the day, I just want them to be happy.

Cheers,

Shannon Richard

ShannonRichard.net
Twitter @Shan_Richard
Facebook.com/ShannonNRichard